Fallen Angels

Vicky Fox

DEDICATION

This book is dedicated to people who love to paint, and those who adore
the history of the British Isles

CONTENTS

1   Portsmouth   1

2   Brotherhood   48

3   Discovery   151

4   Searching   181

5   Finding   230

Acknowledgements

The knowledge that is on the internet and the committed people who post
it there

CHAPTER ONE

'Mr McKinley, what a terrible odour you have created with your turpentine.'

'I beg your pardon Ma'am, but it is the cost of having your portrait taken with oils.'

This was her second sitting that day, for in the morning he had made preliminary sketches and chosen a position where the painting was to be created. There was a window with a northern aspect to retain consistency of the light, but he knew it would exaggerate every vertical line on her face. So by placing an oil lamp on the other side the effect would be to soften those shadows. The lamp would also introduce a warm glow in contrast to the cooler tones from the natural north facing light. He would make much of her large pale eyes and, he suspected, rouged lips.

Robert McKinley enjoyed portrait painting but a commission such as this was done for money. He worked silently and thought about the pleasure he would have that evening watching a touring company of actors' production of 'A Midsummer Night's Dream' at the Portsmouth Theatre. It was his favourite Shakespeare comedy and, even if they performed it badly, was bound to be entertaining.

His charcoal sketches were pinned to the easel for reference so he knew exactly what he could achieve and today he would make the first marks on his canvas in oils. The family had allowed him to use their dining room with its red wallpaper and a fire had been made up to take any chill off the room. He had been shown in and assisted in the setting-up by the family's maid, a dark-complexioned girl, whose bone structure and warm skin tones fascinated him. He could hardly take his eyes from her and made a note to ask her to sit for him when he was in funds. She seemed oblivious to the attention and his study had been interrupted by madam bustling into the room with her companion and waving the girl away.

By contrast Mrs Bartleby had a flat face and slightly disagreeable expression. He would earn his fee with this assignment, but her husband had offered him a generous payment when they met near Kidderminster and McKinley desperately needed money to set up a studio and start painting subjects of his own choosing. He had painted Mr Bartleby in his factory and now he would paint a companion piece of his wife during her summer holiday in Portsmouth in the new middle-class district of Croxton Town. This family wanted oil paintings to confirm their status as members of the new middle class in Victorian Britain and as decoration for the house that Mr Bartleby was building near his factory.

She sniffed and beckoned to her companion, a small sharp looking woman of about forty, to open a window. How different they are, he thought. One rounded like a ship in full sail and the other pointy and thin as though the sails had been taken in. As he watched Miss Salter's quick movements, fussing around the mistress, he wondered idly what they each ate and how they slept and was beginning to imagine them as animals in clothes, a bad habit he had had since childhood. She was a seal in repose on a rock, and the companion was a crab scuttling about the room, when Mrs Bartleby said: 'How long shall I have to sit?'

He expected this question and said 'I would like one half hour and then you shall rest for ten minutes. Then another half hour and again a rest. In all I should like you to sit for me four times this afternoon. I will then require the paint to dry and return next week to resume the sitting for the same amount of time. It should then be necessary for one more visit to complete the work.'

'My husband says that I cannot view it until it is finished?'

'That is customary Ma'am. An oil painting is comprised of layers and begins very dark. It is only at the end of the process that the sparkle of light, and indeed life, is added. You have seen the drawings?'

She grimaced. He groaned inwardly and knew that she did not see what she had expected. Every person with the luxury of a looking glass sees a face that they present to themselves, and they begin to believe that is how they look. McKinley knew this was not what the world saw. He had drawn and painted himself on many occasions for want of a sitter. The intense look and piercing eyes in his self-portraits were not what he saw when he brushed his hair in the morning. He called it 'the mirror face' and he wondered what portraits would emerge from the new image-maker - the daguerreotype. Its subjects were required to stay still for a few minutes, but his sitters had to endure far longer.

He would normally converse easily with his sitters, but it was not so easy with this lady and Miss Salter, so he allowed his thoughts to wander. When he had received these funds, he would leave Portsmouth and meet an old schoolfriend, another artist, who was setting up a community near Guildford where they could create a new type of art inspired by the period before the renaissance. They would paint as simply as people did in the middle ages without the idealised muscularity of classical Western art.

McKinley accepted that for too many years he had been lazy, besotted by one woman or another, steeped in the romantic poetry of Keats and searching for something elusive. He had drifted from one assignment to the next, content to illustrate journals and books simply to pay rent and feed himself.

His family had money, but his father had made it clear that there would be no more handouts. He was now twenty-seven and as a graduate of the Royal Academy he should be able to make a decent living from his craft. He was lucky to have friends who knew people who would pay handsomely to have their portraits painted, and that he was possessed of an unusual skill in capturing a likeness. This source of funds may not be available for long. The recent innovations in photography were making a new means of reproduction more accessible, and it might become both popular and widespread. Time was of the essence, and he focussed on the woman sitting in front of him.

She wore her hair in the style favoured by Queen Victoria, parted in the centre and swept back over the ears and to this she had added an indoor cap with fine lace and ribbons. Her gown was dark and designed to give the illusion of a sloping shoulder and a nipped-in waist. As a portrait artist he needed to understand the artifice of a gentlewoman's attire, the multitude of petticoats to give the exact bell shape for the dress and how to render in oil paint the best quality silk. It bore little resemblance to the dresses of the poor working women that he saw on the streets of any town or village. Cloth was expensive and it was always reused by someone; the styles of many years ago could be glimpsed occasionally among the whores in the backstreets and taverns. He was amused when he and his friends saw a doxy wearing regency stripes while at the same time he was appalled at the thought of how many bodies had worn that garment.

By the end of the day's sessions he had a good likeness with very little colour but a fine composition and he knew that his client would be happy with the end result. She bustled out in relief at being away from the smell of paint and sent the little maid in to help him clear away. As he packed up the big canvas into its carrying case and wiped his brushes, he struck up a conversation with the girl.

'Have you work long for the Bartlebys?' he asked.

She was folding the floor coverings and smiled up at him.

'No sir. Just this last month. They began renting this house in April and my mother did some sewing for the mistress.'

'So when they return to the Midlands you will need to find further employment?'

'I might help my mother in her work. She is a seamstress and if she doesn't have any commissions then she makes lace that we sell. That's my mother's lace the mistress is wearing in your picture.'

'And exceptionally fine it is too. Is there a spare piece I can borrow so that I can paint in the detail before next week's sitting?'

'I'll ask the mistress,' said the girl. She left and returned shortly with a sample. 'She says she wants it back and not smelling of the turpsichord.'

'Turpentine,' he said smiling. 'You have most distinctive features and colouring. I wonder if I might make a sketch of you in the charcoal before I leave. It will only take a few minutes.'

They heard and saw the lady of the house and her companion leave to take a walk, no doubt clearing the smells of his turpentine from their noses, so she agreed provided that the older women did not return. In the fifteen or so minutes he took to render the charcoal sketch, they talked freely and with enjoyment. Her name was Mariel, she was fourteen years old, and her father had been a lascar sailor, one of the many skilled but poorly paid men that the British navy relied on. She remembered him as a tall dark-skinned man from the Bengal region of India. McKinley knew that such sailors were well regarded by their naval superiors, but they were never paid or treated as well as a British sailor. He had often seen them looking for work near the eastern docks in London.

Mariel told him that her mother had married against her parents' wishes and they had disowned her, his race and status was an affront to their society. The couple had lived quite comfortably until the merchant ship on which he had been serving reported him swept overboard during a rounding of the Horn when she was eleven. Mariel was her mother's only surviving child. They lived in Portsea and she made a living altering the clothing of naval officers' wives, and also by lacemaking which they sold in the markets or by hawking it round the better streets.

McKinley gave the girl sixpence and she helped him carry his equipment to the waiting cart. It would take him from the middle-class area of Croxton Town to his lodging house on the other side of Portsea. He was lodging in Landport near the house in which the renowned Charles Dickens had been born. He asked Mariel what she would spend her money on and was surprised when she responded enthusiastically that she would buy a penny dreadful to read when she had finished the day's work.

'What do you see in those things?' he asked, not mentioning that he had illustrated quite a few of them himself.

'I like the mysteries and the supernatural. My friend likes the murders. We take it in turns to buy a paper and exchange with each other. Sometimes we read them out loud and act out the drama.'

'Surely they are intended for boys. Is your friend a boy?'

'No. We don't see why girls shouldn't enjoy them as much as boys, and I can read,' she said. She did not seem offended, merely puzzled that he should expect her to behave in a demure or ladylike manner. McKinley reminded himself that these girls worked as hard as boys, and perhaps a little escapism was not a bad thing.

'Wouldn't you prefer a romance?' he asked.

'Only if it had horrible monsters in it too,' she said.

'So, what is your favourite story?'

'I like Varney the Vampire, and my friend likes Sweeney Todd, the murderous barber.'

'Good grief!' he said, 'So much blood.'

Mr Hatley, the wagoner, overheard the conversation and added:

'That's a true story, that bloodthirsty barber. He were a sailor from Portsmouth who'd had enough of the way the officers had tret him so he took out his revenge when he were on dry land.'

As they stowed his equipment on the wagon they carried on a lively conversation about the truth or otherwise of Sweeney Todd's existence. Mariel enjoyed every gruesome detail and stored titbits that she could share with her friend. The jollity was curtailed when Mrs Bartleby and the wizened companion bustled into sight.

Hatley exclaimed: 'Enemy off the port bow. All hands on deck.'

Mariel bobbed a curtsy and vanished into the house. Hatley gathered up his reins and McKinley doffed his hat as the ladies swept past him up the villa's sparkling steps.

The covered cart trundled slowly northwards from green open spaces to the overspill from Portsea where housing was provided for working people. Times had changed since Nelson's victory at Trafalgar had made Portsmouth and Britain the powerhouse of the seas. The Portsea houses were crowded, and as they progressed past the new railway line McKinley became more aware of the stink of cess pits. The June weather was hot and the odour would only increase later in the year. He mentioned this to Hatley, a suntanned broad old man with an enormous grey beard who had been recommended as one who was slow but reliable. His piebald horse was well treated, and he lived in the village of Buckland not far from McKinley's lodgings.

'Twill get worse than this sir,' said Hatley. 'The night soil collectors can't keep up with the numbers of people and the foulness builds up in the ground which do reek of filth.'

'I heard that last month the Queen herself was here to open the steam ship basin at the dockyard?' said McKinley.

Hatley grunted.

McKinley wondered about this response then said 'I presume the expansion of the navy and its accompanying services will bring more people to Portsmouth. Is no provision to be made for the sewage they produce?'

Hatley chuckled 'I'm surprised you can smell anything at all with the pungent smell that follows in our wake.'

'I can assure you I much prefer the smell of linseed oil and turpentine. And yes, I'm sure that I stink of the stuff but that is the price of my calling.'

'And I stink of horse dung' said Hatley. 'But at least that's good for the roses!' He gestured behind the cart where some urchins were scooping up dung from the road to take home or sell to neighbours.

They plodded along for a while, then McKinley said, 'Do you know if a member of the royal family will be present for the opening of the esplanade along the Southsea seafront?'

This enterprise was part of a scheme designed to claim the marshy and unhealthy land south of the new suburban villas, such as the one he had been visiting today. The seaside might then become an area fit for recreation and healthy walks. The esplanade was being built by convict labour, considered beneficial to both the convicts and society; at least they would be in the fresh air. They were usually housed on prison hulks, old wooden warships, demasted and permanently moored in Portsmouth and Langstone harbours.

Hatley said, 'They say it will be opened by the Lieutenant Governor Fitzclarence, and named for him too. You can't expect royalty to come all the way down here to support a project led by a Jew.'

McKinley looked sharply at the driver.

'Why do you take that attitude, and what do you mean?'

'Don't you know that the Clarence promenade was suggested and promoted by Emanuel? A Jew. And he did much of the fund raising too.' He spat into the road. 'But mostly I blame him for abolishing the free mart fair last year. We have few enough things to look forward to here.'

'I didn't know there was a fair here in Portsmouth. Was it a charter fair?'

'King Richard gave us common folk the right to have a fair every year. It's a tradition. Now it's been stopped. There won't be one this year.'

Hatley seemed extremely put out by the abolition of this excuse for debauchery, but from what McKinley had been told by the woman who ran his lodging house it was a drunken scene of lawlessness. It was held in old Portsmouth where smart houses now abutted the dens of vice that every dockside supports.

'Surely there are plenty of opportunities for drinking in the town,' McKinley said. He was put in mind of Shakespeare's quote from Hamlet 'more honoured in the breach than in the observance'. He said, 'As you know Mr Hatley, I've only been in Portsmouth a few weeks. Which King Richard was it that granted the tradition of a free mart fair?'

Hatley paused for a minute or two as he thought about this, then he grunted 'How many are there?'

McKinley had to dig again into his schoolboy memories of Shakespeare.

'Three, I think. The third who was killed at Bosworth, also known as the Crookback.' No response. He continued. 'The second who was a boy when he came to the throne and was deposed in favour of his cousin. And of course, the Lionheart ....'

'Him. It was him, the Lionheart. I'm sure of it and his wish should always be obeyed, for he was the greatest king we ever had.'

'Indeed' said McKinley. 'He was a very brave warrior and led a number of Crusades to the Holy Land and made peace with Saladin himself with mutual respect on both sides I believe.' Hatley was satisfied with this description of his hero, and his companion had to bite his tongue before he revealed the less savoury aspects of the king's life. He asked what it was about the fair that Hatley most enjoyed.

The old man drew on his pipe and thought about it. He took so long that McKinley wondered if he had offended him, or perhaps he had fallen asleep. Then he slowly said, after much consideration.

'It was all marvellous. The stalls with goods from all over the country for sale and some quite cheap, and the menageries with the wild animals in cages. But Portsmouth being a seaport we have all sorts of birds and animals brought here. Sailors love a monkey or a parrot what they've tamed. The circus horses was alright and the performing dogs. But animals in cages don't have much choice do they, it's like they're in jail for the crime of being an animal. No, I treat my old horse Patch here like he's one of my friends.'

He continued 'No what I enjoyed most was the freaks. What I liked best was the strange people, the twins stuck together and the bearded woman, the dwarfs and the rubber jointed man, and the giant; you just don't see them very often.'

Hatley became enthusiastic. 'You ought to paint them sir! Then they would be for everyone to see!'

McKinley agreed reluctantly, 'But would my viewers believe my rendition Mr Hatley? Or would they accuse me of fanciful or inaccurate depiction?' The other man thought about it and had to agree. McKinley concluded. 'No I think I will have to leave the immortalisation of such beings to the creators of the daguerreotype.'

They carried on for a companionable ten minutes then Hatley said:

'Of course, it was the Vauxhall that did for the fair. When they brought that big tent and had all night drinking and fornicating, that was the end of it.'

'It wasn't just Mr Emanuel then?' McKinley asked.

'I reckon he didn't like it all going on outside his shop in the High Street.'

McKinley knew that the town had a reputation in that respect. He had avoided areas of the docks known to be dangerous. 'Surely there are enough bawdy houses in Portsmouth? And public houses too?'

The other grunted, and conversation lapsed after that, so he was relieved when they arrived at his lodgings.

After Hatley helped him move the equipment into his rooms he paid him, and as there seemed to be no ill-feelings they arranged another journey to the Croxton Town villa in a week's time. Shortly afterwards McKinley looked out of his window and saw the man stroking and making much of his horse whilst filling his pipe. His landlady came out to talk to him and soon a girl arrived with a pail of water for the horse to have a drink. He was evidently a kindly man and well liked and he reflected that it was a shame that the people should not have their free mart fair when so many other cities and towns kept theirs.

He opened his cupboard and removed a small loaf of bread and cut himself a slice that he ate without butter. He had a pot of strawberry jam bought in the market and this luxury was all he needed as he brought out the newspaper he had purchased a few days before and read assiduously. A trip to the kitchen procured him a pot of tea and he was set to relax for the remainder of the day until he could find some supper in one of the nearby taverns.

The world was in a turmoil of change. After the defeat of Napoleon in 1815, Britain had drastically cut back its naval expenditure. It had been a hard time for Portsmouth and its people, but now in 1848 everything was changing and the old enemy across the sea had deposed another king and set up a second French republic during a tide of revolution that had spread throughout Europe.

Queen Victoria and her government could not afford to leave the empire unprotected against possible French aggression and new weapons. The use of exploding shells instead of cannon meant that wooden ships were vulnerable and iron-clad ships were now essential. More navies were beginning to adopt steam to drive warships so that sailing ships, being at the mercy of the wind, could be dangerously outmanoeuvred in battle.

McKinley's spirits were unusually low and he partly attributed this to the heat and the noise from the dockyard. He could hear the clang of metal works and foundries and the sulphurous metallic smell almost overpowered the smell of the ordure produced by the people and animals of Portsmouth. He gained comfort in the smell of oil and turpentine and opened his painting to take stock of the day's work and to allow the drying process to commence.

It was well that she had not seen his work in progress. He had starkly drawn the planes of her face. The heavy eyelids and jowly cheeks, the downturned mouth. This would not do. He looked at the charcoal sketches and began reworking one of them to sweeten her expression. He introduced a lift at the corners of her mouth; he resolved to paint that at the beginning of the next session before the muscles relaxed into their familiar scowl. A tightening of the neck and enhancement of the eyes that would sparkle just as they no doubt had when she was a young woman. That was all it needed. Find the secret of her mirror-face so that she would see what she expected to see in the painting and her husband would pay him his fee.

Her gown comprised a dark dress in shot silk that reflected well in the light, and with it was an elaborate collar of fine lace he knew had been made for her by Mariel's mother. The same lace was on the cap so he would concentrate on refining the detail of both during the week between sittings. He examined it and wondered at the delicacy of the work, how many hours had been spent making it and what sort of payment she had received. He decided to ask the maid to introduce her mother to him so that he might better understand the craft. Mrs Bartleby was rightly proud of the handmade lace she could afford when there were now so many machine-made copies.

He stared at the design until he felt a thumping headache and retired to his bedroom to rest before the evening when it should be cooler and the infernal noise of machines from the docks might not be so insistent. The smell of turpentine had dispersed, and McKinley soon fell into a doze. He dreamed that he was in a deep well, sitting in a bucket and the sky was visible through a small moon-sized opening above him. He was quite comfortable in the bucket and was waiting for someone to pull him up so he searched the little patch of sky for stars because he remembered that you could see them in daytime if you were in a well.

Why was he in the well? He knew that Macey would pull him out and he was not worried until he remembered that Macey was ill and might not be able to rescue him. Panic started, and he was not able to control it. He heard a sound and was beginning to wake up in the certainty that there was someone else in the well with him and he was afraid he might see it in the water bobbing about just beneath him. He woke fully, sweating and with a thudding heart.

The evening light shone through the feeble curtain and McKinley realised that the sound was a donkey in the street outside. He splashed his face with cold water and went out to find a clean tavern or chop house where he might buy some dinner.

*   *   *

The little theatre in Portsmouth's High Street was small and gaudily painted with two tiers of upper galleries at the back and sides. The gaslight added to the heat and it was crowded with all sorts of people; some were trying to sell food, and he had no doubt that there would be a few pickpockets among the multitude. There was a more affluent looking group gathering for the dress circle, but he was in the stalls and he did wonder what the hoi polloi would make of the bard's work, yet it was a full house. He scanned the playbill and was bemused to see that there was a cast of only seven.

The house lights dimmed and the audience quickly became silent. In the limelight the curtains parted to the plaintive strumming of a lute and so began a show unlike anything he had ever seen. The opening scene featured Theseus, his bride and the four lovers and a minor character who doubled as the musician. These actors and actresses carried an aura of glamour. They were each at the height of physical perfection, in stark contrast to the audience and the people that McKinley was used to seeing every day. He was fascinated by the beauty of the scene, he thought it might be the light or the makeup, but it cast a spell over the theatre.

They were dressed in pale cream clothes with their faces made up with greasepaint to give them depth in the glare of the limelight at the front of the stage. The men wore hose like Tudor gentlemen and the women wore short knee length skirts, their lower legs were a source of great titillation to the men in the audience. In addition to the three actresses and four actors there was an older bearded

13

man and McKinley could see from the playbill that he was both an actor and the manager of the Prospero Company.

The women were beautiful in different ways. Hippolyta was blonde and buxom, and Hermia dark and sensual, but the one who played Helena caused a surge of feeling in McKinley. She was tall, slim and fair skinned with auburn hair that curled softly, and from where he was sitting, he could see that she had eyes as green as spring leaves. The repartee between the characters was delivered with speed and clarity so that the archaic language seemed natural, and the audience was entirely charmed. He was unable to take his eyes from her whilst she was on the stage.

Then the scene ended and there was a collective sigh from the audience and applause, but McKinley noticed a change in atmosphere to one of excitement as the scenery was subtly changed to enable the entry of the 'rude mechanicals' and a cruder comedy, written for the groundlings of Shakespeare's day. A roar went up as they entered, and McKinley was astonished to see that they were large puppets clothed in earthy colours and with faces over-sized and full of character. Each was so distinctive, and their padded bodies, enormous hands and faces were as you would expect from a carpenter, weaver, joiner, bellows-mender, tailor and tinker. They walked or swaggered or minced onto the stage with immediate presence and personality to the great delight of the audience.

When you watched the movements of the marionettes it was easy to forget the operators standing behind them; the strings were invisible and they seemed more alive than the humans who had played the stock characters of lovers in the first scene. The operators were those same actors and actresses who had played the main parts, but with hoods over their heads concealing their faces. The audience adored it. The puppeteers exaggerated their roughness and the characterful creations gyrated to shouts of laughter from all parts of the house.

McKinley was curious to see the changes of scenery and he was surprised at how little there was. The first scene had been all red drapes, and these were whisked away for the scene with the earthy puppets so that the operators' stone-coloured clothes blended with the dull backcloth behind them. Behind the scenes someone was playing music and in the first scene this was the refined plucking of a stringed instrument, but this changed to a jaunty rude pipe when the mechanicals appeared.

As the play progressed, he was caught up along with the rest of the audience in the story of the star-crossed lovers and marvelled at the way that these actors had become skilful puppeteers. He wondered how the woodland would be depicted in the next scene when the faeries appeared. The audience held its breath as each distinctive and fantastical faerie, a puppet, was revealed. They were not based on any living thing. If they could be said to resemble anything it was insects or marine creatures, and each brought with it a piece of the wild wood that it deposited on the stage. They floated, crawled, and flew about the stage, vivid and ethereal. They came apart and joined together to represent a variety of creatures. The music, if it could be said to be music, consisted of percussion and bells.

The audience gasped at the extraordinary shapes and queerness displayed by those peculiar marionettes. Again, they were operated by the actors, but the mechanism was so remote that it was possible to ignore them completely. Such was the involvement in the drama of the performance that McKinley forgot that each had a person behind them and that their voices and movement were not their own.

The magical evening ended with the mixture of actors and puppets when the mechanicals perform their play for the Duke and his bride, and it was all the funnier for the mixing of players and puppets. He knew that the actor-manager had taken liberties with the text but as a piece of entertainment that revelled in the lyricism of Shakespeare's writing he could not fault it.

The curtains were broken five times that night to enthusiastic applause and the theatre's manager and staff had to usher out the house. McKinley was exhausted and elated. His face ached from laughing and his mind was filled with the wondrous things he had seen, but his heart felt excited and full; he was infatuated with the auburn-haired actress. He went straightway to the stage door to see the actors leaving but, although he waited for twenty or more minutes no one appeared except the watchman who told him that they had left as soon as the curtain closed.

That night he slept fitfully, and a green-eyed redhead was in his dreams, smiling at him as though she knew how he felt. Whatever was happening around them she looked at him and smiled, and he had a feeling of euphoria and surrendering to bliss. He woke with a pleasant feeling of anticipation. He had to see her again; he would visit the theatre every night until the show was finished.

McKinley struggled to work on his painting and walked out into the streets hoping he might see her in the town. His obsession led him to imagine her face on every woman he glimpsed from a distance or out of the corner of his eye, until he saw that it was not her. He called at the theatre hoping to meet members of the company and pass on his congratulations. The box office clerk told him that this touring group were new to them, and they met no one and only came to the theatre at night to perform. They came in costume and left immediately afterwards. He was unable or unwilling to provide any more information and McKinley gathered that they did not stay in any of the usual lodging houses. He left a note for the manager of the company, begging to be introduced. He was determined to return that night and watch it again. Each night he struggled from the packed auditorium to the stage door but each night he failed to see them leave. The only way he could have been sure of catching them was to have missed the performance and he could not bear to lose the chance to watch her on the stage. Several times he felt sure she had looked at him and knew he was there. The playbill gave her name simply as Teresa.

He knew that he had fallen in love with a stranger, a representation of his physical desire, but the intoxication was so great that he did not care. He was addicted to her face and voice; he wanted to be with her and fervently wanted to paint her. Then the company left the town. The theatre could not tell him where they had gone or where they had come from. They were paid a proportion of the house takings and they travelled all together in three wagons; that was all they knew. McKinley vacillated between the euphoria of love and desire and the uncertainty of not knowing how to find her and what her response would be. Pleasure outweighed pain because all might still be gained if he could find and woo her. He had not been rejected. His hopes existed in a dream.

*   *   *

Another sitting in the stuffy Croxton villa gave McKinley all the information he needed to substantially finish the portrait. He managed more work in the second week than the first as he used his painting as a distraction from the folly of infatuation that otherwise crushed him. By the time Hatley reappeared with his piebald horse and cart and conveyed the artist and his carrying frame and paints back to the house for the final sitting McKinley was in a state of despair. He was convinced that he would never find her when he had finished working in Portsmouth and that he had lost his chance of happiness. He asked the old man if he had ever been to the theatre.

'I make a point of attending every playing company that visits the town and especially the Shakespeare. My missus can't see anything in it but I says to her that this is the bard's work and he was the greatest Englishman that ever wrote plays and such.'

'What did you think of the most recent drama? 'A Midsummer Night's Dream',' asked McKinley.

'It was a marvel. Those puppets were almost alive, and those creepy crawly fairies gave me the shivers. Now I've seen them regular, they used to come each year for the free mart fair, so they did, but I've never seen them on the theatre stage before.'

McKinley's ears pricked at this. 'I have tried to find out where they come from but without success.'

'Well they be circus folk and take their homes with them like snails. They'll be staying in a field somewhere, like as not. I reckon they travel from fair to fair throughout the summer and then they goes to ground in the winter.'

McKinley wanted to press him to describe previous shows, but Hatley was keen to recount what he had been doing in the past week. He had plans for a new business venture and he launched into a great description of the new Clarence Esplanade on the seafront between the town walls and the Southsea castle. It would be a place for ladies and gentlemen to walk and take the sea air. He had got talking to a group of the guards watching the convicts as they laboured on the footpath and they were saying that the draining of the Great Morass marshland would be next between the esplanade and the posh streets of Croxton Town.

McKinley was not convinced of the health benefits. 'Surely all that swampland cannot be healthy?'

'Tis better to have the fresh sea air from the south than the stink of the Portsmouth cess pits. And the marsh isn't so bad, it's mostly reeds and fresh water from rainfall. The birds like it well enough, but I dare say the council will drain it like they have the others. What with the esplanade and the villas it will become a place for the well-to-do to be seen exercising, either walking or on horseback.'

McKinley had not seen many Portsmouth ladies hacking out, but he supposed that summer visitors might take a hire if there was nothing better to do. He tried to imagine Mrs Bartleby riding a horse and found it quite amusing, especially as he saw her companion accompanying her on a mule, like Sancho Panza.

'Will you tell me your business plan?'

Hatley continued with pride. 'I thought that I would take old Patch here down to the seafront and give rides to the people that want the fresh air but can't walk along the esplanade.'

'On Patch?'

'No of course not, my pal has a trap that will suit the old horse. I can smarten him up with ribbons and bows. Should be a popular jaunt for visitors in the summer.'

He was so enthusiastic McKinley said 'I am pleased for you Hatley. And I look forward to visiting a Southsea that would be as popular as Brighton or Weymouth where sea water bathing is attracting regular visitors.'

'I don't know about sea water bathing. It didn't do the old king much good, he still went mad,' said Hatley.

'Possibly,' said McKinley. 'Anyway the new railway will bring visitors; but I don't understand why it doesn't go all the way to the docks.'

'Don't want to make it too easy for the enemy. There's unrest among the continentals.' He tapped the side of his nose. 'The last ship that got floated here in March is like to be last sailing ship,' said Hatley. He was proud of his knowledge. 'Steam is the way forward and I've heard talk of iron clad vessels. We must stay ahead of the Frenchies. They've just had another revolution and got rid of their latest king. Last time they did that it meant war.'

By way of changing the subject McKinley asked, 'There is sea bathing in Southsea is there not?'

'Yes, the assembly halls, mostly full of naval officers and their ladies. Drinking, gossiping, and flirting.' He scratched his beard. 'And sea bathing.' He shook his head as though nothing good could come of such a thing. 'But they're officers from the service and their wives. You'll have heard of the duel fought three years ago by two naval officers, no doubt. It was in all the newspapers. Caused a mighty scandal. I'm hoping now that we have a railway coming into the town and even have royal visitors there's no reason gentry from the country shouldn't come here for the season. Like that Mrs Bartleby and her companion, taking a whole house in Croxton Town. They might eventually build down as far as Southsea and a few hotels would be good for business.'

McKinley vaguely recalled the duel. Two officers fighting over a perceived insult to one and involving the gentleman's wife. He sought to confirm the details. 'The duellists fought with pistols?'

'They did, and in Gosport too,' said Hatley as though Gosport was the proper place for a duel.

'And one of them died I believe.'

'Four shots were fired and one struck home. The injured man was brought back to the Quebec Hotel where he languished and died. They even got a surgeon to operate on him but that did no good,' said Hatley.

'Didn't they blame the surgeon for his death?' asked McKinley. The successful duellist had been tried and acquitted although he appeared to have provoked the altercation and had insisted on the duel.

'Shouldn't go poking around in a man's insides, if you ask me,' said Hatley.

A ball to the abdomen McKinley recalled, and the jury found that the death of the unfortunate officer was associated more closely with the intervention of a surgeon than the original injury. He was not surprised. His friend Dr Macey told him stories of surgeons and their cavalier attitude to their craft that made him cringe. He had probably taken an infection from the opening of his flesh by the filthy hands of a butcher in a blood-stained apron. Better to have left the ball in place.

Hatley continued his detailed and salacious account of the duel which had been the principal gossip of the drinking houses, and McKinley let him continue until a companionable silence descended over them again. The thought of doctors caused him to slip into a dark reverie about Macey whose ordeal in the crypt of a church earlier in the year had affected his health. It seemed that he would survive, but much weakened by his experience and the worst damage was to his mind.

McKinley looked around the sunlit fields as they approached the new villas and thought how different it seemed, so modern and with piped water available to the best houses rather than reliance on wells. He had a horror of wells and shuddered at the memory.

'You feeling cold sir?' asked Hatley. 'I hope you don't have a fever. There's been talk of cholera in the town again.'

'No, I was just remembering something unpleasant. I expect it is all this talk of death. Here we are and there is Mariel sent to meet us.' She did not look as carefree as she had the previous week, and he made a promise that he would reward her with a few pennies that she could spend on lurid papers or sweets as she desired.

They unloaded the wagon and set up for a continuation of the portrait. Mariel exclaimed when she saw the depiction of her mother's lace work and she remarked how realistic it was. She asked if she could touch it.

'It would be better if you did not Mariel as I was painting it quite recently.'

'It looks so real, as though my fingers would sense the fine working.'

'And it would.' He moved it to show her the brush strokes that raised the lustrous creamy paint over the darker background. 'You can see it is thicker than the ground and that is because I use megilp, it's a medium that I make myself and helps the paint to dry in this textured manner.'

'Last week you used the large thick brushes but that cannot have made these marks.'

'Quite right. For the large areas I use a hog-hair brush but had you been here during the entire sitting you would have seen me use a fine sable hair rigger to draw Mrs Bartleby's face. It's called that because it is used to depict the rigging in paintings of sailing ships.'

She sniffed the painting. 'And it does not smell so strongly of the turp…. turpentine.'

'I'm glad you like it, and I have you to thank by giving me the lace sample that I could paint from.' He looked at her small rapt face and again sensed that she was unhappy.

'Has something happened Mariel. You seem worried.'

She stepped away from him and said that her mother had been unwell. McKinley noticed her distance and asked.

'Is it contagious?' she nodded 'Cholera?' She nodded again and made to leave the room.

'If there is anything I can do.'

'Please don't tell the mistress.' He agreed and was about to comment that they might guess from her expression when he realised that Mrs Bartleby was unlikely to look closely at servants. He thought that the sharp little companion might be more astute. They nodded at each other, and she left. He laid out his paints that were ready mixed, and mentally planned the painting of Mrs Bartleby's face and hands. He was confident that there would be only finishing touches to be done at the next sitting and that was as well, for he wished to be away from Portsmouth and up to Guildford to join his artists' community.

The sitting progressed well with little spoken and no complaints about the smell of turpentine. McKinley wondered if the megilp was less offensive or perhaps she had heard rumours of the cholera and believed that the offensive odours of solvent might chase away the miasma of sickness. In any event the sessions were soon over, and the ladies left. As he had hoped, Mariel reappeared and helped him to pack away his equipment and rearrange the room.

'Mariel, I hope you don't mind me suggesting this but if you have any free time in the next week I should like to make a portrait of you.' She started and he hastily added 'Please I am not making an improper suggestion, but artists collect images that they can use in their work, and yours is one such.' He was thinking of a romantic medieval scene requiring an exotic face of innocence, but he made light of it. 'Just imagine if I were to illustrate the cover of a penny dreadful and your face would be that of the heroine, or more likely the victim of the vampire.'

She laughed, and he added 'Plus I can pay you to sit for me. So, you might have an afternoon's rest as well as some money to take home. That is if your mother can spare you.'

'We do need the money sir. She can't work at all in her condition, and I am doing all the deliveries. But as soon as folks hear she's sick they will not give her any more work. I am paid for my work here, but I also spend time helping mother and we must be short very soon.'

'Then it is settled. Tell me the times you have free, and I will expect you at my lodgings. I will write the address down. You need not worry about the landlady; she will expect you and the door shall be left open while I work. You will be perfectly safe.'

They carried the boxes to Hatley's wagon and he waved her goodbye. He hoped that she would keep their appointment because he had an idea that she would be a perfect model as a heroine of John Keats's verse if he ever were able to create a painting based on the work of that romantic poet. He had been absorbed by the book of poems for many months and found it, along with the theatre, to be an antidote to the stress of modern life. A simpler time and a nobler people and one in which skills and crafts had not be supplanted by machines making goods and causing people to starve for lack of work. He could not open a newspaper without seeing accounts of the starvation of people in Europe and Ireland. The revolutions in those countries were also worrying. The French were the greatest worry and it looked as though another Emperor Napoleon might be on the way.

To pass the time going back to Landport he prevailed upon Hatley to tell him stories about Portsmouth. They passed a brewer's dray and Patch was almost frisky as the big horses and their valuable cargo trundled by. He managed to steer Hatley off his favourite subject, the freak shows at the free mart fair, and the old man was persuaded to focus on the production of beer, a subject also close to his heart. The dray belonged to Pike Spicer a large brewery based in Portsea, and Hatley was very familiar with its history and told proudly of the piped water supply from the

Farlington Marshes that was once so filled with sand that it resulted in the spoiling of a whole batch of beer. He was partial to a shant of local beer and would never drink water as it was 'not good for the physic'.

'Shant?' said McKinley. 'I presume that's a local expression. Do you never frequent the coffee houses or drink tea?'

'You don't know what's in those concoctions. The brewing of beer is known to make water fit to drink and the wells on the island are none too good, being so close to the sea, like.'

The stinking cess pits would not help, thought McKinley. The place was as densely populated as London and without the Thames and tributaries flowing through it. He had to admit that the great river also stank. Especially in the summer. He thought of Mariel's mother and asked if he had heard of any fever or other sickness.

Hatley growled and said: 'There is some sickness down by the docks. Don't know yet if it's the cholera has returned; and that's another reason not to drink anything other than beer if you ask me. Nor to go about washing too frequently.'

'They must have strict quarantine procedures when a ship comes in,' muttered McKinley thinking of plague rats from the past, and also the pigs and other animals he had seen in the streets in close quarters to the general populace. The more he thought about it the keener he was to leave the town and get out into countryside. He realised that he did not have any way of contacting Mariel and he was worried about her circumstances. Mrs Bartleby would probably let her go if she became aware of contagion in the family and then what would the girl do?

He had planned on going to the theatre that evening although the Prospero Company had left, and an assortment of acts were filling the void. But after they had unloaded the painting and equipment he decided to walk into the fields and try to find some fresh air. His mind was in a turmoil, and he lay down under an old tree and considered how his soul seemed torn in two. The era of sailing ships was coming to an end, Hatley had said. A wooden frigate named Leander launched in March would be the last to be produced and from now on ships would be fitted with steam engines and driven by screw. Hellish noise and fire and stink where once there had been the whistling of wind in rigging and the rushing sound of the water as the hull breasted the waves.

But in classical myth Leander had drowned and his lover Hero threw herself off a cliff. Doomed lovers are the subject of so many stories, they must appeal to something in everyone, even those who live their lives in strict obedience to society's rules. Mariel's mother and father versus the Bartleby's propriety. Lying in the afternoon heat under the tree's dark shade McKinley felt in a liminal state, between two worlds. He was living among the drear noise and stink of an industrial town like Portsmouth and was drawn to the erotic mystery of a red headed girl who seemed to embody the natural spirit of earlier times.

His mind replayed the Dream that he had watched and listened to six times, and the voices and cadence of speech seemed to fill his head so he was startled when he realised it was midsummer and this was like a dream. The words that he had heard Teresa speak was the language of Shakespeare he knew, and the play had been written in about 1600 when mystery and magic were accepted by everyone, from queens to commoners. Science and technology had not yet imposed the grind of manufacturing onto men and materials alike. He was drawn to paint pictures of those lyrical times, to recreate that simplicity and beauty, forgetting the hardship that a pastoral life could force upon those who lived on the land. With that he fell asleep and dreamed of Teresa and was woken only by the munching of cattle that had moved into the shade with him.

*   *   *

The next day was overcast but dry and he took a little exercise before his Sunday dinner. Most people were making their way to the big tent that housed the unitarian church so popular with the common people. McKinley was not a church goer and although he was a believer, he felt distanced from the Anglican church.

Everyone was in their Sunday best, chatting and excited to be seen taking the air, and it made him feel oddly detached. His eyes still sought her auburn hair and green eyes among the crowds, and he was hoping he might see her again. He would work today, and Mariel said that she would come to his lodgings for sketching in the afternoon when she had finished her chores at home. He fervently hoped that her mother was recovering from her illness.

He found a small restaurant and ate a roast dinner with beer, as recommended by Hatley. Then he almost reluctantly went back to his rooms, dreading that Mariel would not turn up. But she did, as promised, and even earlier than agreed. The landlady examined her carefully, to make sure that her gentleman lodger was not entertaining a woman of ill repute but was soon satisfied by the obvious innocence of the girl herself and McKinley's promise to leave the doors open.

He sat her in an upright chair and instructed her to look out of the window at anything of interest and not to move. Then he began a detailed pencil drawing of her face. He always drew at his best when he loved the thing he was depicting, whether it was a vase of flowers or a person. He was completely absorbed when he heard the unmistakable sound of a rumbling stomach. It could not have been his as he had recently eaten, and he quickly suggested a break and offered his sitter a slice of bread and jam and ran downstairs to request tea.

When he returned, she was looking at the picture and her face was wet. She had no expression just tears overflowing her lashes.

'My poor dear girl. Sit down and tell me what is the matter. It isn't the drawing is it? I'm sorry I should have asked after your mother.' He gave her a rag to wipe her eyes and blow her nose and waited while she gained control of herself. The tea arrived, and the landlady, torn between kindness and accusations at McKinley, made a great fuss, which instigated the shedding of further tears.

Eventually Mariel explained 'It's mother, she's no better, and I don't know how we will survive without her earnings. I can live in as a servant if necessary, but who will look after mother?'

'Don't let them take her into that new workhouse, my girl' said his landlady. 'I'd rather be in the graveyard than that place.'

'That's not helpful, thank you. It won't come to that,' McKinley said. 'Mariel will be fine now, and she will be paid for today's sitting and I will take her home.'

She bustled off and Mariel said 'I'm sorry for making a fuss. I was looking at the drawing and I thought how I look so innocent, young and pure. It felt as though that would be the last image of me as a child. I sense that everything is going to change and I am going to be corrupted.'

Before he could reassure her she said, 'The only way that I can earn enough money to pay our rent and get someone to look after mother is if I go to work in a brothel. My youth and innocence will carry a high price - at least for a while.'

McKinley was shocked and said, 'You have been approached?'

'Most girls in service are approached, sir. There is a ready market for young flesh in Portsmouth. I don't blame the madams of the better houses; there are many young officers without families who must get what pleasure they can on shore. They say the French might attack again soon and these boys and men may never return.' McKinley was horrified that she might be considering selling herself in this way.

'No, you cannot do this. There must be some other way to earn a living and look after your mother.'

'Bless you sir, but I am the lowest type of servant there is, apart from young children and there are plenty of those scratching a living.'

'But you can read,' said McKinley. 'You are not a street urchin.' He thought guiltily of the children he had seen begging in the streets, sweeping the horse dung from the paths of well-dressed people, seldom receiving more than a farthing or a halfpenny. Sleeping in hovels or leaning over a rope in a doss house.

She continued, 'Disease is the greatest fear even in a well-run bawdy house and then, of course, succumbing to drink to forget. I don't want to end up as another 'brute' down at the wharves, I've seen plenty of those who have lost their looks and their health. It's a wretched life.'

'It shall not happen,' said McKinley speaking more confidently than he felt. 'We will go right this minute and see your mother. I will provide whatever is required.' He brushed aside her objections and they descended to the ground floor kitchen where his landlady and her servant were preparing vegetables.

'Mrs R I am sorry if I was a little short with you earlier. You are quite correct that Mariel must not allow her mother to be placed in a workhouse, it would be the death of her. I will go and see her now and I wonder if I might buy anything you can spare to feed the poor lady who has known better times in the past.'

The kind woman provided them with the remains of a beef joint on the bone, and some vegetables. 'I was planning to make a soup tomorrow,' she said. 'But I can purchase other things for that.'

She thoughtfully minced the beef and packaged up the bone with instructions to Mariel on the cooking of a nourishing soup for her mother.

'Do you have tea, Mariel?' McKinley asked and was not surprised to find that she did not. It was a costly commodity, and he purchased a small quantity from his landlady. He told her that it was a wholesome drink and stimulated the nervous system.

With their goods they walked across the town towards the poorer streets of Portsea. It was not far, but as he walked he felt a renewed awareness of his surroundings. They did not speak. He knew that conversation would distract him from this sharpened perception of the world in which he lived. It was true, there were well dressed people, some undoubtedly poor, enjoying a walk on their only day off; many having been to church and living, no doubt blameless lives. But in the shadows, he now saw the thin and ill, old and young, exhausted from life's burden and he could not ignore them.

Mariel pulled at his coat. 'Here sir, is where we live.' He followed her into an alley and a small pig ran past and stopped when it smelled the food that McKinley carried. Mariel shooed it away. She opened a wooden door and they stepped over a threshold into a dark room with one small window. As his eyes adjusted McKinley became aware of a pot stove, unlit, a bare table and a bench. In the corner there was a single bed on which lay a figure huddled in blankets.

'I'll light the stove,' said Mariel and began to pile kindling and wood into the blackened opening.

McKinley remembered his time looking after his laudanum-addicted friend when he had stopped using the drug. He picked up the chamber pot.

'No sir. You mustn't do that.' She was horrified and he could see that she was ashamed.

'I've done it before Mariel and will doubtless do it again. And I hope that if I am ill, someone will do it for me. Where is the latrine?'

She gave him directions and he completed the task. He found a pump nearby and was able to refill the water jug from the kitchen.

'Do you have any soap?' He was used to cleaning up after his painting work and when Mariel brought out a square of soap he grated it and began softening it in the water.

'Mariel, is that you?' The person in the bed stirred.

The daughter ran to her and bathed her face whilst soothing her mother. She was obviously very weak and when a candle was lit he was appalled at the shrunken form, the pallor and looseness of her skin. She was so different from her daughter in looks but when she spoke there was a similarity in her tone of voice and she was obviously educated and probably the person who had taught Mariel to read.

It seemed to take a long time for the kettle of water to boil and all the while the daughter talked calmly to her mother, explaining who McKinley was and trying to persuade her to take some food. He would not let them drink water until it had been boiled and a weak tea was brewed that the poor woman seemed to enjoy. She was prevailed upon to take a few mashed cooked vegetables and Mariel promised to make the beef into a tea.

A motherly looking woman appeared at about seven o'clock and brought some milk and bread. She was a kind neighbour and knew of their plight, but McKinley doubted it would be of much comfort. He made Mariel promise to eat something and to let him know in the morning how her mother had spent the night. He walked back to his lodgings thinking that it could not long before Mariel would be alone. He had paid her as promised so her Monday rent for the week would be met and she would have her work at the Croxton Town villa, at least whilst the Bartlebys were there. He resolved that she would not disappear into the stews of Portsmouth.

*   *   *

When he rose the next day, he could not wait to hear her news and walked to the alley that she had led him to the previous day. The door was locked, and no one responded to his knocking. The same neighbour who had been so solicitous the previous evening appeared. She introduced herself as Maud Kelly.

'Mrs Banerjee died in the night and the body is still in the house. The landlord's agent wants Mariel and the body out as soon as possible.'

'But she has the money to pay him!' said McKinley.

'He wouldn't take it, sir. Says they don't want the likes of her in the street lowering the tone. She has to go, and her dead mother with her. God rest her soul.'

'God rot his soul!' said McKinley. 'Where is the beast? I will knock him down! And where is Mariel?'

'She has gone to her mother's family to tell them that their daughter is dead. They have disowned her, but Mariel thinks they may take her back now that she's dead and it is a better resting place for the poor woman than a pauper's grave. Or, God forbid, the dissector's table.'

'Good God yes. What will she do if they disclaim her completely?'

'Mariel will go to the Poor Union for help in getting the body buried in a consecrated graveyard,' said Maud. 'And I daresay there'll only be a few people that will attend the funeral. Despite all the service and excellent needlework she's supplied them over the years, rich folk keep their purses closed.'

'Tell me where to find the landlord's man. I will settle him so that Mariel shall not be disturbed in this period of mourning.'

'I'll come with you,' the woman said, and she quickly scuttled into her own hovel and returned with a bonnet and a basket. 'You never know what you might find when you're out,' she said by way of explanation when he looked surprised at her basket.

'Mrs Banerjee made the most beautiful lace. All the lacemakers I've known have ruined their eyes with the close work,' she told him as they bustled along the dirty streets to the shabby rooms where the rent man lived and plied his trade. 'And do you know, some of them ladies tried to haggle the price down. Saying that they could get such a piece so much cheaper that was made on a machine. There's no comparison between the fine handmade and the machine-made pieces, and how is a poor woman to earn her bread when those with money are so mean? Someone even offered to give her an orange for a piece of lace that had taken days to make. Fortunately she knew what an orange was, having been given one as a child, and watched it go soft and ruined before she could eat it.'

McKinley was amazed that she could walk so fast and speak without seeming to draw breath. He was working hard to keep up, both with her pace and with the speed of her thoughts when they arrived at a mean terrace with a lean menacing looking dog tied up outside. It growled as they approached.

'He's not there. Must be out collecting rents,' said Maud.

'But surely that's his dog?'

'No that's the dog he leaves to guard his rooms. He takes the savage dog with him when he's collecting. I'll ask around.'

McKinley noticed that there were not many people in the vicinity, and usually the back alleys and squares in the corners of Portsea were busy with folk. 'Where is everybody?'

'It's rent day. They're making sure they've got the money or they're keeping out of his way. They're not going to make it easy for him.' She collared a young barefoot girl who was clutching a few bunches of watercress.

'I'll have some of that.' They haggled briefly and then she asked the girl with a wink and a scrape of the nose where the rent man was. She pointed and said, 'He's in Smelly Alley missus.' It was not a road with which McKinley was familiar.

They set off in that direction and he was alarmed to find the streets even more narrow and filthy than the ones they had left. A slamming of windows and screaming came from ahead and they slowed slightly. Maud said, 'He's up ahead and someone's in trouble.'

A distressing sight met them as they rounded a corner into a small dirty square cluttered with broken barrels and wood piles. A thick set man with a big belly was throwing rags and bundles through the open windows of a hovel and two small children were pinned against a wall under threat of a large brindled cur of the bulldog type. Their mother shrieked as most of her belongings were stripped from the house and the door fastened shut. A policeman and a bailiff stood by so that no one dared to intervene. When it was done the bailiff summoned a thin man with a handcart and they piled the goods onto it. The rent collector called off his dog and the children ran to their mother only to be dragged from her and put onto the cart.

The bailiff announced to all the assembled householders that they would now be taken to the workhouse in Milton where the children would be fed, clothed and educated and the woman could find work to help pay for their keep. They would not be abandoned to the streets but would be brought up to know God's intentions for even the poorest among us. They would be taught from the bible.

McKinley got the impression the woman was about to spit, but she obviously thought better of it and, the fight gone out of her, she joined her children at the cart as it was wheeled away. The policeman and bailiff went with them. The small crowd hissed at the rent collector as he called his dog and walked towards Maud and McKinley. He stopped when neither moved to let him pass and the people turned back and fell silent at the prospect of more entertainment.

'Let me by, will you?' he said with a surly snarl. But he stopped and tempered his manner as he took in the way that McKinley was dressed. His clothes were good quality and his linen clean. He was freshly shaved whereas the rent collector was scruffy and his clothes ill fitting, his complexion pale and unhealthy looking. 'You can't have business with me?'

McKinley raised his voice so that the watching residents could hear him clearly. 'Today a woman lies dead awaiting burial and you intend to evict her corpse and her daughter, even though her rent is paid.'

The rent man looked at Maud, recognising her from the morning's altercation and she loudly claimed. 'She's barely cold you callous bastard! A hard-working Christian woman who always paid her way. You've got no soul; you blood-sucking vampire.'

The crowd murmured their disapproval and shouts of 'Shame!' and more direct expletives caused him to claim loudly, 'She hasn't paid her rent!'

'Only 'cause you refused to take it,' Maud shouted back even louder, then to the crowd: 'She's a pretty young girl. I reckon he want to see her on the streets. Maybe he's got designs on her 'imself.'

That was enough to provoke a threatening murmur from the crowd who, emboldened now that the policeman and bailiff were gone, could see the chance for some sport at the rent collector's expense.

McKinley thought it wise to step in and he said firmly 'Here is her rent money. Now will you accept it and let her stay until the proper arrangements for a decent funeral can be made?' After a fearful look at the mob the rent collector nodded and got out his book. McKinley watched as he recorded the payment, to the great satisfaction of the crowd, who waited for the man to exit with his dog the way that the cart had gone. The dog was wagging its tail, but the man had his own between his legs, metaphorically at least.

McKinley turned to little woman at his side who was shaking her fist at the retreating figure.

'Thank you, Maud. I couldn't have done it without you.'

'He's got no friends round here,' she said. The glee at the banishment of the rent collector being marred by the eviction of the poor woman and her children earlier, the people of the square dispersed into their hovels. It was only one small victory in a tide of misery.

'You can't save them all sir,' she said. 'Let's see if Mariel has come back.'

They walked slowly back through the dirty alleys to the room that contained the corpse of Mariel's mother. There they found the door open and an undertaker's man standing outside.

'Mariel?' called Maud. 'You in there?'

'This is a private matter woman,' the man said, then he looked at McKinley and changed his tone. 'Might I enquire what business you have with the deceased?'

'I have no business with the deceased,' said McKinley, 'but with her daughter. Is she in the room?'

'We're ready' said a voice inside and the undertaker stood back to allow two plain clothed men carry a coffin through the door. It was of good quality and they showed proper respect for the dead woman. McKinley removed his hat and Maud said a quiet prayer to herself and the little cortege turned and began to walk up the alleyway. When it had gone, they realised that Mariel stood just inside the doorway in the darkness of the room. Her eyes were swollen from tears already shed.

'Mariel, who are they and where is your mother being taken?' said McKinley.

'I went to see her family. The one that disowned her when she married my father. Now that she's dead her parents will take her back and bury her in the family plot in the graveyard.' She stopped, struggling to hold back tears. 'I couldn't let her be put in a pauper's grave or used for cutting up. I couldn't afford a funeral and the rent man said we had to be gone.'

'You have the room until the end of the week Mariel and in that time we will find a more permanent and suitable residence for you.' He looked at Maud. 'That rogue won't return I hope?'

'No, you saw him off, good and proper.' She turned to the girl. 'You should have seen it lovely. Let me help you tidy up.' They went into the house, then Mariel turned and said:

'I still have tea sir, would you like a cup?'

'I won't thank you, but I will see you soon as I shall be delivering the finished painting to the Bartlebys. I take it you are still engaged by them?'

'I'll be there later today sir. They know about my mother and the Missus gave me the morning off.'

'How generous!' He was about to say more but continued, 'You will have this room for the next week and I promise to see you soon.'

He left and walked quickly back to the main road. The cortege was gone but, after asking a small boy who was playing with a dead rat, he discovered in which direction and set off in pursuit. They should not be travelling fast, and he would soon catch them. He intended to find where and when the funeral would be held, and he was determined that Mariel should not miss it.

*　　　　　　*　　　　　　*

He soon caught up with them and after speaking to the undertaker, he paid a visit to the family of Mrs Banerjee, although they insisted on calling her Miss Reid. The family comprised her parents whom he thought must be in their fifties, and a son and daughter who were married and established in the local society. They lived in a well-appointed house in Portsmouth High Street. The curtains were drawn and a tidy little maid answered the door, she reminded him of Mariel, but pale skinned. He presented his card and she showed him into a drawing room that was dark and filled with objects from around the world. A painting of a Royal Naval Captain hung on the wall and what he supposed was a mirror had been covered with black crepe. McKinley noticed in the oppressive silence that the big grandfather clock had been stopped.

A gentleman entered. He was stern and grey-whiskered and respectfully black-suited and was obviously the man in the portrait, some years older. He contemplated McKinley silently.

'You are Captain Reid?' McKinley gestured to the portrait and the other man nodded. 'Forgive me for calling on you unannounced in your time of grief, but I am aware that a lady I visited last night has passed away, and I was present this morning when her body was removed from her lodgings. The undertakers said that she was being brought here.'

'Are you a physician, sir?' The old man looked at McKinley's card, which told him very little, but his clothing and demeanour persuaded him that he was one of their own class. As an artist he possessed an indifferent status in this society, but he had turned on the charm and exaggerated his obvious education and his background as a gentleman of means.

'I encountered Mariel at a villa in Croxton Town.'

The old man said nothing but scowled.

'She was working as a housemaid,' McKinley continued, 'I was intrigued by her obvious intelligence and education.'

Then Captain Reid said: 'Then perhaps you and your wife would take her into service?'

'But she is your own granddaughter, sir.'

'It is all she is fit for.'

'Do you not intend to make provision for Mariel yourself, sir?' he asked.

The old man stiffened and beckoned McKinley to sit. 'Do not think so harshly of us. We did not know how far Alice had fallen, and a Christian burial is all that we can do for our daughter. The girl you speak of was born of sin and must make her way in life. And in the society that her mother chose for her.'

Before McKinley could respond he continued, 'Alice Mary was our eldest daughter and we sent her to Italy in the company of a maiden aunt to recover from an illness that we were afraid might be consumption. It was a disaster; the aunt fell in love with an Italian and is still there as far as we know. We insisted that Alice be sent back to us on a ship that I knew of but we were too late. Her head no doubt had been turned by Italian notions of romantic love and, whilst sailing back to Britain, the foolish girl fell under the spell of an Indian sailor, a lascar, serving on the merchantman. Despite entreaties from all her family and friends, and the stern rebuke of our vicar, she disobeyed everyone and undertook a marriage service at the unitarian church, hoping no doubt that we would be reconciled to her in due course.'

'She was properly married in a Christian ceremony?' said McKinley.

'The child was born within five months of the wedding so it was obvious that she had sinned against God and her family whilst on the ship, and we could not welcome a fallen woman, let alone her seducer, back into our home.'

'You were a seafaring man and must have interacted with people of many races and religions.'

'And they should be kept apart, the proper place for the coloured races is in service to the white ones. Even had she repented and given up her husband, the child would not have been accepted into our own circle as it was a different colour. Her face would have been a constant reminder of the shame she had brought on the family.' The old man was stiff with bigotry and pride.

'That is harsh sir.'

'We settled a sum of money on our daughter and the lascar went back to sea. My wife insisted that they move way from Portsmouth as part of the settlement and they went to Chatham. She was dead to us then and we grieved for her. Now we are grieving again.'

He continued. 'Alice returned to Portsmouth after the man was lost at sea. We found this out when my wife's friends saw her selling lace. Soon after that she tried to ingratiate herself with the family; but the damage could not be undone. You are a man from our class and must see that it would have meant disgrace and my wife would not have been received among her social circle. It would also have been unfair on our son and younger daughter. He is in the Royal Navy and his career progression will take into consideration the probity of his family background. Fortunately, our other daughter made a good match, despite our problems with Alice, and her in-laws will not countenance a half-breed as a relation. We have several grandchildren.'

McKinley received the impression that the female side of the family was more determined to keep Mariel out than her grandfather. He also realised that her mother's influence would account for why Mariel was well spoken and could read. The reduction of their means may have been quite recent, and he saw no benefit in pointing out that their appalling living conditions must have considerably shortened the woman's life.

'Well, your daughter is really dead now Captain Reid. Cholera, from what I could see. Where and when is the funeral? I should like to attend, and so will her daughter.'

The old man stood and walked to the fireplace and McKinley thought he was going to refuse to tell him. Then he picked up a small lace doily from the mantle and turned it over in his hands.

'She made this for my whisky glass when she was ten years old. She was my little girl.' There were tears in his eyes.

'Mariel is only fourteen and she is innocent. You know what cruelty and abuse awaits unprotected girls in our society. Please don't abandon her to this unforgiving world if you are a Christian.'

McKinley knew that the forces ranked against him were greater than one sentimental old man.

'The funeral is on Thursday at St Thomas's church at three o'clock. Bring her, but I will not tell my wife so do not expect that she will be welcomed by our family. I will consider what you say.'

*   *   *

On Thursday 29th June 1848 Robert McKinley accompanied Mariel Banerjee to her late mother's funeral at St Thomas's church in Portsmouth. They did not follow the hearse with its dark horses, plumed and shining in black livery in the hot sunshine. A funeral director walked respectfully in front carrying his top hat, and the mourning family walked behind, the ladies' faces were heavily veiled so that their expressions were not visible. Two smartly dressed small boys wept; but they were paid to do so.

Mariel stood next to McKinley at the back of the church and she wept quietly as the service proceeded with no mention of the dead woman's husband and child and nothing personal about her after the age of seventeen. It was the funeral they would have held in 1834 if they had had a corpse. It was a small gathering with no extended family or friends. Alice's mother and father, the son and the other daughter with their respective spouses and children came to pay what respects they could muster. They filed out passed them and he could see that they were all dry eyed. Most avoided looking at their dark-skinned relative, but he thought he detected a look of hatred from one young girl, no older than about twelve. She was a plain, pasty faced child and she must have envied the looks of the other girl, for despite her plain and poor clothes Mariel was a beauty.

At the burial no one remained by the grave after the rites were concluded. It was as though there was a collective sigh of relief and they turned and with undue haste hurried away. As they left

Mariel stepped forward and said a few phrases in her father's native tongue in clear melodic tones. She cast a yellow flower onto the coffin and the vicar gasped in shock at what he may have assumed was some unchristian sentiment. She translated it for him. The family had stopped and turned back at the foreign language but seeing the priest relax they began to hurry away again, muttering to each other.

As McKinley turned and looked around the graveyard, he noticed a tall man in dark clothes who seemed familiar, and who stood some way off, obviously fascinated by the scene. He asked Mariel if she knew him because he appeared to be studying her. She said not and McKinley still could not place him; he was on the point of recalling him when he caught the eye of her grandfather who had stopped at one of the graveyard yews. He was waiting for them so they approached.

'What did you say in your heathen language?' he asked sternly.

Mariel looked up at him and said, 'It's a prayer for the dead in my father's Bengali tongue. Wherever he is I believe he and mother are looking down on us this day and that we are all equal in the eyes of God.' She paused then said, 'Oh God forgive her transgressions, have mercy upon her and wash away her sins that she might dwell in your kingdom in blessed peace and happiness.'

There was an awkward pause then the old man said, 'I can see nothing of my daughter in you except the wilfulness that caused her to defy her parents. However, out of pity for your age and circumstances I have found you a position in service to a family who live some miles away in a country house. They don't know who you are but I have stood as a reference for your good character and honesty. You will live in and be paid £12 a year. Will you accept it?'

She looked at McKinley. He asked, 'What sort of people are they?'

'The captain is Royal Navy and at sea most of the time. He has a wife and three daughters and a staff of three plus a nanny and workers from a nearby village attend to the grounds. The house is from the last century, not large but he has undertaken some improvements to the stables and gardens I believe. What do you say? I need to know now because his ship is in port and he will be travelling home in two days' time after naval business is concluded, and you can accompany him.'

McKinley could see she was thinking seriously about the offer but he could not read her solemn face. Surely she would agree to avoid having to live a precarious existence in a callous world?

She said, 'I accept.'

'Be at the coach yard by eight o'clock on Saturday morning and I will introduce you. You may bring one box.' He turned to go.

Mariel said: 'Thank you grandfather,' and he almost stopped but carried on walking though perhaps slightly bent. It was impossible to read his feelings.

McKinley turned to her and said, 'I will find out what I can about this family to ensure that you will be safe with them. It is probably a good outcome, given the circumstances. Perhaps you can rise in their service with your skills as a seamstress and your education. I think your grandfather meant well.'

'Thank you, sir.'

They walked back to the hovel that Mariel now occupied alone. He noticed that she had put it in order and it did not smell so bad. Her neighbour came out as soon as the door was opened and McKinley left them discussing the day's events and the prospect of a new life. He went straight to the naval base and made enquiries about the family that would now employ Mariel. He was pleased to find that the Captain was a well-regarded individual, that is, he ran a tight ship and was not known for undue cruelty to his crew.

Feeling happier in the knowledge that Captain Reid had found a good establishment for Mariel he returned to his lodgings and scrutinised his painting. He felt sure that the Bartlebys would be satisfied, even happy, with the final work. He felt an affection for it himself, although it was one that he did not feel for the sitter. Did he imagine it, or was there a glimmer of Mariel's tranquillity in the bulging blue eyes of that middle-aged matron?

The following day he had set up the painting to be viewed in the drawing room of the Bartleby's villa. He stood back to admire it. Did that face contain Mariel or was it perhaps the influence of Teresa who was even now fading from his mind? He imagined the sitter as a creature of such ethereal beauty that he smiled on her and was startled as the door opened and the subject walked in.

'Well, I don't know what to say Mr McKinley.'

He was suddenly nervous; then the companion entered and hovered as Mrs Bartleby stared at a likeness that was herself but a little younger and more likeable somehow. Mr Bartleby then strode into the room causing the companion to flee and knock over several small tables with the stiff capacity of her skirts.

'Watch what you're doing woman,' he bellowed, all whiskers and red face, then with a beaming smile as he looked at the painting. 'Ah, you have perceived Mrs Bartleby's qualities admirably McKinley. She looks as radiant as when I first courted her. You have seen into her very soul. Wonderful. Now you are captured forever my dear,' he said and he embraced her in a boisterous hug as he kissed her blushing cheek. 'It will match my own portrait and take pride of place in our new house near Kidderminster. Which I am pleased to say is coming along admirably.'

McKinley glanced at Mrs Bartleby and was rendered speechless by her reaction. She had transformed into a coquettish girl and simpered under the uxorious love of her husband. She actually resembled the woman in his painting.

'You will have your lunch with us, I hope,' said Bartleby.

'Oh yes, do,' enjoined the lady of the house and the companion ground her teeth and regretted not having committed herself to admire the painting straightway. McKinley accepted and as the Bartlebys led the way into the dining room he offered his arm to the companion and she reluctantly accepted with a scowl. As he towered above her, he noticed the redness of her neck and the angry pulse that moved her dry skin. She was probably a poor cousin, he speculated, and had missed any chance of marrying so she was the old maid companion of a wealthy man's wife. What choices did she have? He felt sorry for her and smiled with pity, but she looked up at that moment and mistaking his smile as one of triumph she pinched his arm quite viciously. It was painful but also surprising. He was curious how she had fallen into such habits.

'Are you related to Mrs Bartleby?' he asked with watering eyes. She squinted at him but being within earshot of the other couple she had to reply.

'I am her cousin and they very kindly gave me a home when my mother died.' Mr Bartleby looked back approvingly. She felt that she must continue. 'My brothers found employment after my father died and I looked after our mother until she died too.' She did not say she was without an income but her mother's pension as a widow must have ended with her death. He pushed her chair in for her and took his place.

He wanted to ask if none of the brothers could have taken in their sister when Mrs Bartleby, having waved in the servants said: 'You didn't get on with your brothers did you dear?' She turned to McKinley. 'They fought like wild animals when they were children; kicking under the table and pinching when they could not be seen.'

McKinley moved his legs away from the little woman and she looked at him resentfully. Mr Bartleby said grace and they enjoyed a tasty meal of mutton with onion sauce and greens.

To make conversation McKinley asked how long they would stay in Portsmouth and was told that although the villa was taken until August they would likely remove earlier as the new house was able to be occupied.

'Then you will not stay to see the Clarence Esplanade opened?'

'That will depend upon our children,' said Bartleby. 'They have spoken of visiting us and taking up sea bathing, I believe that my son considers it to be of great benefit. I am not convinced.'

'I will stay for some time whilst my grandchildren are here, but then I can leave if it becomes too crowded or boisterous. Or if the contagion spreads. You have heard that there is cholera, I suppose?' said Mrs Bartleby.

McKinley thought that Mariel's mother's death was no longer a secret, so he said:

'I attended the funeral of Mariel's mother at the church of St Thomas a Becket yesterday.'

'At St Thomas? How did she afford that?' said Mrs Bartleby.

'Mariel's grandfather is Captain Reid formerly of Her Majesty's Navy. He wished to bury his daughter and Mariel had few other choices given their present state of poverty.' He heard the companion breathe in sharply.

'But she's dark skinned,' said Mrs Bartleby.

'Her mother married an Indian gentleman and that was unacceptable to her parents, so they disowned her,' said McKinley.

'That is very sad,' said the companion, to his surprise.

There was a silence as they digested this information but only McKinley knew of the dreadful circumstances of the woman's death and the plight of her daughter.

'What will she do now?' It was the companion again.

'Her grandfather has arranged for a live-in position with a family some distance from Portsmouth.'

'That is why we had a new girl this morning. Such a shame. Mariel was a good worker and her mother made the most beautiful lace,' said Mrs Bartleby.

They finished their meal agreeably enough and McKinley took his leave of the ladies who proceeded upstairs. He bowed to Mrs Bartleby and was about to do the same to her companion when the strange little lady thrust out her hand for him to shake. For an instant he feared she might be about to pinch him again, but she shook his hand warmly and looked at him gratefully, as though she had seen something in him that she appreciated.

He walked back to his lodgings with a cheque for thirty guineas in his pocket. He felt rich, but he also felt chastened. He had formed preconceptions about the Bartlebys. The bluff industrialist who loved his wife and the maternal woman who doted on her grandchildren. Even the hostile companion had softened towards him at the end when she knew that he had helped a young woman in straitened circumstances, rather like herself. He resolved to waste no more time, but to pack up and move to Guildford where his friend promised him a new painting establishment. Now that he was in funds he could do so.

He spent the rest of the day packing away his paints and cleaning his equipment. It was late when he realised that if he caught the mail coach in the morning he might also see Mariel and meet her new employer. Early the next day he hired a couple of men to take his trunk to the coach station and he settled with his landlady. He was about to leave when she said:

'Oh good lord! I've quite forgotten to give it you!' She rushed over to a big teapot on the mantle and produced a letter from behind it. It was from Mariel. He read the following.

June 30th

Dear Mr McKinley

I am much obliged to you for all the kindness that you have shown me over the past two weeks and for speaking with my grandfather. I have decided not to stay in service, but to go to Brighton on the train where I will try and find work in one of the shops.

I hope that you will not judge me too harshly. I have been educated above that of a maid of all work, my mother taught me well, and I can sew and make lace. I want the chance to make my own way in life without being under the disapproving eyes of the Reids of Portsmouth.

I am very grateful.

Yours truly

McKinley was disappointed and concerned that she may not have properly thought through this decision. He had been looking forward to travelling with her for a few miles and talking to her about her prospects. He said his goodbyes at the lodging house and sprinted after his trunk, carrying his hat in case it fell. He caught up with the trunk as it approached the coach station and then he searched for her.

There was no sign of Captain Reid or the potential new employer and he supposed she must have written to him too. Not finding her he ran to the slum where she had been living. There was no answer when he knocked and on opening the door he found the room clean but cold and empty. Only the most basic items of shabby furniture remained, and presumably they belonged to the landlord. He went to the next house where Maud opened her door.

'Where has she gone?' he asked. 'Did she give you a forwarding address?'

She laughed 'Bless you no sir. I can't read or write. She gave me all the bits and pieces that wouldn't fit in her bag. Wouldn't take no money for 'em. Said I'd been a help, but what else could I do, all on her own?'

'She's only fourteen. She had a job in service not far from here. She could have been safe there.'

'Or not, as the case might be. She'd be a skivvy all her life or worse if the master took a fancy to her.'

'She sent me a letter. She says that she's going to Brighton. Do you know where?'

'She went yesterday. I don't know if I should tell you, but a gentleman came round and helped with her bag. He introduced himself as Mr Ede. Mariel said that he had offered her employment with his company as a seamstress. She seemed very pleased.'

'And that was in Brighton?' She nodded. 'What was he like?'

'Elderly. Grey hair and beard. But very upright and with a strong voice and well spoken. He brought her a travelling cloak. Good quality too by the look of it.'

McKinley sagged with the acceptance that she had disappeared forever. He had thought that one day, if he married, he could find her and bring her into his household to look after his children and be … he thought, what? Part of his family? Or a servant?

'Never mind love,' said Maud seeing his disappointment. 'She's a bright girl and I think she will do very well for herself. Better than this anyway,' she gestured to the hovel that she called home. He thanked her and pressed a few coins into her hand, then turned and walked back to the coach and his journey to Guildford.

CHAPTER TWO

Approaching the Hall from the main London to Guildford road he became aware first of the chimneys of Pitdown. They could be seen above the trees that separated the Hall from the neighbouring farms. They were beautiful trees, a mixture of deciduous and conifer so that the privacy in winter was balanced by the fresh display of leaves in springtime. A visitor could leave his luggage in the gatehouse and a servant would collect it and then he could walk up the pine scented drive as it snaked up to the front of the house.

The Hall was built around 1530 and seemed to emerge from the southwest end, stretching itself northeast. At some time, as though in an afterthought, an additional wing was added branching out northwest at an angle, to make a chapel. As if it were not imposing enough the Hall's many corners had been fortified with semi-Gothic spirelets. There were few of the stone mullioned windows and McKinley thought it must be dark inside and not helpful for painting unless larger windows existed at the back of the building. He had been assured that this was a serious artistic endeavour and was looking forward to the creative freedom it should give him to explore his imagination and skill.

He mounted the half dozen steps to the Hall door.

'Robert, I'm so glad you are here!' Jack Seton bounded into the imposing hallway. He was a slightly built man about the same age as McKinley with pale skin and light brown hair. He had always been ascetic in personal inclination and was drawn to the constraints of formal religion. 'It's been, what, three years since we last saw each other?' He warmly shook McKinley's hand and gestured about him at the imposing carved wooden staircase and the landing above.

'I see you're impressed by the place. Gloomy, isn't it? It's Tudor in origin, hence all the dark oak. We find that it gives us a sense of timelessness.'

'How did you find it?'

'The building is currently held by a trustee for some minors whose guardians are disputing the disposition of an estate. A rum business, in and out of Chancery; but good for us as they let it cheap.'

'It's impressive Jack, but surely a bit cut off for a studio. Unless you bring the models in from London or pay the locals. Are the others here? How can you paint without models?'

'More about models later. It's got nine bedrooms including servants' quarters. There are five of us and we each have a room of our own. Come and see the studios.'

He led the way through a long dining hall to the northeast corner of the house and there, in hideous splendour, was the ugliest orangery that McKinley had ever seen. Before he could say anything, Seton said:

'I know, isn't it marvellous? Doesn't suit the house of course but it was constructed about twenty-five years ago and we have cleared out all the dead un-watered plants so we each have a section, there are partitions, see? Unfortunately, being last man in you have the centre one as it was not chosen, but then again you have escaped most of the preparation. It means people will be in and out because your studio is a bit of a corridor ...' Seton tailed off.

McKinley looked at the large clear space with double doors behind him into the house and double doors in front of him and out onto rolling downs that were bathed in sunlight. The orangery was cool and well ventilated; the air was fresh and clean after the stink of Portsmouth. He turned a beaming smile onto his host.

'I think you like it. Yes, he likes it chaps!' he shouted to the three other young men who had filtered from the staircase and through the dining hall. They stepped into the light room and Seton introduced them.

'Robert McKinley I'd like to introduce to you John Millais, William Hunt and Gabriel Rossetti. They have recently left the Royal Academy and, I think, you may have some ideas in common.'

The four men shook hands. McKinley was surprised at their youth and confidence. Millais had dark curly hair, large expressive eyes and a long nose. He seemed the friendliest and smiled as he welcomed a stranger to their close-knit group; he immediately invited McKinley to see what he was working on. Hunt had a boyish face with straight hair and a turned-up nose; he wore a thin moustache, probably attempting to make himself look older. Lastly was Rossetti, a long-haired, full-lipped and sensuous looking man, and McKinley felt that he was suspicious of the newcomer and would hold back his welcome until he knew him better.

'Rossetti wants to be called Dante after the great medieval poet Dante Alighieri, so we humour him, but surnames are fine amongst ourselves,' said Seton.

'Just like school,' said Millais and the others groaned.

'I'll get your things brought up from the gatehouse,' said Seton as he turned and went back into the house.

'Do excuse me but I'm in the middle of writing,' said Rossetti and held up ink-stained fingers before retiring back into the house.

'We'll show you round,' said Millais and led him into the jungle of easels and tables that made up the painting areas. They passed through a space that was full of charcoal sketches and empty canvas frames.

'We have an outbuilding where we make our frames and stretch the canvases. Otherwise it takes too much room. There's a gardener who's happy to lend a hand for a few coppers.' He paused. 'You are in funds I take it?'

'Fortunately, yes,' said McKinley 'I was paid for my last two commissions and have drawn some money to use whilst I am here. Where do you get your materials?'

'We send up to London monthly,' said Hunt. 'We have an account at Reeves and pool our resources for that and other costs. The cook is fairly good, and the establishment runs itself.'

'As long as you like bully beef and potatoes' said Millais 'The ladies don't approve much when they come down.'

'Ladies?'

'Yes. Rossetti's sister comes occasionally. She paints and writes poetry, so we have amusing evenings telling stories,' said Millais. 'Quite often they are stories of the mystical variety.'

He looked quickly at Hunt who asked, 'I believe you have some experience of that McKinley? According to what we have read in the newspapers.'

'I do,' said McKinley.

'That's not why we invited you,' Millais hastened to reassure him. 'Seton remembered your dissatisfaction with the stuffy, convention-bound way the RA taught. He said you were the person who introduced him to Giotto and the early frescoes in Padua. He went to see them, you know. He says they shine with freshness, so directly do they speak to the viewer.'

His earnestness convinced McKinley that they had not invited him merely for his ghostly experiences earlier in the year and he said, 'I shall be happy to speak of the hauntings at St Jude's church, but my friend's situation was serious and I will not see it made light of.'

'Be assured that we are not sensation seekers. We do not indulge in the thrill of the Gothic,' said Hunt.

'It is our aim to recreate the truthfulness and beauty of art before the all-pervading classical style favoured by Raphael and Michelangelo was forced upon the honest folk of Europe.' Millais was sincere in his reassurance and the three men continued their tour of the studios and the house and grounds of Pitdown Hall.

*   *   *

His bedroom was on the second floor of the house and was reached from a smaller staircase hung with gloomy portraits of the long-dead ancestors of the hapless children now locked in a dreary legal argument via the proxies of their guardians. McKinley hoped they were being allowed to play in the sunshine somewhere other than this sepulchral mansion. He thought about the paintings he had seen as Seton and Millais had shown him around the studios. Jewel colours and flat shapes that shone like tableaux under the lights of a theatre. That was it. He was reminded by their paintings of the performance of the Dream that he had seen in Portsmouth. They were luminous, as though lit by many lanterns. He remembered Teresa's beauty and experienced again that longing for the unattainable, unknown woman that he had fallen in love with but never spoken to, nor even seen when not on the stage. He realised how ridiculous his infatuation was, but he still indulged the thrill of ecstasy that she had cast like a spell upon him.

Fortunately, he had told no one of this obsession and he justified it as if he was a medieval knight and the ideal love would be an inspiration he could use in his art. He had been quite cheerful as the two young men had shown him the grounds. Most of the land was tenanted and used to graze sheep but there was a walled garden and a pool where some lichen covered nymphs attempted to insinuate themselves into the landscape. The artists would have preferred that their pastoral view did not have slavish copies of some Greek demigods.

Millais had explained his fascination with the water and the reeds and yellow flags that grew around the edge. There was a simple voluptuousness in the lily pads and small native flowers spilling in profusion from the overgrown lawns. The grass was long, and wildflowers were currently blooming. The solstice was past, but the heat would increase and fruits begin to ripen as June ended and the height of summer stretched out in front of them. McKinley realised that this setting was ideal for painters, with the garden and the cool interiors.

He looked out of his bedroom window to the back garden and the vegetable patch. Perhaps they would need assistance in weeding and tending it. He somehow could not imagine young Rossetti carrying out manual labour. He thought that if they would permit it he would begin by drawing each of the artists and perhaps make a single painting of them in an exterior setting. This would be a chance to paint from nature, he realised. The pool would make a perfect backdrop. He unpacked the few clothes he had brought and as he did so, he thought of Mariel. Where was she at this minute? Unpacking and cleaning for someone else? Perhaps the mysterious Mr Ede?

It was time he put aside the influence of his stay in Portsmouth. He would take stock of his painting supplies and see what he could purchase from the group's store and offer funds to Seton to pay his way at Pitdown. The dinner gong sounded, and he carefully found his way down the back stairs to the big landing that led to the principal bedrooms and the main staircase, and then descended to the long dining hall. The table was laid for five but only Seton was there. A rich odour of beef and cabbage permeated the lower floor of the house.

'Hello McKinley,' said Seton 'I'd show you the kitchen but better to wait until the morning when cook is not up to her armpits in steam and boiled puddings. We normally get our own breakfast and eat it in here.'

McKinley noticed that his friend had not dressed for dinner and his hands were quite stained from the work he had returned to that afternoon. A plump dishevelled woman bustled in and placed a large steaming dish on the sideboard. A smaller maid followed with a similar dish although smaller in dimension and a young man followed with the largest dish of all and placed that next to them. Cook wiped her hands on her apron.

'Help yourselves. Ring the gong when you've finished, and we'll bring the pudding.' She almost curtseyed and, as one, they marched away.

'Let's have a glass of wine then I'm sure the others will join us. The gong can be heard from all parts of the house,' said Seton.

They were just pouring the red wine when Millais and Hunt came in together soon followed by Rossetti who professed to be starving and they sat down to a hearty if plain meal of boiled beef, cabbage, and potatoes. The conversation was centred on art and whether they would have enough materials because Rossetti's sister would not be able to join them in the foreseeable future, but she could arrange the delivery of supplies.

'She has been trying to round up some models, but they seem to be a bit chary of finding themselves stuck in the middle of nowhere in a house of young men,' Rossetti said.

'I am thinking of asking cook to pose for me,' said Hunt, chewing on a particularly tough piece of meat. He gave up and spat it back onto his plate. 'I'm sure they save the best cuts of meat for themselves.'

'I don't think we do too badly considering how much we give them for housekeeping. Though it is a pity that the game has now all gone. Lamb might be available soon.' Seton was always the apologist, thought McKinley.

'What would you have her model for?' asked Rossetti, 'The Female Vagrant?'

There was guffawing and muffled laughter at this, but Hunt said 'Why not? Wordsworth looks at the natural world. Perhaps the gardener would pose for the Leech Gatherer.'

McKinley enjoyed the food; it was tasty, the journey had made him hungry and the company was lively. When they had finished and seen off a monstrous boiled pudding that was served with heated jam, he felt that his trousers might burst and was pleased to note that they all were easing their waistbands.

'Doesn't matter how much I eat, there's always room for pudding,' said Hunt wiping his mouth.

'Men have two stomachs, like cows,' said Millais, 'and one of them is exclusively for pudding.'

When the plates and dishes had been cleared away, they sat at the table drinking wine because they had no port. As the sun set behind the hills the room became darker and they lit a few candles.

'I have seen nothing of your work, McKinley,' said Rossetti and the young men glanced at each other. 'Except this!' Rossetti mischievously flourished a penny dreadful which had been illustrated by their guest and they all laughed, though Seton looked a little anxious. It was a drawing of Varney the Vampire, Mariel's favourite.

'I'm mightily proud of that. I'll have you know that I have a following of adoring young people who cannot wait until the next instalment. Or I did until I gave it up. That edition is, I think, about two years old,' McKinley replied smiling.

'That would explain why I obtained it from the gardener's boy. He and his friends share the cost and pass them around. It seems they are particularly fond of this one with the drawing of the pretty young virgin being devoured by the evil blood sucker, who reminds me of a master I had at school, by the way.'

'Perhaps we went to the same school. Albeit a few years apart,' said McKinley.

There was a pause then Rossetti said, 'You had a real supernatural experience I understand.'

They all looked at McKinley, but he had prepared himself for this interrogation. It seemed to have been a condition of his invitation to the house and he knew that most of the details had been made public at the time it happened.

'Last year I was employed by a Hampshire newspaper to make drawings of an archaeological excavation that a friend of mine was conducting. A church had agreed that the grave of a martyred child could be opened to determine its historical provenance. It was the church of St Jude near Winchester and had a history of a particularly nasty medieval murder.'

'They permitted a saint to be exhumed?' Seton was horrified.

'Saints have been moved and exhumed numerous times over the years,' said McKinley 'Cuthbert was carried around in Anglo Saxon times like a talisman. In fact, being broken up and distributed throughout Christendom in reliquaries seems to have been the fate of most saints if the claims of various shrines are to be believed. But Little William was not a saint, he was the victim of a brutal killing and mutilation. He was treated as a martyr because his murder was attributed to local Jews who were accused of using his blood as a sacrifice in their religious rituals.'

'And did they?' asked Rossetti.

'Probably not. There were a lot of instances of accusations against wealthy Jews in the thirteenth century. The church wanted them gone from Christian countries, they were rich and powerful and an easy target. Whether they did kill him or not, they were hanged, and their property was confiscated to the benefit of the state and the local landowner.'

'What did you find?' pressed Millais.

'His grave lay under a brass plaque near the altar and when my friend and his manservant opened it they found a small skeleton covered in a shroud. He had been only nine years old. I didn't see it until the next day when I rode up from Winchester.'

They waited for him to continue.

'As I am sure you know, the surprising discovery was that there were a number of other skeletons in the grave, and much more recently than 1275. And they were those of babies.'

'But the newspapers said that they were old and only of historical interest.' Seton had made some study of the circumstances.

'That was said to avoid a scandal. They were quite recent burials, and before you exclaim in horror, think about the situation of a parent whose dead baby cannot be buried in consecrated ground because of the constraints of the Church.'

'Illegitimate, you mean?' said Hunt.

'Quite likely,' said McKinley. 'The mother would still mourn the loss and it is understandable that a grieving parent might want to entrust the little body to a child martyr.'

'But these children were born outside wedlock which is a fundamental teaching of the Christian faith. They had not been baptised in Christ. It's sinful!' interjected Seton.

'Seton's thinking of converting to Catholicism,' said Hunt, opening another bottle. 'He's preparing himself for wine to be actually converted into blood by the intercession of a priest.' The others laughed.

Millais said, 'Why would anyone want to actually drink the blood of another? Even that of Christ?'

'Varney the Vampire would,' said Rossetti and they burst out laughing. When the laughter had died down, he said to McKinley. 'What about the man who died?'

'Well, that was a mystery. It happened the night before I arrived, and my friend, Macey, had become separated from his servant when he accompanied the Coroner's officer and the clergy away from the church with the little corpses. Rudd was supposed to look after the gravesite.

'When he returned late at night the man had disappeared, so Macey spent the night at the inn, where I met him the next day and we both went up to St Jude's expecting him to reappear at the church. But he did not.'

He looked around at their expectant faces. It was now dark outside, and the gloomy old house was silent as though it was reluctant to interrupt.

'We found him in the churchyard well,' said McKinley.

'Drowned?' asked Millais.

'Completely ex-sanguinated.' There was a sharp intake or exhale of breath, he was not sure which. 'But before you ask, Varney the Vampire had been nowhere near him. There was a deep cut in the inside of his upper thigh and my friend concluded that he must have bled to death, in the well.'

'That's terrible,' said Millais. 'Do you know how it happened?'

'That was the mystery. There was no blood anywhere in the church or the churchyard and we could find no signs of a struggle. Apparently he was a practical and rather unimaginative fellow, not normally given to superstition, but he had been shaken by the sight of the dead babies,' said McKinley, thinking back to the previous October.

The young men waited for an explanation, but nothing was forthcoming.

After a short pause Hunt said, 'You believe it is unlikely that he fell into the well by accident and I take it there were no other marks on the body, so something frightened him to the well…'

'It was by the lychgate on the main path to and from the church,' said McKinley.

'So he was fleeing and it caught him and threw him in the well?' offered Hunt.

'Or he jumped in to escape it,' said Rossetti. 'Because he was frightened out of his wits.'

McKinley continued. 'He was alive and conscious in the well because he had tied the rope around his waist. That was how we were able to pull him out.'

Seton asked, 'How did he get the wound on his leg?'

'A chisel was missing from the tool set and never found. We assumed that he had cut himself as he fell into the well. It was a long way down, the area is chalk so the wells are deep, he could easily have inflicted the wound by accident and the chisel is probably still at the bottom of the well.'

'The interesting question is what chased him out of the church,' said Rossetti and the others nodded. 'Wasn't there a rumour of ghosts being seen in the area?'

McKinley nodded. 'The newspaper reported such sightings after the events I have described, but you must remember that they are all about sensation and anything that will sell the paper. Newspapers become more like penny dreadfuls by the day. I had left the establishment by that time so any illustrations they published were not from me.'

'Your friend found his way into the crypt I believe, and was trapped there,' said Rossetti.

'Yes, earlier this year we returned to make further investigation as we found no crypt during our first visit. We did find it, it had been bricked up and was concealed by the door into the tower.

Macey got in through a buried window. There was an earth fall and we had to break through to rescue him. The crypt had been sealed because it contained pagan stones and a slaughter stone. 'It was a dangerous, primitive place.'

Seton shook his head. 'Digging up the remains of holy martyrs, whether they are saints or not, is dangerous. I do not hold with this scientific approach to the old times, analysing everything and slicing it up. What happened to simple faith and a childlike gaze upon the beauties of the world.'

'Hear hear,' said Millais and the others nodded. 'You know that we are trying to adopt a medieval approach to art. Our inspiration may be drawn from the bible but also it may be drawn from literature such as the work of John Keats. Beauty and truth are our joint ambitions.'

'Millais is our child prodigy,' said Rossetti. 'There is nothing he cannot depict with paint and canvas. So he paints everything, and here in the glorious English countryside he will capture the romantic soul of England.'

'Or Italy,' said Millais.

'Or Palestine,' said Hunt.

'It's more a matter of representing people truthfully,' said Seton. 'Sometimes pale and thin and not always like muscular gods or plump goddesses. We don't want the classical form anymore. The creatures we paint will be alive because they will be natural.'

McKinley was relieved to have left behind the memory of ghosts and he enthusiastically joined in the discussion of subjects and techniques for the rest of the evening. Millais explained his ideas behind the part completed work 'Isabella' based on Keats's poem and Hunt set out his project to depict a scene from a recently re-issued novel set in medieval Italy. Bright sunshine and colour made him think again of the stage of the Portsmouth theatre on which the vivid scenes of 'A Midsummer Night's Dream' played out before his mind's eye.

The following days were at times both stimulating and soothing as he drew up plans for a scene from 'A Midsummer Night's Dream' and walked in the fresh fields to gather flowers and inspiration. The leaves were turning a dark green and the meadow flowers were running to seed, as July came in with its heat and slightly burnt air. It was a relief to be away from the noise of machinery that resounded in Portsmouth, but it was not much quieter, especially at five in the morning when the birdsong of the last few weeks of the dawn chorus was enough to wake him.

In terms of his work, he felt that he was less prepared than the other artists, they had made multiple drawings of models whilst in London and he only had a few sketches of Mariel and the Bartlebys. He could work from imagination, but he would prefer a live sitter. The classical statues in the grounds would simply not do, they relied too much on the art of Greece or Rome.

On his ramblings he found a charming statue of a hound called 'August' with an inscription that read 'Goodbye old friend. My faithful hound will no longer to me bound. I bury his heart in this stone, but wish he were still flesh and bone.' On a close examination McKinley was intrigued to find that there was a patched area on the left side of the stone body, where the dog's heart must have been placed.

He asked Seton about it when they went to Guildford to buy provisions; they travelled in the cart with cook and the gardener's boy. The gardener's boy confirmed that the heart of the hound was entombed in the statue, and that it was from some time in the last century. An owner of the house who loved hunting had wanted to remember his faithful animal and, according to gossip had continued visiting the statue when his hunting days were over to sit and reminisce with the shade of 'August'. McKinley and Seton talked of the dogs and horses they had known as boys. McKinley remembered first meeting young Seton aged seven when they were both new boys at school, and his awful homesickness for his dog more than his mama.

'Are you really thinking of converting to Catholicism?' McKinley asked his friend.

The other inclined his head and said 'When you look at the proposals to sever the connection between Anglicanism from the British state and you see the increased acceptance of other Christian churches, there is so much more freedom to choose one's own path. Anglican high church isn't that different to the catholic church, but as a catholic you have the advantage of a direct connection to Rome and to centuries of tradition and faith.'

'And dogma,' said McKinley.

'Perhaps,' conceded Seton. 'I just feel that I might belong there, somehow. As a group of artists aren't we looking backwards for our inspiration to the time before the Renaissance and before the Reformation? That makes me look at the single religion whose stories were told in the frescoes of Cimabue and Giotto. If we are being honest then surely that can extend to our religious views?'

McKinley thought about this and about the subject that Seton had chosen for his painting and submission to the Royal Academy exhibition the following year. He said, 'You have chosen a deeply spiritual subject for your painting.'

'Christ in the Garden of Gethsemane,' said Seton with reverence. 'As you know it was a moment of profound agony when our Lord knew that he had a choice whether to be offered as a sacrifice for the sins of the world, but ultimately he accepted it. The joy of living and the knowledge of death is a sublimely pivotal point in anyone's life.'

McKinley had noticed an air of melancholy about Seton in contrast to the other young artists, and to it he attributed his attraction to Catholicism. He had always been a serious and ascetic person seldom indulging in the common pleasures of youth.

Seton paused then seemed to lighten. 'Holman Hunt and Millais have both chosen secular stories set in the middle ages. Rossetti is focussing on poetry, but his mind is following the same path. I think he might join me in returning to the Roman church.' He turned to McKinley. 'What are you composing? I see some delightful sketches of an exotic young woman.'

'That is Mariel. She is a maid I met in Portsmouth, the daughter of a lascar sailor and will one day be a beauty I have no doubt. She is now an orphan and I worry about her safety. I wish I had brought her with me, we could have found employment for her here.' He regretted trying to push the girl into service with strangers. There was something attractive about her that he could not explain, an intelligence and calmness beyond her fourteen years. If she were older he would have felt romantically drawn to her.

Seton continued, 'I also noticed some very strange drawings of creatures that one can only describe as fantastical. Is it a pagan scene that you concoct? The others are expecting something dark and gothic, so they have speculated on the pointed ears and wings on your creatures.'

McKinley laughed and explained about the performance of 'A Midsummer Night's Dream', the extraordinary puppets he had seen in Portsmouth where people could be hired quite cheaply. He began to lament the lack of models in their Pitdown studios.

'Yes, it is a problem being so far from town and the family members we could call upon who modelled for nothing. Perhaps we could make enquiries in Guildford and see if any young men or women would be willing to earn a little money by posing for us,' Seton said.

Cook, sitting up front alongside the gardener's boy, turned and gave them such an old-fashioned look that they lapsed into silence and tried not to laugh. After a short interval they resumed their conversation quietly.

'We must go to the station and collect the materials sent from London and it might be worth putting up a notice to advertise for models,' suggested McKinley.

'You realise that we will, like as not, attract ne'er do wells and it might give notice to unwanted attention from the local burglars. No, I don't think we can risk it,' he insisted. McKinley was about to argue that they would find no valuables to steal but decided that as the lessee Seton was responsible for the Hall and its contents. He reluctantly nodded and they continued with no further discussion.

After they had dropped cook and the boy in the town, they took the cart to the new railway station to enquire of their artists' supplies. Seton went into the office and McKinley wandered about on the platform inspecting notices and timetables. A small figure came out of the office and they both stopped, open mouthed, and stared at each other.

McKinley recovered his wits first. 'Mariel, how are you here? I thought you went to Brighton?'

'Good morning sir,' she bobbed a curtsey but seemed unembarrassed. 'I was intending to sir, but we went to London instead.'

'We? Is this the man called Mr Ede?' said McKinley seriously. 'Who is he and are you being treated with respect?'

Mariel chuckled 'You have seen him sir, he was at my mother's funeral, standing some distance away and we did not speak to him. The letter I wrote for you was the day before I was going to leave for Brighton. I had decided not to stay in service, but thank you for trying to help. I hope you are not angry that I didn't go into service at the Captain's house.'

'Of course not Mariel. It was just a way to ensure you did not fall prey to the purveyors of flesh in the bawdy houses. You haven't have you?' He cared more than he expected that her innocence was intact, but he felt doubtful, finding her alone in a place such as this.

'God save you, no sir. In the end I didn't go to Brighton on the train because that evening Mr Ede found me and said he heard that I could sew and would I like to make costumes for his company. I said yes and we went in the wagons to London. Mr Ede thought he would be able to secure some work for us in the London theatres, but they were very disdainful of a travelling group. They called us gypsies because we travel to the fairgrounds, and we live in caravans.'

'My dear child, a travelling circus is not a respectable occupation. You were a maid in Portsmouth until two weeks ago.'

'Not any more sir. I thought Maud Kelly would have told you. I joined a theatre group called the Prospero Company.' She drew breath and said proudly. 'I have been on a train now though. I came down from London on a train today. It was very exciting and so fast, it took my breath away and I'm covered in smuts.' She looked down for little particles of soot on her clothes.

McKinley felt his heart race and was suffused with excitement. 'Did you say Prospero Company? A group of actors and actresses who perform with puppets?'

She nodded. 'I'm making arrangements for a campsite in this area where we can stay until we go up to Mitcham in August.'

Just then Seton came out of the office with a sheaf of papers.

'Seton, this is Mariel.'

'The dusky maiden of your drawings,' said Seton as she curtsied. 'I see you captured her. How do you do my dear.'

'She is part of a travelling theatrical group, and they are looking for somewhere to stay for a few weeks before their next show. They would be the perfect models for our artistic compositions. They are mostly young and able to take on any persona that is required. What do you say?'

Before Seton could reply, Mariel stuttered, 'I don't think it's that simple sir. You see I was sent here to make enquiry of St Catherine's Hill in particular.'

'We are not far from the hill. I am sure it would suit us all,' said Seton.

She thought for a few seconds. 'Let me go and ask Mr Ede and see what he says.'

Seton smiled. 'We can pay you for your work as models, if that helps.'

McKinley wrote the address of Pitdown Hall on the back of his card and gave it to Mariel. 'Do you go back to London and speak with him. Here is our address. Send a letter to me as soon as you know and if he is agreeable then tell us when they can be expected.' She nodded and left to go about her business in the town.

'Do you suppose the others will mind?' asked Seton.

'You haven't seen them,' said McKinley, hardly able to contain his joy at the thought of seeing Teresa. 'They are a small company of four men and three women plus extraordinary puppets, a musician and now a seamstress. Also, as it seems they are coming to Guildford it would be wasteful not to engage them for our purposes.'

Seton agreed and they loaded their goods, collected cook and her wares, carried loyally by the gardener's boy, and returned to Pitdown Hall.

*   *   *

McKinley was so excited at the prospect of seeing the young woman he adored that he had to fight against disappointment when nothing was heard in the following days, but then on Tuesday 11th July he was about to start painting after a short morning walk when he heard Rossetti shout from his bedroom overlooking the drive.

'There's a rather lovely gypsy approaching the house. Is she selling pegs or some other trinkets!'

The thought of seeing someone other than the four men or the servants appealed to him, so McKinley took off his smock and walked through the cool and shady house to the front door, just as Rossetti and Hunt appeared, their curiosity also piqued. In the doorway they saw the silhouette of a slim figure in loose robes flowing from sloping shoulders and shortened to just below the knee showing shapely legs and sturdy boots. She wore a large broad brimmed hat tied under her chin by a fine scarf and she carried a wide, shallow basket of the sort you might use to collect flowers.

Rossetti had seen her in sunlight, so he was not surprised at her unusual dress, and he greeted her with:

'My mistress' eyes are nothing like the sun;
Coral is far more red, than her lips red:
If snow be white, why then her breasts are dun;
If hairs be wires, black wires grow on her head.'

McKinley did not recognise Mariel at first and a confusion of thoughts filled his head until she stepped back outside the doorway and he saw her properly. She looked as though she might run, and little wonder as Rossetti was examining her with delight and Millais and Seton also came to the hall door.

McKinley went through the door and placed himself between Rossetti and the girl.

'Mariel. How did you come here and dressed in such an unconventional fashion?'

'Sir, I came to find you and you told me I should,' she said, 'There was not time to write so I walked from St Catherine's Hill.'

'But your clothes.'

'I'm dressed like this because it's hot and I had to climb some stiles. And none of the other women in the company wear stays. You don't know what a relief it is to be able to be comfortable in summer.' She looked suspiciously at Rossetti.

'Oh don't worry about him. He hasn't seen a woman for weeks. Except cook and the maid and they are off limits,' said Millais and smiled at her with his youthful charm.

'He said breasts, and something about them being 'dun' – like a horse, I suppose,' Mariel shot back. The others laughed.

She is not intimidated, thought McKinley, she is just cautious. But she had always been respectful and now she seemed to have courage.

'It's a quotation from Shakespeare. Sonnet to a Dark Lady,' said Rossetti.

'Shakespeare is it? Well, I suppose you think that excuses making remarks about the breasts of a fourteen-year-old girl?'

The young men were shamed by this, and Rossetti mumbled an apology.

Mariel spoke to McKinley, and she was more polite if also slightly embarrassed. 'I've come to ask if we can take up your offer of a place to camp until August. We will be prepared to model for your paintings as long as they are decent.'

He turned to the others who brightened at the prospect of female company and models and they agreed readily. It had been discussed at length when first suggested and they were all disappointed that no one had showed up. They invited her to take some refreshment and as they went to the east terrace to sit, McKinley asked her why she had not written to him when she had returned to London.

'Mr Ede preferred to use the old camp site of St Catherine's Hill so we went straight there; but when we got to it there were navvies everywhere. They are digging a tunnel for the railway that will go south to Portsmouth. So, it wasn't suitable you see.' She hesitated then said, 'And I have to ask, do you have a cellar in this house?'

'Why, yes I think we do, but I don't know what state it's in. They might store the wine down there but the house itself is wonderfully cool. Why do you ask?'

She seemed relieved but would only say 'I think Mr Ede would like somewhere to store the puppets so that we have more room in the caravans. They are valuable and he doesn't want them to get damaged or stolen. Apparently he normally would keep them in the caves on St Catherine's Hill.'

He thought of the extraordinary marionettes he had seen on the stage in Portsmouth and could perfectly understand this anxiety. As they sat on the terrace he said:

'Your new style of life seems to suit you Mariel and I really approve of the style of dress you have adopted. So unique, and the fabric is rich. Is that brocade?'

She smiled and smoothed the beautiful fabric. 'Mr Ede has a warehouse in London where he has materials stored that he collected from all over the world. We use it to make costumes for the shows. In fact the women of the company are dressed in a unique fashion, with loose gowns and tabards and no corsets. They are quite relaxed in all things.' She noticed his sharp look. 'Not in terms of morals though.'

'Are they God fearing people then Mariel? Your hosts at Pitdown will not countenance anything else. The Hall has its own chapel and my friend Seton is particularly devout.'

'Mr Ede reads to us from the bible every Sunday, or asks one of the company to do so. We don't go to church as we move around and our dress is peculiar so we are regarded with suspicion. He has a lot of books, I would like to read some of them but they are very old and, he says, fragile so he keeps them locked away.'

'I am looking forward to meeting him, he sounds to be an interesting gentleman,' said McKinley.

'Oh, he is,' Mariel replied, 'When you pointed him out at my mother's burial, you said you thought you recognised him, but could not place him. You saw him watching us.'

McKinley recalled the tall figure in the churchyard and the older actor in the Dream, but obviously with a false beard on stage. Why had he been there? Was he watching Mariel or was this as a result of the note he had left at the stage door? It did not matter; he would meet him soon enough.

Seton joined them with apologies from the other artists but with an invitation to tour the studios before she left. They drank wine and ate biscuits and Mariel chatted happily about her experiences in London.

'We all slept in the warehouse for a few nights, or the others did, and listened for rats and ghosts and I was not afraid.'

'What made you so brave my dear?' asked Seton.

'Mr Ede explained that rats are clever creatures made by God to clean up after human beings and ghosts are manifestations of the human soul not yet ready to move on.'

'If you saw a ghost would you not scream and faint?' asked Seton.

'If I saw a ghost I should know that it has its own agenda and is unlikely to communicate with me unless it wanted me to perform a task that it cannot manage on its own,' she paused looking earnestly at Seton. 'Having no corporeal form of course.' This met with approval from her host.

They finished their refreshments and before she walked back to St Catherine's Hill they made a visit to the studios in the orangery. Rossetti was working on a composition he called 'The Girlhood of Mary Virgin'. He was quite chastened by his encounter with Mariel and apologised again for his remarks.

She professed to being entranced by his composition and the unusual subject matter and was obviously relieved that there was no unnecessary flesh exposed. She asked very perceptive questions about the small objects in the painting, and he complimented her on her appreciation of symbols.

In response to his compliment she replied, 'Mr Ede says that everything has a place whether in the heavens or down below and nothing should be wasted. If it is true then it is beautiful, and if it is beautiful then it is true.'

'I think you'll find he got that from Keats,' said Millais appearing from his studio.

'Maybe Keats got it from Mr Ede,' said Mariel, obviously unaware that John Keats had died in 1821. But then again, thought McKinley, perhaps they had been contemporaries.

'Come and see what I am working on,' said Millais 'It's a scene from one of Keats's poems. This is Isabella and this is Lorenzo who has fallen hopelessly in love with her. It's hopeless because he is a servant, a clerk, and her brothers are not happy about their love for each other, so they murder him.' He waited for a reaction, but she continued to gaze at the details of the design. He continued 'Isabella digs him up, cuts off his head and plants it in a pot in which she grows basil.'

'What's basil?' asked Mariel.

Rossetti laughed. 'She takes the murder and gruesome mutilation of a body in her stride. Then asks about basil. This is a rare and strange young woman you have here McKinley.'

Mariel cast her dark-lashed eyes at Rossetti. 'These things are always happening in Shakespeare's plays. Every night one of the company tells us a story from a tragedy or a comedy. In one play a woman is forced to eat her own sons, baked in a pie.'

He threw up his arms.

'She has you there Rossetti,' laughed Millais.

'I like your painting very much Mr Millais. It reminds me of a stage with all the players in character and ready to take their particularly nasty actions,' Mariel said.

They moved on to Hunt's work in progress 'It shows the Roman tribune Rienzi vowing to obtain justice for the slaying of his young brother. It's based on a novel and set in medieval times.'

Mariel peered at it with an intensity that her hosts found amusing. 'That looks like you,' she said pointing at Rossetti.

'Quite correct,' said Hunt. 'We are short of models, so we have to make do.'

Seton had sketched a biblical scene of the Garden of Gethsemane, which showed a strong resemblance to the grounds of Pitdown Hall. In his drawing of the figure of Christ there was a hint of self-portrait and the torment of indecision, which McKinley knew he was presently experiencing. The disciples looked like frightened sheep and in the background could be seen Roman soldiers being led by Judas.

Mariel had tears in her eyes when she turned to the artist.

'You paint from the heart,' she said and touched Seton gently on his arm. They were all moved by such gravity from one so young, and McKinley was reluctant to break the spell. 'Where is your work, sir?' she asked him.

'I have nothing to show you,' he said 'except what you have already seen, but I promise that I will make very good use of your actors' company in a composition based on 'A Midsummer Night's Dream'.' He chuckled 'Do you think I might impose upon the puppets to stay still for me?'

'I'm sorry,' Mariel said quickly, 'The puppets will not be available. Too valuable, and difficult to repair.' She was obviously embarrassed and soon afterwards she made her apologies and left them, promising to return, if possible, later that day with the company, or tomorrow if not.

*   *   *

Dawn broke light and hazy the following morning and McKinley was woken by a door slamming inside the house and running footsteps. He walked out in his nightshirt to find Seton bounding up the stairs in his shirt.

'They're here!' he said. 'It's just gone seven and they've turned up. They must have set off at the crack of dawn. I've told them to go to the paddock. I'll put some clothes on and then show them where things are.'

'I'll come with you' said McKinley and ran back to his room. He must have taken longer with his toilette than Seton because by the time he descended the stairs and sauntered out into the morning sunshine, the little wagon train had parked themselves in the small field and were feeding and watering their horses. Faced with the prospect of meeting the object of his passion he had been disturbed to find his hands shaking and an undertow of nausea as he washed and carefully dressed, wishing that he had more clean clothes with him and that they had been better pressed. His hair was brushed and he was roughly shaved when he approached the tall thin man he now recognised as the visitor at Mariel's mother's funeral and the actor-manager of the Prospero Company.

He introduced himself and they shook hands. He was aware that the other man had a cool appraising eye and very cool hands, unlike McKinley whose hands were, he realised, appallingly sweaty. He did not spend much time studying Jonathan Ede as he struggled to keep his eyes from scanning the other figures that were busy establishing the little settlement or tending to the horses.

'You desired to meet me I believe, Mr McKinley, when we performed our 'Dream' in Portsmouth. I am sorry that I could not accommodate you at that time. Our arrangements are quite complex, and we seldom find time to be sociable when we are working.' His voice was deep and well-modulated, as one would expect from an actor and it brought McKinley back to his senses.

McKinley stared at him, suddenly aware of his disadvantage. He knew nothing about these people and would have to control his desire to meet Teresa.

He composed himself and said, 'I am an artist sir and was very keen to draw some of the actors and actresses. Indeed, we are all painters here and our themes are often based on bible stories or the tales told of medieval times, when life was simpler.' He looked at the pastoral scene of the wagon encampment and the men in practical clothes, the women with long hair braided and wearing the sort of loose dress that Mariel had worn the day before. He continued 'I have the feeling you are similarly affected by the stamp of industry that blots out the beauty of our green landscape. As artists we have been repelled by the loss of innocence found in heavily stylised classical art.' He was floundering now. 'Where will it all end?' He swallowed awkwardly and cursed his lack of preparation.

Ede smiled, 'When we have settled ourselves, I shall display my people for your consideration and you may discuss which models may be most suitable for your projects.'

McKinley was relieved to see Seton, Mariel and another woman walking from the yard at the back of the kitchen with various containers filled with water. She was there, her red hair plaited and a green dress loosely fitted, quite old yet timeless. She looked at him but showed no recognition. Mariel smiled and he waved and tried to cover his disappointment.

'Good morning Mariel. I am so pleased to see you and hope you will all soon settle in.'

They looked around as the other artists strolled out of the house, in various states of dress and some yawning and stretching. Seton made their introductions to Jonathan Ede and then the manager introduced his company. To McKinley's delight Teresa smiled at them when her turn came. It was obvious that Rossetti was smitten, but then he was taken with all three women. The dark-haired girl who had played the part of Hermia was named Lily and the flaxen headed woman who had played Hippolyta was Katherine. They were ordinary women and yet they each had a beguiling beauty, without artifice, in humble surroundings and simple clothes.

Ede introduced the three actors as Avery, Walter and Thomas. The first two were evidently tumblers and proceeded to demonstrate part of their routine with handsprings and backflips, followed by a bow. Thomas was older and looked strong; he simply bowed and resumed his duties with the horses. The last member of the company was an older man, less pleasing to the eye and slightly bent over. Ede called him Jonah and to demonstrate his talents he produced a small flute and played a melodious series of notes that carried through the warm summer morning.

'Jonah is mute, but can play almost any musical instrument, and he does so by ear,' said Ede as he bowed. 'Well, you have met our little company, now tell me what five young men are hoping to find in this quiet and antique location. Do you not crave the clamour and bustle of London with its markets in culture and flesh?'

There were various reactions to Ede's provocation; Rossetti folded his arms and scowled, Hunt and Millais were affronted, but Jack Seton took the lead and said:

'I am the leaseholder of Pitdown Hall and it is my intention to start a colony of likeminded painters and, I hope, writers. We have decided to shake off the stale and established 'markets' as you call them, of London and especially the Royal Academy.' The others voiced their agreement, 'which imposes its stultifying prejudices on young minds. We prefer to look for inspiration among our people and times and avoid the slavish admiration of all things Greek and Roman. We find the muscular figures of Michelangelo to be grotesque and prefer the ethereal creations of painters like Botticelli. We also look to the nature inspired work of Durer and the simpler style of medieval paintings. A setting such as this house is perfect for our inspiration.'

Ede studied the tall, unusual building and nodded his appreciation. 'This was built during the reign of our last King Henry, the father of the noble Queen Elizabeth, if I am not mistaken. Yes I will be interested to see the paintings you are working on. Perhaps I can be shown around your studios later today. For now, we must put up our tent, with your gracious permission.'

The two groups separated, the artists returning to their work and the troupe carried on establishing their camp. The horses were tethered, and a large marquee was erected. McKinley lingered to watch, and Mariel joined him.

'The women are beautiful, are they not?' she said.

She smiled at him with a knowing smile, and he looked down at her, although it cost him to take his eyes off Teresa and as soon as he could he looked for her again, but she had gone into one of the wagons. Not being able to see her, he then was compelled to talk about her.

'What is she like? Is she married?'

'I presume you mean Teresa the redhead?' she teased. He blushed and she continued. 'None of the women or men are wed in the conventional sense. I think they are all somehow in a state of uxorious love for the company and the plays that we perform.'

This was such an extraordinary statement from a child that McKinley gave his whole attention to the girl and found that she had a place in his heart so that he received almost as much pleasure from her company as he imagined he might receive in the company of Teresa. Her vocabulary had increased surprisingly since they had first met.

'What do you mean 'uxorious', that applies only to love within a marriage.'

'Mr Ede says that we are married to our profession and that the shows are the only time when we are really alive. Of course, it doesn't apply to me yet, I have only had a walking on part, and my needlecraft is my main contribution, but I can understand what he means. It is as though the time when we do not perform is like a dream time and is a shadow of the energy and excitement that suffuse our bodies when we are lit by limelight and hear the laughter or sobs of the audience.'

'I think you have been absorbing too much of Mr Ede's teachings,' said McKinley.

'Everyone says it is so. They all are just existing until they can tread the boards again. Every exercise and study that they make in the so-called real world is just a practise as they hone their skills for the performance. Without our art we are just empty husks.'

'Stop it Mariel!' He spoke to her quietly but sharply. 'This is wrong and it is a dangerous philosophy. There is so much more to experience in life than theatre.' As he said it, he wondered if he was correct. She pulled a child's petulant face at him and ran off and he almost called her back, but knew he was conflicted. Perhaps there was some truth to the statement, but it was a borrowed wisdom that she wore like one of those antique dresses, so obviously made by someone who had lived for a long time. Turning to the old crumbling Tudor house he walked into the dark hallway and wondered if life would mean so much to him if he did not have paint and his skill so that he could fill his own world with vibrant colours.

*   *   *

If his conversation with Mariel had troubled him he did not let it impede his plans to create a major work using the acting troupe as models. He had decided to draw upon Keats's poem of the Eve of St Agnes where a young woman could summon a dream of her future husband by obeying certain rituals before she went to bed. He intended to show the moment when the heroine, believing the presence of her lover to be the continuation of a dream, welcomes the living man into her bed.

The immense popularity of Keats's poetry and the burgeoning fascination with the medieval should assure him a showing at the Academy next spring and, with luck, assure him a sale. He would start by sketching Teresa and he spent the remainder of the morning preparing his canvas and working up a composition. He was about to give up when Seton appeared and shouted to all the artists to make haste to the tent where a circus was in position for them to draw. If they were interested.

McKinley suddenly realised that he would have to compete, and he would be devastated to find her already occupied and being drawn by that genius Millais, or worse still, by Rossetti with his good looks and Italian charm.

The campsite was quiet and seemingly deserted when they approached carrying boards and drawing materials. The big tent was at the centre of the living arrangement, and he could hear voices inside. Seton pulled aside the flap, they entered and were astounded to discover every actor and actress standing in the centre of the space, in costume and holding dramatic poses. A hole in the roof allowed light to fall on them creating dark shadow and clear highlights.

Ede stood to one side and announced. 'They will hold this pose for one half hour then they will move and hold another for the same amount of time. This is to thank you for your hospitality. When you have considered who you wish to paint, they will pose in here or outside in the garden by arrangement for the usual fee. If you cannot agree then I will arrange an auction and the man with the deepest pockets will have his pick.'

The atmosphere of excitement was tempered somewhat at that, and Rossetti said, 'You don't own them sir, surely they have free will. They are not marionettes.'

At this last statement there was a flurry of unease among the actors until Seton said 'You are free to find your own models Rossetti. Don't let us detain you.'

Mr Ede simply smiled. 'I can supply a marionette. Perhaps Mr Rossetti would prefer it.'

'No, please let us proceed as you suggest,' Hunt was placatory, and Millais agreed. McKinley found himself a bench where he could draw Teresa and he started sketching. The clock was running, indicated Ede, holding up a large pocket watch and the others started working as fast as they could. At first he did not notice that Mariel was absent. But when he did he reckoned it was because she was not part of the acting company so that could be explained.

Teresa's hair was loose and naturally curling under a small V-shaped coronet that sat low on her brow. She wore a medieval styled green dress that matched her eyes with an elaborate embroidered belt. It had bell sleeves that left part of her arms bare. He had never seen such creamy flesh. She must take particular care to avoid the sun. A few flowing lines were enough to capture her elegant shape; and then the time was gone, and she moved to the other side of the formation of models. Leaving a muscular young man in front of McKinley.

Perhaps this could be the dream husband he thought and drew the martial figure as a stalwart knight might look in the Keats poem. At the end of that half hour he looked at the two images together and they felt somehow wrong, as though two languages were present together. He rejected the man and would work more on the figure of the girl.

'I shall use poetry as inspiration for more work with models like these,' said Millais, full of enthusiasm.

'I believe the company has a great deal of Shakespeare they could show us,' McKinley was keen to relive the entrancement of 'A Midsummer Night's Dream'.

The models moved again and the dark-eyed beauty Lily was before him. Her hair was calf length, and she wore a bright red cloth wrapped around her twisting body that emphasised the pose and enhanced her voluptuous look as she stared at him provocatively. 'Lamia', Keats's poem came into his mind. A woman who has been cursed to live inside a snake's body is changed by an enchanter back to a woman's form and meets her lover resulting in blissful happiness for both. At a banquet she withers under the scrutiny of a 'wise' old man and dies; then her lover dies of a broken heart. McKinley was becoming calmer and more measured in his drawing now and taking time to use his charcoal with economy. The tent was silent, the artists completely absorbed in their work.

Another turn and Ede announced that they would be allowed to rest before modelling in pairs. Mariel appeared with beer and wine for refreshment and the separate groups of artists and models began to mingle as they had not before. The actors were obviously comfortable in their bodies and the artists, perhaps except for Rossetti, seemed young and less secure and keen to make an impression, chatting about the work they were planning to create.

It should be the other way round, thought McKinley sitting as he sorted out his drawings. The actors were itinerant players, with no home and little money, whereas he and his fellows were of a higher class, better educated, and had mixed in well-connected circles. He looked up and saw Lily making her way over to him, her eyes never leaving his. He made to rise but she pushed him back down and sinuously ducked under his arm so that she was in front of the sheaf of papers in his hands. She sat between his legs on the ground in front of him. He had no choice but to remain there, his arms around her smooth bare shoulders, exhibiting his work.

'Your dress will be ruined,' he stammered. He dared not look at the other artists, but he knew they were smiling or sniggering at his predicament. It would be rude to get up and abandon her and he would look a coward, he had to act as brazenly as she.

'This dress has seen far worse treatment. Show me the picture of me,' she said.

Clumsily he leafed through them, trying not to brush against her bare flesh, but feeling a surge of excitement every time his shirt sleeves moved back to allow his forearms to touch her warm skin. She seemed to glow in the diffuse light of the tent and he could smell her scent like a dark exotic flower. She gazed at the drawing for what seemed a long time. He was sweating and knew that his face was flushed, and he wished this to be over whilst acutely aware of the pleasure it gave him. She leaned back and tilted her chin up, so that her long neck stretched back and he saw her face upside down looking up at him.

'I think you have made me look too beautiful.'

This was his cue to say: you are very beautiful, Lily, and you have bewitched me and I desperately want you, come to my bed. But instead he said, 'It was easy, you held your pose very professionally.'

She was quiet for a minute, as though she could not understand what he had said, then she sat up, took hold of his left hand and removed it from the papers, pushed them aside and stood in one flowing movement and walked away. McKinley sat and realised that his hands were shaking. He quickly put aside the drawings because they made his tremors look worse. When he felt sufficiently composed he looked up and noticed that only Seton was still watching him and his expression was unreadable.

He was reticent about joining in and sat alone for a few minutes, watching Mariel's grace as she made her way around the tent, ensuring everyone was well supplied.

McKinley smelled her before he saw her. She smelled of green fields and he turned and saw the green dress, like newly mown grass at his side. She said nothing but sat next to him on the bench, and offered him a glass of yellow wine. He knew it had the fragrance of springtime before he tasted it and at that moment he was again lost in the perfection of her mouth. She brought him back to the formality of their situation with the calmness of her gaze and said:

'Are we suitable, as models? Do we please you?'

He was lost for words. He would have liked to sit looking at her for the rest of the afternoon, for the rest of the summer, but he managed to stammer:

'You are wonderful, you all are perfect, well absolutely excellent. Oh dear. Look at my drawing of you. I was trying to work up a composition for a painting based on Keats's poem about the Eve of St Agnes. Are you familiar with it?' She shook her head. He continued, 'Maybe a different poem would be more suitable. What about 'La Belle Dame Sans Merci' that's quite famous and … I think I've a copy of it in my room. Not that you would want to come to my room, that wouldn't be seemly…' He realised his heart was thudding. To collect himself he explained the story of Keats's poem.

'It begins 'Alas what ails thee knight at arms, alone and palely loitering, the sedge has withered from the lake, and no birds sing.' Of course I would paint the main story. The knight has fallen in love with a faerie girl met in the meadow, he has taken her and then she has taken him under the faerie hill where ghosts of long dead warriors and kings lament their fate at her hands.' He stopped, blushing, and realising for the first time that the attentions of the knight may not have been welcomed by the woman. It may have been rape, and this was her revenge on powerful men.

He lapsed into silence and she picked up his drawing of Lily, and moved closer to him so that they could examine it together. He was almost overcome with desire for her and with embarrassment, but he took a few surreptitious deep breaths and looked at his drawing. It was good. It was dramatic and he had captured the lithe movement in the position of her body. The twisted fabric and the direct look from her almond shaped eyes promised everything.

'Please model for 'La Belle Dame',' he said. With a shiver he saw that she would be perfect as the faerie woman from a different world who could entice a man to fall in love with her and then destroy him. Oh, how he wanted to be destroyed.

As he gazed on her and waited for her reply, Ede announced that they would resume. She smiled and left him, and he gathered his material and papers fixing a large sheet to a board for the next session. With no discussion the men and women moved into position as three pairs and stopped as though they were statues. It looked as though Rossetti might object to the arrangement that was in front of him, but he thought better of it when he looked at the hooded eyes of Mr Ede. His gaunt figure seemed to preside over the tent as though he were the sorcerer Prospero and able to bend them to his will.

If the artists had expected three sets of man and woman they were surprised to find two men wrestling, two women braiding each other's hair and a man and a woman in a passionate embrace. They were all sitting and, McKinley realised, were expertly arranged to make lyrical statements of drama. Ede must have planned it and the artists gave it their most rapt attention in absolute silence for almost an hour. How could they hold those poses for so long? When he thought about it later it did not seem humanly possible. He attributed it to the rigorous training they had subjected themselves to as performers.

When their time was up both artists and models were exhausted. They walked about the tent and stretched their limbs. Then they showed their drawings to each other and to the models with much admiration especially for Millais's exquisite detail of hair and clothing. Rossetti's work was like him, brooding and dramatic with the glamour of romance and slightly dishevelled in appearance. Hunt's drawings captured the solidity of flesh and the expression of the poses leading one to wonder what would come next. McKinley looked with interest at Seton's sketches, but was disappointed to find that they were partially drawn and did not even attempt to find a statement to express. He had drawn Lily first and that was the most complete. She looked even more serpent-like in his drawing than McKinley remembered, and her presence was disconcerting. He suspected that Seton had worked on it at the expense of the others.

'You have captured the essence of her,' said Ede looking over their shoulders.

'He has given her a darkness of the soul,' said McKinley.

'Oh, that could never be,' said Ede as Lily joined them. He put his long hand on her head, and she rose to it like a cat enjoying the caress of its master. 'For that she would need a soul.' They both laughed and he led her away.

McKinley was annoyed at this exhibition and turned to Seton to find that his friend's face was distraught, but he covered it by turning the drawing away and beginning to pack his materials. Unable to put his sympathy into words, he too resumed packing his papers and materials. He would speak to him about it later, he decided, when they were alone and perhaps could take a walk on the nearby hill as they sometimes did in the evening after supper. He would confide his own love for Teresa and that might prompt a similar confidence by his friend.

He looked up to find that all the Prospero Company were gone, even Mariel who had removed the detritus of their refreshments. Hunt and Millais were effusive in their compliments of the models and the absolute stillness they had been able to maintain. When they were back in the orangery studios, they lost no time in pinning up their drawings and comparing the work with plans to create large oil paintings to astound the Academy next year. They all agreed that they were better suited to dramatic subjects than religious studies. Shakespeare and Keats were among their favourites and McKinley stated his intention to paint 'La Belle Dame' using Teresa as the principal model. He could not decide who should portray the stricken knight.

'You should include yourself in that regard,' said Millais, 'you look at her like a moon-struck hare.'

'You are in thrall, Robert. It is the divinest form of inspiration – make the most of it,' said Rossetti and the others agreed.

Seton kept quiet and to distract attention from himself McKinley said: 'If I am in thrall to Teresa, then Seton is definitely smitten by the lovely Lily, or Lamia as I have renamed her.' He held up his drawing of the twisted sinuous body and hypnotic gaze and laughed and most joined in, but Seton was affronted by the comparison of the woman to the serpent creature in Keats's poem.

'Don't say that about her. It's bad enough that their manager acts like a sinister puppet master.'

'Come on Seton, they're actresses. They're as good as doxies as far as I'm concerned,' Rossetti was no more worldly wise than his young companions, but he effected greater confidence.

'I have seen more of the world than any of you, and I would say that despite appearances these women are not for sale.' McKinley would not allow such a comment to stand uncorrected and he feared for the reputation of his young friend Mariel who could be tarnished by association.

'Why don't you paint Lily as Lamia, Seton?' asked Hunt.

'No, I have decided to paint her as the Magdalene. She has a dark colouring and I am sure that I can portray her as a penitent. Perhaps a triptych from prostitute to acolyte to the woman who first sees Our Lord after the Resurrection for Noli me Tangere.'

'I should be interested to see that, young man.' Jonathan Ede was standing in the doorway from the dining hall. His presence cast a cooling air over the young artists, as though they were especially conscious of their lack of experience in the world when faced with this old man who looked both fragile and powerful. Courtesy won the day and they welcomed him and explained their ideas and plans and made arrangements with him for sittings on the following days, the only person not available would be the musician and Ede himself. Mariel was also to be excluded as she had much sewing to do for the upcoming shows.

Then Ede said, 'I require a favour from you as I need to store our marionettes in a cool and secure room. I understand that you have a small cellar?'

'Yes there is such a place but it is damp and I should have thought the chapel would be a better area, we keep locked and it is ….' Seton started.

'Not the chapel,' interrupted Ede. 'That would not be suitable for these particular examples. They have a unique quality that prefers to be stored below ground. They are very old, you see.'

'The cellar it is,' said Seton. 'I have the key and perhaps Hunt and I can bring up some wine before we lock it up.'

'Admirable,' said Ede, 'I will have them brought over in the next half hour.' He bowed graciously and left.

Rossetti said, 'Well he makes them sound quite mysterious. You've seen them McKinley, what are they like?'

'I have only seen the large human style puppets who played the mechanicals in 'A Midsummer Night's Dream' and the faeries who were extraordinarily flexible and whose likeness was based on insects. The human ones were caricatures with huge hands and feet and that worked well for Bottom, Peter Quince and the others. The skill is all that of the puppeteers who operated them.'

'And didn't you say they were the men and women we have been drawing today?' asked Millais.

'Yes, they have extraordinary abilities,' said McKinley.

'Well, I hope we will be permitted to watch one of their rehearsals. Will you ask him what they present at the next fair they attend?' said Rossetti. He turned to Seton who nodded and beckoned Hunt to join him in bringing up wine into the dining room.

The remaining three did not speak and McKinley thought that he should retire to his room and finish a letter that he had begun to Macey the previous day, but he was curious to see the puppets again and he imagined their workings would be apparent in the light of day, without the glamour of the stage. It became clear that they all had the same idea.

'Come on,' said Millais and they dashed through the dining hall and out of the front door to encounter a solemn procession starting from the caravans. It had the air of a funeral. The entire company carried between them boxes, not unlike coffins that were draped in an ancient fabric, threadbare in parts. They walked slowly, so that the contents would not be jostled. Silently, almost reverently they mounted the steps into the Hall.

The young artists stood aside as Ede led them to where Seton indicated the cellar entrance and they processed into the dark and quiet space, lit only, as far as McKinley could see, by candles. When they had all reappeared Seton solemnly locked the door and for a moment it seemed that he might hand over the key to Mr Ede.

Instead he said, 'I shall keep it in a locked drawer in my bedroom. You can be assured that your props will be safe here.' There was a slight exhalation of breath as though someone was suppressing a laugh, but it was not clear who.

Mr Ede said, 'Excellent. I shall go back to my caravan and take a nap. Thank you for your courtesy gentlemen.'

The company of actors and the musician and Mariel walked into the sunshine. As soon as they had left the Hall the musician pulled out a pipe and played a merry tune, they began chatting and linking arms, even adding dance steps to their walk away from the building.

It was in a state of anti-climax that the five painters retreated to their studios. Before this interlude that space had seemed so full of promise but now, when the objects of their inspiration, having entered Pitdown Hall, had left it, the orangery seemed lifeless and ugly again.

*   *   *

That evening, after dinner when his fellows were writing letters, or poetry, or planning their compositions in the studio, McKinley was in a welter of melancholy because she had not flirted with him, like Lily had, but she had chosen to sit with him. What did that mean? Did she like him or not? He decided to walk off his dissatisfaction. There seemed to be a weight inside him, and it might have been the large suet pudding served by cook at a time of year when fruit was plentiful. They had all eaten it out of habit whether they were hungry or not. He would look for some wild strawberries seen growing along the drover's way, eating them might help to physic the humour that weighed upon him.

He knocked on Seton's door to see if he wanted to accompany him, but there was no reply. He noticed the scent of woodsmoke on the air and he thought that must be the cooking fires of the encampment. He did not want to be reminded of her proximity although he desperately wanted to see her. The troupe seemed self-sufficient, would he be able to impress her with his painting and cause her to fall as much in love with him as he was with her?

The sun was still hot and the shadows lengthening when he reached the drover's road. The sandy soil was warm from the day and a gentle buzz of small insects gave a soothing sweetness to the sound of birds preparing for a short night. He stopped abruptly as he saw a female form kneeling at the bank of strawberries he had noticed earlier. Teresa was about the same business as he intended but she had a basket and was picking a feast to be shared with her fellows. A sudden thought to flee was replaced by a strong desire simply to be with her.

She heard him approach and smiled up at him.

86

'Hello. Would you like some strawberries?' She held out her basket to him and he knelt beside her.

'I was coming to gorge myself on them, but I see you've beaten me to it.'

'There are plenty,' she said, 'and there are more further along the track. These must have ripened today in the sun. They should be eaten because overnight the mice will finish them off.' They picked fruit together in silence and he helped to load her basket. He was aware of her gentle breathing, the sounds of the evening becoming quieter and the scent of her body as they worked side by side.

After about twenty minutes her basket was almost full, and they both reached for a dark red fruit further up the bank. Their hands touched and he did not withdraw his but caressed her wrist. She hesitated, then plucked the berry and brought it up to his mouth. He smelled the fragrant strawberry and the earthy smell of her fingers that had been pulling plants aside to find the fruit. Should he accept it or insist that she eat? He was opening his mouth when she crushed the fruit between her fingers. She smeared the red juice on his lips and then onto her own. They both smelled the intense fragrance and licked their lips to taste its sweet flavour. He thought she might kiss him and reached for her, but she lithely stood.

She said, 'I must go back. They'll wonder where their pudding is. Meet me here again tomorrow. More will have ripened by then.' She turned and ran almost skipping back down the path until her form was lost in the shadows of the trees.

He knelt heavily, his body riven by the weakness of love and the hardness of lust, his mind filled with what might have been. He waited in the growing darkness until bats flitted overhead and the sound of a nightjar whirring in the sedge woke him from his reverie. The words from 'La Belle Dame' seeped into his mind and he resolved to fully explore that dark story. He would draw her, he would paint her, he would examine every inch of her face and her person, her body would be as familiar as his own. He was blinded by the sweetness of obsession as he walked back to the Hall, but as he entered the darkest part of the path, now so dark that he could not see his way, he heard a sound.

It was not much more than a sigh at first then it grew into a moan and he discerned that it was a little way off the path, amongst a coppiced hazel thicket. It might be an animal in pain. Curiosity drew him closer and it became clear that there were two creatures, making a sound in unison. He stopped for a few seconds and listened, then he recognised that it was two people in the act of copulation. They paused, as though realising they were being observed, but almost immediately resumed, their lust heightened. He painstakingly retraced his steps and crept away, knowing they had heard him. The sounds increased in urgency as he retreated and when he was sure he was back on the drover's way again he covered his ears and ran down to the Hall to get away from their cries of ecstasy.

Unwilling to pass the encampment of licentious creatures – how long was it since his own licentious thoughts – he entered the house through the orangery. Hunt and Millais were drinking wine in the dining room, discussing the qualities of the models and the values they would bring to the paintings from medieval inspiration. They had decided to adopt a name – the 'Pre-Raphaelite Brotherhood' and he could join them if he liked. Their art would be natural and lyrical using light and colour to illuminate the real world, not mired in classical tradition and irrelevant imagery.

McKinley was barely listening. He poured himself a large glass of wine and tried not to think of those sounds. He thought that it must have been Rossetti of course, his hot Italian blood, it must have been him with one of the women. Then Rossetti walked into the room holding an empty glass and noticed that McKinley was out of breath.

'Are you alright? You look as though you've seen a ghost. You haven't have you? If you have, take us to it so that we might all experience the supernatural,' he said and the others joined in encouraging the red-faced McKinley.

He shook his head but as the wine weakened him he blurted out, 'Not a ghost, but I heard something in the woods. I am embarrassed to say what it was.'

As they realised the implication Rossetti said, 'Was it a man and a woman, two men or two women?'

This provoked an uproar and Hunt said: 'Must be a couple from the company. Let's see who's missing from the campsite.'

They rushed to the front door and then strolled nonchalantly over to the camp of actors and their fires. McKinley regretted his indiscretion. Mariel and the musician and two of the women were present so as they enquired after the evening and surreptitiously identified those present, Lily came through the picket gate. She confidently walked to the fire and sat beside Teresa and begged tea from her. She was bright eyed and flushed and McKinley realised that hers was one of the voices he had heard. They were told that the other men were out catching rabbits for the pot so they could not identify her mate and at length the casual conversation ran out and the four artists returned to the Hall.

'It couldn't have been the old man, Ede,' said Hunt, 'but either of the young men might have been the other person you heard.'

'Or the strong fellow who looks after the horses,' said Millais.

'It was definitely that little hussy Lily,' said Rossetti, 'I could smell it on her.' He turned to McKinley. 'Who did it sound like? What sort of voice? Did he say anything?'

McKinley bridled at this crudity and muttering something about having letters to write, he left them carousing and speculating further in the dining hall. He walked upstairs trying not to replay those sounds in his head but then he stopped, and his jaw dropped at the sudden realisation that the man he had heard in the throes of ecstasy had been his friend Seton. The epitome of an ascetic who valued the spirit more highly than the flesh. A man whose sense of virtue and propriety seemed to outweigh all else had been engaging in animal sex outdoors with a woman he had met that very day. He did not know whether to be outraged or jealous. He was both.

He hesitated at Seton's door. Should he take him to task or congratulate him? As he could not make up his mind he hastily walked up to his own room where he paced to and fro, unable to settle to any writing or drawing. Luckily his room did not face the encampment, or he would have been tempted to look out all night long and watch the movements of its occupants. As it was, he fell asleep and dreamed of Teresa sitting serenely by a campfire and smiling at him. The dream was spoiled by the knowledge that behind her in the darkness two unrecognisable forms were rocking and crying out in their obscene act. Instead of admiring her beauty he tried to see past her, he wanted to be part of their endeavour and he struggled to see them. The night seemed to be very short, and he awoke spent and exhausted.

*   *   *

In the morning Hunt and Millais were finishing their breakfast and Rossetti had not yet risen; there was no sign of Seton and they had not seen him. McKinley hoped that they would leave, and he might have a few minutes alone with his friend to clarify what had happened last night. It was so unlike Seton, the high churchman, to compromise his beliefs in this way. Of all of them he expected him to behave with moral rectitude and he was troubled, and not a little curious.

As McKinley chewed the stale bread and jam alone, he heard Seton descend the stairs and enter the dining room. He went to the table of food and began to fill a plate without looking at McKinley.

'Good morning Seton,' he said calmly. The other turned slowly and he saw with surprise that he was unshaven, and his lower lip showed a bite mark. 'What the hell did that, man?' He had an idea but somehow could not stop himself from exclaiming.

'I hit myself in the face whilst opening a bottle. It's no big deal. It'll go away in a few days.'

They sat and ate in silence. McKinley knew that this was his opportunity to raise the matter and after a few minutes he said quietly 'If you want to talk about her, you can trust me.'

'So it was you who told the others and gathered a party to hunt the culprits, then.' Seton's eyes blazed.

'No. I mean yes, but I didn't want them to …. I didn't know it was you.'

Seton's face was white, his bruised lip stood out vividly 'Stay out of my personal life!' He held McKinley's gaze as he bit into a large piece of white bread, red jam oozed onto his fingers and he was evidently in pain, but he seemed to relish it. 'Now fuck off!'

McKinley stood and went through to the studios. He wished that his studio was tucked away somewhere quiet, he did not want to spend time in the company of Seton or the others today because there was bound to be some banter about what he had overheard in the woods. He was a fool and should have kept his mouth shut.

He had a primed canvas and tacked it to a board, then mixed a combination of earth colours. As he was doing this there was a light tap at the door and through the glass he saw Teresa waiting in her customary green robe and carrying a basket covered with a cloth. He was pleased to see her but shuddered at the recollection of her friend's behaviour the night before. She smiled at him and the sickness in his stomach gave way to butterflies and hope. He would treat her differently and all would be well.

He opened the door and smelt the fragrant fresh air.

'Let's go out and find somewhere to begin the painting outside,' he said, 'I'll pack up my essential equipment and we can explore. I think there is a pond further down the hill, it will make a fine setting for our composition.'

'Our composition?' she said, 'I am just the model.'

He gathered everything he had prepared and pulled on his hat. 'If you are modelling for me then we are both in this together as equal partners.'

'You are a strange man Robert McKinley.'

'I see you know my name,' he said.

'And when the painting is finished you may know mine,' she said and set off ahead of him.

They walked for about half an hour until they came to a pond filled by a stream off the hill and dammed to provide water for livestock that had left a trodden area but under the shade of some elders there was a natural bower covered in wildflowers. She stopped suddenly turning to one side. 'Look, in the hedge.'

They stood still and he was amazed to see a dozen or so little field mice running and jumping about.

'What are they doing?' he whispered.

'Enjoying the weather and the plentiful food. Life is good for them, so they celebrate it.'

They crept away quietly and chose a shady area where the water cast a reflective light on Teresa and he could position her comfortably. When he looked up from arranging his materials he saw that she had woven a garland from the wild flowers and placed it on her head. She wore no shoes and her hair was loose, she looked as though she really could be a faerie's child. He longed to read the poem to her but he wanted to maintain her innocence; if she tried to assume a pose, she may play the part rather than be the natural muse he was looking for.

They spent the day at that quiet spot, broken by a visit from some cattle and in the regular company of a heron who stalked the reeds at the water's edge like a grey assassin. They ate cheese and biscuits that Teresa had brought, and McKinley walked to a nearby farmhouse to buy a couple of bottles of beer.

The day's work was pleasing to both of them and as they walked back to Pitdown Hall he said that he would not meet her that evening. She agreed and said she felt tired, but McKinley was disturbed by the noises he had heard in the coppice of hazel and the effect it seemed to have on Seton. He would not stir from his room after dinner and would write to all those he had been neglecting recently.

The atmosphere at the evening's meal was subdued. It was a cold plate of beef and salad items from the gardens and fruit for their pudding which was a great relief to McKinley; he assumed someone must have mentioned the heaviness of the previous day's meal to cook. Conversation was scant and more polite than usual, and he could only guess that any mention of carnal exploits was reckoned to be taboo. Seton's bitten mouth was less swollen but was still coloured, and he retired to his room as soon as dinner was concluded.

After McKinley had written letters to his family and to George Macey, now almost fully recovered from his ordeal, he became aware of a sound through the open window. It was like singing but they were not voices, rather like small pipes with an occasional sonorous undertone like that of a bagpipe. The light breeze that picked up from the northeast seemed to carry the thin sound and he wondered if it was from the town or a village, but as he listened it faded and died. The other occupants of the house would not have heard it as their rooms faced the front and his bedroom being on the second floor was probably the only one high enough to receive that breeze, for which he was grateful.

After a night of restful sleep, he met Teresa again and they walked to the pond to continue work on the painting. He told her that Mariel had mentioned stories being recounted by company members in the evenings and asked what they had discussed the previous night.

'We recited Mr Blake's poetry. Mr Ede is very fond of it.'

'I can understand that as William Blake was both an artist and a poet,' he paused and then asked, 'Were you playing music at the campsite last night? I am sure I heard strange music. It sounded like tiny pipes and almost tinkling. I can't quite remember it, but I am sure I heard it.'

He was studying her feet and did not see the fleeting expression of dismay that crossed her face.

'No. I heard nothing.' She changed the subject. 'Mariel told us how you helped her after her mother died and the landlord wanted to throw her out onto the street with her mother's corpse lying not yet cold in the parlour.' He was surprised at the edge to her voice, looked up and saw that she seemed upset.

He said, 'She had no one else, except a kindly neighbour who she had little of her own to spare.'

'It's hard for a woman with no family to even survive. A woman with no family is like a goat driven into the wilderness to be torn apart by wild beasts,' Teresa said coldly.

'Like the scapegoat in the Bible you mean. Taking all the sins of the tribe on its head and driven out as a sacrifice?'

'That's it - a blood sacrifice.' She considered this and then said, 'The sin of Eve, women and blood and death. Someone to blame for the sins of the world.'

'I thought Jesus had taken the world's sins upon himself, at least according to the gospels.'

'That doesn't mean we are not blamed for the loss of Eden. Along with the serpent of course.'

McKinley looked at her enquiringly. 'That means as a society we haven't come very far in two thousand years Teresa. Is that even your name I wonder?'

Her face relaxed again, and she said, 'You can call me Eve if you like. Or La Belle Dame Sans Merci, at least for now.'

I don't know you at all he thought. And he was glad.

'Tell me about the individuals who make up the acting company. Did they acquire their puppetry skills whilst working for Mr Ede, or does he hire men and women who have already been trained? It really is an extraordinary show you perform.'

'Apart from Mariel we have all been with him a long time. Each year comprises seasons and we tend not to see our lives in terms of years. What year is the one we are in?'

'1848,' he laughed at the game she played. She could not be above one and twenty he thought, so a few years would be a long time for her. She may have joined the troupe at Mariel's age, only fourteen. He would try not to interrogate but could play along. 'So you travel from fair to fair, matching your locations to the places where there will be people to pay to watch the shows? I suppose that would include the Lady Day hiring fairs in March and I know you used to perform at the Portsmouth free mart fair.' She did not respond so he said, 'I saw you in Portsmouth. How did you enjoy performing in a real theatre?'

'We didn't enjoy it. It was too restrictive. We are people of the land and sky. I didn't like the industry, the smells and the noise of machinery.'

'But you go to London?' he asked.

'Mr Ede has property there and some business that requires his attention. I cannot say more than that.'

'Of course. I do not wish to pry. I enjoyed 'A Midsummer Night's Dream' very much.' Again she did not respond so he continued 'I daresay most of your performing is in the spring and summer.'

'And the autumn fairs. We do well in the time of harvest when there is usually produce to spare, and the people of the countryside are happy and willing to celebrate plenty before the sharpness of winter and the hunger of Lent. The Sloe fair in Chichester is the one I look forward to most. It is a prosperous town, and our Shakespeare is well received. It provides our stock for the winter.'

'Where do you spend the winter?' he asked.

She hesitated. 'Usually in the west country. Sometimes Cornwall.'

They settled into a pleasant silence, and it allowed him to reflect on her replies as he worked upon her figure and painted in the small flowers amidst the deep shadows from the trees and grasses. She was a mysterious girl and her colouring made her seem otherworldly. She had none of the full-fleshed voluptuousness of Lily, nor the cool iciness of the blonde woman Katherine who seemed older than the other two. He looked forward to putting the finishing touches to Teresa's green eyes. They would be looking out at the viewer, bewitching and tempting, but innocent too.

He thought about the travelling folk who have always populated this land, not only the gypsies, but the migrant workers who go where there is seasonal work. Their labour was marketed at the Lady Day fairs on 25th March, probably the Prospero Company's first engagement of the year. McKinley was concerned that so many people were being drawn into the towns and cities to labour in mills and factories. He thought of his erstwhile patron Mr Bartleby and his carpet factory in Kidderminster.

There were large movements of people in parts of the country. He knew from newspapers that Liverpool had seen an influx in Irish migrants escaping the starvation of the potato blight famine. Hadn't Mariel told him that the digging at St Catherine's Hill was by navvies? They were probably Irish. The men who built the canal navigations were now building the railways. The countryside was changing irrevocably. He did not expect that she was following such matters, she was a country girl.

'Why do the women of the troupe not wear stays like decent English women?' He burst out on impulse. Dear God, he thought, how could I say something so crass? But she just laughed.

'Do you think women have always worn such ridiculous garments? It is men that have confined us in vice-like fastenings so that we appear to have tiny waist and enormous breasts.'

He blushed in embarrassment 'I'm sorry I don't know what made me say that.'

'Perhaps it was because you were looking at my body,' she teased, adding to his confusion. 'Did the women in biblical time wear corsets? Or even in medieval times? I think not.' She was laughing as she said this, and he smiled wryly.

McKinley reflected that those young men at the Hall who were planning on returning their art to the days before Raphael had something in common with the free spirits of the Prospero Company. He thought of Seton with confusion. The liberation of his baser instincts did not seem to have made him happy. He had noticed that yesterday's work was shocking. His painting was becoming visceral and vivid. The colours almost pure and recklessly applied. He would have suspected the influence of J M W Turner except that he knew Seton did not value Turner's contribution to art and looked upon him as a man ruled by passion not intellect. His friend was showing signs that he was changing, and it was disturbing.

He felt his mental irritation in his brushstrokes, so he stopped painting and said to Teresa, 'Let's take a break and walk to the farmhouse for refreshment. They will likely sell us ale or milk if you prefer it.'

She agreed and they strolled side by side, not quite touching, to a ramshackle building with outlying barns and barking dogs tied up in the yard. Chickens, ducks and geese were plentiful, and milk churns indicated the location of the dairy and they found a woman making butter inside. She greeted McKinley in a friendly manner, and he remembered her from the previous day, but when she saw Teresa she crossed herself and told her to leave. She covered the butter churn with a worried look.

'Is there something wrong?' he asked. He saw that Teresa had skipped away back to the path that led them into the yard and was now walking away, her head covered with a shawl.

'She'll not come here again,' said the woman, a red-faced matron. Strong and healthy-looking but evidently afraid of the willowy auburn-haired girl. 'She's fae. The butter will spoil if she so much as looks at it.'

'I can assure you she is no faerie.' But as he said it, he did wonder at its truthfulness. There was something not human about her, and he was painting her in his work as a faerie's child.

'She has the green eyes and the red hair. She has been marked as the devil's own. I will sell you whatever you want but I pray that you do not bring her here again.'

McKinley bought beer, cheese and bread and returned the previous day's bottles and they parted. Teresa was nowhere to be seen and only when he was out of sight of the farmhouse did she appear from the hedgerow, making him start. They walked back to the pond and ate in silence. He resumed the painting but could not settle.

'That woman thought you were fae and that your presence might stop the butter from churning.'

She nodded and thought for few minutes before evidently deciding to tell him her own story.

'It's not the first time. It started at home in Wales when a cow got sick and the bitter old maid that owned it blamed me. Even my family suspected me when objects were lost and then found in strange places. Eventually the whole village turned on me after a baby died and its mother blamed me. She said I had looked at it sideways and it sickened from that time on. I was thirteen and had just started my monthly bleed. Eventually there was talk of witchcraft and my brother told me to pack a bundle, he would take me to a town where I would be a servant and people weren't so superstitious. I could 'blend in' by covering my hair and becoming anonymous. We rode for hours into the mountains. There are no towns there. He left me on the side of a mountain to die of exposure.'

McKinley was shocked.

'That's terrible,' he said, 'how did you … survive?'

'The hills and mountains are the places where the fae now live, having been driven from their homes by men. So they took me into their faerie glen for a year and a day. They fed me and showed me their magic and the time passed as though it was a few weeks.'

McKinley looked at her in amazement and she held his gaze until she could not continue and burst out laughing. 'Alright. A shepherd found me and took me to his hut.'

'That was lucky, and you not more than a child. Did he and his wife raise you as their own?'

She became quite matter of fact as she continued her story, showing little expression on her face or in her voice as she said, 'I doubt he told his wife. He kept me prisoner in that hut for a year and a day. So you see the year and a day bit was true.'

McKinley frowned in incomprehension. 'Why would he do that?'

'So that he could rape me repeatedly when he visited his sheep. They got a lot of attention that year. But he brought food and drink and kept me alive.'

McKinley felt as though the world had fallen away from him. He wanted to hold her and comfort her but was appalled that it might be seen as abusive. Especially as he wanted to do the same thing to her that the shepherd had done and his mind kept picturing it and it made him sick, and yet it made him excited. He did not know what to say or do, he felt guilty by association. Could any words be sufficient?

'That's terrible, terrible. I am so sorry.'

'Do you know what the worst of it was?' she said.

'I cannot imagine anything worse,' he said.

'After a few days alone, when I was lying there shackled to a stone by my leg, I would pray that he would come and use me. Because then I would eat.'

He waited for her to continue; there were tears in his eyes, but none in hers.

'He used to unshackle me when he was there so I could clean the place. One day the shepherd died while he was at the hut, and I was able to take his pony and ride away.'

McKinley wondered how the man had died but he somehow knew it had been a violent and probably painful end.

'Eventually I reached a town called Oswestry where I sold the horse and in the late afternoon Mr Ede saw me fighting off the attentions of drunk men. They drink all day when there's a fair. Mr Ede saved me.'

There was a lot more that McKinley wanted to ask but he considered himself lucky she had trusted him with that awful story. She continued:

'I have faith in some men now because of the way he treated me. Otherwise, I would have a stone for a heart on which I would hone the sharpest of knives the better to destroy those who prey on women.'

'I would never … '

'I know. I have spoken with Mariel and I can see your heart Robert McKinley. It is honest and kind.'

He had never been a rakish ladies' man and he feared that women thought of him more as a brother than a lover, but he had to ask the question. He would accept the answer if she gave it.

'Could you love me?' he said simply.

There was a long silence in which his heart at first so hopeful began to sink and she did not look at him but studied the water at her feet. When he could bear it no longer, he said:

'I'm sorry I should not have asked. Forget I did.' He began to pack up his paints and wipe his brushes and palette. There would be no more painting today.

When they were ready to walk back, she said, 'I could love you, but it would not be right for us to fall in love. We are not the same, you and I. We are from different worlds and there would be consequences. It would be unnatural.'

He was shocked at that word. 'How could it be unnatural? I know that Seton and Lily are behaving in a very carnal way but ….' He turned as she stepped back from him, fear in her eyes. 'I would marry you.'

His last statement took some of the fear from her face, but she approached him and took his arm. She said quietly 'Lily is playing a dangerous game. She and I are different, and she will harm your friend and care nothing for it. She has needs that she allows free rein, men are meat and drink to her, he will be a husk when she has used him to sate her desires. You must warn him Robert, if you love him, send him away from Pitdown Hall. No good can come of this affair.'

He believed her to be earnest but how could he tell the man who had rented the house that he should leave it and how could the girl damage him? Most young men would consider him to be fortunate to have a lusty and beautiful young woman to satisfy him.

'Does she have the French pox?' he said, and she immediately withdrew from him and walked off back up the track towards the house. 'I'm sorry but I cannot understand the danger.' He gave up as she did not turn and would not speak to him again.

When they had reached the house, she relented and said, 'Do you want me tomorrow? I have chores that must be undertaken.'

'No,' he said, contrite. 'I could perhaps paint one of the men as model for the part of the knight. Will you ask if anyone is free?'

She nodded and left him and he wanted to shout: I'm sorry I love you I love you; and he said nothing except 'Thank you.'

*   *   *

At dinner that evening the general atmosphere was subdued and Seton was uncommunicative and had been so since swearing at McKinley over breakfast the previous day. He ate steadily and prodigiously and had abandoned his usually fastidious manners. There was some discussion about progress on paintings and ideas for exhibitions the following year. All the artists were positive about their prospects except Seton who barely spoke at all.

'I say Seton, your work is taking a completely different direction from the religious tone you originally planned for it,' said Rossetti. 'I thought you were going to paint that dark little beauty as the Magdalene but she is looking more and more like Lamia the snake woman from Keats's poem. I didn't know you had it in you.'

There was a hush of anticipation and while most eyes were on Seton, McKinley stared fixedly at his plate. When he did look up he saw that Seton was relaxed and his eyes hooded as he drank deeply of the wine and poured himself more. Eventually he spoke, in a voice thick with satisfaction.

'You're all fools, thinking that you can dabble with your fingers at the edges of a world of darkness and magic. You see the pulse of a vein or the flush of blood beneath the fair skin of a girl and you daub away. What you create is immutable, but you fail to capture the rush of life in those veins, the pricking of sweat through the skin, the panting search, the throbbing and the rubbing and the inexorable ending.' His face was flushed, and the other young men were torn between amazement and suppressed laughter.

'We all know about sex, Seton old man, but we paint something esoteric, more aesthetic. A tuppenny whore can be had on any street corner in London.' Rossetti looked at his fellows for support but they were embarrassed.

'A whore looks upon a man as a source of money,' said Seton. 'She does not participate as an equal with her entire body and her soul. Love is all consuming. It lifts me beyond earthly life into a heaven that I did not know was possible.'

McKinley was tempted to repeat Teresa's words about Lily but the passion in Seton's eyes deterred him and he was mindful of the conclusion of Keats's poem about Lamia. When the lover's elderly teacher looked at Lamia and saw her for what she was, a serpent in human form, she shrivelled and died. The young man was found lifeless the next day. This love was like a drug, perhaps a drug like the laudanum Macey had become addicted to and that had almost killed him when he gave it up. He knew that the Prospero Company would only be with them for July, then in August they would move on to the next fair.

'What will you do when the company moves on?' he asked.

Seton looked as though he had been slapped, but eventually he answered 'I will ask her to marry me of course. I will …' He stopped.

'Make an honest woman of her?' Rossetti continued. He looked as though he might snigger but then reflected. 'Why not, you are a good fellow and perhaps she has never had such an opportunity before. I wish you well.' He raised a glass to the blushing Seton, and they drank his health and that of his putative bride. Only

McKinley felt concern at the matter, but he joined in, and the five young men managed to pass a reasonably pleasant evening.

The weather was becoming humid and sultry so that even when McKinley opened his bedroom window there was little breeze to relieve the stifling heat; he found sleep elusive and was troubled by the things Teresa had told him during their day together. During the night, when he was half asleep, he again heard the strange music and he looked out of the window to see a bright moonlight obscuring the stars. Despite some unnamed fear he was restless enough to try and track down the source of the sound. He pulled on trousers and shoes and went down the flight of stairs to the first floor of the house. One door was ajar, he looked inside. Seton's room lay empty, but he could hear the music more clearly now. Perhaps he too had gone in search of its source.

He left the bedroom and the music faded. He re-entered and it became clear again. McKinley raised his candle and looked around the room. It smelled of sex. She had been here, he thought, and he was tempted to leave; but there was no one in the room and he was drawn to the sounds. He avoided thinking what he would say if Seton appeared. He followed the sound to the fireplace and noticed a narrow doorway to one side that was half open and appeared to be disguised by the oak panelling. A priest hole. Of course, Seton would have given himself that room when allocating bedrooms. It was a connection to the Roman Catholic history of the place and therefore had been dear to his heart.

There was a staircase, and a cool and slightly damp draught reached his face; it was welcome relief in the stifling night. He could retreat and spend all night wondering what was down that staircase, or he could descend and discover. It was sweet music and a friend that he was likely to find in that cool passage, not a crypt and some unholy relic, so he quietly entered and softly descended into the darkness.

He reckoned that he must have passed the ground floor down the uneven brick stairway, roughly spiralling anti clockwise. The air grew cooler and his candle guttered. He stopped and was aware of movement ahead. It was very quiet, perhaps a bat or a large moth. A pair of bright eyes raised up in front of him. Lily's face, her long dark hair loose about her shoulders. She smiled secretively and blew out his candle. In the darkness he hardly dared to breath. He could sense her presence, the warmth of her skin in the cool air as she took the candle from him and placed it on the steps. Then she took both of his hands and, turning, placed them on her shoulders where he became aware that she was naked.

She led him down the remaining steps until they arrived at a beaten earth floor, quiet underfoot and coolly dank. His eyes became accustomed to the darkness so he could see in the faint moonlight that ahead of them stood a man, also naked, and McKinley realised it was Seton. His back was to them, and she led him forward until they stood looking at what the man could see.

When he thought about it afterwards Robert McKinley could not recall in detail what he saw. It was dark and the only light was moonlight that came from a barred window high up on one side. From this borrowed light he thought he could see that the boxes containing the puppets had been opened violently. Splintered wood and charred remnants were strewn about the floor. He could not see the marionettes but could hear a faint humming and felt that something alive was now in the boxes. The tiny silvery voices and deeper notes swept around the room longingly but as they looked, the moon passed on and the light faded, and as it did so the music ebbed. When it had become completely silent and very dark McKinley felt a shiver from one of the two naked people he stood with. They turned and moved away and he was obliged to follow the sound of their footsteps mounting the stairs. He kicked his candle and picked it up and at last emerged into Seton's room.

The couple were on the bed wrapped in a sheet. He opened his mouth to ask what they had just seen but she said, 'Close the door.'

He did so and turned.

She continued, 'What you have seen is forbidden. You must never speak of it or great misfortune will fall upon us all.'

'The marionettes?'

'Never speak of it. There are curses you cannot conceive that will be unleashed upon the world if you betray it. Now please go. Unless you want to join us.' She opened the sheet so that her beauty was exposed to his eyes. Seton gazed upon her proudly. McKinley fled.

*   *   *

He was greatly disturbed, whether by what he had almost seen or by his cowardice when invited to join in their debauchery. Was it a dream? Between the time he had fallen asleep in the early dawn and his awakening to the sounds of the house rousing itself he had slept so deeply that it could have been a fantasy and seeing Seton at breakfast tucking into slices of meat and cheese seemed to compound that. He sat next to him with tea and bread and Seton looked up and smiled happily.

'I'm ravenous. Everything tastes so good today.'

McKinley whispered, 'What did we see last night? Shall we tell the others?'

'Don't be ridiculous man. They can't know about this unless they have been chosen by the angels themselves.'

'Angels?'

'Yes,' said Seton. 'They were obviously angels, didn't you hear the singing? It all makes sense when you understand that God intends the Prospero Company to look after them until such time as he chooses to reveal himself to us again.' His face lit up with the bliss of a fanatic as he thought about it. 'The second coming is imminent. No one is allowed to know because it will be a revolution; a new order will be created and the old ones thrown down. It is as Blake said: that in some places voices of Celestial inhabitants are more distinctly heard and their forms more distinctly seen.' This is one such place, d'you see McKinley? We are blessed. Here is paradise on earth and free love as experienced by man and woman in the Garden of Eden.'

McKinley was speechless, but he had heard the singing and perhaps he was right. Seton continued:

'Blake will be my inspiration. I have this day written to London for books containing his poems and engravings. I am on fire with passion for this. It is a great day for us; but you must not tell the others. If they have not been summoned by the songs then they must remain in ignorance until their time is come. Do you promise me?'

He was so earnest that McKinley agreed. It could do no good to involve the other men in this mystery and he had been chastened by his experience two days before when he had mentioned the noises heard in the woods. They had become carried away and things had quickly got out of hand. When the books on Blake's work had arrived they could all study them, but he would leave it to Seton to proselytize if he wanted to. Still, in the back of his mind he had Teresa's words of warning; he would have liked to speak with her but today she was not available. He left the dining hall with his breakfast as the others came down and he set about preparing for the day's work.

*   *   *

The man who came to him was one of the younger actors and he took an interest in the role he was being asked to model. He gave his name as Avery and asked to read the poem a few times so that he might understand the character. They sat in the garden and discussed it, as one might analyse a text before rehearsing a play.

Avery said: 'If I am meant to be a knight then I should be wearing armour and a surtout. We have some wooden breast-shields painted silver and helmets that we wear for Shakespeare. If

I speak nicely to Mariel she might lend me some tights, though it is really too hot to be wearing them.'

McKinley's spirits were lifted at the prospect of seeing Mariel again and he followed Avery to the camp where they found the girl fitting Teresa with a man's outfit.

'I am to be Rosalind again,' she said by way of explanation.

Mariel was happy to oblige with the tights and Avery found the wooden armour and a sword and they set off to the house. He looked back and saw Teresa and Mariel gazing after them. He waved and they both waved back, and for a confusing moment he was not sure who he was waving to.

He gathered his equipment and they walked to the pond, discussing the meaning of the poem, Avery happily carrying as much as McKinley. It was refreshing to talk to a normal man, the other artists were young, and Seton was now definitely odd. He showed the other man his painting so far, the position of the faerie woman and the pose he hoped that Avery would assume.

'In the poem,' McKinley said, 'the viewer finds the knight after his encounter with La Belle Dame. He is sickening and not far from death. She has beguiled him, he has made love to her and gone with her to a faerie realm. There he has seen the ghosts of kings, princes and warriors that have gone before him. If I am to paint the lady and the knight then he must be hale and hearty, not yet sunk into despair, but I must show by sign that he will become entrapped and brought low or the picture will not have the air of tragic romance that makes the poem so haunting.'

They stood together and looked at the canvas.

'I thought you might kneel at her feet. She is looking out at the viewer you see which gives the feeling of her power even though she is slight and barefoot, and he is powerful and armoured.'

Avery knelt in the position he indicated, and McKinley gathered flowers for him to appear to weave into garlands; they agreed it was suitably incongruous an occupation for a warrior. He was still too imposing, so he asked him to stand behind her leaning forward as if to tempt her with the garland and quickly sketched him. When

Avery saw it he took off the helm and the sword and placed them on the ground before her feet. 'A symbol of his surrender,' he said, and McKinley agreed that he would be emasculated by her as she took revenge for the way warriors had treated conquered women over centuries.

They worked all day, walking to the farm for provisions for lunch, the farmer's wife looked suspiciously at Avery but could find nothing supernatural about him. When the shadows were lengthening and they returned to the house, McKinley was delighted with the progress made and hoped that he could work on the painting with both models the following day. Avery promised to try to arrange it and they shook hands.

After cleaning his brushes and palette McKinley walked wearily through the hall and was surprised to find the door to the cellar open. He was hesitating, reluctant to go alone into the dark space with the broken boxes and whatever they held. All day he had succeeded in putting the night's experience and his encounter with Seton this morning out of his mind, but now it rose as a nagging worry. Whilst he dithered, he heard Mr Ede's voice saying:

'They shouldn't be any trouble now Mr Seton. You were quite right to tell me; no one else needs to know.' He then appeared with Seton behind him. They were both smiling, and he nodded to McKinley then left.

Seton took McKinley to one side. 'I haven't told him that you know so you mustn't say anything. The celestial beings are safely tucked away and the moonlight will not disturb them tonight because we have covered the window. So no singing, you see? And no danger of alerting anyone else ahead of time.'

'Are you sure? Have you actually seen them? I don't see how they can be angels,' McKinley said but Seton would not hear it, he was still ecstatic that the 'angels' had revealed themselves to him. His commitment to his sexual affair with Lily was firmly established in his mind as the epitome of Eden that should again fill the world after the second coming. Weary from his day's work

McKinley retired to his room to wash and lie on his bed until the dinner gong sounded.

As he lay staring at the dirty yellow ceiling, he thought of those puppets he had seen on the stage in Portsmouth. Were they the same creatures that now lay in the boxes in the cellar? The ugly marionettes dressed as Peter Quince, Bottom et al? And worse, the weird insect like things that played the fairies Oberon, Titania and Puck? He had enjoyed the performance because he imagined they were controlled by the skilled puppeteers. It was part of the fun. If they were angels the entire show became a mockery and he felt cheated. They must be something else. Seton's epiphany must be the result of his strong attraction to religious faith combined with his discovery of physical pleasure in the arms of Lily. Perhaps at her suggestion he had conveniently connected the creatures in the cellar with the teachings and writings of William Blake the mystic artist and poet who believed in free love and had once had a vision of angels in a tree in the village of Peckham.

He studied his hands. They smelled of turpentine and his fingernails were never quite clean. His fingers tapered and his palms were square, and he wondered why some people could create art and others not. Millais was a child prodigy; he had been admitted to the Royal Academy schools at age eleven and the detail in his paintings was marvellous. Rossetti did not possess the same skill but there was a spiritual quality to his work that lifted it in the viewer's sensibility to an equally effective level. Holman Hunt's work had a similar spiritual quality although it seemed more laboured somehow. Seton had been the most laborious of all of them but now he had broken into a feverish style of paint application, the face of his subject was delicate but the garments she wore were tumultuous, the background a maelstrom, and the oil paint applied so thickly it seemed it would never dry.

McKinley thought about the upbringings of each man. Seton was born the son of a parson in the South West and had been intended for the church until the spiritual beauty of early renaissance religious art had swept him off to the Royal Academy.

Millais was born in Southampton but raised in Jersey until his mother's ambition placed him at the RA. Hunt was from a family successful in trade and reflected the odd position of the artist in society, neither upstairs nor downstairs. McKinley thought the faces he painted all looked alike but there was no denying the ambition of his storytelling.

Dante Gabriel Rossetti was the most mysterious and romantic of the four. His father was Italian and his mother was the niece of John Polidori who had written the story of the vampire that McKinley had illustrated. He smiled as he remembered Mariel's enthusiasm for the penny dreadful and he realised that he had been neglecting her and he regretted it. Although still a child she had found a place in his heart and he had not realised how much he missed her when she had disappeared. He idly wondered if he and Teresa could adopt her when they married and he imagined their wedding and the sun shining on smiling happy faces in a garden. He was tempted to continue the daydream but forced himself back to the present dilemma.

There was something nagging at his mind and it was linked to the stories that Polidori, Byron, Shelley and their wives and mistresses had written in the Villa Diodati in 1816 during that dark summer when crops failed and people starved. They had created some of the foundation stories of Gothic horror. He reflected that this was what he and his companions were now doing in paint, their work inspired by the unusual models they had acquired through his connection with Mariel.

Then he remembered: it was the story that Mary Shelley had written about a young doctor who gave life to a dead creature, made from parts obtained from dead bodies. The concept of animating a dead thing; was that what had been done to the puppets? He had read that book and thought it better than others of its genre. He was particularly touched by the predicament of the creature, thrust fully formed physically into a world that could not accept it. It was born as an adult but was as innocent as a baby, unloved and unlovable because of its appearance. He tried to recall the story but found himself dozing and pleasantly relaxed.

He awoke to the sound of the dinner gong and was hungry. He tried to rise but his arms did not move and he could feel that they were flimsy as though made of cloth with nothing alive inside them. What had happened to his muscles and bones? Had he become a marionette? With a jolt of fear he realised that he could not move his hands on his own. He was very hungry. He tried to call for help but only a dry whisper came out and he was afraid then that no one would understand. If they found him like this they might mistake him for … a dead thing, or a puppet?

He woke fully and realised that his arms were behind his head and had become numb and lifeless and his open mouth dry and his tongue papery. With an effort his flopped onto his front and worked the blood back into his arms, he drank tepid water from the jug that was placed on the washstand. He looked at his haunted eyes in the mirror and realised that he had felt like a puppet. Or a creature. He was no longer hungry but sick. Had the gong sounded? He should probably eat. He went down the stairs to see if the other fellows had gathered, and they were just entering the dining room.

It was a relatively subdued affair, they were all at a difficult stage of painting, needing it to dry or unhappy with the composition. They were tired and McKinley was glad to leave them drinking together in the sitting room while he walked out to the camp of the acting troupe to arrange matters for the following day. They had just finished a meal of stewed rabbit he guessed from the rich scents lingering by the fire. Mariel was scouring a pot and he walked over to her.

'Are you looking for Teresa?' she asked. 'She's in the tent rehearsing 'As You Like It' with Mr Ede and some of the company.'

'I was going to try and arrange tomorrow's sitters with her and the fellow Avery who is the model for my knight at arms. But it is a pleasure to see you Mariel. Tell me how you are getting on? Do they always have you serving them and cleaning up for them?'

She bridled slightly at this.

'They are working you know. They spend many hours learning lines and if I was not cleaning up after them, I'd be cleaning for someone else. At least they treat me as an equal.'

'I'm sorry,' he said chastened. 'When you see them can you just say I would be honoured to have either or both of them tomorrow at the usual time. Please.' He sat on the ground beside her and rubbed his face and eyes. They were quite alone and he decided to ask the question that had been gnawing at him since the night before.

'Mariel, what do you know about the puppets that are stored in the cellar of the house?'

In the growing gloom her face was unreadable and she took a few seconds to think about the question as she finished the pot. Eventually she said, 'Why do you ask about them?'

'I have heard them singing and I know that they have broken free of their boxes. How can that be if they are made of wood and cloth and controlled by strings?' He said this in a whisper but urgently.

'They belong to Mr Ede. He has their management and we all do as we are told, and we leave them alone. You would do well to do the same.'

'Seton thinks they are angels.'

He saw her smile at this, and she said, 'I very much doubt that.'

'As do I,' he said, 'but they have some sort of motor. Are they automata? Does someone wind them up?'

'That had not occurred to me,' she said.

'But do you know how they move? They seemed to be puppets when I saw them in the Portsmouth theatre, but they must be extraordinary ones.'

She smiled at him. 'Yes they are extraordinary puppets, and it is Mr Ede who controls them.'

He pressed her. 'How does he control them?'

'With something he calls alchemy. He is a very clever man you know. He has rescued us all and he has made some very special puppets.'

She seemed unwilling or unable to say more so he rose to go but said to her 'Promise me that you will be careful Mariel.'

And she laughed and said, 'These past few weeks have been happier than most that I have known since my father died, Mr McKinley. I miss my mother, but I have found a whole family of siblings in the troupe and Mr Ede is like a father to me. I am, as always, grateful for your concern about my wellbeing.' She stood and gave him a hug and a broad smile. He wanted to keep her with him, but he felt awkward and so merely patted her shoulder. He was overwhelmed by the strangeness and weariness of the day and bade her goodnight.

His mind was empty as he trudged up to his attic bedroom and looked out onto the bright yellow moon low in the sky and listened for the strange unearthly music. All was silence except for the bark of a dog fox and the noisy calling of owls in the trees. He fell asleep quickly and woke once in the night to the sounds of Seton and his woman noisily making love in the room below him. He closed the window and put the pillow over his head cursing the concept of 'free love' and trying to ignore the hushed rhythmic intrusion and its effect on his imagination.

Eventually he slept but as he did so his mind worked over the last day's incidents and his conversation with Mariel. She had used the word 'alchemy'. He woke to a silent room, where he lay quietly and contemplated the eery thought that Ede had done something unnatural to the puppets. What if he had imbued those wood and cloth creatures with life as Frankenstein had given life to the monster he had built from dead human body parts? It seemed a more rational explanation than keeping angels locked in boxes in a cellar, and angels would surely be happier in a chapel. Ede had rejected the chapel out of hand when it was suggested.

He thought about the things he had seen on the stage. Were they mechanical or were they inhabited by some sort of life force? They had jointed arms and legs and they appeared to be held up by strings, but that was probably illusion. They had no real facial expressions because they wore masks, but their bodies expressed their emotions as clearly as their faces would. How powerful was a tilt of the head, a slow turn to one side or an elegant hand gesture? This would take enormous skill by the puppeteer and as he thought about it he could see the disconnection between the operator and the puppet. They seemed to be alive - because they were alive.

Why did they have to be locked up? They were small and biddable so they could not be dangerous like Frankenstein's creature, but you would not want them running around the place frightening people and livestock. They were locked away in a secure cellar, and they had been singing so they must be happy. He felt relieved that he had found the reasons for the strange events, but he was worried about Seton and it was clear that Ede had not disabused him of the notion that he was hosting angels in the cellar.

After giving the matter serious consideration he decided not to inform Seton of his conclusion. The man was in a state of bliss and his Blakean explanation satisfied both his spiritual and carnal needs. The Prospero Company would only be here for a few more weeks so Seton would have to move on from his affair then. He thought, with a pang, of Teresa and tried not to draw a comparison between their situations.

*   *   *

The morning was even hotter than the previous days, with no wind and a stifling humidity. The gardener said:

'There'll be a storm today, I've no doubt. The farmer was top dressing his fields yesterday so he's expecting a downpour.'

McKinley thought that would account for the rich odour that had wafted from the west yesterday. It was not unpleasant, certainly when compared with Portsmouth's cesspits. He asked the gardener when this was likely as he was painting outside, and the old man said later in the afternoon, though if clouds built up they had better come back inside before the heavens opened.

He thought that he would welcome rain to cool and clear the air but he would not have long if both models turned up; and so they did. Avery carrying his armour and Teresa in her green elfin dress with her auburn hair loose and a garland of flowers on her brow ready. They made such a beautiful couple that McKinley felt a twinge of jealousy, and they seemed happy in each other's company which made it worse.

They walked to the pool discussing the weather and the abundance of midges and other flying insects. The elder tree should keep them at bay said Teresa as they set up, and the poolside was a pleasant spot. She sat in her usual place staring at him from her garlands and with her bare feet whilst Avery bent over her, his helm and weapon at her feet. She so fragile and otherworldly and he so strong and full of flesh but soon to be reduced to dying man 'Alone and palely loitering' in a dying landscape.

He worked quickly with light touches of paint, each one conveying something he had not seen when he painted them separately. It had been easy to paint Avery with large strokes, robust and sculptural, using all the techniques he had learned at the Royal Academy schools. The garlands of flowers had become bonds and she appeared to be his captive. As a soldier he would have felt entitled to rape the women of defeated enemies. McKinley was uncomfortable when he recalled the story Teresa had told him of her previous life, and if it was true he suspected she had killed her rapist. There was an obvious parallel here because the faerie woman would turn the tables on the armed man and ultimately destroy him. The slight smile on her face indicated that after her ordeal she would take her revenge.

His mind had wandered on to the possibility of La Belle Dame having vampiric qualities, did she feed on his blood? The vampires he had drawn for the penny dreadfuls were all men, when Avery said:

'I'm sorry Mr McKinley but I must move. My joints have seized.'

He realised they had held that pose for several hours, a superhuman feat given the position the poor young man was in. Teresa was seated and could have continued for longer.

'No no, I am sorry Avery. I lost myself in the moment, or rather the hours and the sun has moved quite a long way across the sky.' He looked up and noticed on the Western horizon huge white clouds with dark undersides. 'I think we can finish now. It would be better not to be caught in the storm.'

They packed everything away and began the walk back to the house.

'What goes through your mind as you sit for so long?' he asked.

Teresa said, 'I am running through my lines and as much as I can remember of other actors' lines too.'

'Same for me,' said Avery, 'and trying to sing the songs in my head. The notes sound so pure, it is a shame that I can't reproduce them with my voice.' They both laughed and Teresa began singing 'It was a lover and his lass,' and they sang together as they walked the overgrown path, uninterrupted by birds or other animals. McKinley had noticed the silence; he thought they have all gone for a nap or were anticipating the coming storm.

They walked on ahead of him and he saw their lithe bodies in step, arm in arm and they seemed to shimmer in the heavy air. They were bright like ethereal beings floating between heaven and earth and singing like the creatures in the cellar. The equipment weighed him down and it was hard to breathe.

He was in shade now, the earth pressed into his cheek, and Avery was calling him and Teresa fanning him with her hat. He felt slightly sick and between them they helped him and his painting back to the Hall where he sat in the cool sitting room as his sweat dried. They fetched him tea and biscuits. Millais brought wine and the young men put him to bed. He slept heavily but woke to vomit. Then slept some more.

He did not hear the thunderstorm as it raged over the Hall, rain seeming to steam off the chimneys and the tall roof. The campers had stowed their belongings in the caravans and taken shelter in the tent. The horses put back their ears as the lightning flashed and the thunder made them plunge like boats in a storm, but they could go nowhere and soon grew used to the noise and welcomed the rain and began cropping the grass again.

He did not hear the rain on the orangery roof cleaning the stains of birds and algae and pouring out of the broken gutters so that a river ran around the building. He did not hear the creatures in the cellar as water came through the barred window and surged across the earth floor.

Seton heard them, and unlocked the door to the wine cellar. He returned from his inspection to ask Millais and Hunt to help him carry the boxes into the chapel where it was dry. His thinking was clear: the 'angels' would be happy in the chapel. He had wrapped the boxes in canvas, so the contents were invisible to the men who carried them up the stairs.

When they had been placed in front of the altar, he sent the two young men away, they needed to ensure there were no leaks in the studio areas. Seton knelt in front of the boxes and intoned as many prayers in Latin as he could think of. He assumed that they would understand the language of the ancients and the Roman church. He stayed with them for several hours, until the gong for dinner sounded and the storm was just a distant rumble. He locked the chapel and left.

Later in the night the moon and stars were occasionally obscured by a passing cloud, and McKinley was woken by a cool breeze on his face. It felt pleasant and he was refreshed and encouraged to leave his bed and look out of the window. He heard a chuckling and assumed it was an animal on the ground, but he could see nothing and the sound was closer. Perhaps it was a night bird, like an owl on the roof above him. He could see by leaning out and craning his neck upwards. He could make out the clouds now and he knew that at some point the moon would appear if only briefly. The chittering continued and he opened the casement wide, sitting on the windowsill and leaning out as far as he dared.

There were two gabled dormer windows to his attic room, and he heard the sound from the other and knew whatever it was must be perched there. He looked with anticipation as the cloud cleared. He saw a gargoyle; but there were no gargoyles on Pitdown Hall. He stared at it and it sighed with pleasure at the moonlight. Alive. It was alive and moon-bathing. He must have made a noise for it turned its head and looked at him. A look that was unsurprised and full of knowledge.

McKinley said 'Hello,' but the creature looked back at the moon and ignored him. Unwilling to intrude on its moment of freedom, and somewhat uncomfortable hanging out of a second storey window, he eased his way back inside and closed it firmly. Whatever happened he did not want it joining him. He also closed the curtains and put a chair against the door.

This meant that the creatures, whatever they were, had got out of the wine cellar and that is not what Ede intended. Perhaps Seton had released them. If Ede was their creator then presumably they would owe him some kind of loyalty for giving them life, and he hoped that Ede had behaved more kindly to them than Victor Frankenstein did towards his monster. The thing on the roof had seemed relaxed but it must be incredibly strong and agile to climb all that way. He heard no more that night from the creature, but he took paper and ink and attempted to sketch it from memory before lying on the bed and trying to sleep.

He was woken in the morning by raised voices and the slamming of doors as the household was roused. Seton and Ede were arguing at the top of the stairs to the cellar. By the time McKinley had made it down to the ground floor they had moved into the chapel and two of the Prospero Company's men were standing in the doorway preventing Hunt and Millais from entering.

'What's going on?' said Hunt. 'We're doing you a favour allowing you to keep those things here.'

'We had to save them from the flood yesterday by moving them up from the cellar to the chapel,' added Millais. Rossetti came partway down the stairs in his nightshirt.

'What is this confounded noise?'

Seton came out of the chapel upset and white-faced. 'I thought it best to move the puppets from the cellar because it was in danger of flooding, and we put them in the chapel. The door was secure, I am certain of that.'

Ede appeared and spoke quietly to the men. They went inside and closed the chapel door. He addressed the gathering of tousle-headed, fractious young men.

'One of the marionettes is missing. It is the oldest and the most valuable. It is irreplaceable. We shall move them all to the caravan.'

'You surely cannot think that one of us has stolen it?' said Millais. Ede shrugged but looked at each in turn with a piercing eye. Only McKinley quailed under that glance as he remembered the thing on his roof. The others looked at him.

'I didn't take it. I've been ill. You are welcome to search my room if you don't believe me,' he said in the embarrassing silence.

'I believe you,' said Ede and McKinley knew he was perfectly aware that the creature had escaped on its own. 'We will make enquiries in the local area. If someone came and took it they would not find it easy to sell. With your permission I will speak to the servants and then we will widen our enquiries to the farms and towns nearby. I fear we may have to leave sooner than I had hoped. This marionette is vital to our company.'

He swept out and his men followed with the boxes wrapped in the canvas that Seton had provided. Hunt, Millais and Rossetti were outraged.

'He thinks one of us took it,' said Rossetti. 'Seton old man, I'm thinking of going back up to town. If the models aren't here, there's not much point staying. Sorry.' He looked at Hunt and Millais and they said nothing, but doubts had been sown. The three of them went back to their rooms to prepare for whatever work they would achieve today.

McKinley turned to comfort Seton, but he had to follow him into the chapel where he closed the door and said with tears in his eyes:

'I tried to save them. How could an angel be missing?'

McKinley decided to tell him 'There was one on my roof last night, but honestly Seton it didn't look like an angel.'

'Have you seen an angel before?'

'No ...' he had only seen representations of angels and if these beings had been trapped on earth a long time then they may have lost some of their lustre. He decided to tell Seton what he had deduced from his discussion with Mariel and from what he had seen on the roof.

'I think they are creatures made by Ede and imbued with life using the magic of alchemy.' Seton's jaw stiffened. His beliefs and theories were being attacked by his oldest friend. He would have none of it.

'No, no, they must be angels, you heard them singing. Would something created from wood or cloth be able to make such a beautiful sound?'

'I don't know much about alchemy but it does use natural principles. The idea is that 'as above so below'. Surely that can mean that the magic of the heavens is reflected in the magic of ordinary things so why not wood and wool? Or paint and canvas?' McKinley could remember little from his study of alchemy except an understandable interest in turning base metal into gold or finding the philosopher's stone that would prolong life. 'You know that the great physicist Sir Isaac Newton wrote more manuscripts on alchemy than the mathematics and physics for which he is now famous.'

His friend sat and covered his eyes, repeating, 'They are angels. They must be.'

'Seton, scientists acknowledge that there is much that we cannot understand, and it may be that there is a heavenly connection with these creatures but it seems to me that they cannot possess free will. They are obliged to perform in fairground shows, they are kept imprisoned in boxes and locked cellars. They are controlled by Ede; and now one of them has escaped,' said McKinley.

'You said it was on your roof,' Seton stood and held his friend's shoulders. 'Did you see its wings? Were they feathered like angels or leathery like demons? Perhaps they were demons.' He let go and walked to the front of the chapel tearing at his hair. 'Oh God I have sinned and now the spawn of hell has come for my damned soul.' He threw himself onto his knees and began to bang his head against his clenched hands resting on the back of the pew.

'Stop it!' said McKinley. 'This will achieve nothing. Whatever they are Ede has the secret and he must be prevailed upon to give it up.' Seton stopped banging but wept bitterly.

'I have sinned,' he said. 'I have surrendered myself to the most basic carnal desires. I have revelled in my lust.'

McKinley could see that he would be useless in any communication with Ede and the company. He put a hand on his shoulder.

'Why don't you spend some time reading your bible and in prayer? I am sure that is the best thing you can do now. The sinner who repents is always welcomed back to Jesus.' The sobbing subsided and he thought seemed a little calmer. 'I will find out what is to be done.' He left Seton kneeling, muttering to himself in the quiet chapel and closed the door on him.

He went through the ground floor of the house and found only Millais at breakfast. He looked glum.

'The others are talking of leaving and if the Prospero Company is going then there doesn't seem much point in sticking around.' McKinley looked at the open face of the curly haired young man.

'You won't leave right away surely? Try and persuade them to stay a few more days. Seton is distraught. You know he has been consorting with one of the actresses?'

'How could we not? To be honest it has been an ordeal the last few days. His behaviour has become very peculiar and quite unlike him. He is usually such a steady fellow, a bit like a father figure to us. Now one minute he is all religious morality and the next he is mired in fornication; noisily too.' Millais shook his head. 'I'll speak to the others and perhaps we could wait until next week. We can hire a wagon and take everything at once.'

McKinley thanked him and sat and had breakfast with him. Then he walked over to the camp site to talk to Ede.

The tent had already been dismantled.

'God, that was quick,' he said to Avery who was strapping the thing onto a cart.

'We have to strike camp very quickly sometimes,' the young man said. 'I'm sorry but I'll have to ask you for payment. We won't be around to finish your painting. Are you feeling alright now? Looked like heat stroke to me.'

McKinley decided this was an opportunity to find out as much as possible from Avery. They seemed to have formed a good relationship.

'I'm happy to settle up, both you and Teresa,' he said. 'Can you come with me now to my room where I have my funds?'

They walked up to the Hall and then climbed the stairs to McKinley's attic room and he went to the desk. He turned to the young man.

'What are they? The marionettes?'

Avery lowered his eyes. He was trapped and he wanted the money; he also did not want to lie to McKinley who he thought of as a sensible man. McKinley continued:

'There was one perched upon my roof last night. I saw it in the moonlight. It looked at me and I saw intelligence in its eyes, but it was not a beast that I recognised, nor was it a man.'

Avery blanched and crossed himself. He sat heavily in the chair and evidently tried to decide how much to reveal. After a few seconds he said, 'They belong to Mr Ede, he has had them for as long as I have been with the troupe and he controls them with something called alchemy.'

'Yes, but are they demons?' asked McKinley, the other man shook his head. 'Angels?' He shook his head again.

'Then it is as I thought: they are creatures he has made and given life to.'

Avery shrugged. 'I can't say what they are but they have the ability to appear to change shape, so they are very useful as actors in a performance and the audiences love them.'

'Are they free to leave?' asked McKinley.

'Of course not,' said Avery 'People would be afraid of them. They are kept captive for their safety and the safety of the common man. We do not handle them without Mr Ede's say-so and they must be kept locked up.'

'Prisoners, poor things,' said McKinley; he turned to Avery. 'And now one has escaped. What will it do? Where will it go?'

'It will try to go home I suppose.'

'Where is that?'

Avery shook his head 'I don't know. Only Mr Ede knows that.' He took the money owed to him and Teresa, and went to leave. As he approached the door he turned and said, 'Teresa might know more, she's been with the company longer than me.'

'Teresa?' asked McKinley as a thought struck him. 'How long have you been with him?'

'Fifty-odd years,' said Avery with a sly smile. 'Since the reign of King George, the one that was mad.' Then he left.

McKinley felt the world fall away. Close to collapse; he sat on the bed and tried to make sense of it. What he knew about alchemy was mainly the philosopher's stone and the secret of an unnaturally long life? He knew that there was a long history of alchemy and it was kept as an occult activity and hidden from normal people by cryptic and coded writings. Queen Elizabeth I had relied on the advice of her astrologer John Dee and the influence of alchemy had pervaded the writings of reputable scientists like Newton. The other main attraction was the ability to turn base metal into gold and it was linked to magic and to astrology and the names he recalled were Nicolas Flamel, Doctor John Dee and his associate Edward Kelley.

'As above so below' was the fundamental principle and he could see that if an alchemist discovered the secret of long life he would not make it widely known. It occurred to him that Jonathan Ede might be John Dee; the names were very similar and for some reason he had taken to the road and was wandering England with his group of actors and marionettes. Why not sell the secret? As he thought it, he remembered that alchemy was a cabbalistic science and not to be shared. Perhaps there were religious reasons why it must be kept hidden. Certainly the persecution of witchcraft in the seventeenth century would have caused anyone practicing magic to conceal it from the authorities. He needed more information.

He could hear the other painters gathering downstairs and preparing to say goodbye to the actors. He suddenly thought about Teresa. He must speak to her before they left. He ran down the stairs and started towards the company as it prepared to leave. From the side of the house he heard his name being called, and Teresa was there in the shadows.

'I had to say goodbye,' she said, and he could think of no reply but took her in his arms and kissed her mouth. The smell of her skin enchanted him. They clung to each other.

'Stay with me, I will marry you.'

'I cannot,' she said, 'but every October I visit a grave in a churchyard in Chichester. We attend the Sloe fair and Mr Ede lets me do that.'

'You mean Doctor Dee?' he said.

She gasped. 'You cannot tell anyone,' she said. 'Please, we are all in danger if you do. The world cannot know what exists here. We do no harm. Promise me that you will say nothing.'

'Will you come with me and marry me?'

'I cannot. But I will meet you at the church of St Andrew's in the Oxmarket at noon four days before the fair starts. Please I will explain all then. You know that one has escaped and he must be caught or we will all be at risk.'

'I love you,' he said. She kissed him again then pulled away and ran into the sunshine to join the troupe that was harnessing the horses and preparing to leave. He stood for a few minutes in the shadows until he had regained control of his emotions and then he sat on the steps of the Hall. He would not wave them off. There was a noise behind him and Seton ran out of the door.

'No no they cannot be leaving so soon,' he cried and ran to the lead horseman. 'Lily, where are you?' He went from wagon to wagon and tried to get into the covered vehicles. The men pulled him off and he flung himself at them to no avail. Each one of them was stronger than him.

'Where is she? She would not leave me by choice. She loves me. We love each other.' A tall figure appeared from the last wagon and dragged Lily out. Her hands were bound in a cloth and she had obviously been beaten. Her clothes were torn and her hair wild and tangled. McKinley was shocked to see she had a swollen eye and bloody lip.

'Take her,' said Dee, 'if you still want her. But know that she has been used for pleasure by every man in this company and many more besides.' He released the cloth and pushed her from the wagon.

'Lily, what has he done to you? I'll kill him!'

'She has betrayed me and is of no further use. Take her if you must or let her die in a ditch like the animal she is.'

Millais, Rossetti and Hunt moved forwards as if to attack him, but the men of the troupe moved to meet them and Dee held up his hand, a movement that stopped them all. Seton carried Lily away from the departing wagons. They left slowly. McKinley saw Mariel look back at him, but Teresa was focussed on the way ahead. She knew to conceal her feelings and he was sure that he would find her again. Hadn't she told him when and where?

They helped Seton bring the injured woman into the house and took her to his room.

'He must not be allowed to get away with this,' said Millais as they went downstairs.

'Who will prosecute him?' said McKinley. 'These women are his servants. He would be allowed to beat them if they were his family and you saw how the other men roused themselves to protect him. No, he cannot be touched.' He shuddered at the thought of both Teresa and Mariel being in the hands of that brute, but Teresa had survived a long time and Mariel had made her own choice. He decided to question Lily as soon as she was fit to be interviewed. Seton was with her and was bathing her wounds. McKinley went and knocked on the door.

When Seton answered he carried a bloody cloth and came onto the landing, closing the door.

'She's resting. This morning I told her she should not go back to him. That is how he knew I had moved the angels. Sorry, the creatures. She did not know what I had done and when I told her this morning she immediately went to tell him. If one had not escaped, then all would still be well.'

'You know that one escaped?'

'Yes of course, it must have done. I had the key and I knew that none of us would have stolen it. Ede came at me with fury in his eyes and accused me of taking it. I knew nothing about it, how could I? They were in their boxes and I had wrapped them in canvas to protect them from prying eyes. The door was locked, it was as secure as the cellar but not as wet. I had thought to earn his thanks but when I told Lily she seemed shocked and left straight away. Why did he beat her?'

McKinley said, 'She showed them to you when they were singing didn't she? She took you down to them and let you believe they were angels?' Seton nodded. 'So you naturally thought that a chapel would be a good place for them. But if they were comprised of different matter, something that would detest a sacred space, then that would disturb them and as we know, one of them escaped. That was the disaster that brought on his ire.'

'Yes, yes. I see now.' He glanced back towards the darkened room. 'I must find some clothes for her. We will marry as soon as we can. Poor girl, poor girl.' He opened the door.

As McKinley was leaving the woman on the bed cried out and Seton rushed to her with soothing words. He left them and went to see what the other men were planning to do.

They were packing up their equipment.

'I'm sorry McKinley,' said Millais 'but we have decided to return to London as soon as can be arranged. Cook and the maid have just arrived. I'll speak to them and let them know that we shall only be here for two more nights.'

'I'll speak to cook,' said McKinley. He thought that he would need to explain the situation with Lily and Seton and perhaps she could suggest a place where they could buy clothes for her.

*　　　　　　　*　　　　　　　*

That evening dinner was a subdued affair. The painters had packed away their materials and Rossetti and Hunt had gone into Guildford to arrange transport to London. They would leave in two days' time, but they were keen to assist as much as possible in the restoration of Pitdown Hall and in Seton's care of Lily.

'Does he realise that marrying a woman like that will put him completely outside social circles. His family will disown him and no one will engage his services. The Academy will cut him and he will never receive any of the appointments that he could otherwise expect.' Millais thought he was making a foolish decision.

Rossetti expressed admiration for his romantic spirit. 'He is living up to the ideals of romantic love. Of course, it would be better if she died and then he could paint tragic portraits of her forever and write beautiful poetry.'

'Like Dante and his lost Beatrice,' said Hunt. 'I fear that would mean a trip to hell, but in the long run I agree with you.'

McKinley listened to the debate and thought it ridiculous; he said nothing. He was afraid that the woman upstairs might not be all that she seemed. He did not know what effect the loss of Doctor Dee's alchemy might have on her when she was no longer part of his retinue. He feared it. How old was she really and would she age in front of their eyes? He half expected to hear a cry of horror from Seton as his lover grew old and withered whilst in his arms.

He did not see Seton that night as cook had sent food up to his room. She had promised to find some dresses left behind by an earlier occupant of the house before it was rented out. Probably the old woman who had died here and left it to the distant family that now fought over it. He had no doubt that cook would make Seton pay handsomely for the unwanted clothes of a dead woman.

There were no cries in the lengthening dark night, either of horror or of ecstasy. He did not look out of his window for creatures sitting on the roof in the moonlight, but sleep was a long time coming and when it came it was uneventful, seemingly dreamless and he woke relaxed. As memory returned so did the fear and the horror of the last twenty-four hours. He must formulate a plan.

He decided that as soon as he could leave Seton, he would pursue the Prospero Company and he must carry out research on John Dee. If his suspicions were correct the man must be hundreds of years old. As well as his alchemical expertise and the loyalty of his troupe, whose lives had been prolonged beyond nature, he was knowledgeable and experienced. If McKinley intended to take him on he would have to try to find his Achilles heel and the things in the boxes held the key.

Seton did not appear for breakfast that morning and the three younger men went out to sketch the house and surrounding countryside on their last day. Cook said that she had taken breakfast to the couple and that the young woman's condition seemed to be serious.

'Did you see her?' he asked.

'No, I couldn't see round Mr Seton and the room was dark.' She bustled away shaking her head.

McKinley decided that he had to go and speak to his friend. He needed help and Lily was his best source of information if he was ever to find Mariel and Teresa. He knocked on the heavy oak door to Seton's bedroom. He heard whispering and then the door was unlocked by key and opened a few inches.

'How is she? Is there something I can do? Do you need the advice of a doctor?'

Seton opened the door a little wider and slipped out. 'I don't think a doctor would know what to make of it.' He was pale and obviously tired, but he looked shocked.

'She has changed Robert, virtually overnight. I have bathed the wounds she received at the beating and they will heal I am sure, but she is lethargic.' He looked downcast.

'She's had a beating, man, what do you expect? She's been cast out of her home and from her family. She is bound to be traumatised.'

Seton looked around miserably like a cornered animal.

McKinley said, 'You will help her?' He closed the door. 'Do you still love her?'

Seton squirmed slightly and did not reply. It was clear to McKinley that the lust had abated and perhaps the glamour cast by Dee's alchemy had been instrumental in causing the passion, and now that had been removed. He had a fleeting doubt about his own feelings for Teresa, but he had been nurturing them for many weeks and they had not been satisfied in sin.

'Can I speak to her?' he continued, even more curious to see the effect that the loss of alchemy might have on a woman who had lived goodness knew how long within its orbit. 'I promise that I will not judge her Seton, or you, but I need to ask some questions about the company and its origins.'

'She led me to believe that they were angels. She did not tell me that they were demons or base things animated by demonic magic.' He sounded like the mealy-mouthed parson he had almost become before these last few weeks. McKinley wanted to slap him. He put a hand on his shoulder.

'Let me in and I'll see if I can help.'

They went into the dark bedroom. The wash basin was coloured with blood and McKinley told Seton to take it downstairs and bring up fresh water and towels if he could find them.

When he had gone, he cautiously drew aside the curtains and the room was flooded with morning light. Lily lay on her stomach with the sheets wrapped around her. Her hair was spread wide and it was clear that Seton had been brushing it. Despite her condition it had a lustrous sheen and a curl. She was awake and she slowly sat up with her back to him and began to collect it over her left shoulder. The sheet slipped down and he saw that she was naked and the bruises on her body were turning a mottled purple and red against her amber skin.

'Pass me the brush please,' she said and held out her left hand. She did not turn to look at him or try to tempt him with her body and she seemed subdued. McKinley passed it over and she brushed her hair and started to plait it.

'I am sorry for your situation Lily, but I need to speak with you.'

'I think you have come to ask questions about John Dee. You know who he is, don't you?' She continued plaiting her hair.

'I guessed when the word alchemy was mentioned, but I can't believe he could still be alive after all these years,' he said.

'He discovered the secret of long life in 1605. He was fortunate to escape the purges of King James and to avoid punishment for his sorcery.'

'How did he escape?'

'By dying of course. With the help of his daughter and the dismissive contempt that society holds for the old and poor. Nobody was interested at the time.'

'You have been with him a long time,' he said. It was a statement and he knew the truth of it.

'Yes.' He heard the smile in her voice and she continued. 'He has drawn those of us who were useful to him into his power and kept us prisoners, like those poor creatures that are locked in the boxes.'

'What are they?'

'I've never known for sure,' said Lily, and he knew she was lying. 'I wasn't really interested. He saved me, you see.'

'Saved you from what?'

She ignored his question. 'I loved the freedom of the open road and the power that we had over audiences when we performed. It was the only time we really felt alive. It was the only time those creatures were allowed to be seen. He has them tightly in his thrall.'

'But not the one I saw on the roof,' said McKinley. She turned sharply. He saw that she was still beautiful and bewitching despite her blackened eye. Her bruised, swollen mouth looked more voluptuous than ever, like a fruit begging to be eaten. Her full, firm breasts bore as many bruises as the rest of her body but her nipples were pert and dainty like purple flowers. She was not embarrassed. He sat next to her and collected a few loose strands of hair for her plait.

'You saw Gilgoreth?' she said.

'On the roof. Lily, what is it? It looked at me and he had intelligence.'

'He can fly you know,' she said.

'Is that how he escaped? Flew to the roof of the chapel and found some exit hole? How can a marionette fly?'

'They are the old ones. That's all I know about them. I don't know how long he has had them,' she lied again but seemed regretful now that she was parted from them, and because of that, or because he was kind to her, she began to weep softly.

McKinley felt sorry for her. He looked at her lowered head, she seemed vulnerable and feminine.

She said, 'They could heal you if you were ill.'

'Where will they go?' McKinley asked. 'I must follow them.'

'For Teresa?' she said turning her wet face up to him and appealing with her eyes. She had completed her long dark plait and she twisted it around her neck like a scarf. Then she lay down, onto her back so that she lay naked in front of him. 'Don't go to her, stay with me. I am free now and I'm tired of Seton. I will give you pleasure that you could never know was possible.'

She pulled back the sheets so that he would be able to see her intimate parts and moved her hand down to caress herself as she made to open her legs. She tried to open them. She moved both hands down to her thighs and tried to open them. They lay heavy and unresponsive. She did not cry out but opened her mouth, arched her back and writhed on the bed.

Horrified by the sudden change, McKinley went to the door, 'I'll fetch Seton.' As he opened it he heard a thud and looking back he saw her clawing her way across the floor towards him dragging her lower body like a serpent. Her pink mouth was open in a silent scream.

He ran down to the kitchen where Seton was looking at a black dress held up by the maid that cook had found for him. They were haggling over price.

'You must come. She's lost the use of her legs.' They all dashed from the kitchen and stopped at the bottom of the stairs. At the top Lily was draped over the newel post. The exertion had brought more colour to her skin and the bruises were multicoloured and patterned, seeming to be all over her body. She saw them at the bottom of the stairs and reached out to them. Cook gasped in horror and the little maid screamed.

'No,' said McKinley as she slipped over the banister. Her heavy body fell, and the plait caught on the post. She only moved a little, then twisted round so that they could see the staring sightless eyes and the protruding tongue. The maid fainted.

*   *   *

She hung like a carcase on a meat hook, twisting slightly, her eyes glassy and hands limp. The hair that had hanged her creaked slightly as she moved. There was no other sound until cook ran back to the kitchen.

The men were only then able to tear their eyes from the body and Seton dropped to his knees. McKinley thought with irritation that he was praying but he knelt over the unconscious maid. McKinley felt obliged to try and recover Lily's body. He leaned over the banister and wrapped his arms about her waist. She was hot to the touch and her skin soft and fragrant in a musky, animal way.

'For God's sake Seton, leave the girl and help me with this!' He was able to swing her legs onto the banister and held them there. Cook appeared from the kitchen with a large knife and McKinley was alarmed until she mounted the stairs and cut the plait that had looped itself over the newel post. It took the strength of both men to bring the body onto the stairs. They looked at her naked form, her spread arms and her closed legs.

'Don't stand there gawping!' said cook. 'Get the poor creature back into the bedroom and cover her up. I'll have to report this to the magistrate. Goodness knows what the owners will say when they hear of it.' She accompanied them as they carried Lily back into the bedroom. She threw a sheet over her and said, 'Now out of here. I don't want any men near her. She'll have as much respect as we can give her in death.' She shooed them out of the room and took the key and locked the door.

The men made for the brandy that was kept in the sitting room. After a few gulps Seton said: 'She … she told me that she was a whore in London after the plague and the great fire when Ede, sorry Dee, found her. She was sick with the French pox and near to death. His alchemy saved her and gave her back the beauty she once had. She didn't know how old she was, but she had been sold as a child to men who liked little girls. Every day she drank a potion that Dee gave her to renew her beauty and keep the disease at bay.'

'Poor child,' said McKinley.

'What if I've got it? What if the whore passed the pox to me?' Seton began to curse and sob.

McKinley slapped him hard. 'Stop it!' he said. Then more gently, 'You're in shock but you must pull yourself together and prepare to be questioned by the officers of the law. There will likely be a Coroner's inquest and we know nothing about Lily. You can't tell them she's hundreds of years old. The Prospero Company has gone, leaving no trace of their whereabouts.' He thought with foreboding that this looked like an abused woman beaten and murdered by her lover. Thank God the cook and maid had witnessed her accidental death. Cook seemed to be a sound person and would likely be known hereabouts, he thought. She will tell the truth and be believed.

Seton drank two more glasses of brandy and McKinley left him in a chair and went to find cook. She had sent the gardener to Guildford to tell the parish constable about the death. He would no doubt visit and examine the body then speak to the witnesses and the other occupants of the house. McKinley needed to inform the other artists as soon as possible and he found the gardener's boy talking to the maid in the scullery, trying to get details of the accident whilst pretending to care for her.

She was pale and wide-eyed. When she saw McKinley she stood up shakily and he bade her sit. Then he told the boy to look around the grounds and tell the other residents that there had been an accident and a death and that they should return to the house at their earliest convenience.

He sat next to the maid. 'Tell me what you saw, please, in your own words.' He wanted to ensure that she and cook had seen the same as he and Seton. There was no telling if the effect of glamour might be different on men and women. They may have seen something else in Lily and her appearance.

'Cook told me I shouldn't say as what she weren't wearing no clothes, but she weren't were she?'

'No, she was naked, having just got out of her bed and having been very ill in the night-time.' McKinley thought it right to bring the context to the fore. 'Go on.'

'Well, she were leaning on the bannister at the landing. No clothes but her hair in a braid wrapped round her neck. Her legs looked funny.'

'Funny?'

'Like they were stuck together and painted red and blue and green. The ankles were bent back so she was resting on the tops of the feet. They looked uncomfortable.' The girl closed her eyes. 'Her face was terrible, all purple and white and I've never seen nothing like those eyes. Her mouth was open.'

'Did you hear her say anything?'

'No, but it was wide and red, filled with horror,' she was warming to her task now. 'She held out both arms and that made her slither over the banister. That's when I screamed. But her hair was caught on the post and it jerked her back. She spun, then she hanged, moved a bit and then she was dead. I don't remember any more. They say I fainted.'

'I'd say you remembered very well. Thank you. That is how I remember it too.' McKinley was relieved that no glamour had distorted his own eyes. 'That is exactly what you must say to the coroner's officer when he questions you. Leave nothing out and don't add anything that isn't true. Her nakedness is a matter of fact, ignore cook's prudishness.'

'But why was she all those colours?' asked the girl.

'She had been cruelly beaten by her previous master with the travelling theatre company. Mr Seton had been looking after her and he was fetching a dress for her when this terrible thing happened.'

'Oh yes, I was holding the dress when you came in. But sir, what happened to her legs?'

McKinley frowned at his recollection of the attempted seduction and her sudden paralysis and how he had fled. He should have stayed and looked after her; he was guilty of neglect. 'She discovered that they were paralysed whilst I was talking to her and I came to find Seton. It must have been because of the beating. If only she had remained on the bed…. I am so sorry you had to see that.'

He heard voices as Millais and Rossetti returned, the gardener's boy and Holman Hunt were not far behind. He thanked the maid and took the men into the sitting room where Seton sat with his head in his hands. McKinley explained what had happened.

After a few moments Hunt said: 'The scandal will ruin us. We must be kept out of this at all costs. I am planning to return to London tomorrow, that won't be delayed, surely?'

Millais looked sad but Rossetti quite buoyant. 'It was never going to end well for that woman, she used her charms on us all didn't she? You're lucky to have escaped Seton. I suppose you're heartbroken.'

Seton looked up and smiled oddly. 'No, I think that you are right, old man. I had a lucky escape,' he glanced at McKinley, 'and we have the cast iron witnesses of cook and the maid to ensure that we are held blameless. Don't you think so McKinley?'

Despite his friend's callous attitude he had to agree and kept to himself the queer onset of paralysis and her reaction to it. From the moment of its discovery on the bed, when she was attempting to seduce him, her voice had become as useless as her legs. Her screams were silent as she pursued him across the bedroom floor and as she died.

'I don't suppose we could have a look at her,' suggested Rossetti. 'It'll take a while for the parish constable or whoever, to come up and we could make a few quick sketches. For art's sake.'

Seton replied 'You'll have to ask cook. The door is locked and she has the key.'

They thought better of it.

*   *   *

No one had entered the bedroom when the coroner's officer appeared in the trap with the gardener, his sturdy cob trotting behind. He was a competent-looking man of about thirty-five and began carefully making notes of all their names and addresses. McKinley saw that he was very observant and methodical as they showed him the site of the accident; then he and cook took him into the old study for privacy while everyone else waited in the sitting room and made free with the brandy.

McKinley began to describe what had happened and suggested that cook tell him if she disagreed with any of it. He was able to start the tale earlier with the background to the Prospero Company and the relationship between the artists and the actors as models. He did not mention the marionettes but thought it necessary to disclose Seton's affair with Lily and described that as the reason Mr Ede had beaten her and thrown her out of the caravan. Cook knew nothing of this but confirmed that there had been a relationship and an almighty row when the 'gypsies', as she called them, left. The officer grunted and made notes at this, and it was clear that he was inclined to blame the travelling folk; it was likely to move the matter out of his jurisdiction and would save the magistrate the cost of an investigation.

After he had satisfied himself that the other young men had not been present, he spent some time with Seton and then gently interrogated the maid who repeated what she had told McKinley, but without the awkward questions. He then asked to view the body and was taken by cook in the presence of McKinley, who had witnessed the death, and Seton, as the lessee of the house, to the bedroom. She produced the key and gave it to the officer who checked that the door was locked then unlocked it and opened it.

Cook now opened the curtains to show that she had swaddled the body in sheets so that only her face was showing. 'Naked, you say.' If he was disappointed that she was no longer in that state, he did not show it. Her long plait that had been cut to let her down from the newel post was laid on the bed beside her.

'And this is what strangled her?' He picked it up the thick brown braid, at least a yard long and was examining it. Something, perhaps the warmth of his body, made it move and curl itself around his wrist and arm. 'Get it off me!' he gasped and stepped backwards shaking his arm.

Seton cried out and shrank against the wall, even cook was shocked. McKinley picked up a cloth from the washstand and, using it, he removed the rope of hair and laid it again on the white sheet. It returned to a limp state as soon as it was away from the healthy skin of the horrified man. He was not inclined to look at the body on the bed in any more detail, being satisfied to note the discolouration of her bruises as evidence of the beating by Ede. They all left the bedroom, and he locked the door, giving the key to Seton.

'I will make my report and if the coroner decides then we will undertake a search for this Mr Ede. Do you know where the company has gone?' he said.

'They were intending to perform at the Mitcham fair in August I believe,' said McKinley. He hoped that they might be found and Ede, or Dee, taken up by the police but he was not optimistic. The man had avoided the authorities for two hundred and fifty years, what chance did the newly formed constabularies have? 'What shall we do with the body? The warm weather will quickly corrupt it.'

The officer thought about this. 'I expect it could be collected tomorrow for a pauper's grave, unless you want to pay for a burial elsewhere.'

'Can't you take it now?' said cook.

The man shuddered at the thought. 'I've got my old horse to ride back and I've got to leave now as I must make my report, in writing. No, tomorrow is the earliest you'll be getting rid of that.' He gestured in the direction of the bedroom. He went down the stairs, avoiding touching the newel post but looking again at the scene of the accident.

Cook turned to Seton. 'I'll be staying at my sister's cottage in the village,' she said, 'and the maid will be coming with me. I'll lay out cold cuts and pickles for you men.' Seton and McKinley agreed, and as the coroner's officer prepared to leave, they went back to the other young men and recounted the events of the last two hours. They were fascinated by the animation of the braid of hair.

'It was probably the attraction of electricity from the body of the man. It creates a form of magnetism,' said Hunt.

McKinley helped himself to brandy and went to ask cook for tea and something to soak up the alcohol. When he returned, they had decided to go and draw the body.

'It's an opportunity not to be missed,' said Rossetti.

McKinley declined. Seton had the key and all four of them took sketching paper and pencils or charcoal to record the scene. He considered his squeamishness. Until last year he had been employed by a newspaper to draw scenes of disaster and the dead. He had drawn the skeletonised remains of a medieval child martyr when it was exhumed for archaeological reasons. But there was something unholy about the way that woman upstairs had died, and he did not think that even now she was at peace.

The brandy made his eyes close, and he lay on the leather sofa and slept. He was woken by Seton shaking him. 'Come and get some supper old man. You've been asleep for a long time.'

They joined the others at table. It was seven thirty in the evening and the sun was sinking behind the hills. After dinner they proudly showed him their artwork and he had to agree it was impressive. They had made her look as beautiful as she had been in life. Her large eyes were closed and her fine nose undamaged, but her mouth had been bruised and was now returning to its former size, not yet shrunk back from the teeth in death. He was particularly interested in the way they had treated her hair.

Millais had drawn it in exact detail, her cropped hair spread on the pillow like a dark halo, the severed plait starkly separate next to her; she looked like a desperate dead woman who had been lovely in life. Hunt's picture was more spiritual in conception; she looked startled and her eyes seemed slightly open, as did her mouth. One might expect her to take a breath and then awake in surprise at finding her plait cut off.

Rossetti's drawing was the most voluptuous; her lips were parted, full and dark and her eyes closed as if in ecstasy. He had drawn the plait, not separate, but wound around her long neck as though by a lover and her neck was slightly arched. It was Seton's portrait that disturbed McKinley the most. Lily did not seem dead at all. Rather she was basking in the sunshine of their attention and she smiled with her eyes and her mouth. He had drawn the bruises on her skin vividly so that she looked as though they had been painted on her like stage makeup and it reminded McKinley of the first time he had seen her at the theatre in Portsmouth.

'Isn't it awful to know that right now she is physically changing as we sit down here contemplating these images,' said Millais.

'And it's so awfully warm,' said Hunt 'Do you think we should move her into the chapel? It's cooler in there, on the north side of the house. Your bedroom gets the full sun during the day, Seton.'

'I won't be sleeping in there tonight,' said Seton, 'But yes, let's move her to the chapel. I'll unlock it and prepare a table for the body.'

Millais, Rossetti and Hunt went up to the bedroom with the key and McKinley followed Seton into the chapel. It was dark and cool and suitably quiet for a mortuary and McKinley looked about to see if there was a slab of stone that she could be laid on. They had not been there long when Millais burst through the door.

'You – must – come,' he gasped. 'She's …' he could not find the right expression, '…. not all there.'

McKinley had visions of dismemberment by a creature; perhaps the flying thing had returned and found its way into the bedroom and begun to devour her. They ran up the staircase and into the large room. The curtains were flung wide and the lamps lit so they were able to see what was on the bed. The men had begun to lift her wrapped body but the form of the woman had collapsed as though it was an empty husk. Her head and face were still visible, exactly as they had left her.

'Touch her face,' said McKinley to Seton. He backed away.

'No, no, I can't. Her hair clung to that man. What if she isn't dead?'

Rossetti made as if to poke her with one of Seton's brushes. 'I'll do it,' said McKinley.

He drew the back of his hand across her cheek and, as he had expected, it collapsed, drawing with it her entire face so that she looked like a deflated balloon. There were gasps of horror and curses.

'Unwrap the body,' said McKinley and they carefully unwound the sheet from the corpse revealing the skin of a woman but no flesh and no bones. When they were satisfied that she was not going to rise up and attack them they searched the room for the rest of her corpse. McKinley beckoned Seton and took him to the concealed door that led to the cellar; it lay open about ten inches.

'I don't know how she did it, but I think she has gone through here and down to the cellar.'

'She? What do you mean?' said Seton. 'No! How could she? Somebody has been here, skinned and taken her.'

The others heard this exchange and Rossetti said: 'Was it that bastard Ede? Has the devil stolen the body leaving only the skin? What in hell's name is going on?'

McKinley hesitated but he had to tell them what he was thinking, crazy as it seemed. 'I think she has shed her own skin and slithered down to the cellar in the form of a serpent.' There was nervous laughter and incredulity. He turned to Seton. 'You saw her as Lamia, a snake woman, and I have a suspicion that she has been

141

transformed into that creature. Losing the use of her legs was the first change, then her voice was lost, and she interrupted the metamorphosis by hanging herself accidentally. Now it is complete. I believe if we go down to the cellar we will find a large snake.'

The laughter subsided to an atmosphere of serious consideration and an awareness of danger.

'How can such demonic magic be possible?' asked Rossetti.

'There are things about Ede that you do not know. He practices the science of alchemy; I am sure you are familiar with that expression. Their belief is 'As above so below' – the mysteries of God, angels, demons, and other things that walk the earth invisible to us are known to them. The practitioners of alchemy are secretive and have long sought the ability to prolong life. It is possible that the Prospero Company actors and even the marionettes have been contaminated in some way by receiving alchemical treatment from Ede. Don't you agree Seton?' He looked at his friend willing him not to say too much about John Dee's prolonged life and Lily's history.

'She led me to believe something like that,' he mumbled.

While the young men were dazed by this revelation McKinley continued, 'We must be practical. She cannot be allowed to escape. Hunt and Millais do you find wood and anything heavy and block up the one window to the cellar. There is a board in the way, but I would prefer it to be strong enough to withstand the pressure of a large animal. Seton, is the cellar door locked? Good. Then we must shut this door to the priest-hole and move furniture in front of it so that she cannot escape this way. I assume no one wants to descend the stairway to see if she is there rather than in the cellar?' No one responded. 'I thought not.'

They set about their tasks and eventually McKinley was satisfied that all precautions had been taken to keep Lily confined until the morning when the coroner's officer would return with his conclusions. There would be undertakers expecting to remove the body and he had no idea how they would explain its disappearance.

A great deal of wine was drunk that night and they all decided to sleep in the sitting room with one person keeping watch. She was probably a large and dangerous snake and they had no way of knowing if she might be venomous. McKinley had estimated that the hidden stairway might descend next to the dining room so at the last minute they searched for a concealed door and pushed heavy furniture against the place where they deduced it might be.

He did not sleep. They did not know where a snake might be able to hide itself in a house like this. Were there more hidden passages and stairs that led to other rooms? His own? The kitchen? That was usually warm, and snakes liked warmth. Eventually exhaustion and alcohol pulled him into a fitful sleep filled with small snakes that wriggled away as he approached them, unsure if he was hunting or being hunted. He must get weapons. He only had a paintbrush to defend himself and if he found the Lamia, huge and beautiful in her coloured skin, he would be at her mercy. Terror and desire made him sweat and he woke in a panic with a dead weight on his chest. She had him and she was crushing him. A swift shove revealed Seton who had fallen asleep next to him and whose head had fallen onto his friend.

The noise woke everyone and McKinley asked Hunt, who had been on watch, if he had heard anything.

'Only snoring from those of you lucky enough to be asleep,' he replied. They could hear birds beginning to sing and light appearing in the east.

'You can sleep now,' said McKinley. 'I'll wait up until dawn. Does anyone have a gun?' No one did but he remembered that the gardener had been carrying a shotgun the previous week. He picked up the poker and positioned himself on a chair near the door.

The minutes passed slowly, and the breathing of the other men settled into the strange shallow rhythms of sleep. He tried to stay awake without disturbing them but must have dozed because he woke with a shock. It was dawn and he was looking at the empty black hole of the fireplace and in the half-light, he imagined the head of a serpent appearing. She could get in that way. He walked over to it and stared at the light-absorbing blackness, he squatted to get a better look, then prodded with his poker into the darkness. A sudden fall of soot made him fall over backwards. The other men stirred.

Lying on the floor feeling foolish he looked to one side and saw her under the chaise longue. It was dark and he could only just make out her form, but he saw the glassy orbs of her eyes and she looked at him with intelligence and he felt sorry for her. She must want the company of her fellow creatures to come to a room full of men who would hunt and kill her given the opportunity.

'Something there McKinley?' said Hunt.

'Just soot,' he replied and slowly got to his feet. Seton was lying on the chaise and he had been sitting there himself earlier.

'I think we should leave this room and go to the kitchen and get some breakfast,' he said. He did not know if she could understand language, better not to mention knives. He also did not want a bloody fight in the sitting room without having planned it and, he realised, he felt sorry for her because she was utterly alone. Most of the men had sore heads from the brandy and the prospect of food and tea was attractive so it did not take long to usher them out and shut the door.

'She is in there, under the chaise,' he told them, 'I don't know how she got in but she didn't attack anyone.'

'Then we should get in there and kill it,' said Millais. McKinley beckoned them away from the door and spoke in a low voice.

'I think we should keep her alive and trapped until the coroner's officer and the undertaker arrive. We have no dead body to give them but we have a large snake and we can say that the woman was eaten by the snake.'

'Why are you whispering? You don't think it can understand us do you?' said Seton. 'Dear God, it's not natural, it's an abomination.'

'You're the only one who has seen it,' said Rossetti 'How can we know if you are telling truth?'

'Keep your voice down,' said McKinley, 'and go back and look under the chaise.'

Rossetti opened the door and all four of them crept quietly into the sitting room. The light was poor and they peered cautiously under the furniture, and on the furniture, finally above the curtains and drapes and the lights.

'There's nothing here,' said Millais. McKinley stepped into the room and as he did so his eye caught movement by the door.

He stepped back and said 'Look.' They turned and froze. They saw a thick stream of coloured scales and muscle moving silently through the doorway, and it seemed to go on for a long time. Then a tail flicked through, and it was gone.

Millais said, 'I didn't see the head, but it must have been twelve feet long.'

'More like fifteen,' said McKinley. 'Come with me.' They followed him outside and he led them to the gardener's cottage and found the man preparing to work on his own vegetable patch.

'We need to borrow your gun,' said McKinley. 'There's a large snake in the house, it must have been part of the menagerie that the theatre company owned and we may have to shoot it.'

The man was amazed, but he had heard of the previous day's goings on and was prepared to believe it. He brought out the weapon and his box of cartridges.

'I only use it for vermin but it might be useful if you know how to shoot.'

McKinley said he had experience of shotguns from his father's estate, and they told the man not to worry, the officer of the law would return to take away the woman's body today and between them they would catch or despatch the creature. They returned to the house and went to the kitchen to find food, and knives with which they might defend themselves. They stayed in pairs as there was no way of knowing where the snake had gone, and it would have been easy to be ambushed in that old Tudor hall with its many dark corners and heavy drapes that could make an ideal camouflage for a snake.

McKinley was haunted by the eyes he had glimpsed, and he forbade the hunting forays that the younger men were keen to pursue. He stressed the need for the thing to be seen by the authorities to explain the disappearance of the body, so it must be prevented from escaping. They sat outside the Hall at two corners of the building and kept watch on the windows. In the middle of the morning they heard horses approach. He stood and was preparing himself with an explanation to greet them, when he was struck by a thought.

'I'm a damned idiot! Lily's skin is still on the bed!' said McKinley.

Seton was with him. 'I'll get rid of it into the hidden stairwell. I've got the key to the room, just let me have the gun.' They were alone on the front steps, the others were positioned around the house so he loaded the shotgun and gave it, broken, to Seton. 'Don't worry I know what to do. You and I are the only ones who know what we are really up against here.' He seemed calm and McKinley was reassured that he had recovered from the horror of what they had witnessed. Neither cook nor the maid had appeared that morning. Seton went into the house.

The coroner's officer rode around the final bend of the drive and behind him came the wagon of the Guildford undertaker with two men sitting up front. McKinley brushed himself down and tried to look less dishevelled after the disturbing night. He walked down to the men and spoke to the officer as he dismounted, explaining that the body had disappeared and that a large snake had been seen in the house, probably left behind by Ede's travelling players. They suspected that the snake might have eaten the unfortunate woman.

There was a moment's silence when the man looked suspiciously at McKinley. 'We all saw it and we have taken positions in pairs around the house to prevent its escape.'

The man nodded and beckoned the undertaker's men. 'It seems you'll have to wait before we can go inside.' Then as an afterthought, 'Have either of you had experience of handling or killing snakes?'

One said he could not abide the creatures and the other just shook his head. As they walked to the house he said: 'The magistrate has decided it was an accident, but this is going to complicate matters. You think the creature has eaten her?'

'I suspect it,' said McKinley. 'We have not slept much since we discovered her gone last night and we all saw the creature in the house. It's big.'

'How big?'

'I estimate about fifteen feet long and about a foot thick in places.'

'Dear God!' said the man 'How are we going kill it?'

'We've borrowed a shotgun from the gardener. Here are the others who saw it, so that you can confirm my story if you wish.' McKinley took him to meet the young men who described what they had seen. As they did so he realised that Seton had not reappeared.

'Where is the gun?' said the officer.

'My friend Seton went inside with it a few minutes ago.' He avoided looking at the other artists. 'Perhaps we should arm ourselves with staffs and knives and go back in.' It was becoming a dangerous situation and he cursed himself for having let Seton have the gun and go back into the house.

'Well I don't know what's more dangerous,' said the officer 'A large snake or a nervous young man with a shotgun. Do you want to wait for him?'

McKinley weighed the odds and he was not happy with the amount of time Seton had been gone, he may be trapped and in danger.

'No, I think we should proceed. I will go first and I'll call his name so he knows it's me. Do you stay behind me. I'm pretty sure he went to his bedroom. If anyone wants to wait out here they can do so.'

None of them wanted to miss the adventure so they crept behind McKinley and the officer and entered the hall. It was dark and they waited until their eyes had adjusted to the gloom while their ears strained to hear any sound in the silent building.

When he was prepared to move forward McKinley called, 'Seton? Where are you? We are coming in, don't shoot us.' Then he listened and there was no response. 'Let's go upstairs.'

They mounted the stairs slowly, the light from the front windows illuminated the landing, and they passed the post on which Lily had hanged herself. Seton's bedroom was the largest and closest to the stairs, the door was ajar but it was dark inside. McKinley beckoned the others to stay back and gently pushed the door open.

'It's just me Seton. Are you in here?' There was no reply but he thought he heard a sound, perhaps it was a movement. 'I'm coming in.' He slowly walked into the room and could see that there was something on the bed. He heard a whimper.

Holding his breath, he drew aside the curtains and there was a cry from the door; he turned to see the officer in the room and the other men standing in the doorway. They were white faced and staring at the thing on the bed. He saw it and stifled a scream.

Seton lay on the bed, his clothing was dishevelled, his eyes large and his face flushed. She lay entwined around him, the sound he had heard was her body shifting against his. He knew that she could crush him in an instant. She was blue and violet with streaks of yellow, the colour of a bruise on a woman's face. She rubbed her head against his and her tongue flickered as she smelled his skin. She would have been beautiful if she did not hold the life of a man in her lethal embrace. Somebody in the doorway moved and she tightened her grip, Seton whimpered. He could do nothing more, his breathing was entirely within her control.

They regarded each other for several seconds but it seemed like an age to McKinley who decided to try and speak to her.

'Please let him go. You don't need to do this.' He thought he saw a glint of recognition in her eyes as she looked at him, and then it disappeared, and she opened her mouth impossibly wide and plunged it over Seton's head. The suddenness and the speed meant that they could not reach him before her jaws had totally engulfed it and he emitted a thin scream with what little breath he had.

With shock McKinley saw an arm emerge from the writhing coils and it held the gun. He was about to try and grab it when Seton's shoulder dislocated and he was able to turn the gun towards his own head. He pulled both triggers. He blew his head apart along with that of his tormentor.

*   *   *

The horror of the event had been witnessed by the coroner's officer as well as the other occupants of Pitdown Hall. They were all anxious to leave, no one else could bear to stay another night in that awful place. The undertaker's men had a body to remove. The officer had four statements to add to his own and McKinley had a difficult letter to write to Seton's sister, his only remaining family.

The wagons hired by Rossetti and the others came to the Hall soon after the incident and they were cleared to leave provided McKinley promised to stay for the inquests. His spirits sank in the knowledge that he would not be able to pursue Doctor Dee until they were over. He would move to lodgings in Guildford and whilst waiting he would discover as much as he could about Ede and the travelling players he called the Prospero Company.

By six that evening everyone had gone and the gardener's boy waited with the trap to take him to Guildford. Cook and the maid had shrieked when they saw the blood and brains on the bedroom walls. They would clean it up, he knew. And the old Hall would stand gloomy and quiet and silent once again with its secrets. He had a sudden thought about Lily's skin. Was it in the hidden stairwell? Or would the cleaners discover it? He could not bring himself to return and search. They would have to make of it what they could. He was moving on.

CHAPTER THREE

The inquest had been brief. The body of a large snake had been examined by the authorities together with the remains of a man and the witness reports of five men, one of whom was an officer of the coroner and a constable. There was outrage locally that such a dangerous creature could be allowed to escape from its cage and take two lives, and a countrywide notice was issued to detain the Prospero Company and Mr Ede if they should be found at a local fair. McKinley was satisfied that this would disrupt Ede's plans but he was afraid that he might not see Teresa again, and Mariel, if they did not visit the Sloe fair in Chichester in October. The scandal was diverted to fuel the increasingly heated debates in the press and in Parliament whether to ban ancient fairs on the grounds that they brought drunkenness and lewd behaviour and did not have a place in modern times.

Privately McKinley was relieved that no one had tried to find Lily's body inside the snake, she had no family pressing for a funeral. Only one man had pointed out that it was usual for a reptile to rest for a long period after eating, he having returned lately from India. The attempt to eat Seton was attributed to the stress of being cornered and no more was said.

McKinley was in London staying at the house of an uncle called Ewart McKinley. His correspondence with Seton's sister resulted in the removal of his body to her husband's house and thence to a church in Wimborne where his parents were buried. The sister was on the point of confinement with their third child and her husband made the arrangements. He did not want any of Seton's painting materials or finished canvases, so McKinley was sitting in his room in London contemplating his friend's portrait of Lily as Keats's Lamia. It had been prescient in its subject and execution and he was stunned when he thought back on the previous few weeks.

He felt that he should burn it, but it was beautiful and full of colour and life. It reminded him of his friend so he was determined that he would keep it and if the occasion ever arose where it could be seen without renewing interest in the circumstances of its execution, he would try to have it exhibited. His own painting of 'La Belle Dame Sans Marci' was unfinished, and whilst he was pleased with it, he had not the heart to continue. His mission was to research the life of Doctor John Dee and to find a way to release those he held against their will. He was in London because the library of the British Museum offered the best way to do this, and it was a relief to his heart and mind to throw himself into long hours of reading and note-taking. Returning to his uncle's house exhausted every evening meant that he did not need to dwell upon the horrors he had seen.

Inevitably he was obliged to explain what had happened at Pitdown Hall; he was invited to dinner parties by people he hardly knew. The national newspapers ran the story at every opportunity and the publishing house that produced the penny dreadfuls McKinley had illustrated found out where he was staying and offered him generous amounts of money to write and illustrate the horror. His mind was already prone to conjure the dreadful images without needing to recreate them for the titillation of the masses. He knew that eventually they would tire of it and it would be replaced by some other salacious gossip.

McKinley's uncle was an unmarried gentleman in his fifties who kept his own substantial library on matters of natural philosophy. He had travelled extensively, he gave that as the reason he had never married, and his modest house in Aldersgate was decorated with stuffed specimens of exotic animals, including several from Australia. There were no snakes, McKinley was relieved to find.

Uncle Ewart had listened to his nephew's story with no interruptions. He wondered if the older man had fallen asleep, his eyes were closed. When McKinley had finished, he quietly said:

'Would you show me the painting of the Lamia, dear boy?'

His nephew obliged. He brought down the painting and revealed the vivid swirling dress of red silk embracing the voluptuous figure of Lily with her amber skin and calf length hair plaited and falling over her bare shoulders. McKinley remembered the sensation of those warm shoulders under his hands in the dark staircase at Pitdown Hall when she had stood naked in front of him. The background was indistinct but seemed to be the green of a jungle with some vague purple flowers amongst the leaves.

They sat in silence looking at Lily's extraordinary portrait.

'The serpent is found in Greek mythology on the staff of Asclepius and associated with healing; and you say that Lily was much older than she looked?' Uncle Ewart filled and lit his pipe.

'That was what she told poor Seton, after the man I now believe to be Doctor Dee had abandoned her,' said McKinley. 'She suggested two hundred years.'

'Good grief.'

'She also said that she had been near to death and that his potions had healed her, restored her beauty and given her many more years of life.' He lit his own pipe. 'I suppose it is possible that he gave her a potion derived from snakes and that this change she suffered was the long-term effect.'

'Or the withdrawal symptom,' mused his uncle.

'So he knew what would happen and he caused this terrible thing deliberately!'

'He may not have known that she would transform into a serpent, perhaps he thought she would die, or age, given the additional years she had lived. You say he accused her of betraying him?'

'Yes,' McKinley thought of his exact words. 'He said she had been used by many men – that must refer to her being a prostitute, and that she could die in a ditch like the animal she is. That suggests he knew the effect of the potions in turning her into a snake.' He thought about it. 'I assumed it was a commonplace insult.'

153

'Possibly,' said his uncle 'If his company were with him for a long time he may not have been aware that the metamorphosis would be so very drastic and with such terrible consequences. He almost certainly was condemning her to death for betrayal, but I cannot believe he wanted to hurt any of you.'

'Why do you think that? He seemed to be a man of few emotions, cold even,' McKinley said.

'And yet he saved the lives of the individuals you spoke to in the company: Lily, Teresa and even the young man.'

'Avery. And he seems to be well regarded by Mariel.'

Ewart enjoyed his pipe for a few minutes. 'He would not want any harm to come to you because he could not afford the attention of the authorities into his affairs. I daresay he expected her to age and then you would have a deceased old woman on your hands, not so very unusual.'

But very embarrassing, thought McKinley.

His uncle continued. 'I'm interested in this man. Doctor John Dee was renowned for trying to converse with angels in the last few decades of his life. It was one of the reasons that he fell out of favour at court; that and James I's suspicion of anything relating to demons. The king wrote a book about it you know, a Dissertation on Daemonologie in 1597.'

McKinley said, 'I've been reading up on that period. The king obviously believed in witchcraft and all sorts of occult things. He describes the various types of spirit that can cause trouble for men and should be discouraged, if not actually stamped out, but no one prosecuted Dee for his pursuits.'

'He was protected by the high men of England at the time of Elizabeth. James was only king in Scotland until she died in 1603, by then Doctor Dee was living in obscurity and poverty, apparently,' said Ewart.

'What do you mean – apparently?' asked McKinley.

'Well, we know that as an alchemist he was intent on discovering how to turn base metal into gold and prolong life; and we know that he was very secretive. If the man you met is Dee he has certainly achieved the latter. He was also famous for having acquired a large library,' said his uncle.

'Mariel said he has books in his caravan, but she is not allowed to read them.'

'That many books would require more space than a travelling wagon. You say he lives a nomadic existence, but I think you mentioned a warehouse in London where fabric is stored. Yes?'

'That's right,' said McKinley 'It makes sense - his father was a mercer, and he was able to join the Worshipful Company of Mercers by reason of patrimony. They imported and stored velvets, silks and other fancy notions used to make clothes. He must have retained a warehouse. Goodness knows what else is stored there.'

'You're in luck my boy. I have a friend in the Company of Mercers; we share an interest in natural philosophy and have both travelled widely. John Dee wrote books on navigation as well as astrology, and he was an accomplished mathematician.'

'I can't seem to square the acquisition of occultist knowledge with the pursuit of science. Newton was similar I believe,' said McKinley.

'You must remember they were just emerging from the very rigorous control of the Catholic church. Science was expected to accord with accepted Christian dogma. The notion that the earth was not at the centre of the universe was considered heresy, as Galileo found to his cost in 1632, and belief in God and angels and the teachings of the bible were not to be disputed.' He paused to relight his pipe. 'I think your friend's belief that he had heard angels singing is quite a reasonable assumption. What else could they be?'

'Poor Jack Seton was convinced of William Blake's theories that angels walk among us. But uncle, these creatures were being held prisoner and forced to perform in public in the guise of marionettes. I don't see how they could be celestial beings.' McKinley remembered what he had seen on his roof. 'The thing I saw bathing in the moonlight, after it had escaped from the chapel, was not as I would expect an angel to look.' He fetched the sketch to show his uncle who studied it with interest.

'Extraordinary and most disturbing,' said the older man. 'But there is a wisdom in its eyes, don't you agree? It seems to be old and yet there is an alacrity about it. It flew up to the roof you said?'

'According to Lily it could fly and there may have been wings, but I didn't notice them. The shock at seeing it nearly sent me backwards over the window ledge.'

'Yet it did not attack you, and presumably it could have done.'

'I think I said 'Hello,' but it ignored me. If it had been a demon,' said McKinley 'It could easily have hurt me.'

His uncle stood up. 'Your story has intrigued me Robert. Alchemical texts are written in a cryptic code and use glyphs and cannot be interpreted without a key, we will need help deciphering them, assuming we find them of course. If you will allow me I will contact my friend this evening, he may be at his club.'

'Should I come with you?'

'No need. If I am right, then tomorrow we might meet with him and find out what we can about Doctor John Dee. But for now, I suggest you eat some cold cuts my housekeeper has left for us. You really should try to be here in the middle of the day. She cooks my hot meal then because with my old man's digestion I really cannot eat much at night.' So saying he took his hat and cane and left the house.

*　　　　　*　　　　　*

The following day it was hot, and a stink arose from the Thames that McKinley had never noticed so strong and he was reminded of Portsmouth. It was the middle of August 1848 and there were rumours of cholera that had led many of the wealthy classes to quit the capital. He remembered Mariel's mother and her recent death and was anxious to finish his research and begin a physical search for the Prospero Company. As they walked to the Mercer's Hall he mentioned this to his uncle.

'Did you know that Shakespeare probably based the character of Prospero on Doctor John Dee?' said Ewart. McKinley had to admit he was not aware of the connection but it made sense. No doubt they performed 'The Tempest' with as much brilliance as the 'Dream'. His mind turned to the use of puppets on the stage in Portsmouth and he tried to explain to his uncle how effective they had been and how the audience loved them.

'Of course,' said his uncle. 'The company seeks to appeal to country folk by and large, not scholars or the sort of people who attend the theatre to be seen by their peers. From what you have told me they perform in a tent to folk who might never have heard of William Shakespeare otherwise.' They walked a little way in silence. 'Tell me again what is your theory about these creatures.'

McKinley took a deep breath and tried to sound as logical as possible in explaining his fanciful notion. 'I think they are like Frankenstein's creation, except they are built from bits of wood and cloth and perhaps metal and then animated with the same alchemy that keeps the people about him alive.'

'Do you refer to the book by Mary Shelley?' asked his uncle. McKinley nodded. 'But Frankenstein is a work of fiction, Robert.'

'Yes, and a quite recent one. Doctor Dee has been about this mischief for a long time.'

'And when you saw them perform did they seem animated?'

McKinley replied, 'I did not doubt that they were brilliant marionettes. I assumed they moved with marvellous realism because a skilled puppeteer gave them life, animated them in a way that I simply could not see. These creatures moved like puppets but with little apparent effort on the part of the puppeteers.'

'Did you recognise the one you saw on the roof as being one of the creatures you saw on the stage?' his uncle asked.

'It was about the size of a mechanical, say Bottom, but its face and hands were different. It must have been wearing a mask, gloves and a costume.'

'As you would expect,' said his uncle. 'But did it speak?'

'Oh God,' said McKinley. 'Of course it spoke. I hadn't realised until now. Those strange voices that we in the audience thought were the actors ventriloquising and disguising their own, they were the voices of the creatures.'

'So,' said Ewart, 'it is a natural creature, either angel or demon and Doctor Dee has power over it.'

McKinley remembered something else Lily had told him. 'She said that the creatures have their own power too because Dee uses their healing power to prolong life.' He realised that this did not accord with his theories, but they were approaching the Mercers Hall and there was no time to debate it.

His uncle said, 'We must be circumspect about this. Let me do the talking.' So, attended by the liveried servants, they were shown into a club room and McKinley was introduced to his uncle's friend, a Mr Weber. He was a small old man, almost hairless except for a quantity that grew from his ears, and he was obviously profoundly deaf. A servant wheeled him to join them and made him comfortable with whisky and cushions and a large ear trumpet. McKinley wondered what he might have looked like as a young man and found it impossible to imagine him as anything other than this strange, almost alien creature.

His disrespectful thoughts were interrupted by Ewart launching into a description of some new natural specimens he had received from abroad. If the language of the alchemist was arcane so was the language of the natural philosopher. McKinley could understand little of what was said, except that it related to the fossilized remains of giant birds from the antipodes.

After the niceties had been got out of the way the two elderly men turned to the question of Doctor John Dee and his warehouse.

'I am only disclosing this information because I have known you a long time Ewart and I trust you implicitly. Your nephew seems a pleasant young man and there is little benefit to be had from the information in any event,' said Mr Weber.

McKinley's heart sank.

'I have looked at the archive and it is among the oldest of accounts managed by the Company and the property itself has changed several times. Original records go back to 1667, when they were, in part, re-created following the Great Fire and there is no information on the original owner.' He brought out a small piece of paper and a large eye-glass. 'There is currently a warehouse in Wapping and it was set up, we think, by a very old family in trust for a mysterious beneficiary before the common law restriction on trusts in perpetuity. It is called the Monad Trust, not that that helps. We always seem to manage to find the beneficiary if it becomes necessary and the path is smoothed over, as it were.' He smiled at them and said conspiratorially, 'Occasionally funds are required to pay for some repair or other bill and an attractive woman brings the money, in cash to the bursar to meet the expenses. It is a trivial sum in relation to the fabulous wealth of the Mercer's Company but always noteworthy for the beauty of the woman.'

McKinley wondered if it had been Lily or perhaps Teresa.

Ewart considered this and then carefully asked, 'When money is required how do you contact the owner?'

'We contact the trustees; they are a firm of lawyers. We know that the original settlor was a member of the Company, but because the records were burnt we don't have a name. It is possible the trustees have a copy of the trust deed, if it still exists, but we no longer do.' However deaf and decrepit this man might be, his mind was sharp and his memory good. 'I suppose you want their name; but I doubt they will give you any information.' He waved a feeble hand and his servant came forward with a small escritoire. A short note was enough to send the Company's servant scurrying off to the archives.

In the lull McKinley could not resist asking: 'How beautiful? How beautiful was she? The woman?'

The old man chortled, and his face flushed. 'Suffice it to say that when a visitor from this particular client is expected the club is far more popular than usual.'

'Please describe her.'

'It's not always the same woman.' He closed his eyes, the better to picture her. 'I don't think she is a lady. The last one had red hair and green eyes and she smelled of springtime and flower meadows and grass.'

McKinley said to Ewart, 'That's Teresa.'

The old man continued, 'The previous woman smelled of spice and incense and musk roses. She was dark.'

'That must have been Lily.'

'My eyes are not so good these days, but my sense of smell is excellent. Which is a great pity on a day like today. How I wish I could spend my last days in the countryside, but alas I must remain in town.' He closed his eyes and seemed to doze. His ear trumpet rested on his lap, so McKinley said to his uncle:

'Do you think he'll tell us where the warehouse is?'

'I think, my boy, that we must begin with the lawyers. You don't expect the troupe to be residing in the warehouse, surely? It sounds as though it is a storage facility only.'

McKinley thought about Mariel's account of the night she had spent in the warehouse. 'They do stay there sometimes and there might be evidence of necromancy and the occult,' he said, quietly.

'And then what? It is 1848, we do not burn or hang witches. I don't think that involving the authorities will help the creatures he has in his thrall.' Ewart thought about it as he filled and lit his pipe. 'He is an expert at covering his tracks and they are all actors, from what you say. They are probably a family of tinkers by now or picking fruit in Kent.' He puffed out clouds of fragrant smoke.

'That's wonderful,' said the old man. 'You've masked the damnable stink of the river! I can't smoke any more, but I love that memory.' He opened his eyes. 'I think I may have dozed a little. I had a dream in which I recall a few years ago when one of the fragrant women, having been followed by a man who waited outside for her, was accosted by him as she emerged from the hall. There was quite a fracas. Fortunately, her going was being observed by several members as usual, and it took no time at all to grapple the fellow to the ground, but when they turned to ask if she was alright, the woman had vanished. They brought him inside to find out whether he was a danger to the general populace, or a robber, and he raved about grave-robbing and raising the dead. Well, and I think this is relevant, it was shortly after William Godwin's book 'Lives of the Necromancers' had been published and there were one or two copies in the building so the man was interrogated further.'

They waited for Mr Weber to continue.

'He alleged that his brother had been exhumed shortly after burial by a group of travellers with whom the brother had been consorting. There was general disbelief at this as it was after the Anatomy Act of 1832 and corpses could be obtained legally by the medical schools so there was not much of a market. Yes, now I think of it, this happened about 1842, not so long ago come to think of it.' He paused.

'Weber, what happened to the man?' prompted Uncle Ewart.

'It was quite sad. He began to weep and said that he would never find them again. It was only by chance that he had seen the woman that day and recognised her striking looks. These travellers had befriended his brother, an impressionable young man in his early twenties, he was probably attracted by the girls. He admitted his brother was a petty crook but never violent and he liked the company of women. He had been with them for a few months when he was knocked down by a horse whilst under the influence of strong drink. His family scraped together the money to give him a Christian burial.'

'What made him think the travellers exhumed him?' asked McKinley.

'A vagrant boy saw them and described the women and the master in charge. He was too afraid to give evidence to the authorities,' said the old gentleman.

McKinley was sickened by this, but his uncle was unperturbed and asked, 'So you let the fellow go? And what did you, and the other members make of the explanation?'

'Well, we looked at the necromancer's book and it seems the occultists believe that the recent dead are able to forecast future events and so these travellers may have been doing that, talking to him. To gain some advantage one supposes. Perhaps a wager on a horse race.'

'It's blasphemous whatever their motive. What did they do to the body, did they take any body parts?' asked McKinley.

'I don't know, the man seemed more distressed at the removal of the corpse when he came here, it was the main cause of the fellow's grief, that he could not visit his little brother's grave. Terrible thing. I changed my will after that and asked to be buried in a metal cage to make it difficult to get at me.'

'It is as I suspected,' McKinley turned to his uncle. 'He is animating marionettes or other creatures, perhaps animals, or composites of both and then he has control over them.'

'Or he is using the dead to converse with angels or other supernatural beings,' said his uncle.

The ear trumpet waved between them. 'Who is?' shouted the old man.

'Doctor John Dee,' said Ewart after a pause, and to McKinley. 'There's no point hiding it from him. He may be the greatest help we can expect.'

The ear trumpet had dropped into his lap as Weber thought about the disclosure. 'So, you are on the track of Doctor Dee? Interesting. He is reputed to have discovered the elixir of life, in Glastonbury Abbey and to have used it on himself and his accomplice David Kelley. I read it in Godwin's book. It would explain why he is still alive. If you find him …' he stopped.

'Are you thinking you would like it?' asked Ewart McKinley.

'..... No, I think I'll accept the natural way of dying. Living that long must have an effect on a man. It would, I think, etiolate the soul, stretching it too far so that it grows pale and thin.'

Ewart looked his nephew. 'Does that accord with the man you met?'

'Possibly,' said McKinley. 'He is still a man of intellect and vigour but if a soul is what makes someone human then I think he has lost or is losing his humanity. He treated Lily worse than an animal, he beat her and discarded her like a used rag. She, also, was something other than human. She preyed on men and did not seem at all surprised that Dee treated her so badly. We were told that she had lived for an unnaturally long time too.' He thought about Teresa. If she had been coming to Mercers Hall to pay bills then she must be older than she looked. He quietly said into the ear trumpet, 'Did anyone comment on the apparent similarity of the women coming to bring funds and whether they did not appear to age?'

'It was mentioned, yes, but we assumed that they were a family and so bore a resemblance to each other. There might be fifteen or twenty years between visits and memories cannot always be relied upon.' At that moment the Mercers Hall servant came back with a leather-bound ledger and presented it to Weber. He called his servant from the corner and then made use of an eye glass to look through the book. His servant held it as it was too heavy for his frail arms and at last he stopped searching and beckoned for paper and an ink well. He laboriously copied down the name and address and his servant handed it to Ewart.

'Thank you, dear friend. Will you let us buy you dinner?'

'No, thank you. Sadly I only eat pap these days. I am like a butterfly sucking my food in liquid form through a proboscis. It is not a pretty sight, and I would not inflict it on you. But promise me that when this business is done you will come back and tell me how you fared. I can only live vicariously now and your story has intrigued me.'

They made their farewells and McKinley said to his uncle as they walked back to his house 'What a wonderfully wise old man. How long have you known him?'

'I've known Nicolas all my life, dear boy. He is my older step-brother from your grandmother's first husband. He was much older than her and Nicolas is fourteen years my senior and more like a father to me, or an uncle. I lived with them until I went to school at seven years, and he was then twenty-one and left to make a life for himself in India. My homesickness was much abated by being able to write to him, although it may have been as much as several months before letters were delivered. He always filled my dreams with strange plants and beasts and is the main reason I became a naturalist. Your grandmother produced children over a thirty-year period from the first in 1772. She was lucky to survive her child-bearing years, so many do not. Your father was one of the last in 1800.'

McKinley wondered when Teresa had been born as they walked on.

*   *   *

The paper that Nicolas Weber had handed to his younger brother contained the name and address of solicitors in Chichester in the county of Sussex. It was the very city that Teresa had named as providing the opportunity for them to meet in October when the traditional Sloe fair was held. They studied William Godwin's 'Life of the Necromancers' for information on John Dee and even visited his house in Mortlake. Whatever remained of the original Tudor house built at the time of Henry VII had been incorporated into a public house called The Queen's Head and sat very prettily at the side of the Thames.

Weber had provided them with the address of the warehouse and with the assistance of the constabulary and the report from the inquest the lawyers might be prevailed upon to disclose some information that would enable Dee and his people to be discovered. The more that McKinley thought about the actors, and in particular Teresa, the more he was afraid of the resulting severance of the people from the source of their longevity, if indeed that was possible. Would she metamorphose into an animal?

The diminishment of the soul through a long life may have changed Lily but she had been with Dee since the time of the debauched court of Charles II, almost two hundred years. She had worked as a prostitute, but from what Seton had told him she was forced into that profession whilst still a child. That surely would have an effect on her character? In contemporaneous reports Dee was said to have been a gentle and charming man and well regarded in Tudor times by the court of Elizabeth, but the man McKinley had met was obsessed with power over people; and over whatever those things were in the boxes.

Teresa had said that she had been with him a long time and she had been cruelly used by a man before he rescued her. It was likely that she had committed murder to escape from her shepherd captor. She had sometimes been distant with McKinley and perhaps that was because she could not love him. He had wanted her to love him more than anything and he had to acknowledge that it might not be possible. If he could not save her then Mariel must be the reason he would find Dee and stop his dangerous business, whatever it was.

He was not surprised when one morning he received a letter from his old publisher, the one that had commissioned the penny dreadful illustrations and was trying to persuade him to return to them. But it contained another letter. He glanced at it then read:

August 30

Sir

I have been approached by a young blackamoor girl of extraordinary attire who importuned me on several occasions to provide her with your London address. As you know we are reluctant to breach confidence in these matters and I steadfastly refused.

However in light of your recent adventures, which you know are of the greatest interest to us, and because so importunate was she, visiting my office daily and speaking to anyone she happened to chance upon in the vicinity, I have agreed to pass to you a letter that she has apparently written.

To make matters worse she professes to being a regular reader of the magazine and regards it highly. I trust sir that this will not be a recurring matter.

Yours etc

Algernon Dalrymple Esq

McKinley smiled broadly at this description of Mariel and her persistence and he was relieved to have some communication from her. The letter was sealed and folded small within the other. The envelope read '*Only the hands of Robert McKinley can open this seal*' and was signed with a strange glyph. So she was now using magic; or she had become adept in the art of the bluff. He prised apart the seal and there was no flash of light or puff of smoke, but then he was the intended recipient and he did feel a tingling in his spine. Clever Mariel.

Dear Mr McKinley,

I have seen a newspaper and I know what happened after we left. I am so sorry that you had to go through that and the horrible thing that happened to Mr Seton and poor Lily. She was not really a bad person and could not have been kinder to me since I joined the company. I know that you will be worried for the safety of me and Teresa but I can assure you that we are quite safe. I cannot tell you where we are but you will not find us nor will the constabulary which we know are looking. You will not give up I know this and I will help you because we have not found the bosky and the others are pining for him. I am to take on ~~the~~ Lily's role in the Dream and this means I must learn how to handle them as though they are puppets. They are sad and unwilling to work and Mr Ede is angry and impatient with them which makes things worse. They come and hold my hands when we are alone but they are afraid of him. I want to help them and to do that I need your help. They are held in some powerful spell and must do as Mr Ede demands but the loss of Gil has weakened his hold over them and I am afraid that some of the frailer ones may die. They are fading. Teresa tells me that there is something called a ~~greemo~~ grimoire and that it holds the masters spells. He only has a few books with him and she says he does not have it and lost it some years ago. It must be destroyed to release the boskies. Please try and find it and meet us in October.

Your humble servant Mariel

McKinley read the note several times and took it straightway to his uncle who was both fascinated by the young woman who had composed it and intrigued by the revelations regarding the creatures.

'She calls them boskies, uncle,' said McKinley, 'what does that mean?'

'It means wooded or relating to wood. Can they be made of wood and enchanted into life, do you think?'

'The thing I saw on the roof, she calls it Gil, which I assume is short for Gilgoreth, that is what Lily called it.'

Ewart reread the letter as they sat at breakfast. He had obviously been considering the creatures for some time.

'Robert, you have said that you surmise they must be made of wood, fabric or metal, but wasn't that because you were assuming they were puppets? What if they are organic, for example, a type of already living creature that we have simply never seen before.'

'Alive?'

Uncle Ewart continued, warming to his argument. 'In the latter part of the sixteenth century explorers were discovering countries that had never been visited by western people. Look at Australia and its extraordinary marsupials. Have you ever seen anything like the duck billed platypus? If I described it you would think it made up of several different animals and yet it is completely natural.'

'So you are surmising that they were brought back on a ship, somehow purchased or obtained by Dee and then forced to do his bidding.'

'Well your young friend says he cast a spell on them. A pretty powerful one at that and recorded in the man's grimoire.'

McKinley asked, 'What is a grimoire?'

'It's a sorceror's book of magic spells.'

'And how is it that no one else has since found these extraordinary creatures in this mysterious land?' asked McKinley.

'Ah. Magic?' suggested his uncle. 'Perhaps he has kept it hidden like Prospero's island.'

'If he is capable of that then we stand no chance of defeating him.'

They lit their pipes and smoked in silence.

*   *   *

The next day he received a letter that further frustrated their efforts to find Doctor Dee and his travelling company. It was the end of August and the Mitcham Fair had been held and attended by an officer of the district with instructions to look out for any of the described members of the Prospero Company. McKinley read it to his uncle.

August 28

Dear Mr McKinley

We followed the trail of the Prospero Company on a progression south but that vanished at the Devil's Punchbowl near Hindhead. From that point my officers could draw no information from the local people. It was as though they had disappeared off the face of the earth.

However as suggested by you I have sent officers to the Mitcham Fair in the hope of sighting the man Jonathan Ede and members of his acting company. I regret to inform you that no one was found or had been seen matching the descriptions and drawings you provided.

When the young constable reported back he was asked to discover whether any new entertainment had been found this year. His enquiries revealed that a man selling patent remedies for boils and ulcers had done a brisk trade and he had never been seen at the fair before by the other stall holders. He searched for the man but he and his stall had gone so he was unable to confirm if this was Mr Ede or some innocent man plying his trade.

We will continue to watch for this person and his gang but I must conclude that the trail is now cold.

Yours etc

'Gang?' said McKinley, 'they are victims of this man's lust for power.'

'I bet it worked,' said Ewart.

'What?'

'The ointment. I bet if Doctor Dee made an ointment, it would cure any boils or ulcers.'

'If they have gone to ground we will never find them,' said McKinley. 'My only hope is that he would not leave Gilgoreth at liberty in this world.'

McKinley read through the letter again but could find no solace, and he sat drinking coffee and thinking of Teresa and Mariel. If he had been torn between finding them and the potentially damaging effect of severing the link between Dee and his followers, he was now determined to heed Mariel's plea for help in releasing the boskies, whatever they were, from slavery. His uncle put down his newspaper and said:

'It looks as though we should contact those lawyers in Chichester. Shall we write to them or pay a visit?' Before his nephew could reply he said, 'I feel restless. Let's pay a visit to these pettifoggers and find out why they need to keep everything so secret. Shall we pack and take a coach? I understand it's a beautiful old city with a fine cathedral.'

McKinley enthusiastically agreed but prevailed upon his uncle to take the train to Brighton and then along the coast to Chichester. They made arrangements to travel the next day out of the stink of London and through the beautiful south downs to the coastal city that had commanded the ancient harbour where the Romans had made a great base at the time of Vespasian. They found a comfortable lodging house in the South Pallant and took a turn about the city before retiring.

The following day they discovered that the lawyers' offices were not far from their accommodation and they were directed there as soon as they had breakfasted, passing by the old Roman walls to an attractive building of brick and flint that dated from the time of the Georges. The lawyers were called Penny and Penny and comprised a father and son and several clerks. One of the clerks, the youngest judging by his ill-fitting clothes and spotty complexion, bade them sit on some hard chairs, while he took their cards into the partners.

After a short while the youngest Penny emerged and attended to them. He was obviously impressed to have a gentleman in his waiting area of Doctor Ewart McKinley's academic standing, with so many letters after his name and he had read one or two of his books having an interest in natural philosophy himself. The ice thus broken, Ewart requested a meeting in private which was arranged for that afternoon.

'That's the easy bit done,' said his uncle as they left, 'now we have to squeeze the information out of them.'

'Perhaps we will need to threaten them with the force of the law to find out how much they really know. They seem to have an established legal practice, surely they would not want to be associated with the scandalous affair at Pitdown Hall. The younger Penny seems a nice enough fellow. We shall have to see what the older one is about.'

They presented themselves at the offices of Penny and Penny promptly at three o'clock and were shown into a cold and dingy room on the east side of the building that would have benefitted from an open window. Young Mr Penny stood and introduced an older Mr Penny who bowed and then indicated an even older Mr Penny who was sitting in a bath chair next to a small coal fire, It was August and warm outside but McKinley concluded that this room seldom became warm and was probably the recipient of icy east winds.

The room was lined with shelves on which there were volumes of bound law books and others that bore the deeds upon which the practice prospered. McKinley had agreed that his uncle would present their request, having the gravitas and the connection with the Mercer's Guild. He expected him to introduce their mission with subtlety and finesse, but Ewart had other plans.

'Is Penny and Penny a trustee of the Monad Trust? Or is it the solicitors for the trustees?'

There was confusion on the face of the youngest Penny and the older Pennys glanced at each other. Eventually the middle Penny said, 'My father is a trustee and the firm acts for the trust in matters of law.'

'If I were to tell you that there is a warrant out for the arrest of an individual in relation to an unlawful killing, and that we have reason to believe that the trustee is in contact with said individual, what would your firm advise your client?'

A flicker of alarm passed through the middle Penny's eyes and he turned to his father who seemed to be made of wax and sat staring at the fire. If they communicated it was by telepathy and eventually the middle Penny said:

'I would advise him to provide all assistance necessary to assist the authorities whilst serving the best interests of the trust.'

'That's gobbledygook,' said Ewart.

'Where did you obtain our name?' demanded middle Penny.

'From the Worshipful Company of Mercers,' said Ewart. 'The guild to which Doctor John Dee belonged in the sixteenth century and where he hides his wealth to this very day.'

The youngest Penny gasped. 'No, that's ridiculous.'

'Be quiet,' snapped his father.

McKinley spoke for the first time. 'Have you ever watched a man, your friend, being devoured by a giant snake? Crushed in its coils and swallowed whole so that he is driven to blowing his head off with a shotgun?'

Young Penny blanched and the others glowered but said nothing.

'We will find Dee and whatever he travels with, that is not human, but is alive. We will find them and you will have the might of the law brought down upon your heads unless you help us,' said McKinley.

The oldest Penny spoke for the first time, his voice was like the bellows of an ancient church organ. 'You'll never find him. He will have gone to ground, and he can stay there for years. You'll both be dead before he comes out.'

Both McKinleys rose and made to leave, then Ewart turned and said, 'He may escape justice in his hidey-hole, but you will not. I will bring this house of cards down about your heads.' They walked out and the door closed just in time to obscure the furious argument that followed inside the room.

As they walked back up the South Pallant towards the market cross Ewart said, 'I don't think young Penny had any idea about the necromancer and his alchemy. That was his voice raised after we left.'

'What did he mean 'he will have gone to ground'? I was told that they winter in the West Country, I suppose he might have property that they can hide themselves in.' McKinley's voice hardened, 'but he can't do that and look for Gilgoreth, so he must be above ground at least for the present.'

They looked about the small city and visited the cathedral. Then they retired to the lodging house to freshen up before taking supper in a chop house, Ewart grumbling about his digestion and insisting that it must not be late.

They were surprised to find a note waiting for them at the lodgings. It was from young Mr Penny and he wished to meet them that evening in a tavern in an area known as The Hornet. They wasted no time or energy speculating but found themselves an early meal and armed with Ewart's sturdy walking stick and McKinley's pocketknife that he used for sharpening drawing pencils they surreptitiously entered the Half Moon alehouse. They immediately attracted stares from everyone in the room for, as well as being strangers, they were not working men. The silence must have alerted young Mr Penny because he popped his head out of the snug and beckoned them over.

'I thought we had better meet here.' He closed the snug door and the landlord appeared at the serving hatch. They ordered ale and sat around a table in the small but confidential room. The McKinleys waited for him to begin.

'I have often worried about the client you mentioned this afternoon, the Monad Trust, but my father refuses to discuss it with me, or allow me to see the files. My grandfather has actually met the beneficiary, but it was many, many years in the past and I have always assumed that the named beneficiary Jonathan Ede had a son of the same name and so on.' He paused and took a draught of ale. 'Today my grandfather told me that the true beneficiary has always been Doctor John Dee under his assumed name, and incredibly he has perfected the method of prolonging life and vigour and still lives.' He searched their faces. 'I think you already knew this.'

'What made you decide to contact us? Are you prepared to disclose where the group has gone to ground?' said McKinley.

'They didn't want to tell me at first, father was very angry, but grandfather said it won't make any difference, you'll never find them they will be under the ground and every day they stay there will be many years in this world.'

Ewart gasped and McKinley looked at him quizzically, but they said nothing.

Penny continued, 'If I tell you where they have gone, will you promise not to involve us in the police investigation into the poor man's death? I read the newspapers and I know what happened. Terrible. Keeping dangerous animals should be illegal and those responsible must be held accountable.'

Ewart turned to his nephew. 'What do you think Robert? Are we obliged tell the constabulary everything we know?'

'Would they believe us if we did?' said McKinley.

'If you give us the location of his bolt-hole then we will not implicate your firm. I don't know what they might find if they executed a warrant on his Wapping warehouse, do you?' said Ewart.

Penny was flustered for a moment then said, 'As far as I know it just contains fabrics and possibly a few books that he cannot take on the road.'

'As we thought,' said Ewart, 'no wild beasts kept there then.'

'Good grief, I hope not, he would need keepers …. and it is unattended, I believe.' Penny slipped his hand into his coat and brought out an envelope. 'I copied this from the file.' He handed it to Ewart. 'It contains the poste restante addresses that we use when sending letters to Mr Ede. We are obliged to use a cipher, but I have no access to the code. I hope you find what you are seeking and that it does some good.' He finished his ale hurriedly and left.

McKinley made to rise but his uncle said, 'No, we must read it here. If it is stolen from us then we at least have the information in our heads, assuming our heads remain intact.' He opened the envelope and read the contents, then handed it to his nephew and waited for him to read it.

'There are seven locations,' Ewart said, 'all over the south of England, and some in the Midlands. Look, there's one in Worcestershire.'

'That may be close to my friend's family home, he will be familiar with the area,' said McKinley.

'This one is in London - Greenwich and also Glastonbury, yes I would have expected that. Nicolas said he and Edward Kelley claimed to have discovered the secret of immortality there and tried to sell it to European monarchs.'

They considered the seven locations and Ewart pointed out that they were all close to ancient burial sites or henges. St Catherine's Hill near Guildford had been spoiled by the construction of the railway tunnel and they were not familiar with the sites that might be linked to others: Salisbury, Petersfield, Findon and Kidderminster.

'Do you understand the significance of the years exchanged for days?'

'It means nothing to me,' said McKinley, 'but you obviously know something about it.'

'It is in the folklore relating to the fae,' said Ewart. 'And it is one day to seven years.'

'The fae?' McKinley laughed. 'You mean faerie lore? Magic?' He shook his head with incredulity. 'No, that thing I saw on the roof can't have been a faerie,' he whispered to his uncle, afraid of being overheard. 'I suppose it could have been a goblin but it was quite big.'

'Some of them are supposed to be the same size as humans,' said Ewart. Then asked, 'But you now believe it could have flown up there?'

'According to Lily, and its name was Gilgoreth. It had no wings that I could see ....' He stopped, 'But that means if Mariel goes into the underhill world it will be seven years before she comes out.' He thought in one day*I will be thirty-five and she will still be fourteen. Why is that so important to me?

'Assuming she stays for only one day. Robert, I suspect this may be part of the secret of Dee's long life and that of his people. The fae have a powerful magic of their own.'

'But it doesn't explain what happened to Lily – the metamorphosis,' said McKinley.

'Perhaps faerie magic will do that. We must go back to London and carry out more research.'

They left the Half Moon and walked back to their lodgings without incident and returned to London the next day.

*   *   *

The seats of the new first-class carriage they travelled in between Brighton and London were upholstered but still uncomfortable, and they were fortunate in having the carriage to themselves.

Ewart McKinley said to his nephew, 'I think one of us should go to Oxford and research the information that is held by the Ashmolean Museum. I read that Elias Ashmole acquired many of Dee's writings on the occult through his son Arthur Dee. I suggest you travel onwards and I will remain in London. There are some gentlemen I know that might be of use in this venture.'

'Ah yes, I remember the Ashmole connection.' McKinley thought for a minute. 'Uncle, it occurs to me that some of the acting company might have been his children, don't you think he would have preserved their lives too? None of them seemed to favour him in face or body. And Dee himself looked to be about fifty years but he was eighty-one when he died, and portraits of him show an old man with a thick grey beard.'

'The effect of his magic and the faerie influence might allow some 'glamour' to attach itself to his appearance,' said Ewart. 'I doubt we shall ever know. Did he move like an old man?'

McKinley tried to remember his impressions when he saw him in the churchyard at the funeral, he had a cane and moved quite stiffly. Yet in the caravan he seemed to be possessed of vigour, although he did not undertake the physical tasks of the encampment and left it to the younger men. He tried not to think of him with the women.

'Occasionally he seemed older but, as you say, it might be faerie glamour. Perhaps his son, Arthur did die a natural death.'

'Ah,' said Ewart, 'there is a story attached to that. You have read about Edward Kelley?'

'He was the disreputable man who became Dee's partner in persuading wealthy patrons to pay for their services as clairvoyants and who did the so-called speaking to angels that Dee then wrote down.'

'Yes, he was the skryer in England and on the Continent and Dee wrote down and interpreted his conversations with 'angels' or whatever they were. Sometimes Dee tried to make do with poor Arthur when Kelley was indisposed or uncooperative, and he was a troublesome man by all accounts. They were both married men and at one point Kelley prevailed on him to exchange wives, or rather to share their wives in common.'

McKinley said, 'That sounds unnatural ....' He felt the heat of jealousy. 'Do you think that's what they do now, in the Prospero Company?' he asked.

'It's not so far from the free love preached by William Blake, Robert,' Ewart chuckled. 'You're an artist yet sometimes I think you have the soul of a clergyman.'

'I want to protect and care for the woman I love, is that so strange?'

'No, dear boy, it is commendable. But we digress. The point is that Dee had no children with his first two wives and eight children with his third wife who was twenty-eight years his junior. In most societies having children is the natural way to build a support network. They may or may not have been his natural children.'

'But you would expect him to take one or two with him, assuming he knew what was going to happen when he entered the faerie world,' said McKinley.

'Exactly, 'assuming he knew what would happen', though the time disparity is a common theme in stories of faeries it may have been outwith his control. And faeries practice illusion with regards their promises of riches. They are known to be tricksters.'

'And we don't know how long he spent in the other world, if what appears to be one day is equivalent to seven years in the mortal world,' said McKinley. 'Historians think he died in about 1608 or 1609, no one knows exactly where he is buried, and his daughter was looking after him in London. He would have had to gain access to the other world.'

'That might explain why there is a London site on the list,' said Ewart, 'Greenwich Park would be easily accessible from the river and Dee's house in Mortlake was also on the Thames.'

'If he entered in 1608, when he is presumed to have died, he may have stayed for what seemed to be eight days and re-emerged into an England after the civil wars and during the restoration of Charles II in 1664.' McKinley looked at his uncle. 'Eight days for fifty-six years. If he was not fully aware of the disparity of time he may have missed the chance to save his family.'

'I don't think we can assume anything about that man,' said Ewart. 'Doctor Dee had disappeared before, in his lifetime, and it is clear that at that time, or subsequently, he learned something that enabled him to acquire a measure of control over it, or over the creatures that ruled the world he had entered.'

'The Fae,' said McKinley, struggling to accept such things. 'They were the creatures with whom he was conversing. So, when he was trying to talk to spirits, or angels, he reached a realm that we have known about through stories and myths for generations. He found something quite different.'

His uncle said, 'And has made it work to his advantage. Some people believe that faeries are fallen angels; but what we do know is that they exist in many different cultures and take many different forms.'

'Like the damnable .... sorry, like the poor creatures that Dee now holds in his power, wherever he may be.' McKinley stared out of the train window and it occurred to him that the passing countryside might contain thousands of unknown living things. He said to his uncle: 'You're very open to the possibility of magic, considering you have always been a man of science.'

'Not to be open to things you cannot see would not make me a very good man of science, Robert. The genius of Newton and others was to deduce the existence of things we cannot observe from things we can observe.' He paused and lit his pipe. 'Do you believe in God?'

'I was brought up a Christian,' said McKinley. His uncle coughed contemptuously so he admitted, 'Yes, I do, and no He has never spoken to me directly, but recent experiences have opened my mind to things that I could not have dreamed of a year ago.'

'Quod erat demonstrandum,' said his uncle, closed his eyes and puffed contentedly on his pipe.

McKinley closed his own and recalled his research into Dee's life. Why would he be digging up ancient sites in the seventeenth century when such artifacts were considered pre-Christian and the devil's work? Macey often lamented the deliberate destruction by pious local people of ancient stones and burial mounds, but Doctor Dee's imperative seemed to be a need for money. At some time he had petitioned William Cecil, Elizabeth's senior adviser, to give him permission to search for buried treasure. He alleged that he had a scientific method of finding it and this would bring much needed wealth for the Crown.

It was common practice to bury your valuables when there was no banking system. If it was buried in times of trouble, say during the many wars of the medieval period, then the owner may have perished and been unable to return. He remembered the odd fact that, in his diary, Samuel Pepys claimed to have buried his cheese when he fled London at the time of the great fire.

Where the original owner had been unable to return, because of death or banishment, it was considered 'treasure trove' and the precious metals and jewels belonged to the Queen under common law. It would make sense to try and do a deal with Cecil that assured Dee of his own share in the bounty.

The other circumstance was that the owner had deliberately discarded it, intending never to see it again and had no intention of retrieving it. Then it belonged to the finder. That gave McKinley some disturbing thoughts as it might include the robbing of graves. Did the necromancer dig up the recent dead to use them to talk to spirits or to avail himself of personal items that were interred with them? He thought of the man who had accused the woman at the Mercer's Hall of being associated with grave robbers and it disturbed him that Teresa might have been involved. He spent the rest of the journey gazing out of the window at the peaceful landscape, looking for ancient hill forts and burial mounds, while his uncle slept soundly.

After a couple of peaceful days at Ewart's house in London, McKinley was dispatched to Oxford to research John Dee in the Ashmolean Museum. He and his uncle were conscious that one of the older Pennys might have decided to warn Dee of the closeness of the investigation using the established method of sending messages to him post restante and in a coded language. If Dee was desperate to find the missing faerie, would he bother to check for letters from his lawyers? They must assume so and be prepared for an intervention if they came close to finding his secrets.

CHAPTER FOUR

The Ashmolean Museum in Oxford was opened in 1683 and named after its founder Elias Ashmole. There were exhibits on the ground floor and a lecture theatre on the floor above, but it was singular in having a chemistry laboratory on the lower ground floor, intended for the practice of alchemy. Ashmole was fascinated by the generally accepted science of alchemy and also by sigils which were talismanic objects that could be carried on the body and possessed magical powers. He was from the trading class and became a lawyer in London, married well and moved to Oxford at the outset of the English Civil War in 1642 where he developed an interest in horoscopes and astrology.

It was a time of great uncertainty and superstition, but Ashmole ultimately did well from the war as a supporter of the royalist cause. He acquired the papers of Doctor Dee from his son with the intention of writing a biography, but he never wrote it because at about the same time he inherited a substantial collection of manuscripts and curiosities from another estate.

The classical buildings of the Ashmolean Museum were familiar to McKinley from previous visits to Oxford and he quickly established a rapport with the curator of mystical artifacts. He was an odd young man who professed an interest in the work of the museum's founder, and that man's study of Dee. He proudly informed McKinley of this with little prompting. Mr Loveday was a thin man whose voice indicated that he was apparently of a similar age to McKinley, but was slight and pale as though he disliked sunlight, in contrast to McKinley's stocky good health. But he was delighted to show him the archive that was not on display.

'What are you actually looking for?' asked Loveday as he led him through the basement corridors.

McKinley had prepared an answer, 'I have been commissioned to paint a large picture of faeries and other supernatural beings so I am researching relevant folklore.' The young man stopped suddenly and McKinley walked into him, almost knocking him down.

'I don't think there is anything about the faerie in Doctor Dee's papers. He spoke with angels and used the sigil as a defence against the demons that he found whilst seeking them.'

'That's what people think,' said McKinley, 'but my patron is especially keen to explore the possibility that the fae are fallen angels, or angels that chose not to return to heaven at some point or for some reason ...' his explanation tailed off.

'Who did you say was your patron?' asked Loveday.

'I am not at liberty to say,' replied McKinley. 'He has an interest in medieval imagery, or older if possible. Possibly even pre-Christian. A reaction against the classical.'

'I understand,' said Loveday and tapped his nose. 'You need the Cadwallader collection.' He turned about and made off in a different direction.

'I think Doctor Dee is what I am really after,' McKinley said as he hurried to catch up with him. 'Burial mounds and hills that.. that...'

Loveday turned and said, 'Lead to the faerie realms?' he smiled conspiratorially. 'You want to try and enter, see what it is like, what they are like.'

McKinley paused, 'Well if it was something that Doctor Dee would have considered, then yes it would be relevant. He will be the main subject of the painting you see,' he improvised. 'Doctor Dee among the fae.'

'The grey folk.'

'Grey folk?'

'Yes they don't enjoy sunlight any more, so they avoid it,' said Loveday.

'Am I to understand from your knowledge that you have made a study of the fae?' asked McKinley hopefully.

'It is a neglected area and there is much material in the Ashmolean that supports the comprehension of these beings, mainly the writings of alchemists who sought to make contact with the realms above and instead uncovered the realms below, so to speak.'

'But not Dee?'

'Oh yes Dee, but he didn't leave much behind in terms of writings about the fae.' Loveday turned to look at him.

'But someone else did?' said McKinley.

'And you were too embarrassed to ask for it. Well, that is understandable, and in any event, we don't have Doctor Dee on the fae. But we have John Dastin's Dreame as part of the Cadwallader Collection and nobody ever asks for that.'

McKinley could not reply. He was bemused and running out of breath as he followed Mr Loveday deeper and deeper into the depths of the Ashmolean Museum so that he became aware that they had long ago left behind the modern, recently constructed basement. They were now in a warren of dark corridors with a stone floor and shelving up to the ceiling. It was dry and tidy but looked as though it had not been disturbed in a long time.

Loveday stopped and turned around. 'Welcome to my world.' He gestured to a desk, a lamp, a truckle bed and a large comfortable chair. There was even a spirit stove and a kettle for brewing tea.

'Do you live here?' asked McKinley.

'Lord, no. But I live in lodgings and occasionally I need to get away from them, and here I can pursue my studies in peace. If I lived here I'd be as grey as a faerie. Tea?'

As he made the tea McKinley studied the pictures pinned to the walls of the office. He pointed to a strange watercolour of tiny creatures that could have been, but were not quite, human.

'Ah yes. Sad case, poor chap murdered his father and is now locked up in the Bedlam. Richard Dadd. Interesting man, vast memory, but he saw too much so it drove him mad. You know the story of the midwife who was asked by a faerie man to attend his wife's lying-in? She did so and delivered the baby and as she lifted it some of the birth fluid got into her eye. She thought nothing of it but a few weeks later she saw the faerie man going about his business in the market and she said to him: how's your wife and the baby? He asked if she could see him, which she obviously could, and then he covered one eye and she could not see him. It was the eye that got the birth fluid that enabled her to see the faerie realm. So he blinded her in that eye and she never saw him again.'

'That's quite horrible,' said McKinley.

'They're not nice creatures, but why should they be? They were living in this land for thousands of years and then men came with metal swords and drove them underground. They don't like us and they won't do us any favours.'

'Have you ever seen one,' asked McKinley.

'Not to my certain knowledge,' the other replied, 'why, have you?'

'I think I may have, but I did not think 'faerie' when I saw it.'

Loveday smiled and beckoned for McKinley to take the chair whilst he perched on the truckle bed and they waited for the kettle to boil. McKinley described how he had heard singing and that somehow the moonlight was associated with this phenomenon and that he had seen a creature the size of a twelve-year-old child sitting on a dormer roof, three stories above the ground. It looked like an old man but grey and slightly leathery and wore a few rags. It had pointed ears and little hair, and long hands and fingers. He had seen no wings but was informed that its name was Gilgoreth and that it could fly.

As Loveday made the tea he seemed to be musing over what McKinley had described.

'I think it was a Puck,' he said as he handed a mug to McKinley. 'They're to be found all over the country and are able to fly, quite large too. Did you see evidence of any magic?'

McKinley was reluctant to speak further of the events that had occurred with Seton and Lily, but this young man was apparently well-versed in folklore and open to the supernatural experience, so he said:

'I saw things that cannot be accounted for without there having been magic of some kind. Can I be frank?' He took a deep breath and told Loveday that he was searching for Doctor Dee and his troupe of actors and actresses. 'They have been touring the country under the name of the Prospero Company, and I have reason to believe that Dee has captured a number of the faerie creatures and holds them against their will.' He observed his companion's face for incredulity or laughter.

'Held against their will,' repeated Loveday, 'and you could see them?'

'It's worse than that, they are being forced to perform as puppets in shows for the public.'

'That is interesting. One thing all the fae have in common is that they can be invisible to humans, and only seen if they choose to be. You said the creature on the roof appeared to be old.'

'Ancient and quite leathery,' said McKinley. 'I only saw the others and possibly Gilgoreth on the stage in Portsmouth performing in 'A Midsummer Night's Dream', and they wore masks and costumes.'

'And you say Doctor Dee controlled them?'

'He goes by the name of Jonathan Ede and if the rumour is true then he has sustained himself and his troupe for hundreds of years.'

'Fascinating,' said Loveday. 'I wonder how he caught the fae.'

'He likes to keep them underground and we know that he moves about the country between caves or hills that might give access to their world. They seem to have power to heal sick people, but do you know if the faeries themselves die?' McKinley asked, mindful of Mariel's letter.

'There is little about that in the documents I have seen,' said Loveday. 'The story of the faerie midwife I told you earlier is a bit unlikely as faeries don't seem to breed. Maybe they did once, before men came, but now their numbers are dwindling, they are moving away from populated areas into the west, into Wales and Cornwall. And the changeling story is commonplace all over the country. The fae take a baby from its cradle and replace it with an old or sick faerie. It's probably just an explanation for why a child has sickened beyond the control of its mother.'

'Why would they take a human baby?' asked McKinley, 'and what do they do with it?'

'No one knows, but John Dastin thought they kept them until they were grown and then they were sacrificed as part of a tithe to hell. You know the story of Tam Lin? He was a knight who fell from his horse and was saved by the queen of the faeries and lived in luxury until the night that he was to be sacrificed. Now, those faeries have monarchs and a class structure and ride around on horses, so we can assume they would be full sized. Dastin was a cleric and faeries were little more than demons to him.'

'Was he a contemporary of Dee? Another alchemist?'

Loveday stood and began rifling through a trunk of papers. 'These were collected by Obadiah Cadwallader. There are some of Dastin's writings, he lived in the fourteenth century, we think he died around 1386 and not much is known about him, but Doctor Dee knew of him and he acquired his papers from Nicolas Flamel in Paris. Am I going too fast?' He brought out a bundle of manuscripts on vellum tied up with ribbon.

'Yes, but please carry on. You have papers here at the Ashmolean? And you have made a study of them?' said McKinley.

'I have been translating them from the Latin. Are you able to read it?' said Loveday laying out a sheet in front of McKinley. The writing was tiny and spidery, McKinley thought it might have been written by the faeries themselves. It was indecipherable to him, not a scholar at the best of times.

'I think I shall need your translation Mr Loveday,' he said, but his heart sank when the young man brought out an even bigger bundle of papers. 'Oh dear, I feel I need to explain the urgency of my position as I fear there will not be time to make a study of these works. It is September tomorrow and I have been asked to find

Doctor Dee's grimoire before October 20th when the annual Sloe fair is held in Chichester.' He ran his fingers through his hair. 'When you were reading them, did you find any reference to a grimoire?'

Loveday shook his head, 'Oh dear me no. These are Dastin's papers. Unless Doctor Dee used a grimoire created by Dastin then we shall not find it here, and I do not believe he would have created a book of spells, he may have believed in alchemy but he was not a necromancer.'

McKinley wondered whether to disabuse him of this impression but decided to listen instead.

Loveday continued, 'But he read Dastin's papers on faeries and perhaps he found a way to see them and to communicate with them.' He began to burrow into the papers.

'I did find something interesting about an object that was used as a protection against faeries and was acquired by John Dastin and may have been of special interest to Doctor Dee.' He found a single sheet of paper. 'Yes, he collected stories from common folk and gentry alike about their experiences with the fae. He was told by a knightly family that before the Normans came a ritual was carried out at a river crossing place in the fens. It was a dangerous place because travellers and their horses were frightened by creatures from the other world, attacked even with what they called 'elf-shot' and the unfortunates were then robbed of any silver they carried. The ritual was a votive offering of a sword thrown into the water at the crossing point and it had to be a good sword and an heirloom and probably bore a name, such was the habit of warriors at the time.'

'Was this during Christian times?' asked McKinley.

'Possibly,' said Loveday. 'But the offering was not necessarily made by Christians. The Romano British were Christian but replaced by the Anglo Saxons who were originally pagan, then later converted. Apparently the ritual worked and the fae stopped attacking people at the ford and appear to have left the area. The interesting thing is that Dastin took men with him and searched for the artifact, and they found it.'

'What was it like?' asked McKinley.

'Much of the iron had rusted but the silver and bronze remained intact and the pommel was a hollow flask. There were no Christian symbols on it but rather a runic script that he has not translated, but he kept it in a reliquary as one of his treasures. Here is an illustration which I have copied, it is very simple. Swords of this period were usually heavy and required a heavy handle to balance them but some warriors carried lighter swords that they wielded with great speed.' He handed over the drawing of a pommel with flask end in silver and bronze.

McKinley stared at it and knew that he had seen it before. When Mr Ede had thrown Lily from the wagon his shirt had not been buttoned up and this had been hanging on a chain around his neck. Was he imagining it? He closed his eyes and tried to picture that awful day, the violence and the fear may have clouded his awareness at the time, but he had registered the amulet and part of his brain had stored it.

'I have seen Dee wearing this recently,' he said.

'Then he wears it as a sigil,' said Loveday. 'That is most interesting. The description says it is primarily silver and bronze but it has an iron heart. It would both attract and repel the fae. And the flask may contain something that has a special significance too. It might be the source of his power over them.'

'How could he have obtained it?' said McKinley, 'unless it was among the papers that Nicolas Flamel sold to him in Paris.'

'I have a theory about that,' said Loveday. 'John Dee's father, Roland, was a mercer and was appointed as one of two packers who checked all merchandise shipped through London and its suburbs during the dissolution of the monasteries. We know that his son always took an interest in oddities and, as the runic inscriptions were evidence of an older provenance for this sword hilt, it is possible that it might not have been disposed of like the bones of saint, on a midden, and Mr Roland Dee acquired the reliquary and its contents.'

'So the acquisition of the documents came after the acquisition of the treasure itself.'

'Quite possibly,' said Loveday and he sat back. 'There is another book you should read before you undertake your search for the fae. It is by Mr Jabez Allies and was published two years ago and sets out a comprehensive catalogue of the types of creatures that you may come across.'

'Do you have a copy? Can I buy it from you?' asked McKinley. The other man agreed after a little thought and explained that as it was printed recently he could acquire another. They agreed a price and then spent several hours discussing how best to search for the grimoire and how to deal with any fae McKinley might come across. He received the impression that Loveday was thinking of asking something, but hesitating.

'Would you like to accompany me?' McKinley asked eventually and Loveday said he would consider it but had to finish some curating he was in the middle of for an exhibition. His employers would not take kindly to him gallivanting around the countryside, if that was McKinley's intention.

In fact he had not thought much about what he should do after the Ashmolean, but as he was halfway to Worcester he felt drawn to see Macey at the family estate and to try and find any likely hills that might contain faerie folk. The latest letter he had received indicated that George was much recovered and that he needed to get out into fresh air as part of his convalescence.

McKinley left Loveday to his work and taking his copy of 'On the Ignis Fatuus, or Will-o'-the-Wisp, and the Fairies', returned to his lodging house. He had not told Loveday about the seven locations where Doctor Dee received his mail, but he was likely to be somewhere near one of those. He hoped to receive some news from his uncle and had arranged the same poste restante collecting points as Dee relied on. They had discussed trying to pass him off as one of the Prospero Company but even if they intercepted a letter there was no guarantee that they could read it, if it were in code.

*　　　　　*　　　　　*

That evening McKinley was fascinated by his book, in which Mr Jabez Allies had compiled an encyclopaedia of the world of faerie. Many were simply different names for the same creatures but found in all parts of the British Isles. They were gleaned from country folk who seldom travelled more than a few miles in their lifetimes yet experienced similar things that they could not explain and gave them the explanation of faerie business. It was only when he came to the Appendix that McKinley saw something that might prove useful if they ever found faeries that were not in Doctor Dee's power and were therefore invisible to the human eye.

The Appendix gave an alchemical recipe for an oil to be applied to the viewer's eyes so that he might see the faeries.

.... taken from Adams Work on Flowers, their Moral Language and Poetry.

We have a precious unguent prepared according to the receipt of a celebrated alchemyst, which applied to your visual orbs, will enable you to behold without difficulty or danger, the most potent Fairy or Spirit you may encounter. This is the form of the preparation:- 'R. A pint of sallet-oyle and put it into a vial-glasse; but first wash it with rose-water and marygolde water: the flowers to be gathered towards the east. Wash it till the oyle come white; then put it into the glasse 'ut supra': and then put thereto the buds of hollyhocke, the flowers of marygolde, the flowers or toppers of wild thyme, the buds of young hazle: and the thyme must be gathered neare the sides of a hill where Fayries used to be: and take the grasse of a fayrie throne; then, all these put into the oyle, into the glasse: and sette it to dissolve three dayes in the sunne, and then keep it for thy use; 'ut supra'.' Ashmolean MSS

McKinley was astonished by this and wished that he had the time and knowledge to concoct the oil. He would write to his uncle the next morning and give him the recipe to see if he knew anyone with the necessary skills, he was bound to have friends or acquaintances at Kew or who had physic gardens of their own.

In that letter he explained his intention to visit each of the poste restante addresses provided by the lawyer, Mr Penny. He would start with the one nearest Worcester, and he also wrote to George Macey and invited himself for a visit. There was no nearby railway station, so it was coach or hire a horse and ride out to these remote places. He opted for the latter and visited the livery stables to find a suitable mount and saddle bags for his luggage. When he returned to his lodgings, he was given a package addressed to him that had been dropped by hand that morning. It was from Loveday.

September 9

Dear Mr McKinley

I have considered your kind invitation most seriously but I am afraid that I have to decline. I am not physically suited to the adventure that must await you when you find what you are seeking. However I do have something that might be to your advantage: the Faerie Oil that is described in the Appendix to Mr Allies book. I prepared it some years ago in a moment's idleness when I thought I might one day need it. I enclose it. I do not know how efficacious it might be nor how long it will last once applied but I do hope that it is of some help. I would be very interested to hear of your adventure when you return to Oxford.

Your humble servant

S.P. Loveday Esq

McKinley was touched by the generosity of Loveday's gift. It was wrapped in a yellow cloth and was not labelled but he could see a cloudy substance inside the apothecary's bottle sealed with a cork and slightly crusted at the top. He shook it gently and the oil moved sluggishly inside the vial. It looked as reluctant to be applied as he felt to apply it, but this was better than nothing and he set about drafting a note of thanks and a promise to tell him about it, if he survived.

So far he had not heard from his uncle, and having decided where he was going next he was keen to start. The weather was still fair, but the nights were becoming longer and the wind cooler. The following day, having checked the poste restante he took his hireling from the livery stables, a bay gelding with solid cob good looks and a hog mane. He ensured that the animal's tack was sound and comfortable for both of them and rode out of Oxford towards Worcester.

The horse's name was Marshall, he was about seven years old and the stableman promised McKinley that he was as tough as they come, did well on his feed and never threw his shoes. He was bred in Ireland and could jump if McKinley wanted to take him over a fence or two. McKinley had no intention of doing so but if the horse had been hunting in Ireland he would be sure-footed and that was good enough.

They walked at a smart pace along one of the country's leading green roads, the drovers' trails that enabled animals to be taken to London for slaughter. He knew these were being phased out by increased use of the railways to transport livestock but there were still flocks being driven to markets. They saw the work of the harvest going on in the fields and McKinley wondered if members of the Prospero Company were hidden in plain sight working on farms and in orchards. They stopped in Chipping Norton and then Evesham overnight and by the end of the following day McKinley was drinking tea with the Macey family in their comfortable parlour.

'You look well George,' said McKinley when they were alone. 'Have you told your family what you saw that night in the church?'

'I have told no one and I would prefer not to be thought mad for doing so. As you know, the entrance to the crypt has been re-sealed with a stone wall and whatever I encountered will remain in that unholy place. I know there is something evil down there and if I tell my story then thrill-seekers, or worse, will find a way to open it. Please don't ask me to describe it to you.'

'Then we shall draw a line under it. But I need your help. I have told you what happened in August, and I must find the company of actors in order to ensure the safety of a young woman who is very dear to me. As an archaeologist you may be able to connect these towns with the alchemist Doctor John Dee, astrologer to Queen Elizabeth.' He handed over a sheet of paper that listed the seven locations they had been given by Mr Penny. 'A firm of lawyers that manage a property we believe belongs to Dee sends its letters to those addresses where they are collected by Dee or his acolytes.'

'You think that John Dee is alive?'

'Longevity was an ambition of the alchemist's trade. And yes, I am sure he lives.'

'What is the relevance of these towns?' said Macey

We believe the area contains a hill or some other natural place that is of importance to the fae.'

'Fae? You are seeking the realm of the faerie?' Macey smiled.

McKinley thought he was going to burst out laughing. He said, 'I have seen magic of the most monstrous kind George, and people I care about are in danger.'

'I'm sorry Robert, I should know better than to mock any supernatural manifestation. The servants and the local people hereabout certainly believe in them, at least until they move to a city, then they return with a newfound scepticism.'

'It seems that the faerie is a very old race that lived here before the country was overrun with men and in particular with iron. They seem to have travelled to more remote areas like Cornwall and Wales where the yoke of machines is more sporadic. As for being supernatural, that is a matter of conjecture. My uncle thinks this might simply be nature that we have not yet explored and, if they die out completely, perhaps we never will.' McKinley felt regret that he might be seeing the last remaining faeries in England.

Macey examined the list and said, 'These are all close to ancient hills, some of them were iron age hill forts and may have been used by previous occupants of this island, when bronze or stone was the commonplace tool.'

'We think they are bases that hold some significance for Dee and he may be visiting them to try and find a missing faerie,' said McKinley. 'The creature escaped near Guildford at about the time of the deaths of two people. Officers of the court and the constabulary have been looking for the Prospero Company but I believe the trail has gone cold and they are unlikely to pursue it for much longer.'

'Did the faerie have a hand in the deaths? Was it responsible?' Macey asked seriously.

'No, the creature and his fellows were held in some form of slavery, I am sure of that now, and he escaped to sit on the roof of the house and bask in the light of the moon. I saw it George and it could easily have attacked me but did not. The fae have the power of invisibility but Dee has somehow removed that from the creatures in his control.'

Macey stood and fetched a map of the country; he spread it on a desk and they studied it.

'Here is Greenwich.'

McKinley said, 'My uncle is exploring it with friends of his. We suspect that Dee has a warehouse nearby.'

'The furthest is Kinver, which is in Staffordshire and the hill is Kinver Edge a sandstone formation famous for its rock houses that are currently occupied by several families, I believe. You can reach it via Kidderminster.' He smiled at his friend. 'Perhaps you could call upon the Bartlebys while you are in the vicinity.'

'They were not so bad when you got to know them,' said McKinley thinking of his lunch with the trio in Portsmouth. 'They may not be at home in their new house yet. I must thank your father for the introduction though. It has provided me with funds. I doubt that I shall have time to call on them.'

They continued to examine the map and Macey pointed out that the locations tied in with fairs and other entertainments where the troupe might be working. The poste restante addresses gave him a link with the solicitors but there were probably many other hills and places where the fae might have been found at one time or another.

'If the creature, Gilgoreth, left the house you occupied near Guildford then presumably he would have flown to the nearest refuge,' said Macey.

'That would be St Catherine's Hill, but he could not remain there because navvies were digging a tunnel for the railway line to Portsmouth, and he is visible.'

'To the south is Petersfield which may relate to Old Winchester Hill, although there are many hills and ancient sites thereabouts.'

'The court officers said that he had travelled south before the trail became stone cold,' said McKinley. 'They may have stowed the caravans and disguised themselves, even split up to search for the missing creature. They would have needed to leave someone to look after, or guard, the remaining fae.'

After some thought Macey said, 'As you have travelled all this way we should look at Kinver Edge before you go on to any other place, I'll be happy to accompany you and visit the Bartlebys on the way.'

McKinley was delighted at the prospect of his friend's company.

'That's agreed then,' said Macey. 'Shall we start tomorrow? Is your horse up to it or would you like to rest him and borrow my father's hunter?'

McKinley was delighted by the chance to ride Saxon, a large chesnut gelding with a flaxen mane.

'I'll tell the groom to prepare them for a journey. I am riding the grey mare Czarina almost every day for exercise so it would be good for me, I haven't been to Kinver Edge for years. We will need to stay in Kidderminster and we can call in on the Bartlebys the next morning.' Macey left the room and McKinley continued to pore over the map. This is the furthest from London, he thought, so he would have sent a couple of men on horseback to cover the ground more quickly. He did not want to run into Avery and Walter, or even less strong man Thomas. They should arm themselves and he decided to advise Macey to find a pair of pistols for self-defence. He hoped they would not have to use them.

*   *   *

They rode out to a fresh wind as the days became noticeably shorter; their horses were lively and longing for exercise. McKinley knew that he would have to move down to Glastonbury if he failed to find a trace of Doctor Dee in Staffordshire or Worcestershire. They stopped in Kidderminster and McKinley checked the poste restante and found a letter from his uncle.

September 10

My dear Robert

I have received the recipe for the magic oil that you sent from Oxford and friends at Kew have begun collecting the flowers required for the potion. It should be ready in about three weeks' time. Are we expecting to see more of the fae do you think, or do you anticipate that Gilgoreth will have regained his powers of invisibility, I wonder? There have been no sightings of the troupe in or around Greenwich; I offered a reward for any news and nothing has arisen. However, I do know where the warehouse is; Nicolas's manservant and I went to pay it a visit to search for the grimoire and any other interesting documents. I suppose we were trespassing, but his servant dressed in the livery of the Mercer's company and I attempted to look as bookish as possible so that we would not arouse suspicion. There were any number of books, but none made much sense to me as they were written in a sort of cipher. It was foolish of me to expect the grimoire to have its name emblazoned on the front cover. I plan to revisit it with an acquaintance who has an interest in alchemy and a head for

*puzzles of any kind. Do be careful my dear boy. Give my regards to
your friend Macey when you see him.*

Affectionately

Ewart

He was pleased that his uncle was taking sensible precautions.
The servant McKinley had seen at the Mercer's Hall looked like a
former prize fighter and he had no doubt that he was engaged to
carry his master up and down stairs.

Whilst in the post office he had asked about letters for Mr
Jonathan Ede and he was sure that the clerk had reacted with
suspicion. He questioned McKinley's authority to receive such a
missive and he wondered if this had set alarm bells ringing and
would prove a problem. Feeling increasingly cautious he looked
for signs of the actors among the townspeople but could see no one
that he recognised.

In the tavern where they spent the night, they asked locals about
Kinver Edge, its history and whether there had been any sightings
of ghosts or spirits thereabouts. They tried to appear as a pair of
indolent young chaps looking for excitement. For a few pints, two
of the elderly local men were happy to oblige.

'There's the ghost of Lady Jane Grey. She haunts the
Whittington Inn.'

'She had her head chopped off by bloody Mary.'

'And there's the Faerie Tree where villagers hang presents and
messages for the grey folk in the hope of a magic favour.'

'That's the Witch's Tree fool, that's where they held witch trials
and hanged them, from that tree.' The old man gripped McKinley's
coat sleeve and looked at him through rheumy eyes. 'There's
another tree at the farthest point away from the village, where you
can see the Malvern Hills and almost into Wales. That's where the
faerie live now.'

Most of the conversation was about the machines being
installed in the carpet factories and the new-found prosperity of
factory owners like the Bartlebys. Macey and McKinley let them

talk and did not offer any insight into their own acquaintance with the family whose industrial expansion was providing so much employment to the area and taking people off the land.

The next day they set out again with the intention of visiting the faerie or witch's tree first. A few miles from Kinver Edge, which they could see in the distance, they approached a large set of gates and Macey said, 'Here we are Robert, duty calls. This is New Place, Bartleby's mansion. Let us see what he has made of it.'

They trotted up the drive to a grand neo Palladian frontage and sweeping stairs. A groom came and took their horses and the door was opened by a housekeeper.

'The family's not at home sirs,' she replied to their presented cards. 'There's only the missus's companion Miss Salter.'

McKinley winced at the memory of his pinched arm but felt it would be unkind to leave without offering his compliments to a woman so much overlooked. They were shown into the drawing room. It was bright and clean and not yet overstuffed with things acquired on travels like his uncle's house. He liked it very much and was, for a moment, taken aback when he saw the portraits he had made on either side of the large fireplace.

'They are temporary frames only Mr McKinley,' said Miss Salter as she entered the room behind him. They bowed to each other and he was pleased that she smiled as she greeted George Macey and welcomed him to her cousin's home. 'Please sit. Will you take coffee? Or tea?' she rang a bell for a maid and engaged them in polite conversation while it was fetched.

McKinley revised his opinion of her looks. She had fine skin, perhaps a little dry and it caused her to colour rapidly when she was in a stressful situation. Being Mrs Bartleby's companion was probably stressful most of the time and the position of a poor relation reliant entirely on the bounty of family members must in itself be difficult. She was probably no older than five and thirty and may have been quite pretty in her youth, but the bloom had gone and she was now unmarriageable. He was curious to know if she had had any suitors and what had happened to them.

To his surprise Macey and Miss Salter were soon chatting away like old friends about the folk of the county and recent events and scandals. They drank their tea and explained their intention to ride to the Edge and take the air for Mr Macey's health. She immediately asked them to have dinner with her that night and to stay if they wished. She said that it would be simple fare but nourishing and would enable them to spend longer at the hill if they desired. Macey was happy and it appeared that given the friendship between the two families it would not be an imposition.

They set out towards Kinver Edge and as they passed through the village McKinley could see how the old rural community was being brought into the industrialisation of the nineteenth century with the harnessing of the River Stour and the canal-based transport system. Any fae still in the area would be unlikely to remain for much longer.

The tree they had been directed to was an alder and was close to the village. It had cloths tied to the lower and a few of the higher branches, presumably with offerings or prayers in them. It was very much a human place so they decided to move further up and along the Edge past the troglodyte homes carved into the sandstone. They would ride to the part of the Edge furthest away from people and McKinley would apply the oil to his eyes and try to communicate with whatever creatures still remained.

He had the vial of magic oil wrapped in a cloth in his pocket as they followed the little-used trail up the heathland and among the trees. These were remnants of the Mercian Forest that had covered the country at the time of Alfred the Great. The horses had settled to their work long ago but as they left the noise of industry behind, they became nervous and suspicious of any odd-shaped plant or sound.

'They say that animals can see the fae even when humans cannot,' said Macey.

'Perhaps I should rub the oil on my eyes now. I would if Saxon would settle down, I'm afraid I shall drop it if I try to apply it whilst on horseback.'

At the highest point of the hill they stopped and found a clearing where they were able to tether the horses using the head collars they had brought with them. It was an eery place where the light had a bright quality.

'There's something wrong,' said Macey. 'I have never seen Czarina so jumpy, especially in the company of Saxon. Perhaps there is something in this fae story.'

They walked to the viewpoint and McKinley opened the cloth holding the vial of Loveday's oil. He was not sure if the oil should go into or on the eye, so he dabbed a little on the cloth and wiped it on his left eyelid. He blinked a few times and was about to apply it to the other eye when Macey grabbed his arm.

'Do you know these fellows?' he said.

Approaching them from opposite sides were Avery and Thomas, and there was no escape except over the edge of the escarpment. Avery was carrying a scythe and Thomas, a man of immense strength, wielded a large club. They were about thirty feet away. Fortunately the horses' obvious fear had created enough caution for them to bring the pistols from their saddlebags and load them, so they each had one in his coat. They were pocket pistols used for self-defence when travelling and they had received some training in their use from Macey's father. McKinley was less experienced. He fumbled with the weapon and he was unwilling to fire at Avery who he had come to like during their time together at Pitdown Hall.

The men said nothing as they grew nearer and they were not deterred by the sight of the guns. Macey shouted a warning.

'Stay back or I'll shoot!' At this Thomas raised his club and ran towards him. Macey fired and Thomas's legs collapsed as his body fell backwards. The ball caught him in the sternum at close range.

Avery carried on walking, but McKinley lowered his gun. His eye hurt and cloudy images were swimming through his head. Avery threw away the scythe as he closed in on McKinley and swung a haymaker punch at his head. McKinley blocked and ducked, then he pushed up the expected follow-through body blow and threw himself at Avery knocking him onto his back. The gun fell to one side and McKinley tried to pin his opponent's arms, but Avery was too strong and grasped his throat. He could not dislodge the other man's hands and he was afraid that his windpipe would be crushed. The only weapon McKinley had was the vial of oil in his pocket. He dashed the substance into Avery's eyes and hoped that it would disarm him with the sort of pain he was currently experiencing in his one treated eye.

Avery's eyes were open in a fanatical stare and took the liquid fully. He screamed and clasped his hands over them. McKinley breathed and pulled away, gasping for breath and staggering from the quick brutal struggle. Avery lay doubled over on the ground in great pain.

'Robert, are you all right?' asked Macey. He picked up the undischarged pistol and help his friend stagger away from their assailants.

'My eye hurts, but that poor bugger must be in agony,' he pointed to Avery. 'What about …?'

'He might die. It looks as though the ball has severed his spine so he will be no threat to us. Who are they?'

McKinley said, 'The big one is Thomas, and the other is Avery. I got to know him well at Pitdown and I liked him. I'm sorry this happened.'

'How did they know we were here? And why attack us? We were no threat to them,' asked Macey.

'They must have followed us from Kidderminster where I asked about Dee's post. The clerk seemed agitated, no doubt they paid him well. The rest we will have to discover when we interrogate them.'

'Aren't you going to hand them over to the authorities?'

McKinley grimaced. 'When Lily died she turned into a huge snake and attacked Seton. If Thomas dies, God knows what he might become. I am afraid that it would be impossible to explain the effects of magic to the authorities and they could be in danger.

Imagine if he became a wild beast, such as a panther and stalked the villagers?'

'The horses are still jittery but they didn't bolt at the shot. Why don't I ride down to Kinver village and hire some men to move them off the hill into a secure facility? Would you be all right on your own?' Macey said. 'Or would you prefer to go and leave me here?'

'I have blurred vision in my left eye, so you should go. But is there anything we can do to help them before you go?' said McKinley.

'We might slow the bleeding of the big fellow and wash the other one's eyes. I'll get the water bottle.'

They ministered as well as they could to the men. Mercifully, Thomas was unconscious and Avery stoically bore his pain but his eyes streamed. They tied his hands in case he recovered enough to be a danger.

After Macey left McKinley sat against a tree and contemplated the awful event. The water had improved Avery a little and his breathing grew more measured.

'Avery, I'm sorry this happened. But why did you attack us? You gave us no choice.' There was no reply at first, so McKinley continued to speak to him.

Eventually Avery said, 'What was the stuff you threw into my eyes?'

'It was supposed to be a magic oil that enables you to see the fae when they are invisible. I was given it by a man who works at the Ashmolean in Oxford.' Avery waited, holding his breath.

Avery said 'You used it on yourself as we approached. How do you feel?'

'That eye is painful, but I only put it on the eyelid.' He closed his right eye and looked through the affected one. Colours seemed more intense. He looked back through the trees to the clearing where Saxon was tethered. The big horse was dozing in the sunshine and McKinley could see the shape of his muscles and sinews through the skin. His perception was heightened, he realised. He saw the same things only with more depth and clarity. Even leaves had veins and flaws that he had not observed before.

'I don't see any faeries,' he said to Avery.

'They've probably gone west. We are looking in the usual places for Gilgoreth as he may be searching for his kind. When he cannot find them he will probably return to the boskies that Mr Ede holds.'

'Why did you attack us?' McKinley said. 'We had found nothing, we were no threat to you.'

'You have knowledge, so you are a threat to Mr Ede and therefore to all of us. Now you have the oil as well and who knows where that will lead. Already you have told too many people and once it is out it will never again be secret. Look at what Lily did, showing off to her lover. Her recklessness has released a bosky into a world that no longer recognises them for the natural spirits they are. Eventually some sportsman will kill old Gil and have him stuffed by a taxidermist and exhibit his poor body in a museum like a prize exhibit to prove the supremacy of man over all living creatures.'

McKinley thought he could hear the voice of Dee, but he knew the man had a point. Even human skeletons were exhibited for the so-called benefit of science. His uncle had spent his life collecting natural specimens, why should a faerie be any different.

'He does have magic powers to protect him,' he said. 'I could see him on the roof of Pitdown Hall. How long will he remain visible when away from the power of John Dee?'

'The fae are a very old people, they have lived a long time and have not been able to breed for many centuries. The longer they live the weaker their magic becomes so the more wisely they must use it,' said Avery.

McKinley thought about this, but he was unwilling to accept that the fae held by Dee were not his prisoners but in his care.

'Are you saying that by remaining visible they have lived longer and that Dee is preserving their lives?'

'He has preserved all our lives,' said Avery.

But at what cost, thought McKinley. 'Surely the fae have their own places under the hills where they can live their lives, as nature intended?' he asked.

'You know nothing about them,' said Avery. 'They like to sing in the moonlight and play with wild animals. They like to milk their own cows and ride on hares and play tricks on people as they go about their business. They like to laugh.' He stopped. 'Sometimes, in the old days we could let them do that. In secret places, but there are so few of those now, where men have trampled all before them.'

They were silent for a while. McKinley checked Thomas's pulse, it was weak, but he was still alive.

'What will happen to Thomas's body if he dies?' asked McKinley. 'Will he turn into a serpent or something else?'

'Near death is he? Then I daresay you're going to find out.' said Avery. 'I've often wondered what I will become when I die. I hoped it would be a bird but not if I'm blind. A bird has to have good eyesight. We heard what happened to Lily and that young man, terrible, but she was a passionate woman who gave all and took everything. We loved her and Mr Ede was wrong to cast her out, it was his anger speaking.'

'His name isn't Ede. He is Doctor John Dee - the alchemist, magician and astrologer who pulls all your strings as though you were his puppets,' said McKinley.

'We have lived long and intense lives because of him and we have to pay a price,' Avery said and was about to continue when Thomas began coughing and gasping for breath. His struggle did not last long before his death rattle echoed around the grove of trees. Saxon stirred and snorted causing McKinley to go and comfort him.

'I suggest you hide him somewhere out of sight,' said Avery.

'Why? Tell me what's going to happen?' said McKinley and he gathered the weapons together, well away from the body. 'It took several hours with Lily.'

'Was that a quick death?'

'I suppose it was, she broke her neck in a fall.'

'Thomas's been a-while dying. He might change quickly, it might have started already,' said Avery. His voice betrayed his excitement, but it did not sound like fear to McKinley. He, on the other hand, was terrified. He would have liked nothing better than to mount Saxon and ride hell-for-leather back to the village and the company of men.

He stowed the pistol in his pocket and dragged Thomas's corpse into a thicket of hawthorn and sloes, scratching his face and hands in the process. Then he retreated and Avery called out to him, 'What's happening?'

'Nothing yet. But his body was warm, almost hot to the touch,' said McKinley.

'Then it's started.'

McKinley retreated back to his horse and soothed him as he began to fret and paw the ground. They waited for what seemed like an eternity. A rustling in the undergrowth could have been a bird, but there were no birds singing and the only sounds were those of a long struggle. It was as though the wood was watching and waiting for some unnatural thing to be born.

'I hear it,' said Avery, 'and if you look with your enchanted eye you will see it happen.'

McKinley had no intention of getting that close. He cocked the pistol, and Avery chuckled. The noise grew louder and the struggle more violent, eventually he could hear it breathing, panting as it lay exhausted where the man's body had been. Another struggle and a massive snort and it was on its feet, trapped in the branches of the sloes and thorns, shaking its head from side to side. It reversed out of the thicket, twigs and leaves caught in his antlers - a magnificent buck.

'What is he?' asked Avery.

'A buck, fallow. Tell him to go, not to come towards me or the horse.'

Avery pushed himself to his knees and held out his bound hands. The buck walked to him, the dappled light shone on its fur and it seemed perfectly calm and at home in the woodland. It sniffed the man's hands and allowed him to stroke its muzzle.

'Thomas, my old friend, go and be safe,' murmured Avery. The breeze ruffled the leaves and the deer raised its head and sniffed the autumnal scents. It grunted in anticipation of the coming rut and then turned and bounded from the clearing. Avery curled himself into a ball and wept.

*   *   *

Macey returned with two village labourers who were happy to earn a few extra shillings carrying a wounded man off Kinver Edge. As they were loading him onto a makeshift stretcher Macey took McKinley to one side and asked about Thomas.

'I'll tell you later. Let us just say that he died and turned into a full grown fallow buck and ran off. I doubt that much will be found of his remains, perhaps just some skin and clothes, but they are hidden in the bushes.'

Macey said, 'Nothing you tell me surprises me anymore.'

'What shall we do with Avery? I don't want to hand him over to the magistrate's men and it will tie us up with the authorities when I really want to move on.' McKinley thought for a few seconds. 'We are expected at dinner with Miss Salter tonight. What if we take him with us and lock him up somewhere? He knows a lot about the faeries and Doctor Dee and I think he might talk to us if we can win his trust.'

'I assume he is completely blind,' said Macey. 'We can have a carter take him the short distance to New Place and decide then what to do with him.' McKinley agreed and eventually they rode up to the imposing new mansion with Avery lying in the back of a cart to the surprise of the groom who came out to take their horses.

'Shall I take him to the servant's quarters?' he said looked at the country attire of the young man.

'We need somewhere secure for him,' said McKinley, 'is there anywhere in the stables?'

'There's a stallion's box, never been used. I could straw it down for him, if he don't mind. Has he done something bad. He's not a killer is he?' said the groom.

'That will be excellent,' said Macey. 'He cannot see and is feverish; he could come to harm if he was able to wander around unsupervised. So he must be locked up, for his own good.'

Avery was settled into his loose box among the horses and a maid brought him water and Macey bathed his eyes.

'Is it still painful?' he asked.

'Not as bad. What about your friend can he see out of his eye?' said Avery.

McKinley was standing nearby and closed his good eye. 'My vision is almost normal in the shade but swimming with colours in the sunlight.' He wanted to say he was sorry, but he knew that he would be dead if he had not thrown the oil into Avery's eyes. He was being choked into unconsciousness.

A woman bustled into the stables with a rustle of petticoats.

'My housekeeper tells me you have prisoner, Mr McKinley,' said Miss Salter.

'I can assure you ma'am, he is not dangerous.' He moved aside so that she could enter the loose box.

'But he is injured.' She knelt next to him and examined his eyes. They were puffy and closed but she gently wiped them with the cloth and untied his hands.

'I'm sure this isn't necessary in here,' she said and gave him a drink of water. 'You have neglected your prisoner, he is thirsty.' She called the maid and ordered tea and some of the lamb they would be having for dinner with bread. 'I expect you're hungry,' she said to Avery in the most feminine voice McKinley had heard her use.

She stood and left the box and as she did so Avery said 'Thank you Ma'am' in his resonant actor's voice. Miss Salter stopped and turned, confused, then hurried away.

'What a fragrant lady,' said Avery. 'Where have you brought me and what will you do with me?'

'You don't need to know where you are, but you are safe, and we must speak with you. Have something to eat and drink and we will call in later,' said McKinley.

He and Macey left the groom with strict instructions to lock the door. The stallion box had bars to the ceiling but blind as he was Avery might still find a way to get out.

They need not have worried. They paid their respects to Miss Salter and explained as simply as possible the predicament that Avery was in – a young man accused of theft and now blinded by an ointment he had purchased from a mountebank to relieve painful styes. She was sympathetic and wanted to know more about his past. McKinley explained that he was a Shakespearean actor and so had a peripatetic life and may have been led astray. They ate a simple dinner and Macey and McKinley went into the garden to smoke.

When they did call on Avery they saw a light and heard him talking quietly. McKinley was afraid that the fae had found him, but it was Miss Salter seated on a three-legged stool, telling him about her brothers. He also had come from a large family it appeared, although it was unlikely he had told her when this was. She stood and approached them.

'Gentlemen, I have been telling this young man stories of my brothers, my youngest was rendered blind by a silly dare he had engaged in, he could never resist a challenge. But it was temporary and his sight was eventually fully restored. Good night Avery I will visit again in the morning.' She bustled away into the night.

'I think you have a conquest there Avery,' said McKinley. 'We will try to ensure that you do not die and turn into an animal to greet her in the morning.'

'You cannot protect me,' said Avery, 'whether I am alive or dead, if Mr … Doctor Dee goes underground into the world of the fae I will die if I don't accompany him.'

'Why?' said Macey.

'I am old and have already been close to death.'

'Then how have you lived so long?'

'We have spent some time in the world of the fae and I have eaten their food and drunk their wine. A day with them is seven years in the world of men.'

'I thought you had to stay if you did that?' said McKinley, thinking of the confusion of folklore he had read in Oxford.

'But we have also made a bargain with Doctor Dee to extend our lives. We become animals when we die because our souls have been paid as a tithe to maintain his power.'

Macey sat heavily upon the stool. Dee's remarks about Lily not having a soul came to his mind. 'A tithe. Do you mean to hell?'

Avery shrugged. 'I don't know if there is a hell. There are sources of great power beyond the reach of most mortals and the greatest magicians and alchemists have found a way to use them, at a cost.'

'And your souls have been the price of the bargain. Did you consent?' asked McKinley.

'I daresay you know Lily's story. If you were a young woman of one and twenty and you were dying of syphilis, hunger and years of abuse and a man treated you kindly and offered many more years of a healthy life; wouldn't you?'

'What about you Avery?' asked Macey.

'I was a sailor aboard Bellerophon at the Battle of the Nile. Nelson won the bloody battle but we suffered terrible casualties. They shipped me back home but my insides were eaten up with rot by the time I got to Portsmouth. I was only four and twenty, of course I jumped at the chance of a longer life. I wasn't going to end up in heaven anyway.'

'I take it you don't know what you'll become if you die in this loose box tonight?' asked McKinley. 'You must have seen the metamorphosis take place for others.'

'I have no idea. Perhaps I'll be a stallion and then I'll fit right in. That lovely lady can ride me around the county,' laughed Avery.

McKinley and Macey looked at each other at the thought of Miss Salter being described as lovely.

'I just pray to God I'm not blind,' he finished grimly.

'Do you know what Dee is planning to do if he can't find Gilgoreth?' said McKinley. 'If he does go underground where will it be?'

Avery shook his head. 'There are many places where the grey folk still exist in the hills. You'll know he has gone to ground when I age and die. So currently he must still be searching.'

'Will he go to the October Sloe fair in Chichester?' McKinley decided to put some of his cards on the table.

'Teresa told you about that didn't she? Her son is buried there so it is a pilgrimage for her, and it is usually our last event before we overwinter in the west.' He refused to confirm or deny that they would attend and McKinley was satisfied that Avery did not know what Dee would do. He was not even surprised to hear of Teresa having a son. He really did not know her at all.

'Will he know that Thomas is dead? Either by some magic means or because you have to send letters to him? Do you have a reporting routine that will arouse suspicion if it is broken?'

Wearily Avery replied, 'We only report by letter if we find Gil or hear reports of him being seen. He might be invisible again by now. And before you ask, no we have not seen hide nor hair of him.'

'Where have you been looking?' asked McKinley.

Avery hesitated then shrugged and said, 'Old Sarum and then Glastonbury. No signs at either.'

'Where does Dee keep his books?' asked McKinley.

'I wouldn't know. Book learning was not one of my strong points, hauling on a sheet was.'

McKinley was ready to give up the questioning, but Macey said, 'Where does he keep his grimoire?'

'I don't know what that is,' said Avery. 'He has a number of books and he stores them in lots of places. We used to joke that every great library in the land had one of his books in it, hidden in plain sight as it were.'

Surprised, Macey turned to McKinley who said, 'It is unlikely that anyone would understand them if they are in code, but they would be collectable because they have an antique value as belonging to another era, before the enlightenment.' He opened the door and they made to leave. 'Is there anything you need Avery?'

The man paused and said, 'Your prayers for my soul wherever it may be.' Then he said, 'Are you pursuing him for revenge at the death of your friend Seton? Or because you are in love with Teresa? She is a lost cause, like me; and revenge won't bring back your man.'

McKinley considered this and offered, 'I don't want Mariel to become a victim. There is no need, she can have a good life without Doctor Dee's bounty.' Avery nodded and turned away from them.

They walked back to the house where they had been provided with rooms and they talked quietly.

'It is likely that there are books belonging to Dee in the Ashmolean,' said McKinley. 'Elias Ashmole was collecting them before he died. I will inform my uncle of this information – that the books are spread throughout the land. He can ask his many antiquarian friends to search their local collections. I suppose we can assume he would place them in towns that he visited occasionally. But even if we find the book we have the difficulty of decoding it.'

'Do we?' said Macey, 'I thought you said Mariel wanted the grimoire to be found and brought to Chichester. Perhaps she has a means of using it to defeat Dee's magic.'

'She is a child of fourteen, in thrall to penny dreadfuls. I doubt she knows what it means,' said McKinley feeling hopeless and wondering what they would find when they looked in the loose box in the morning.

He woke late and found Macey in the breakfast room eating eggs and drinking tea.

'Did you sleep well?' asked Macey. 'I have yet to see our hostess but as we are both quite late she may be about her business. Have you had any thoughts on what we should do with Avery?'

'I suppose we shall have to take him with us, assuming he is still there. I am not keen on travelling with him on my own, it would not be safe, he was trying to strangle me yesterday,' said McKinley. 'Do you think there is somewhere at your parents' house where he might be safely held, or would you be willing to travel back to Oxford with me? Though what I shall do with him there I cannot imagine. The effect of the oil on his eyes should be conveyed to Mr Loveday. It has proved toxic and my own much smaller amount has rendered my vision suspect.'

'Have you seen any magic creatures?' asked Macey. His friend cast a few glances around the room.

'Nothing in this bastion of modernity,' he said.

After eating they walked to the stables and met the groom mucking out their horses.

'I've fed them sirs, so you might give them an hour or two before working them. They're fine beasts, proper hunters,' said the young man.

'How is our human guest?' asked McKinley.

'He's gone sir.'

McKinley felt an icy shiver down his spine. A snake would have escaped that loose box easily, or did this mean that Dee and his people were underground and lost for ever? He looked at Macey with despair.

'Where has he gone?' asked Macey calmly.

'Miss Salter came down early and said he has a temperature so she led him up to the servants quarters where she has put him to bed,' said the groom.

McKinley quickly looked into the stallion box and could find no residual skin or suggestion that he had physically changed so they went to the attic of the house via the backstairs, interrupting several servants in their gossiping. Without words they were pointed in the direction of the men's area and heard subdued conversation from a room that had its door closed. Macey tapped discreetly.

Miss Salter opened the door smartly to show there was nothing improper in their tete a tete and smiled at them with a pleasing flush in her cheeks.

'Good morning Miss Salter. How is our patient?' said Macey.

'I believe he will benefit from being away from the dusty air of the stables and I propose that he remain here until he is fully recovered,' she said.

'Will Mr and Mrs Bartleby agree to this?'

'They are away for the rest of September and by the time they return we will know whether the mountebank's ointment has permanently or only temporarily affected Avery's eyes.' She looked at the patient with affection and then said, 'I will leave you to discuss your business with him but I am sure you do not need to hand him over to the magistrate just yet.'

She left the three men together and McKinley and Macey stood contemplating the young man lying in the bed in clean white linen and propped up with pillows.

'It seems you have found a safe port in a storm Avery,' said McKinley.

'She has offered to read to me,' said Avery. 'I only had basic letters until Doctor Dee took me up, now at least I can quote some poetry to her.'

'You sound like young lovers,' said McKinley. 'You do realise she is a plain spinster in her mid-thirties and has lost whatever prettiness she might once have had?'

'Does she realise that I am a man without a soul in my mid-seventies and will crumble to nothing if the charm that keeps me looking like a man is withdrawn from this world?'

'She has a heart, and I would not want it broken,' said McKinley unhappily.

'I will be kind to her for as long as I can,' said Avery. 'I have a heart too.'

McKinley remembered the way he had stroked the buck's muzzle and how he had cried when the animal had run away. 'Promise on everything you hold sacred that you will not deliberately harm anyone from this household, and if you feel a change coming to your body that you will leave the area. You will not stay in the house and hurt people.'

Avery gave that promise, saying he would jump out of the window if that was what it took, and the others went downstairs to the drawing room discussing how much to tell Miss Salter. She was waiting for them.

'It is so good to have a young man in my care again, I used to take care of my brothers when they got into scrapes. He will be perfectly safe with me,' she said proudly.

McKinley said, 'Please don't become too attached to him, there are things about him that you don't know.'

'I realise he is wanted for theft and has not had a proper home for a long time but ….' She took a deep almost shuddering breath and said, 'I am accustomed to disappointment.' She blushed slightly. 'I always fell in love with my brothers' most handsome friends, and they laughed at me. Please allow me to have this interlude of friendship with an attractive man even though it must end in tears.'

As long as it does not end in bloodshed, thought McKinley, and he thought it again as he rode away from the house with Macey and looked back at the windows in the attic, wondering what would happen to the man in that room and the woman who loved him.

*   *   *

Much as McKinley enjoyed riding Saxon he was pleased to see his hired cob turned out in a paddock on the Maceys' farm. His friend was tired by the trip and he could see that some recuperation would be necessary before he could venture so far from home. It was obvious that he would be taking the journey back to Oxford on his own. They talked long into the night about the events on Kinver Edge and the apparent hopelessness of the task that McKinley had undertaken.

He had written to his uncle from Kidderminster with the information Avery had provided: look in a library for a book by Doctor John Dee. Look for a needle in a haystack. And if they found it, a grimoire written in cipher, what then? Somehow it must be passed to Mariel in the hope that she had discovered a use for it. McKinley bade farewell to the Macey family and heartily thanked George for accompanying him and risking his life in a fool's errand.

'I admit I was shocked by the suddenness and violence of the attack, but I feel more alive now than I have done for years,' Macey said. 'Promise that you will keep me informed of developments. I will carry out some research of my own into the sightings of unnatural beings in this area.'

They parted with sadness and McKinley rode a newly frisky Marshall out onto the road to Oxford and arrived there on 18th September. He was sad to part with him at the livery stables and considered buying the horse to enable him to ride out to the remaining hills that had been listed as close to the poste restante towns. He would need to spend at least one night in Oxford to explore the possibility that the grimoire was in the collection. It would then take about three days to ride to Petersfield in Hampshire from which he could visit Old Winchester Hill, a massive escarpment similar to Kinver Edge but comprising chalk not sandstone.

There seemed to be little point visiting Glastonbury Tor and Old Sarum if these had been discounted by Avery and Thomas. First, he must check the post office for letters from his uncle. There were two, and he took them back to his lodgings for consideration.

September 13

My dear Robert

We have made good progress here in tracking down Dee's movements when in London. There are three campsites he uses, among the travelling folk who take their shows around the country. He is generally well liked and his women and men even more so. Apparently he can cure most ills with his potions and his particular brand of entertainment, the Shakespeare plays, do not impinge on the money-making ventures of the other showmen. They tend to exhibit freaks and wild animals. They were curious about the puppets, several of them had asked to try their hand at manipulating them and Dee had always refused saying they were old and fragile.

The Prospero Company has not been seen since July when they left to spend time near Guildford. One man suggested they might be on the south coast where families take the railway to the seaside in ever greater numbers. I cannot believe that the 'bosky' Gilgoreth would tolerate crowds of people and children, but what do I know? It is probable that Dee has sent his people out to likely places to seek the creature in quiet areas as we have discussed, and is now touring a small troupe performing the traditional Punch and Judy to hear what gossip goes around among the travelling folk. I have offered a reward for information and hope to hear soon.

Affectionately etc

McKinley considered this before opening the second letter. What would Gil do? They had assumed he would try to find his own kind in hills and glens where faerie folk were said to live. If he could not find them then surely he would be lonely and seek out the only others he knew and who were in the care of Doctor Dee. There may be a real affection between the people and the fae in their care. Mariel said they held her hands. She must have an affinity with them. She was young, not much more than a child, perhaps the fae were attracted to human children. That might explain why Doctor Dee had wanted Mariel in his troupe, she would please the grey folk.

Another, less welcome, thought occurred to him. Avery had said that he paid a tithe to hell and it was that of a human soul. Could that be the price she would pay for joining his company? If so, Dee had mistaken her character. She would thwart him if she could, and her letter was evidence of that. He opened the second letter from his uncle.

September 16

My dear Robert

I was greatly upset by your experience with two of Dee's men and the violent death of one of them. Are you and George Macey unhurt? I would not have sent you into harm's way for all the world. Perhaps we should cease this hunt and let nature take its course? I have so many questions: did you see the corpse transform into a beast? And what have you done with the other man? I trust that he will present no danger to innocent bystanders unaware of his condition.

If you wish to continue then you should know that my book-minded friend has found a coded book associated with John Dee in the British Museum and my puzzle-minded friend has been examining it at my house. After receiving your letter we have made arrangements to stay at my club where security is on hand at all hours. Please send future correspondence there.

Do be careful and do not put yourself at risk.

Yours affectionately etc

McKinley thought about the woman he had left looking after Avery and sent a quiet prayer to heaven, or was it an oath? At least his uncle had found a book and he would continue his pursuit of a grimoire whilst in Oxford.

The following morning he went to the Ashmolean and surprised Loveday at his desk in the catacomb-like basement. The young man was intensely focussed on a book and did not notice McKinley until he was within his vision, then he gave a great start and almost fell off his chair.

'I've just come to say thank you,' said McKinley. 'Your oil has provided me the gift of magical perception. You would not believe the things I have seen after using your potion.' He placed the vial on the desk and had thought to tease Loveday some more, but he seemed genuinely terrified. 'Perhaps you are not ready for such wonders,' he said. 'How goes the search for the grimoire? Have you made much progress?' He leaned over the desk and looked at the book that Loveday was studying. It was in code and he tried looking with his augmented vision but it simply looked more colourful, the symbols did not rearrange themselves. Loveday recovered his wits and offered the book to McKinley who turned a few pages and sighed.

'I see the oil does not enable a deciphering of the code,' Loveday said.

'Sadly, no. And I don't see any faeries hiding in your office, although I should have thought it might appeal to them, being so buried as it were.' He looked around the office and saw evidence that Loveday had been industrious in his research. 'Have you found anything?'

'I had some luck translating the runic script on the sword hilt,' Loveday said. 'It's not complete but it comes from a Norse runic poem called ...' he struggled with the pronunciation and handed a written copy to McKinley.

Hávamál

I know a twelfth one
if I see up in a tree,
a dangling corpse in a noose,
I can so carve and colour the runes,
that the man walks
and talks with me. i

McKinley read it a few times. 'This is necromancy,' he said quietly. 'The user of this would be bringing the dead back to life.'

Loveday nodded. 'John Dee was very interested in speaking with the dead because he thought they would provide access to the spirits and to the mysteries that lay beyond this life. It was the ambition of all alchemists to discover the secrets of heaven and the other place if it exists. When he obtained this sword hilt he would have tried to translate it and, given that he travelled the continent speaking with people from many races, he probably succeeded.'

McKinley was reminded of the body-snatching that Dee had been accused of on the steps of the Mercers Hall. He wanted to know more about it and resolved to write to his uncle and see if the man's brother could be found. 'I have it on good authority that he exhumed a recently dead man in 1842.'

Loveday's mouth hung open and he flushed unpleasantly.

'Thank you for sending me the faerie oil. Why did you not try it yourself?' asked McKinley.

Loveday did not look at him and said, 'I am a bookish fellow and I do not travel much. As you found for yourself, there is no trace of faerie folk in the modern world.'

McKinley regarded him with new-found scepticism. 'You have used it on yourself, I think. It's painful, isn't it? Is it why you don't spend much time in the sunlight?' Loveday could not meet his eyes. 'Why did you send it to me?'

The young man squirmed in his seat and McKinley had an odd feeling of power that he was unaccustomed to, and which brought with itself a desire to be cruel for the sake of it. As he was striving to control this Loveday spoke in a pleading voice.

'I hoped you would find them and tell me where they are. I knew them when I was a baby you see, and they knew me. You must have noticed that I look older than my twenty-eight years and I have never been in good health. You can't know what it was like; I have never fitted in. My mother said faeries had left me behind in the cradle when they took her real child and that I was a changeling. My mother never loved me. She could hardly bear to look at me.'

'I'm sorry,' mumbled McKinley, his desire to be cruel faded.

Loveday looked up. 'So you see why I have to find them. I have devoted my life to discovering the whereabouts of faerie folk and finding a way to return to my people.' There was such hope in his eyes that McKinley could not challenge his unorthodox beliefs.

'Did you find anything that might be the grimoire?' he asked.

'I did not. But I have not given up looking and I assure you that if I find it you will be the first to know. If you leave me an address, I will write instantly if I uncover that most valuable of books. And I know that you will help me return to my people. You will, won't you?' He added hopefully.

McKinley nodded and they shook hands on the bargain. As he walked through the busy streets of Oxford, he felt guilty at taking advantage of this unfortunate young man whose mother had not only rejected him but tortured him with this nonsense about changelings. He wondered vaguely what the father's position had been, but he supposed that depended on whether he was a strong fellow or a downtrodden husband. Perhaps the mother was an unnatural woman. Whatever the family background Loveday had had a miserable life and was now pinning his hopes on a miracle.

*   *   *

He stopped in the main Oxford thoroughfare when he saw a shop selling paintings and stood looking through the clean shining windowpanes at something that resembled a Stubbs painting of a bright bay cob like Marshall. He had grown fond of the horse and was sad to leave him at the livery stables for someone else to use and maybe abuse. He liked an honest horse and appreciated his company. The cob in this picture had a docked tail and hog mane and was obviously a stallion from the massive crest on his thick neck. He stared out at the viewer in all his glory.

As McKinley gazed, his eyes unfocussed in thought, for a second he thought he saw a small man standing next to him looking at the same picture. His eyes focussed on the reflection and his face must have registered something because the man disappeared and there was nothing but the cobbled street to be seen reflected back. But he knew what he had seen. It was the same old face and clever eyes that he had seen on the roof of Pitdown hall. It was Gilgoreth.

He slowly turned and covering his right eye searched with his left for any sign of the creature. But he had gone and McKinley received the impression that he had flown quickly out of his view. He looked up at the ornate skyline of Oxford where pinnacles and gargoyles were common currency, he would be hidden by now.

McKinley realised that this meant Gilgoreth was now visible to most people and had found and recognised him. It must have been a shock to realise that he could be seen if he thought he was invisible. He needed a plan and that must be something that would entice Gil to contact him and to realise that he was no threat. It was almost lunchtime, and a bakery was selling sandwiches. He asked them to make him one with honey and he purchased a bottle of madeira and took them into Balliol's garden quadrangle. The men were not yet up at their college so it was quiet and as the gardeners went to have their dinners McKinley was alone in the green and quiet space.

He took off his coat and hat and laid down with his picnic beside him. The sun made him sleepy and he must have dozed a little. A light pat on the grass next to him broke into that sleep and he had the wit to keep his eyes closed in case he frightened whatever had landed. It might be a bird he realised and listened for the sounds of pecking and scratching. He heard fingers quietly opening the package containing his honey sandwiches and then sniffing and finally the smacking of lips as his lunch was delicately consumed.

'I hope you're enjoying that,' he said without opening his eyes. There was no reply and for a few seconds he wondered if a stray dog or pauper had taken the bait meant for Gilgoreth. Then a deep rich bass voice said:

'How did you know what I would like?'

McKinley slowly opened his left eye and looked at the creature. He was the same as he had appeared on the roof, old and greyish, but not silvery as in the moonlight, he had a downy fur that reflected golden in the sunlight.

'Something Shakespeare wrote: 'Where the bee sucks, there suck I.' I hoped he had got it right.'

'Very good Master McKinley.'

McKinley sat up, leaning on his elbows and looking around. 'How long have you been following me?'

'I saw you return to Oxford, but I was surprised that you saw me. You gave me a fright. Who gave you the magic oil?'

'I read about it in a book.'

There was a sound like swearing, then Gil pulled the stopper from the bottle of wine and began to drink it. When he had slaked his thirst he said, 'Tell me have you seen any more of my kind as you travelled this realm?'

'I have seen nothing of the fae. But I saw a dead man transform into a deer, and that I cannot understand. Can you explain it to me?' When he did not reply McKinley looked at him and was surprised to see that Gil's face was wet and he appeared to be weeping.

'My folk have gone. To the west, across the sea, or under the earth to sleep. The hares we rode are hunted and their forms are destroyed under the feet of men. Soon machines will do the work of men and beasts. We have no place here now. We are a dying race.'

'What will you do? Will you re-join Doctor Dee?' asked McKinley.

'You ask too many questions.' He stood up and shower of golden dust dropped from his skin and McKinley could smell the sweet decay of autumn about him.

'Please, before you go, you should be aware that at least one other in Oxford has applied the magic oil. A man who works at the Ashmolean Museum.'

'Thank you for that warning. You will find me among the gargoyles of Brasenose.' And he was gone, straight up, no beating of wings.

*   *   *

That evening McKinley wrote to his uncle and explained what had occurred. He was not sure that he could find Gilgoreth again, but it seemed likely that he would make contact and perhaps could be persuaded to accompany him to the rendezvous with Mariel and Teresa in Chichester in October. The book of spells still eluded them and that was what Mariel had specifically requested in her letter; he would need to redouble his efforts to find it among the libraries of Oxford. He also requested that his uncle make every effort to locate the man who had accused Dee of stealing his brother's body. The more McKinley thought about it, the more he was convinced that the man had information that was valuable. His brother had been a petty thief and he may have stolen something of value from Dee whilst in the company of the actors.

He spent three days searching the Bodleian, but without the assistance of someone like Loveday it was like looking for a needle in a haystack. McKinley had to admit that he did not have the mind of a cryptographer and he was quickly bored by the fruitless search. He spent each midday mealtime in the quad at Brasenose College carrying a tempting snack and hoping that Gilgoreth would honour him with his company. The oddly shaped gargoyles were all round him and he could see why he would pass unnoticed on the roofs.

On the fourth day he went to the Botanic garden and sat munching a meat pie and drinking beer without thinking of the faerie. He was disposing of crumbs to the robin that had edged close when he noticed a distinctly autumnal smell.

'Hello,' he said to no one in particular. A deep throaty chuckle came from behind him, and the bird hopped over to whoever was there. He turned and saw Gil holding the robin and feeding it a juicy worm. The bird tilted its head to look at McKinley and Gil imitated it, then placed it on the grass and turned to him.

'I suppose you want to ask me questions?' he said.

McKinley decided to go straight to the point. 'You remember Mariel, the most recent girl to be added to Dee's entourage?' He nodded. 'She has written to me and she says that the fae held by Dee are captives and bound to him by a very old spell. This spell can be broken but to do that we need to find the grimoire that contains it.'

Gilgoreth considered this and said slowly, 'If we are bound by a spell then why did I manage to escape?'

'Perhaps it was the effect of being in a church, it weakened the magic and you were the strongest faerie and you could fly,' McKinley thought Gil had made a good point that he had not considered. He continued, 'Mariel is concerned about the health of the other faeries, they seem to be pining for you.'

'We are all very old and tired.'

'Is that it? You have travelled many miles on your own and you look healthier now than when I saw you at the hall,' said McKinley.

Gilgoreth stretched his hands and feet. He managed to look clothed although it was difficult to describe what he was wearing.

'You could be right Robert McKinley. Perhaps hiding has deprived us of the energy that we would receive from the sun and the natural world.'

'Were you hiding or were you prisoners?' Gil said nothing so McKinley continued, 'Slavery has been abolished.'

At the word slavery Gilgoreth jumped up and stamped his feet. 'Faerie are not slaves, never, never. We work if we chose to and our magic is more powerful than any human machine. We are a noble people, we are a free people!'

McKinley became aware that visitors to the gardens some way away were now turning their heads and staring at him. They looked concerned. Should he pretend to be mad? Gil noticed this and quietened down. 'Just rehearsing a play, learning lines!' he shouted, impersonating Gil's deep voice as best he could.

Gil slumped into a heap.

'Mariel says they come to her and hold her hands. Does that mean anything?' said McKinley.

'They despair of ever seeing me or their home again. I must go to them.'

'But if you do then Doctor Dee will have won. Help us find the book and we will use it to free you.'

The old creature shook his head, 'I cannot help you; I know nothing of books. Faerie lore is spoken or sung, not written. However, if you find the book then I will stand beside you when you confront him. I feel stronger each day I am away from his presence. If I can free my people we will go to Wales or to the isles of Eire.'

'And what about the tithe to hell?' McKinley began to say but Gil had flown, up and away from him. He would have to pursue the grimoire with the help of human enterprise, not faerie magic. He had the feeling that faeries were elusive, never quite delivering what they promised, or you expected. With this sense of dissatisfaction, he headed back to his lodgings via the post office.

There he found a letter from his uncle written two days before.

September 21

My dear Robert

Thank you for your letter. How extraordinary that the little creature should find his way to you and you able to see him because of that poor young man's obsession with being a changeling. You must learn all you can about the magic of the fae and if it can be used to defeat Doctor Dee.

Nicolas and I have pursued the matter of the man who accused Dee of bodysnatching. There was a report made to the authorities when it happened. It was not a significant crime as such because the authorities consider that the dead do not belong to anyone, but if anything was removed from the corpse then that would be theft. It is unlikely that he was buried with valuables because the fellow had very little, and he was buried in a poor man's grave.

His brother stated he had been an associate of the Prospero Company but that he had left their employment prior to his death. There was some confusion over the reason why Doctor Dee might want to question him. Did he know something he should not? Or, perhaps given his previous history, had he stolen something of value? It is likely that necromancy, speaking to the dead, would be the only way to find the location of the thing that he had taken. Which means it must have been important!

The whereabouts of his body was never discovered. It was not found in any dissecting room and I assume you no longer believe that Dee reanimates the dead to use them in the manner of the Golem as in Mrs Shelley's novel - Frankenstein. But I digress. A complaint was made regarding the misdemeanour of interfering with the grave, so we have a record. No prosecution could be mounted, but it did mean that the name of the man's brother was recorded and using an agent we have found an address for him in Reading, Berkshire.

I suggest that I meet you there in four days' time. I shall be at the George Inn and I hope that will be enough time to enable you to complete your research in Oxford.

Yours affectionately etc

McKinley could have made the journey to Reading in a day on the railway, but he decided to see if he could buy the horse Marshall and ride him to the town instead. Apart from his attachment to the animal he thought it might prove helpful to have the means to travel across country when they were in pursuit of Dee.

If he was honest, he was reacting to the instruments of change, the iron rails and the noisy smelly steam engines and fast journeys made him wistful for a slower time. He felt immense sympathy with Gilgoreth and his lost world. He thought the artists he had known for a short time at Pitdown Hall were experiencing the same reaction to change. They yearned for the medieval purity of artistic form before the muscular Christianity of the renaissance. McKinley mourned the passing of a pastoral idyll in a rural landscape before it was carved up by machines. He conveniently forgot the daily struggle of the people who worked in it.

He wrote to George Macey that evening and recounted all that had happened and asked that he write to him in Reading. It helped to see it summarised and he wanted to know what was happening with Avery and Miss Salter. Had the Bartlebys returned and what did they make of the strange young man in their servants' quarters? For the first time he felt the hopelessness of the venture; the shock of the violent events had receded leaving the stark bones of his emotions. They had not found John Dee; Gil was thinking of returning to his captivity; they had not found the grimoire and nor would they know what to do with it if they did stumble upon it. Would he ever see Teresa again and could he save Mariel's soul from being paid as a tithe to hell? He went to bed in a state of depression and fell into a merciful deep sleep.

*   *   *

The next morning he woke as from a dreamless slumber and thought with fresh hope about the horse he had just purchased. He felt like a boy again as he packed up his clothes and books and went out to buy saddle bags and all the kit needed to keep Marshall comfortable. He even bought some apples to refresh them on the road ahead. The livery stable's groom had brushed him and he had been fed so he went in to his stall to check him over.

In the gloom he saw the horse standing very still, his eyes closed as though he was dozing, but his ears were alert and he twitched them towards him when he heard McKinley enter. As he got closer he saw Gilgoreth lying on his broad back and stroking his neck. He may have been singing but it was not a song for human ears.

'I'd be tying faerie knots in his mane, but he doesn't have one. It's a shame that men like to mutilate their beasts, docking tails and shaving manes. Anyway he seems healthy enough. I thought I'd better give him the once-over if you were riding him on from here,' said Gilgoreth.

'Thank you, Gil. And how are you?'

'Going along, you know,' he replied. 'As I left the other day you said something about a tithe to hell. I don't know what you have been told but this is an old-fashioned idea and dates back to the time when there were hierarchies of faerie and they were strictly observed. Each level owed fealty to the next one up, until you had the overall lord - Faerie himself. He is mightily powerful; but how can we pay our tithes when we have no homesteads and no access to the harvests. There hasn't been such a thing for many a year.'

'But you have been a ...' McKinley hesitated, '...out of circulation for hundreds of years. Someone like Doctor Dee may still practice such magic using his human followers as soul sacrifices. Is that why they turn into animals when they die? They have no chance of going to heaven? And do they have a choice?' asked McKinley.

'I wonder if I have a soul,' said Gil and crooned some more to the horse who whinnied softly.

'I don't want Mariel to lose her soul. When is it likely to happen?'

'My guessing would be calan gaeaf, you know it as samhain. The doctor holds to those old Celtic traditions. He thinks he's descended from Welsh kings. I may see you then.' With a final stroke of Marshall's neck he flew out of the stable, seeming to flit along the roof like a bat.

'Bloody faeries Marshall. They never give you a straight or a full answer.'

The horse lifted his tail and farted loudly. 'I knew you'd agree,' said McKinley and began tacking him up.

They left Oxford along a drovers' trail and kept away from the railway line as much as possible, the noise and steam and flying sparks made it seem like a dragon rushing through the peaceful countryside. The boats on the canal navigations were pulled by draught horses along waterways built in the previous century and were havens of quiet compared to the monstrous engines.

McKinley relaxed and enjoyed the fresh wind and good going underfoot. Marshall seemed lively and contented, he wondered what the faerie had been saying to him. They stopped at Wallingford for the night and he dreamed of faeries who all looked like Gilgoreth and enabled a horse to fly with them. It disconcerted him and he blamed the cheese he had eaten for the nightmare.

At the end of the following day he rode into the yard at the George Hotel in Reading and handed a tired horse to the groom for a good rub down and with instructions for his regular feed. As it was clear that looking after Marshall would earn a generous tip the lad jumped to it.

He was ahead of his uncle so he had an evening to think about their dilemma and set it in writing. He slept deeply and woke feeling refreshed.

CHAPTER FIVE

It was a different day that he woke to, with dark yellow clouds requiring the lighting of a candle to enable him to wash, though it was eight o'clock, and there was thunder rolling overhead. He had planned to walk Marshall about the town for half an hour to prevent him from becoming stiff after his work but that would have to wait until the storm had passed.

While he was eating breakfast he noticed an uneasy atmosphere among the servants and an unwillingness for chatter among the guests. He tried to engage them in conversation but they were reluctant to respond with anything other than politeness, and he sensed a certain coolness. He went into the stable to check on Marshall and found him munching on good hay in a fresh stall, his coat was gleaming and his tack had been cleaned.

He found the stable lad and tipped him handsomely.

'Are the guests and servants at the George usually so unfriendly?' he asked.

The boy's ears went red but he said nothing.

'Is it the storm?' persisted McKinley.

'Lord no sir. It's the hanging.'

McKinley sighed, it was a bad day to be in this town. 'Are they always so reticent on a hanging day? I heard that it was quite a public spectacle.'

The lad chuckled, 'They thought you was the hangman sir.'

McKinley laughed at this. 'I can assure you I am not. Who is to be hanged? And why is the town so inflamed about it?' He thought for a moment, 'It is a man isn't it?'

'Of course, sir. But it's an old man with a long grey beard, a stranger and a travelling man and people think he was just blamed for the murder because no one stood up for him.'

McKinley thought of Dee and his beard and age. 'Who was murdered?'

'A beautiful young woman. Her body was found in a hedgerow where the tramper had been seen earlier.'

It was impossible to avoid jumping to the spurious conclusion that Dee had murdered either Teresa or Mariel, and he began to worry. The lad had no more information about the crime, or the people involved, he had seen the drawings on the front pages of the newspapers, but he could not read. McKinley thanked him and left in search of a newspaper. He had never attended a hanging and believed that it could only serve to bring out the baser natures of people, but he would have to witness this one.

As McKinley went onto the wet streets he sensed the undercurrent of excitement. They might not approve of the hanging but that would not diminish the event as an experience to fuel gossip. Were not such executions held in public to keep the lower classes in check and remind them what the powerful would do if they broke the law? There would be preachers at every corner calling the sinners to repent.

He found a newspaper and cursed the cheap drawings they used to convey the drama of the spectacle. He could not recognise Dee from the image, or one of his young women from the melodramatic drawing of a girl begging for her life as a blade plunged into her breast. God, but this was worse than a penny dreadful. The hanging would be in public at noon above the entrance to the gaol, a recent building in the centre of the town. There were no names of victim or killer, apparently the old man had spoken only gibberish. Could it have been the ancient language of the sorcerer? A daguerreotype of the girl's body was available at the police station in the hope that a relative might come forward to identify her.

He walked to the police station but it was besieged by people wanting to see the photograph and being denied by the officers who sensed the mob instinct rising in the crowd. It was impossible to gain access and he went instead to the post office where he found a letter from George Macey. Although he was tempted to open it, the crowds heading to the prison to take their positions for the hanging were now so numerous that he did not want to read it in the street, and all the shops were either busy with custom, or shutting up so that they could attend the event or avoid the base effects of the killing on the roughest elements of the people.

He did not need to know where the prison was as the crowd carried him with them. It would have been a difficult task to fight it and he was glad that he had not ridden out on Marshall that day. The storm could still be heard in the distance as it headed for London, but the rain had stopped and the scents were sharp upon the cleaner air.

By and by they approached the prison gates and saw the scaffold built above them. The crowd was rowdy and diverse, whole families were taking the chance to witness a public death together, and talk was of the beauty of the young woman and the wicked nature of the person who had ended her short life. McKinley wondered if it had been a short life and found himself in turmoil because he wanted it to be an innocent young woman and not someone he had known, and who may not have been so innocent.

The closest places had already been taken by men and women who must have been there all night and were either recovering from drink or still drinking. The comments were crude and not suitable for the children of the better dressed working-class people who had brought their families with them. McKinley thought about the free mart fairs held all over the country and the shows that appealed to the lower orders, together with the debauchery and base behaviour they encouraged. The human beast has a taste for cruelty and death he decided.

A bell rang and a creeping quiet spread across the crowd. The doors opened and the prison chaplain came out with the hangman. The muttered word 'Chalcraft' went around the multitude with barely suppressed excitement. McKinley asked the man next to him why there was such fervour at the appearance of the executioner.

'He makes a great show, strangles 'em on a two-foot drop and then swings on their legs till they dies. Takes a while.'

He tried to turn around but there was no way of fighting through this crowd.

Then he saw them, on the roof of the prison. A dozen or so grey figures perched on the castellated roof like gargoyles. They were too far away to make out any detail but he knew that they were like Gilgoreth. He gasped and looked at his neighbour and gestured to the roof. The man looked and shook his head, edging away from him. It was clear that he could not see them. McKinley felt a surge of feeling that perhaps he would witness the end of Doctor John Dee. Silence fell again as prison guards brought the old man out, his hands tied behind his back. He was bald and hunched and even from that distance it was clearly not Dee.

The chaplain said a few words to the old man who seemed confused by the proceedings and smiled at the crowd. This upset them as they expected to see a murderous villain in the grip of remorse and fear, not a senile old man who thought he was being treated to a show for his benefit. He said something and the people nearest repeated it so that it spread through the masses until he heard 'Is it my birthday?'

There was a surge of anger from the mob and Chalcraft decided not to delay the death. He placed a bag over the old man's head and quickly fixed the noose that was already around his neck to the strap above. With undue haste he pulled the bolt and the trapdoor dropped. It was over very quickly; old bones break easily so there was little suffering. The speed of the killing was a shock, and the crowd were silent. As Chalcraft cut the body down a sound arose like the hissing of serpents and erupted into yells of rage, either at the obvious injustice or the speed of dispatch, McKinley could not tell. The officials hastened inside the prison, and it was clear that Chalcraft could not get away fast enough, fear was on his face.

McKinley was carried away from the scene with other members of the crowd and when he could he turned and looked at the skyline of the prison, but the creatures had gone. Had they been faerie and had they really come to witness the judicial murder of an old man? He must see the photograph of the victim for himself, but he would wait until his uncle arrived and tempers had calmed. It would not be safe on the streets of Reading that night.

*   *   *

He hoped that his uncle would be at the hotel when he returned and so he was, sitting in the waiting area by a fire and listening with interest to the gossip of a pretty young waitress. He had already gleaned the entire story of the case and of the hanging from her, whilst his nephew had learned nothing that morning. McKinley sat down heavily and looked at his uncle's smiling face. He felt that their ages must be reversed that day.

'What is the matter dear boy?' Ewart said.

'I have just seen an old man who was obviously not in his right mind, hanged for a murder he probably did not commit in front of a crowd who seemed to be out for a picnic. What are we doing as a society, allowing this primitive behaviour? And I'm sure I saw about a dozen faeries watching the awful display from the top of the gaol.'

'Really?' said the other. 'So many of the little people in Reading; well there is a large Irish community.'

'Look uncle, faerie like Gilgoreth are not little, they're about four feet tall and don't you think it is rather ghoulish to come to watch a hanging?'

'I'd say it's very human, and actually death is a natural occurrence.'

'But to take pleasure in it!' McKinley buried his head in his hands and rubbed his eyes. He could not get the images out of his mind. He ordered and drank a large brandy. He met his uncle's eyes and knew there was a lecture in store for him.

'Robert, I think you are a romantic. You have been brought up to see the best in people and, despite being raised on the family farm you have been sheltered from the acts of killing and copulation that make life possible.'

'Not for entertainment!' he protested.

'Nonsense, you've ridden to hounds. And don't mumble about it keeping the numbers of foxes down, the fact was that you didn't do the killing yourself. You kept your hands clean.' He called for two more brandies. 'Whether you are a hunter or a husbandman the beasts must die at some point, and if you live in an agrarian society then fecundity is also essential. Yet we pretend that coitus should only be carried out between husband and wife in darkened rooms. The next step is to hide the process of death itself so that no one will witness the passing of the spirit when a life ends.'

The brandy came and they drank it thoughtfully. Eventually McKinley said:

'Gilgoreth indicated that his race belongs in the rural communities and that their time is ending because men and machines are taking over the countryside. In fables they are said to be less fertile and that is why they steal human babies and replace them with changelings. Did I tell you about the young man I met at the Ashmolean. He is convinced that he was a faerie's child!' McKinley shook his head. 'Do you think they are especially attracted to death?'

His uncle nodded and took out his pipe and filled it. 'For as long as there has been human history there have been rituals of killing, and from what you have written to me you seem convinced that a tithe is still expected by hell. If there was a community of the fae in Reading they might see the judicial killing of an old man as a ritual and believe that such a thing should be witnessed. It sounds as though humans and faeries are not so dissimilar.'

He lit his pipe and the clouds of fragrant smoke dispersed some of his nephew's sense of despair. Today they would discuss their findings and tomorrow they would view the photograph of the murdered woman. The newspaper suggested that she was a gypsy girl and no one had claimed knowledge of her. It was likely that she had been dissected as was the custom with paupers since the Anatomy Act. McKinley knew that the old man's body was also destined for the autopsy table.

He brought out the newspaper and as he looked at the drawing, he remembered the sketches made by the artists at Pitdown Hall of Lily's body after her death and before her transformation. He wondered what the Coroner and his men would have done if this corpse metamorphosed into an animal. Kept it from the newspapers he thought.

Uncle Ewart's room had a desk and easy chairs so they sat there to discuss freely what they had discovered.

'The name of the man who recognised the woman at the Mercers Hall was Michael Flaherty, an Irishman who works on the railway. His younger brother Liam had been apprenticed but did not stay to qualify; he was attracted to the bright lights of the circus and the travelling community. We have found out that Michael now lodges near the railway line in Reading and I am sure that we will find him with a few well-placed coins.'

'I take it there is no sign of the book, the grimoire,' asked McKinley.

'I'm afraid not. As you know I made the journey to Greenwich in the hope that Dee had gone there, but it yielded less information than we had hoped. I didn't expect to see any faerie folk had they been around, the oil is still being brewed by my friend at Kew Gardens. However our enquiries at Mercers had given me the address of the warehouse and whilst we were down the river we made an examination of it. It mainly contained fabrics and lace. Apparently the furs had all been eaten by vermin and the cloth was held in metal trunks to deter all but the more ravenous rats, of which there were few. The Mercers Company sends a rat-catcher into the wharf regularly as they manage several of the properties.'

'You mentioned books in your earliest letter.'

'Yes, they also are stored in metal trunks and my cryptographer friend spent several hours perusing them. Some are written in code but most in a strange archaic language that appears to use metaphor to suggest meaning rather than stating outright the matter at hand. I believe the main business of Doctor Dee when in the company of his skryer, Edward Kelley, was the interpretation of instructions and information provided by spirits in the language of Adam and Enoch. As you can imagine, this is not a cipher that needs a key to solve it but a riddle that can have many meanings.' He brought up a leather case and produced two slim volumes that he handed to his nephew.

McKinley said, 'Was this in addition to the alchemy of turning base metal into gold and prolonging life?'

'Making gold was the art that everyone wanted to have, of course, but difficult to produce without committing outright fraud and using sleight of hand. Doctor Dee was in his fifties when he met Kelley and his contemporaries would have considered that a great age, so they might have been swayed by the claim that they had found the philosopher's stone.' Ewart stopped to relight his pipe.

'Spirits,' said McKinley, 'That could mean angels or demons, or I suppose it could mean the folk who were otherwise invisible and around them already.'

'Quite so. Kelley may have been speaking with faeries. It may explain why the messages he received were so varied and sometimes mischievous. He was at times incited to chastise the ruling monarch in European countries, which would not have improved his popularity.'

'What happened to Kelley?' asked McKinley.

'He and Dee spent some time abroad in Bohemia and Poland with mixed results. This was when they exchanged wives, eventually Dee returned home without Kelley and tried to re-establish his own fortunes without success. Kelley was knighted and given wealth and estates in Bohemia but eventually seems to have been found out as a fraudster, at least in terms of the base metal into gold claims, and imprisoned. One story has him knotting sheets together and climbing out of a window only for the sheet rope to come apart and for him to break both legs.'

'I have a feeling his faerie friends would have been quite gleeful about that,' said McKinley.

'Once Kelley was out of Dee's life the old man struggled to find friends, most of his contemporaries had died and then his children and wife succumbed to the plague and other illnesses,' said Ewart.

'But at some point as well as speaking with and seeing the fae he found the means to enslave them.'

'And your young friend Mariel says that this knowledge is found in a book.'

'Which we have failed to find,' said McKinley.

'As far as we know. It is possible that we have it in our possession and my friend is translating it as we speak,' said Ewart, 'let us not be downhearted. You have your appointment in Chichester next month and we will keep it. In the meantime, we must follow the leads that we have and tomorrow we will see what information awaits us in Reading.'

They spent the evening studying the books; one in a cipher and the other in the strange language of the spirits or the mischievous or malevolent fae.

*　　　　　　*　　　　　　*

The following morning they went to the police station and asked to see the photograph of the murdered girl. The duty constable was evidently tired of sensation seekers but the gravitas of Ewart McKinley and his nephew reassured him that they were serious in their concerns. He gave the well-handled daguerreotype to Ewart who handed it to McKinley.

'Is this one of the women, Robert?'

He took the print to the nearest daylight and studied the thin pale corpse laid on the mortuary slab.

'No, this is little more than a child and it isn't Mariel.' He handed the print back to the policeman. 'I'm sorry we cannot help you in identifying her.'

'We think she was a gypsy family's child but they usually look after their own with more care than this,' said the officer.

'May I?' said Ewart and taking out a magnifying glass he examined the corpse in detail. 'Am I correct in thinking that her hands were red and sore from wet work, possibly washing? Not rough and calloused from field work, or tanned by the sun?'

The constable scratched his head. 'I did see the corpse and that could have been the case.'

'This is a slavey, Robert. Probably put into service at twelve years old and forced to do the harshest and most menial tasks. Was she pregnant?'

The constable nodded.

Ewart sighed and continued, 'I deduce that she was put out by her employers with no letter of character and no box containing her personal possessions. She may have been trying to walk home and had been foraging for nuts and berries when she was killed.'

'She was found in a hedgerow where the tramp had been seen earlier,' said the constable.

'That does not make him her killer.' He saw there was no point in pursuing the matter, but said to the constable, 'If you want to identify her I suggest you show this photograph in the houses of those who employ servants, and in particular kitchen maids or maids of all work. If you do that you may be able to locate her parents.'

He turned and walked out followed by McKinley who had never seen his uncle, usually a placid man, so furious in a matter. He wondered if Mariel might have been treated in such a way had she accepted the position her grandfather had found for her. She was a beautiful girl and good company, he realised how much he missed her.

'A child like that should be cared for by her employers not abused and then discarded. They are as much to blame for her murder as the monster who committed the crime.' He marched off at such a speed that McKinley struggled to keep up with him. They did not speak for some time and eventually the pace relented and his uncle turned and spoke with his usual equanimity. 'Now Robert let us follow our second trail and make enquiry of Mr Flaherty about his brother.'

McKinley was not hopeful. 'I can't see why the young man that was exhumed would have stolen a book, surely he would have been drawn to steal money or precious metals or jewels?'

Ewart was more positive and chivvied his nephew, 'Let's keep an open mind. Here is the public house nearest the railway, let us enquire in there.'

At the cost of a few pence and the enjoyment of a few beers the McKinleys were directed to a lodging house in a recently constructed terrace. They were invited to wait for Michael Flaherty as he was working on the railway locally and would come back soon for the hot midday meal that the landlady was cooking for those of her tenants who could return for it. They might join the table for a modest fee and Ewart was very keen to do so as he preferred to take his main meal in the middle of the day.

They were an incongruous dinner party, a lawyer's young clerk, an elderly retired lockkeeper and Flaherty, a handsome man of about forty, who was a skilled carpenter, sitting down with an eccentric scientist and his nephew, an artist. Fortunately the big topic of conversation was yesterday's hanging and as each of the men expressed their opinions the McKinleys listened.

'Course I blame the peelers for taking up that old cove. He didn't know what was happening did he? Shame on them, I says. Could've been me if I hadn't been at work but just happened to be sitting in the hedgerow or thereabouts. They're not too particular who they take up, them constables, long as they get someone condemned,' said the clerk.

'At least that bastard Chalcraft managed to kill the old man quickly. I've seen him bungle more hangings than I care to remember,' said Flaherty. 'Did you see it Bert?' he addressed the waterman.

'No, I stayed away. I was by the Kennet and there was such a terrible silence even the birds were quiet. Then that great hiss that became a roar. I heard it after the deed and I swear there was a flurry of spirits across the river that stirred up the water. I couldn't see anything but something was moving about rapidly. Might have been fish I suppose.'

McKinley looked at his uncle, who was focussed on eating. Flaherty intercepted the glance.

'And you, fine gentlemen that you are, what brings you to Reading? Did you come to see the shame?'

Before McKinley could speak his uncle put down his spoon and wiped his mouth with a handkerchief. 'We came to speak with you Michael Flaherty about your youngest brother Liam. I am sorry to bring it up at table, but you did ask.' He said no more and they all silently finished their meals and went about their business, all but Flaherty who beckoned them into the yard where he filled and lit a pipe.

'So what is it you'll be wanting to know about young Liam? He's been dead and buried these many years, god rest his soul.'

'But he didn't stay buried did he? We have heard that his body was stolen and that you know who did it,' said McKinley. 'We are seeking that group of travellers to call them to account for their various misdeeds.'

'It was the Mercers Hall where you accused a young woman of having been involved, we traced you from that incident,' explained Ewart.

Flaherty pulled across some packing cases and brought out a chair for the older man.

'My little brother, the youngest of six boys and the only one to join me here from Ireland, was dazzled by the bright lights of London, the music halls and the glamour of it all. He drank and went with women who our mother would not have tolerated, God rest her soul. I couldn't control him. Eventually he saw a play by that William Shakespeare that convinced him he was in love and they accepted him into their cursed circle. From that time on he was lost to me. He travelled with them and became their backstage man and he was always good with horses so he was soon useful to them.'

'How long did he spend with them?' asked McKinley.

'About six months, from April to October and he was travelling all over the countryside. Something happened at one of the fairs, I think he fought for money in a bare-knuckle ring and there was a scandal. Liam wasn't above pulling a fast one. After that, the relationship with the troupe was not the same. Liam was no great penman, but he passed a message to me via a mutual friend who travelled the country as a tinker. He said things were going to change, they had something in store for him and he expected to be richer as a result. Ever the one for the money was Liam.'

They waited for him to continue.

'Next thing I heard he was dead, knocked down by a horse and cart in Greenwich and waiting burial, the authorities had found me because I was expected to pay the burial cost. Then, less than twenty-four hours after his grave was covered in, it had been dug up. This desecration was witnessed by a little lad sleeping in the graveyard. He described exactly the people that my brother had been travelling with, and very distinctive they were. The women so beautiful even the lad noticed them. They took his body away and, though I searched the dissecting tables I could find no trace of him. What did they want him for, I ask you?'

McKinley and his uncle had discussed how much they would tell Michael Flaherty about Doctor Dee and his necromancy and because they wanted to know what Liam had stolen they would have to reveal the purpose of his disinterment. Ewart spoke.

'We think that Liam took something important from Mr Ede the troupe leader and they may have looking for that thing.'

'But he was buried with nothing but the clothes he wore,' said Flaherty.

'Have you heard of necromancy?' said Ewart.

Flaherty crossed himself and said, 'Tis the work of the devil, communing with the dead.'

'We think that is what they were about.'

'Jesus, Mary, Joseph, what fiends did my little brother get mixed up with?'

'Do you know what it was that he took? I believe that you made some enquiry into the circumstances of his death,' said McKinley.

'Are you saying they disturbed his rest to question him from beyond the grave? That even his soul was not allowed to rest in peace?' raged Flaherty standing and pacing in his distress.

'At least he still had his soul when he died. If our suspicions are correct then it was intended his soul would have been offered to hell as part of some bargain that had been struck many years ago,' said Ewart quietly.

There was a terrible silence as that statement was understood.

Flaherty said, 'They were going to kill him as a sacrifice?'

'Not exactly, we think that the soul is given up but the body remains alive, at least for some time, but after death there is no redemption and the person is more like an animal.' McKinley spoke gently. 'They did not do it and your brother died as a human being.'

'But they dragged his spirit back to account for what he had done. They are blasphemers.' He continued. 'If you are trying to bring these people to justice I will tell you everything that I know.' He sat again and with an effort, composed himself. 'From talking with his drinking companions I believe that he did take a book. Took it because the cover was encrusted with jewels and bound with gold and silver. He bragged about it when he had the drink taken.'

'What happened to it?' asked Ewart.

'He sold it to a receiver of stolen goods. I went to the man's shop, he was a pawnbroker, but I wasn't able to talk to him because all I found was a burnt-out shell. The man had been in it apparently,' said Flaherty.

Ewart looked at his nephew. 'We have to assume that they retrieved it and then destroyed the evidence of its existence by killing the pawnbroker.'

'What in the name of God was it that Liam took?' asked Flaherty quietly.

'Do you know what a grimoire is?' The other man shook his head. 'It's a book of spells and we believe that this man Ede has power over several ...' McKinley hesitated '... grey folk. We call them the fae.'

'Faeries? You mean like leprechauns?' Flaherty's face was a mixture of scorn and anger.

Ewart quickly said: 'We would not be wasting our time here in Reading if we did not have evidence that they exist and that they are held by the travelling folk.' He leaned forward, 'You are evidently a god-fearing man and you have answered our questions. We will not take up any more of your time.' He stood and so did his nephew.

They were in the process of leaving when Flaherty said, 'Wait. I will take you to the pawn shop. I have some business in London. All I ask is that if you find what happened to my brother you will tell me where to find his remains.'

Ewart nodded, and they arranged to meet the following morning to take the train into London. As uncle and nephew walked back to the George Hotel they agreed that McKinley would ride down to Chichester and take a look at the outlying area. He would contact the youngest Mr Penny at the lawyers' offices and try to find out if Dee had been in touch. They would need to be on their guard, he may have heard about Thomas and Avery by now and he still had two men to do his bidding and the blonde woman Katherine.

McKinley did not fear Mariel and he hoped Teresa could not be forced to act against them.

McKinley accompanied his uncle to the railway station the next day and they met Michael Flaherty there. After a slightly awkward exchange the Irishman agreed to ride in the first-class carriage rather than in the open third-class one as Ewart convinced him that they had much to discuss.

*   *   *

McKinley set off from Reading the same day on Marshall who had been walked about by the stable lad but was keen to get out of the noisy city and the stink of the tanneries. The hearts of both man and beast were uplifted as they moved through the water meadows south of the town and crossed the gentle rolling countryside, past the estate of the Duke of Wellington towards the South Downs. The weather stayed fair until he reached Odiham where he stayed the night and the following day a storm blew in and began painting with the brush strokes of autumn colour on the changing landscape.

The going became harder and he spent three more days before he came within sight of the spire of Chichester cathedral as they descended through the heavily wooded countryside. He was very glad to hand over Marshall to the stable boy at his inn and to change out of wet clothes. He decided to recover before seeking the post office and calling on Mr Penny.

When he woke the next day it was to a sore throat and a temperature. He went to the stables to make sure that Marshall was well looked after and he searched for any sign of Gil. It was warm in the stable and the horse whinnied when he saw him. The young lad appeared and assured McKinley that he would walk him and keep an eye on him. Wrapping up in as many clothes as he had that were dry he quickly called on the post master and collected one letter to take back to the hotel where he had hot water bottles and tea and toast sent to his room. He regretted his venture outside as he felt worse, was running a fever, and took to his bed.

He stayed there for four days, neglecting the search for Doctor Dee, receiving messages via the stable lad to the annoyance of the hotel manager. Another letter from his uncle arrived. He reread the first one.

September 30

My dear Robert

Mr Flaherty and I had a safe and uneventful journey to London and he has now gone about his business in the East End. I feel sympathy for the man, apart from the horror of his brother's death he had lost his wife many years ago when their son was born. His son has been raised by a cousin and is now ready to start working so he needs his father's guidance. Flaherty is a skilled man but the Irish immigrants are now blamed by the English working class because their increasing numbers are driving down wages for unskilled men. Add to this his own situation in which a number of his family members who came to work on the harvest now find themselves with no form of livelihood and he is the mainstay of financial support for a growing number of people who have varying degrees of independence. The famine in Ireland has not been relieved by the scant aid provided by the government and there are many more deaths from starvation than we see reported in the newspapers.

I have asked an antiquarian friend to assist in the investigation into the pawnbroker as he may have some information on the book. He tells me that there are collectors who do not advertise their acquisitions because they have been gained through nefarious activities. It is possible that Dee did not find it.

I will write again when I have more information.

Yours affectionately etc

McKinley opened the second letter and was shocked by the writing. His uncle's usual precise script was untidy and appeared to have been written in haste.

October 6

My dear Robert

I trust that you are well. Please take care when going about your business in Chichester. The cryptographer friend I told you about has been badly beaten by unknown assailants. He was working in the library of the British Museum on some of the encoded books I told you about when he was attacked at his desk. He is an elderly man and I am not sure that he will recover. I feel very guilty. An older man engaged the servant whilst a younger man did the dreadful deed. The book he was decrypting was stolen as were several others from the same collection.

I have been to see him, poor fellow, as white as the sheets in which he lay with dark bruises on his face and hands. He saw the man, a good looking fellow, briefly before his spectacles were ripped off his face and two punches landed. That was all it took to knock him unconscious. The servant found him face down in his own blood and the work he had been engaged in was gone. We must deduce that these were Dee's men and that the stakes have been raised higher. You must take precautions, you know what they are capable of.

I met with Flaherty and he suggested, very sensibly, that the book his brother stole may still be at large and they are desperate to stop us from finding it. We followed my antiquarian friend to several houses where apparently respectable gentlemen became furtive at being asked about their purchases of books six years ago. I was very grateful to have Flaherty with me as he is a substantial fit looking man and renders me less of a target.

Eventually we narrowed the likely receiver of the book to an eccentric man known to only the most dedicated of antiquarians as a collector and we visit him tomorrow. I will not give you his name in case this letter is intercepted but I have lodged it in an envelope with my lawyer, should anything happen to me. I will write again with news. Be safe.

Yours affectionately etc

McKinley was now worried about his uncle's safety and regretted getting him involved in the matter, not to mention feeling remorse at the attack on his elderly friend. He had been lying in bed nursing a head cold while they were risking their safety working on his behalf. He resolved to get off his sick bed and make contact with Mr Penny today. He left a sealed letter at the offices of the lawyers with a request to meet that evening in the Half Moon and acquaint him with the seriousness of the matter. Penny did not show up, and he was driven to keeping watch on the office the next day from a local tavern, but saw no one resembling the young lawyer, although the middle-aged man came and went. There was no sign of the old man.

At about dinner time one of the clerks that McKinley recognised came out into the street and, turning up his collar against the cold wind, went towards the city centre. He caught up with him after a few minutes, out of sight of the office.

'Excuse me, are you one of the lawyers' clerks at Penny and Penny?'

'Who wants to know?' the young man said nervously looking around.

'You may remember me. I came in the summer with my uncle and had a meeting with the Pennys,' said McKinley.

'I remember you and I can't talk to you, on pain of my job.'

'I just want to talk to young Mr Penny.'

'Good luck with that. Nobody knows where he is.' He saw that he was not going to get away without a fuss being made so he said, 'Come into this courtyard.' They turned down an alleyway and arrived into a small physic garden with benches, but currently no visitors, and they sat down away from the biting wind. The clerk continued, 'Just after you left, Mr David, as we call him, that's young Mr Penny to you, began courting. He had been loosely promised to a clergyman's daughter, but his head was turned by this new woman, and he broke that match so that he might marry the new one.'

'Redhead?' said McKinley.

'Blonde,' said the clerk. 'His father and grandfather were furious and warned him that she was just toying with him. Threatened to throw him out of the firm unless he ceased and desisted from seeing her.'

McKinley waited, 'What happened?'

'They eloped, if that's what you can call it when people in their twenties run away together, that was two weeks ago. It's affected the old one particularly badly and he's been seen by a doctor and a clergyman. Of course, if he doesn't return they will be looking to take on a new partner; not that it will help me, I can't afford to buy into the practice.'

'Do they expect him to return?'

'His father says he expects there will be a reconciliation, but the old man swears that his soul will be lost and his body will soon follow. Now you must go, I will stay here until I am sure no one can have seen me with you. They blame you for this! You and the Monad Trust!'

The young man folded his arms and firmly turned away from McKinley so that he had no choice but to leave. And every step of the way back to his lodgings he felt that someone was watching him. He went straightway to see Marshall and to arrange a hack for that afternoon. They both needed some exercise and the dry weather was the time to take it. McKinley asked the lad where was the most interesting country and he suggested a ride along the Lavant river that found its way through the city from the north by passing through Summerstown. That way he could avoid the railway to the south.

He then pointed out that the Sloe fair would be held just outside the North Gate in a short time and how much he was looking forward to it. McKinley decided to acquire as much knowledge as he could of the local area in preparation for any confrontation with Doctor Dee. He felt anxiety when he thought of how they had failed Mariel and the boskies, for they had still not found the book of spells that held them in thrall.

He also needed to take more pains to conceal his whereabouts and staying in a hotel in Chichester would make it too easy for Dee and his associates to find him. After some discreet enquiries he found lodgings to the northwest and left Marshall in the care of the hotel's livery stables. The stable lad would act as his messenger and collect letters for him.

*   *   *

On the 14th day of October he received another letter from his uncle.

October 11

My dear Robert

Firstly let me put your mind at rest, we have suffered no attack from the other party and Mr Flaherty and I have made a great discovery. At least we think it is a great discovery, but it leaves us perplexed.

We have found the book that Liam Flaherty stole from Doctor Dee and sold to the pawnbroker whose shop was destroyed by fire. Or I should say we have found the cover of that book but the written contents were gone. The antiquarian collector swore that he had only received the outer shell which is, I must admit, a treasure of immense value in terms of its historical provenance and precious metals and stones.

The whereabouts of the contents of the grimoire were unknown to its present holder who keeps the cover in a case and looks at it occasionally. That dead end led us to try and find the place where Liam had been lodging when he was in London to sell the book. The other possibilities are that the written contents were in the pawnbrokers shop and were found by Dee or were removed before the valuable cover reached the pawnbroker. It is possible that Liam was aware of the unholy magic power of the grimoire, and he only wanted the precious stones and metals. Michael thinks it quite possible that his brother might have removed the book of spells and there is even a chance that he confessed to his priest at some point before his death. I believe this is wishful thinking on Michael's part as he would otherwise have gone to meet his maker unshriven.

Of course, after six years the lodging house had changed hands but the area has a growing Irish population and very few Catholic churches so we enquired of them and eventually found one where a member of the congregation recalled the young man that had been run down by a horse and then his body stolen out of his very grave. By this means we located an elderly priest who had heard Liam Flaherty's confession and, of course, he refused to speak about it.

By this time I was exhausted so I took a hansom cab back to my club, leaving Michael with his co-religionist to use whatever method he could to determine the fate of the grimoire. Eventually he returned and informed me that by asking general questions and observing the responses he had drawn a conclusion. In theory if a priest found out that a young parishioner was in a possession of a book of dark magic he would be advised to burn it.

So you see although we do not know if he followed the instruction or not, it appears that Dee still does not have it but I am afraid that neither do we. Michael is despondent and believes that he will never find his brother's body and now intends to return to Reading. I will join you as soon as matters here allow me to do so. Leave a note for me at the post office so that I can find your lodgings. Use my brother's name, then no one can intercept it.

Yours affectionately etc

McKinley found Mariel's letter received in London and read it again. It gave the impression that Dee was searching for the book and the boskies believed themselves to be under a spell preventing them from escaping. Yet Gilgoreth had escaped and was moving freely about the country. Was it possible that the book had been destroyed and they did not know they were free? Or was Mariel wrong about it being an essential part of their enslavement.

Perhaps they were free and were too weak to act on it. They were an old and failing species doomed to become extinct and supplanted by men, but they had magic powers and it had taken a man like Doctor Dee with his life-prolonging philosopher's stone and magic to hold them captive for such a long time.

He remembered the figures he had seen on the prison roof in Reading and it occurred to him that the ignorance of the modern industrial man might mean a new freedom for the fae because you cannot see what you do not believe in. Only people who had used the magic oil would be able to see them and that potion and recipe could be quietly forgotten in an age of science and scepticism. They had their own homes under the hills according to legend, perhaps returning them to that place would restore their energy. He had to wait only seven days before he might see Teresa again and he would put them to good use by acquiring a map of the country and the city and exploring as much as he could.

He would begin by visiting the church of St Andrews in the Oxmarket that she had suggested as their meeting place. He left a sealed letter at the post office addressed to Nicolas Weber for his uncle, and in a newly purchased countryman's coat and broad brimmed hat he walked the streets of the city to orientate himself. It was an easy task with the steeple of the cathedral so visible from any point and the cross at the centre of the four roads that led north, south, east and west inside walls that were remnants of the Roman occupation.

The Oxmarket was easy to find and the little thirteenth century church was hidden through a maze of alleyways. It was a small churchyard and he began examining the gravestones. He had no idea what he was looking for; he did not know what her family name was or if she had ever been married and what name would have been given to her son, if he really was buried here. He found that he was looking for the name Ede or Dee as he thought there must be some connection. There were very few recent graves and it was overcrowded, so he assumed new burials were carried out in the numerous other churches in the cathedral city. How long ago had Teresa's son died? Was he a baby, or an old man? His head spun and he looked inside the church to find a small and plain building but with fine windows. He felt safe for the first time since coming to Chichester, as though the people influenced by Doctor Dee could not follow him into a sacred space.

Feeling free at heart, he visited all the many churches in the ambit of the Dean of Chichester, and in each he found peace. McKinley wondered if he was a coward. The fight at Kinver Edge had been forced on him by circumstances and he had never been drawn to violence in the way that some men were. He could not shoot Avery in those circumstances. How would he defend himself and possibly Mariel and Teresa if there was a violent confrontation with Dee and his men? It was possible that young Mr Penny was also now caught up in the influence of the troupe if the woman he had fallen in love with was Katherine. It seemed likely as Dee needed to replace the fallen members of his entourage.

His last visit that day was to the cathedral where he found a clergyman carrying out duties at the altar. McKinley asked if he could speak to him. He was tempted to tell the earnest young priest everything about Dee, the fae and the unnatural prolongation of life. He confined himself to a question about hell.

'This may seem an odd question but if we assume that the devil exists …'

'As he surely does,' said the young priest earnestly.

'Is there any basis in the story that a tithe must be paid to hell at regular intervals?' asked McKinley.

He saw surprise at the question from one so obviously educated but, after some thought, the priest said, 'Well Christians and Jews pay a tithe to their church or synagogue to maintain the good work that they do, so it is natural that uneducated folk assume that the devil would request something similar from his followers. I believe in this case the tithe is not in the form of the harvest and its benefits but in terms of a human soul.'

'Have you ever encountered such a thing?' asked McKinley.

'No no, I am just repeating the folklore that simple country folk may believe. There are no church records of which I am aware, although the existence of devils and demons is enshrined in documents mainly written at the time of the reformation,' said the priest.

'What about faeries?'

The young man smiled. 'We are encouraged to try to prevent sin as our primary duty to our flock. The loss of souls from the intervention of supernatural creatures is extremely unlikely and the realm of fantasy if I may say so. You will have to tell me why you are asking these questions.' His attitude had changed and McKinley saw that he was now suspicious.

'I am translating a medieval story and was just interested in the views of the church,' he said much to the relief of the other who then smiled and said:

'Well if it is medieval you will need to speak to someone of the Roman faith to elicit the traditions that existed then.' He stood, obviously unwilling to continue the conversation. McKinley remained and bowed his head in his hands, appearing to pray but feeling close to despair at his ignorance despite their assiduous research. If only Gilgoreth would answer his questions honestly. He wondered where the old faerie was and whether he would come to Chichester to find his fellows.

Hunger reminded him that his landlady had promised to cook dinner and he must not be late. Perhaps his uncle would soon arrive.

*   *   *

He walked quickly back to his lodging house, paying no regard to whether there were people around him and was suddenly stopped by a man in a slouch cap who pushed him into an alleyway and ripped off his hat to get a better look at his face. He had a knife to McKinley's throat. The suddenness and the violence of the attack winded him and he realised that he had no defence. This might be the end of life.

'Walter,' he said desperately as he recognised him and knew this was personal because he could see the hatred in the other man's eyes. They must have found out about Thomas and Avery.

There was another man behind him, Jonah was keeping watch. 'If you kill me this place will be filled with policemen and investigating magistrates. My uncle will see to that. Dee will not be able to transact whatever business he has here.'

The other man pulled Walter back, and shook his head.

Walter put his mouth close to McKinley's ear and said, 'You need to leave, get out of here. Or I will cut you.' He backed off and was about to go but then turned and violently grabbed McKinley's face and beat his head hard against the wall.

He felt the grip but nothing more until he began to regain consciousness on the dirty ground. He left the alley and made his way back to his lodgings; the fear was now upon him because his legs were at first stiff and then shaky. By the time he had reached the cottage in Summerstown he noticed that his neck felt cold. The maid who opened the door saw him and screamed, he touched his neck and looked at his hand wet with blood. His collar was soaked.

The landlady came out and ushered him into the kitchen where they stripped off his coat, collar, tie and rolled down his shirt. The gash was about an inch long and the flow of blood, which had only been light soon stopped.

'Shall I get the doctor?' asked the maid.

'No, definitely not,' said McKinley, thinking of the rumours he had heard about their lack of cleanliness.

'I don't think that'll be necessary,' said the landlady. 'I've cleaned plenty of cuts and scrapes on my lads with vinegar and clean linen. They survived, and this bleeding is stopping now. I'll put a strip of cotton on it and you must stay still. Your head is bleeding and has a lump on it too. In fact, go and lie down right now. The maid will bring you hot tea with sugar and then you rest and no moving about.'

He did as he was told and lay quietly with a throbbing headache until he fell asleep. He woke reluctantly to find the landlady showing his uncle Ewart into the room. He waved feebly, afraid to start the blood flowing.

'Let's have a look,' said Ewart and peeled back the bandage. 'Oh, nothing to worry about, I've had worse cuts shaving. You'll just have to stay still for a while because it needs to scab over.' He thanked the landlady and promised that they would soon be down to dinner. 'I'll tie it tight and don't move your head. What happened?'

'One of Dee's men – Walter - held a knife to my throat. I threatened him that the city would be overrun with officers and magistrates if he killed me. I think Dee must be carrying out some business hereabouts and would be seriously inconvenienced if he was unable to do it.'

'What sort of business?' asked his uncle.

'It must be connected to the tithe he has to pay to hell in order to keep control of the fae and I'm afraid he might be planning to sacrifice Mariel.'

'According to legend that would be every seven years at Hallowe'en. Do you think the landlady would mind if I smoked my pipe?'

McKinley continued 'Doctor Dee lost the grimoire six years ago when Liam stole it. What if he needs it to make the payment? If he is unable to make the payment he may lose his powers. I imagine she would welcome it, your pipe that is.'

Ewart filled the pipe and sat back 'And the payment is presumably due on 31st October, Hallowe'en, when the veil between the living and the dead is at its thinnest.'

'Possibly that is when the faeries pay the tithe. Today is 15th October and I am to meet with Teresa and possibly Mariel in the church of St Andrew tomorrow. My head aches deucedly. That pipe smoke is going to make me sick.' He vomited into his basin.

'Let me look at your head,' said Ewart. He examined the lump on his nephew's skull and tutted. 'Were you unconscious at all?'

'I think for a few minutes I must have been and saw double when I came round. I only just managed to stagger back.'

'It hasn't bled much and looks clean but there may be damage under the skull. This is worse than the cut on your neck. You must stay here and not move about too much while it heals.'

McKinley struggled upright, 'No, I am meeting Teresa tomorrow, I have to go to St Andrew's Church.'

'I will go in your place and tell her what has happened. She will understand if she is half the woman you think she is.' He helped his nephew drink as much as he needed and dressed the wound with vinegar. He would not be able to do more than lie in bed for several days and only time would tell whether some greater damage had been done by the blow.

The next day his uncle left, and McKinley gave him strict instructions and directions. He prayed that she would be there, perhaps Mariel too, and that she would not be too disappointed that they had failed to find the grimoire to reverse the spells on the fae. He slept fitfully and dreamed that Teresa was a faerie and could not be saved and turned grey and withered in his arms. Then in another dream she was a puppet and when dead she was equally beautiful but a thing of wood and cloth.

He dreamed again and smelled the green fresh fragrance of meadows and flowers and refused to open his eyes so deep was his bliss that the dream must be prolonged. He felt a cool cloth on his brow and she whispered his name 'Robert' and kissed his cheek. This was the perfect dream and he was afraid to wake up, when it was over he knew that he would weep and a tear escaped his closed lid and rolled to his ear.

The kiss moved to his ear and he opened his eyes. She was sitting on the bed and tending to him. After murmured words of endearment and kisses they looked at each other and she forbade him to move.

'Your uncle has told the landlady that I am your wife and I will care for you now,' she said.

'Where is he? And how is Mariel? I am afraid ...'

'Mariel is safe and she is with your uncle. I know you have questions and I am prepared to answer them but first you must eat some broth and drink some tea so that you can regain your strength.' Teresa helped him to sit up and with great reluctance McKinley was prevailed upon to take some of the refreshments offered. He still felt sick and only just kept it in his stomach, he was desperate not to humiliate himself in front of her.

She took the dishes back to the kitchen and when she returned sat next to him on the bed.

'I will be staying with you all night, now that we are husband and wife,' she said. 'You may ask your questions.'

His eyes feasted on her but he was sick and shaking, unable to make her his wife in any other way. 'The boskies are faerie folk aren't they? And Doctor Dee has some hold over them so that they are not free.'

Teresa said 'Yes, he has had them with him for as long as I can remember, and that is a long time, Robert, I am ..'

'Don't tell me. It doesn't matter, I love you for who you are today. Why is the book, the grimoire, so important?'

'No one knows, but it is vital to the seven-year tithe that must be paid at the faerie market,' she said.

'The faerie market? It is here?'

'Near by. There are many such places in this area where the fae can be found, some are more active than others, ours are weakened by their bondage I fear.'

'I have spoken with Gilgoreth,' McKinley said, 'He seems to be growing stronger, but he misses his kind.'

'Were you able to see him? We thought he might have regained the power of invisibility being away from Doctor Dee.' Teresa looked at him closely. 'Ah your left eye has tiny glints of gold that are not in the warm brown of your other eye. You have used the potion. How did you find the recipe?'

'A helpful young man in Oxford had some he had made up and said he was afraid to use. He believes himself to have been a changeling.'

'Strange, that is a story I have never found to be true.'

'I saw a lot of creatures like Gilgoreth in Reading watching a hanging,' McKinley said. 'It was very disturbing.'

'They are an ancient people and live a long time, the sacrifices that humans make fascinates them.' Teresa said, 'But why were you watching it?'

'A girl had been killed and I was afraid it might be you.'

She kissed him again and they sat quietly for a while, then McKinley said, 'Why did you exhume the body of Liam Flaherty?'

She gasped. 'How do you know about him?'

'His brother saw you at the Mercers Hall in London and we have followed the trail left by the records when his assault was reported. He just wants to know where Liam's remains are. But I want to know why Dee wanted to interrogate his corpse.' McKinley's eyes searched her face and she said nothing for several minutes. He did not press her.

Eventually she turned to him and said, 'Liam and I were lovers, but he was tempted by one of the master's books. He stole it and ran away.'

'It was the grimoire, with jewels and precious metals?'

'Yes,' she said and smiled.

He stroked her auburn hair and said, 'He was a fool.'

'He was a fool. He was knocked down by a horse and cart and killed, but the book had disappeared. Doctor Dee thought he could summon his spirit and find out where he had hidden it.'

'He sold it.'

'Yes, we found that out by asking around, but the summoning of the revenant was a ghastly business and it went horribly wrong.' She shuddered.

'What happened' he asked gently.

'The men dragged the body from the coffin the way the old grave-robbers did. They broke open the head of the coffin and tied a rope around his neck and pulled him out. It sickened me.' She continued, 'Then we took the body to a piece of woodland near where we were camped and the master spoke to it in a language we could not understand. After hours of this, and with the stink of the body getting worse, most of us wanted to give up - but then it convulsed.

'I was standing with the other women and nearly fainted, but they held me up. He was not the young man who had been in my bed in the prime of his life, but the terrible thing that arose in front of us was foul and warped and it spoke to Doctor Dee in a strange language. We could see that even he was terrified of it and he began shouting incantations at it. I thought for a moment that he was going to turn and flee but eventually he made the thing subside and the body fall back into a human shape.'

'It wasn't Liam?' asked McKinley.

'No, we hope that it went back to wherever it came from, but I suspect part of Liam's soul came back too.'

'What did you do with the body?'

'It is buried in the grove of trees and a small rowan grows over him. I will give you directions that you can pass to his brother. It is not consecrated ground.' Teresa said, 'I think you should sleep now.'

They lay together but he did not sleep and neither did she, thinking of the horror of John Dee's actions. Nothing was said for a long time until McKinley spoke. 'We found the outer cover of the book but there was nothing inside. If the paper was destroyed does that mean that the fae are free?'

Teresa thought about this, 'Gil escaped so perhaps that is so, but I am sure the book is needed at the faerie market and is always taken there.'

'What happens at the faerie market?' He was equally fascinated and afraid. It might be a place of barter for more than fruit and vegetables. It might be the place where flesh and souls were traded. Teresa could not or would not tell him.

'It is a deal done by Dee and the lord of the fae. He has a magic amulet that protects him from the lord's power and we would not be safe, or so he says. We wait outside the hill until he returns. It is how our kind are made.'

McKinley looked at her and saw that she was not truly human but was alive and warm and he could see the pulse beating in the soft skin of her throat.

She continued. 'Every seven years we add to our number. Liam was intended for this year's tithe but he was either too strong a Catholic or too easily tempted to thievery.'

'It is Mariel this year, isn't it?'

'She has useful skills and a robust physical and mental nature. She has indicated that she is willing to part with her soul, her religious beliefs are different from ours. She thinks it will be a transformation that will benefit her,' said Teresa.

McKinley doubted this, but if he was to save Mariel he might have to keep that secret from Teresa. 'Did you give up your soul willingly?' He asked her as he fought to keep his eyes open.

'Yes, when you have lived with creatures that we consider have no souls, such as animals and to some extent the fae, and see how beautiful and elemental their lives are, you realise that the knowledge acquired by Adam and Eve in the common Christian religion is a curse. Mariel knows that.'

He could think of no reply. He was not a devout church goer and the beliefs instilled by Sunday school and the habits of society had been shaken in the last year so that his mind was a soup of unformed ideas. He lay back and woke in darkness, alone.

Had he dreamed her presence? He carefully sat up and the room spun so it was with difficulty that he did not vomit again. He must have groaned because the door which had been ajar opened and his uncle came in.

'Robert, I am glad that you are awake, but don't move. I'll light a candle and we can take a look at you.'

His heart sank. It must have been a dream, or she was a ghost, how he longed to be haunted by her. 'I thought Teresa …' He could not finish the sentence.

'Oh dear boy she was here but she has gone to make arrangements so that she can stay here with you. You cannot move and I told a small fib and said she was your wife.' Ewart chuckled at his wicked deception of the kind landlady. 'I'll make it worth her while.'

'Christian decency has a very tenuous hold over more people than I ever realised,' said McKinley.

'I have travelled in many countries and seen many religions. They all have their virtues and their faults. Mariel is the daughter of a Hindu and has quite a deep knowledge of her father's religious beliefs. This has opened her eyes to the plight of the fae and she wants to help them.'

'Then you have talked to her?'

'We have talked for hours dear boy and she will take me to meet them soon, when John Dee is otherwise occupied.'

'You know about the faerie market, and the tithe? It is a human soul and it must not be Mariel, even though Teresa says she is willing. And Teresa has no soul. What will become of us?' McKinley weakened by pain and dizziness and hunger felt unequal to the task of helping those he loved.

'I must travel to London to collect the magic potion that will allow us to see faeries, so I will leave you in Teresa's care. You will need to rest while you are in that condition and as you are no threat to him it is likely that Dee and his men will leave you in peace.'

Ewart saw to McKinley's needs and ablutions and then fetched some weak broth that he managed to keep in his stomach. He quickly fell asleep again, knowing that he could do nothing in his current condition. When he awoke he was alone, and he lapsed into a fluid half-conscious state in which people appeared before him amorphous and unshaped but fixed inside their situations as though kept afloat by strength and virtue.

Avery, an outcast and possibly without a soul, was being looked after by a spinster whose chance of happiness had passed her by. She was grabbing life with both hands and he was willing and grateful, so what did it matter that conventional society would disapprove? The human form of Lily sitting between his knees looking at his pictures and touching his skin at every chance, then flowing around him like a serpent. He saw Thomas the fallow buck, free and wild and hunted. What had happened to them? Were they in hell or heaven or nowhere, or reincarnated as Mariel might believe?

At this time he was in such pain from his head wound that the unconsciousness of sleep was a blessed relief and he wished that he had laudanum to ease his suffering. But his uncle had refused to procure it for him and he knew from his experience with George Macey how addiction was easily acquired and how difficult it was to give up the drug.

The next time he woke she was with him and soothed the pain with a balm she had brought with her, a sweet-smelling herb that made him think of moorland and heathers and the Scottish family he had visited but a few times in his life. Now he promised that he would do so again. He wanted to take her to meet his family to show her off to his friends and watch the wind blowing her long auburn hair as the clouds scudded by. So he slept and woke briefly and slept again until she said she had to go and work because the Sloe Fair was opening and they needed her in the show. He did not mind her leaving him as long as she returned and slipped between the sheets to cling to his body as the nights grew colder.

As he grew stronger his desire for her led him to caress her and then the time came when he could hold back no longer, and he took her completely. In the darkness their sighs filled the bedroom and after that they often made love before he drifted into his deepest sleep. It occurred to him that his sleep was drugged but it felt sweet all the same, not the opiate of the nervous system that laudanum provided but something more wholesome, and the days passed without any memory of dreams. One morning he woke to full consciousness after she had left and he heard a conversation outside the door to his room. The door opened and his uncle entered.

'Uncle Ewart, how long have I been here, what day is it?'

'And good morning to you too Robert and I am very well thank you for not asking.' Ewart replied tartly.

'Sorry, my head is so dizzy ...' he stopped. 'No it isn't dizzy at all and I'm absolutely starving.' He carefully sat up. His neck was stiff where it had been cut but his head was clear.

'It's October 29th and the Sloe Fair is over, so Teresa has gone with the troupe.'

'But she was just here.'

'No Robert, that was Mariel.'

He looked at the depression in the mattress where she had lain with him. Surely he had not – she was a child. His strength left him, and an overwhelming uncertainty woke him to the reality of life and cleared the blissful illusions of the previous fourteen days. He stood shakily and washed and dressed with his uncle's help; then he left that room of dreams and took breakfast downstairs.

'I have much to tell you,' said Ewart ruthlessly slicing the top off a boiled egg.

'We have no time, we must act soon; the faerie market will be in two days' time and Mariel's soul will ....' He was mortified that she had been in his bed but could not explain to his uncle. 'She will be sacrificed.'

'We are not too late; the market is on 11th November and I know where it will be held. Your good 'wife' Teresa told me. So, we need to restore you to greater strength and then we, and Michael Flaherty, for he is joining us, will travel to that place along the coast and prevent the unholy ritual.'

'I thought the eve of all hallows was the date the tithe was paid to hell. This buttered toast is delicious.'

'It seems it is not that simple. The seven-year tithe arrangement was made in 1603, but the contract was made under the Julian calendar. In 1750 the Gregorian calendar was adopted and eleven days were lost so the payment must be made on 11th November, by strict calculation.'

'And who is it paid to?' asked McKinley. 'The stories have the fae paying the tithe to hell and substituting humans in place of their own people.'

'My elderly cryptographer friend has recovered enough to tell me that in Dee's notebook he has recorded information from a spirit who says that the lord of the faerie, it appears to be a hierarchical society, has made a pact with a great power …'

'You mean the devil?'

'It's not expressed in those terms Robert. It seems to be a transaction, as you would conduct in a market, but in this instance with a force that we would consider pagan. But then we are steeped in the ritual of a Judaeo Christian society where there is only one god. Previous civilisations believed that there were many gods and these gods could be quite capricious. So the lord of the faerie makes a payment every seven years and the fae retain their invisibility to human kind and he retains his power over them.'

'And that payment is the soul of a human?' asked McKinley.

'That would appear to be a valuable commodity to this pagan deity. It's a very good deal if you are the fae. How else would they be able to live with their troublesome human neighbours and their proliferation and bad habits?' said his uncle.

McKinley washed down his toast with a quantity of tea. 'How does Dee come into the picture?'

'Doctor Dee bought the services of his enslaved faeries by supplying what the lord of the fae needs.'

This was almost too much for his newly wakened state and for a few seconds the world span and he thought he might fall.

'We'll talk about it later,' said Ewart.

'Uncle, I didn't sleep with Mariel last night, did I? She is only fourteen.'

'It was cold Robert, she probably only got into bed to keep you both warm.' Ewart seemed unconcerned and McKinley realised he had been so drugged by the potions they had given him that he had no definite recollection of the past two weeks. They finished their meal in silence because the maid came to clear away and then uncle and nephew took a turn about the city to try and build some stamina in McKinley's weakened limbs.

'When you have regained your strength we will travel along the coast and stay at a small village called Findon. Teresa has informed me that this is where the faerie market is to be held this year.'

His uncle fed him this information as though afraid that too much detail might overwhelm his brain and McKinley began to think that perhaps he had been suffering a brain fever and was out of his mind. Perhaps he had been hallucinating all the times he had lain with the woman he loved and sated his lust with her willing body, enjoying her again and again. It must have been a dream.

When they had checked on Marshall's health and found him well tended and turned out in a small paddock, they returned to the lodging for McKinley to collapse on his bed and enjoy a more natural sleep with no dreams that he could remember. They ate early as it suited his uncle and spent a quiet evening in their rooms. It was clear that no female presence would be needed to look after him now.

'Do you have the magic potion that will enable you to see them?' McKinley asked his uncle.

'I not only have it, but I have used it, although I can't say I've noticed anything different. You didn't tell me it stung so much.'

McKinley looked into his uncle's eyes and saw a few flecks of gold among the faded grey irises. His own left eye remained flecked, and he wondered if the effect would ever wear off. He suggested that they sit in a quiet place where there was a natural stream and try to see anyone who might be passing unseen by humans.

They sat by the side of the Lavant, a small chalk-fed stream that meandered south from the downland and passed in tunnels under the city. It had been like this since Roman times and had probably been a common area for both humans and faerie. It was a dry day and they wrapped warmly and took sandwiches and beer with them. Ewart obviously thought they were crazy to be doing this even on a warmish day on November.

They found a calm area under a willow tree and sat watching the wrens and robins dipping about in the surrounding bushes, busy with the challenge of surviving as winter approached. The cathedral spire lay to the southwest and as noon approached the sun came out and the birds settled for a brief interlude of quiet. McKinley nudged his uncle who seemed to have dozed off; there were half a dozen grey clad men approaching them from the north carrying empty cloths. They did not acknowledge McKinley or his uncle as normal men would, and passed by them silently as they neared the tunnels along the dry river bed. They went into the tunnels without making a sound and disappeared.

Ewart was wide eyed and had to clap a hand to his mouth to keep from crying out. Fortunately they gone past before he was fully aware of them and McKinley engaged his uncle in conversation to prevent him from staring at the creatures. At the sound of his voice the last of them turned and looked at him and McKinley thought that perhaps it knew they had been seen.

'Why didn't we talk to them?' said Ewart.

'We can't do anything to change the way that events must unfold, or we lose the advantage of our knowledge. If they were to change the venue, for example, we would have no way to find Dee and his victim.'

'Of course Robert, you are right. But to be so close to them and not be able to converse! I have spent my whole life seeking and sometimes finding new species and all I could do was watch, listen and then kill them so I could bring back a specimen for my collection ....'

'Perhaps that explains why they are not keen to meet you,' interrupted McKinley.

His uncle grunted. 'You have a point. If I were a different species I would not wish to meet me, in the field, as it were.' He thought for a moment. 'They were definitely fae? Not some small locals or children?'

'I closed my left eye and could not see them. It is quite useful having only one eye anointed with the oil. Shall we go? I am feeling chilled now and some hot tea would be very welcome.' Both men got to their feet and went back to the lodgings. 'Did you notice that the birds stopped singing as the fae went by? And resumed again when they had gone.'

'You think they can see them?' asked his uncle.

'Well my horse Marshall was very happy to have Gilgoreth sitting on his back and stroking him and he could certainly hear him.'

'I should like to know where they were going with those cloths and what they will be collecting to bring back. Shall we go back later and watch out for their return?' Ewart was excited at the thought of hunting the faerie folk and learning their habits.

'Definitely not,' said McKinley. 'I think one of them noticed me looking and was suspicious. We cannot disturb the process. You will have to wait until the faerie market and the sacrifice before you can collect your scientific information.' He did not say that he both longed for and dreaded the event. He would see Teresa again but he knew in his heart that he would also lose something valuable. The days passed and Michael Flaherty came to their lodgings and they hired a brougham and horse and Flaherty rode Marshall. They travelled slowly to the east and stayed two days in Arundel to explore the town before finally reaching their destination.

Findon was a small village situated between two ancient hill forts and surrounded by evidence of thousands of years of human occupation. Ewart remarked about this, and they agreed that human and fae must have lived in relative harmony for millennia, each accepting the presence of the other, until recently when the arrogance of the 'enlightenment' and science shifted the balance in the minds of men and destroyed their ability to live in harmony with nature.

'I am part of the problem,' said Ewart sadly as they sat by the fire in the inn and drank mulled ale. 'I have killed so many animals and brought them home as trophies. All in the name of science.'

'At least you didn't do it for sport,' said Flaherty. 'That's something I can't stand. A man will kill a rabbit for the pot, fair enough, but not just to beat his rival as though it is a game.'

'You are an Irish Catholic Michael, does your church recognise the fae? The reformation seems to have changed the way that Christian folk approach the supernatural,' asked McKinley.

'Your uncle has told me where Liam is buried and I will find him and have his remains transferred to a proper churchyard. I am more concerned about the possibility that his soul has been disturbed and cannot find rest. Summoning the dead is an unnatural practice.' Flaherty spoke with quiet determination. 'As for the Church, well the rural folk in Ireland have their beliefs in the old ways and yet they also believe in the protecting power of the liturgy and the eucharist. There is the natural world and its laws, and they are wise to remember and respect them, and there is the Church and its promise of salvation. When you have as little control over your lives as the rural folk of Ireland do then it is sensible to hedge your bets. Not that it is helping now as so many are starving and having to leave their homes and families.'

Ewart spoke up, 'There have been bad harvests all over Europe in the past few years, that is one of the reasons for the revolutions.

You know most crops recover in the following year but the wretched potato plants have not recovered and our damned Whig government will do nothing about it.' Flaherty nodded. 'Do you know that in 1782 when there were food shortages in Ireland, the ports were closed so that food could not be exported and prices in Ireland fell and disaster was averted? Farmer George knew a thing or two, despite his later descent into madness.'

'Only the British would milk the starving cow until she fell down dead,' said Flaherty. Nobody argued with him, and they stared glumly into the fire until it was time to turn in for the night. The following day they walked around the village and visited the hills that they believed would host the faerie market.

The local people told them about the sheep fair held in September, declaring that in the middle ages the black death had killed so many folk that farming was given over to sheep and no one had ploughed the fields since that time. They were happy to relay stories of ancient peoples that had lived hereabout. Many of the undisturbed round barrows housed graves, they believed and possibly even treasure.

The closest hill was dominated by the church of St John the Baptist and they agreed it would be unlikely as the place where the fae might gather. The best prospect was Cissbury Hill, its top was an iron age hill fort and numerous barrows that suggested bronze age occupation. The locals said they had found numerous examples of 'elf-shot', flint arrow-heads that the faeries had used against animals and occasionally people. No one had encountered any elves or faeries in recent years, but they had tales of agricultural mishaps that were attributed to the intervention of the grey folk. After a pint or two in the Gun Inn the stories were embellished to include changelings.

One story was particularly grim. A woman looked into her baby's crib and saw that the thing there was old and black and she knew that it had been exchanged by the faeries. Her husband looked at it and thinking it was a piece of wood he put it on the fire. At which it screamed and flapped its wings and flew about the room screeching, a large flying thing in flames, until it fell down dead. The tales kept coming thick and fast, some were reiterations of ones McKinley had heard or read before: the faerie midwife and the ability to see faerie folk, the rule that if a human enters the faerie realm they must not eat or drink anything for fear of never being able to return to the world of men. Though some said that it was possible to return but only to sicken and die, for once having tasted the faerie food nothing else would satisfy that hunger.

As they prattled on, encouraged by his uncle, McKinley thought of 'La Belle Dame Sans Merci'; once the human knight had made love to the faerie girl he withered and died. Perhaps nothing would be as pleasurable as the nights he had spent with Teresa, or thought he had. Perhaps every sexual act with another woman would be a disappointment. He longed to see her again, to recreate that ecstasy, and surely that must mean that it was a dream, for did men not tire of a woman's body once they had enjoyed it?

'Robert, Robert! Are you well? You seem pale, perhaps today there has been too much walking,' said his uncle.

'Yes. I shall retire.' He bade them good night and went to bed hoping to dream again of her fresh scent and warm welcoming body. He remembered nothing of the night's dreams.

*   *   *

McKinley fell asleep quickly and awoke on a hilltop with a bright moon above him and his arms and legs bound together.

'I am glad you are awake,' said a deep voice close to his ear. 'You have caused me so much trouble. But I think it will be worth it to see you as my offering to Faerie. For it is he who will attend the market and I want to give him something special. Have you heard of him? He has been lord of all the fae in these isles for hundreds of years and he is not happy that his people flee from the pervasive human plague.'

McKinley tried to turn his head and to speak, but he could not and his voice was just a gurgle.

'Ah, you are still under the influence of the drug. It will soon wear off and then you can speak all you want to your lover. You can tell her how you feel, what she means to you. Promise that you will love her until the moment of your death and then we will see if we can make that promise come true. I have a feeling you will not willingly give up your soul so your life will have to accompany it'

McKinley swallowed the lump in his throat and focussed on regaining his movement and faculties. He told himself not to hope for rescue, to accept his fate and behave with honour. If death was imminent then he would savour every moment of life, look at every star in the sky and even relish the feeling of the hard ground beneath his bones. He thought he heard John Dee move away from him and then the shadow fell on him and he could smell her, green and meadow scented, kneeling above him.

She let down her hair so that it flowed around his head and brought her face close to his. She kissed his paralysed lips and he breathed in her sweet breath. She whispered to him. 'Have faith in me Robert and we will be together.' Then she lifted her head and declared to the sky 'I claim your heart, and your body. No one else will have it.'

She kissed him more ruthlessly, her tongue exploring his mouth as though she would suck his soul from him. He gasped with pain and pleasure. John Dee saw this and laughed.

'You were ever my creature Teresa.'

'I want to have him one last time, under the trees, in the autumn leaves, where the moon cannot see us. It is my right as the one who delivered the lamb.' As she said this, she caressed his body lasciviously.

There was an awkward silence then Dee beckoned his two men and they carried McKinley roughly down from the ridge to a small clump of trees. They threw him into a pile of leaves and left as she began to pull up her dress.

When they were out of earshot she said, 'Can you speak yet? We have some time before the gateway opens.' She brought a knife from her underclothes and cut his bonds. 'I know you can't move much, but the drug will wear off soon and paralysis will buy us more time. I am sorry there was nothing more that Mariel and I could do. We persuaded Katherine to seduce the youngest of the Penny family but Dee refused him as a sacrifice, saying that he needed the lawyers to be on side for business reasons. He will be returned to them soon.'

'Kiss me,' he said. She did so and rubbed his limbs, they huddled together as the feeling returned to him, both were terrified that this was their last time together. A flurry of wind whipped up some nearby leaves and McKinley saw Gil crouched near them.

'Well this is a fine pickle. All you think of is rutting, you humans.'

'Gilgoreth,' they both whispered.

'Can you help us?' asked Teresa, 'Dee is going to …'

'I know,' said Gilgoreth, 'I've brought your uncle and his Irish friend. They are a bit slower because they can't fly, see.' He moved closer. 'Where are my kind? How are they?'

'They are with Mariel. They know that the book that bound them to Dee has been destroyed but they don't know what will happen when Faerie meets him tonight here on the hill,' Teresa said. 'I think they should all come here to witness the event and plead for their freedom.'

Gil nodded and leapt into the air silently.

He had just left when there was a great shout from the hilltop.

'They have seen your uncle and the Irishman. They will fight. Can you stand? We must go and help them.' She did not wait for him but took her knife and ran quickly around the side of the hill towards the noise. He staggered after her, stumbling on the uneven slanting ground.

There was a scream that McKinley knew was his uncle's voice and he saw Teresa launch herself onto the back of Jonah, the mute, and they fell together away from Ewart. Teresa had the advantage and plunged her knife without hesitation into the man's neck cutting the artery in his throat. She clung to his back with her arms and legs and he must have crushed her badly as he fell heavily and writhed violently in his death throes while his life blood spurted from the terrible gash in his neck.

His uncle lay quietly, not moving, and McKinley could see why. The man's knife had penetrated his breastbone, such was the force of the single blow, and it had pierced his heart. He cradled him in his arms and their eyes met. His eyes sparkled with borrowed gold in the moonlight, and as he watched, the gold faded until he held the body of a dead man with unseeing eyes. He closed them and kissed him.

He was roused from this by the struggle between Walter and Michael Flaherty. They were both strong men and fought well. Walter had his knife and Michael a cudgel that might have been a shillelagh. A few feints by Walter were met with quick footwork by his opponent, but the uneven ground made that a risky tactic. But Michael was getting the measure of his man and the next backward slash was intercepted by a crushing blow from the weighted end of the club which had the greater length. Walter gasped as his fingers were broken, but the adrenaline kept him fighting and he tried again, this time the knife was knocked out of his hand and Flaherty coldly followed through by bringing the weapon back across his face and smashing his nose and cheek. He dropped onto his knees but could not rise, then lay on his back, trying to breathe while his airways filled with blood.

There was applause and McKinley turned expecting to have to defend himself from Doctor Dee but instead he saw a shining figure in the moonlight. His clothes glistened as though made of silver and he wore a hat at a jaunty angle. Michael crossed himself.

'I'd have come sooner had I known you were laying on entertainment,' he said to Dee who walked several steps behind him. He looked around and saw her lying under Jonah's body. She was hurt. 'Teresa, the colour of gore suits you. Don't get up.'

McKinley began to move towards her but in a burst of coloured light Faerie was between them.

'You must be Robert McKinley, the artist. Don't worry about Teresa I have no interest in her. It is you I want.' He turned to Michael. 'You are a good fighter but not suitable for this day's sacrifice.' He waved his arm and Michael was wrapped in a binding like thick cobweb.

Walter's laboured breathing became a death rattle and Faerie beckoned with his left hand and four grey-clad men came and removed the bodies of Walter and Jonah. 'Take them to a distant place where they can change into natural creatures.' The faerie folk lifted into the air and were gone.

He looked down at Ewart McKinley and the blade protruding from his breast. He turned his ire on the doctor.

'This is inexcusable Dee. This cannot be undone and will bring attention to the rings of this place. I am displeased and ....' He stopped as six small grey figures appeared up the side of the hill. His anger changed into tones of affection. 'There you are, my old folk.'

They stood facing their lord and several made as if to bow to him but were nudged by their fellows to remind them that this was the lord who had sold them into slavery. Mariel followed and she looked determined not to submit to this Lord Faerie.

Doctor Dee spoke to her. 'Where is Katherine?'

'Tied up in the camp. She is unharmed.' Mariel's voice was hard. She turned to Faerie and said 'My lord, your subjects have laboured too long enslaved in the captivity of Doctor John Dee. They want to be free.' A frisson of excitement ran through the little group.

'They have never been free. They have always owed their labour and their lives to me or my kind. Our society is feudal and they have a duty ....'

'Can't you see how they fade in his service?' Mariel interrupted him.

He looked annoyed but then turned to the poor creatures and studied them. He said, 'How you have changed, you look old and withered, you are weak and dependant. Why should I take you back? You are no use to me in this state.' As he spoke they shrunk away from him and he seemed to grow brighter. Some of them bowed or knelt before him.

Mariel looked at McKinley in despair. His Lordship smiled and even Doctor Dee was beginning to relax when Gilgoreth flew in and stood in front of his lord and bowed a polite but defiant bow.

'I have returned from months of freedom Lord. I was not this creature when I escaped the years of servitude imposed on me by him.' He pointed at Dee.

The faerie lord looked between them then stepped back and said to Dee. 'He is your servant until midnight, when our bargain must be renewed. Make him come into line with the others. Show me how you enforce your feudal duty over a miscreant subject.'

Dee stared at Gilgoreth for a long time but the creature did not cower. Eventually he grasped the sigil he wore around his neck and muttered unintelligible words in the secret Enochian language he used to communicate with spirits. The fae cringed, but Gilgoreth stood unmoved and Faerie smiled with excitement. Nothing happened for several minutes but then McKinley heard the Irishman saying his prayers in a language that was similar to Dee's and might have been Gaelic. He turned and saw what Michael had seen. From the barrows dotted around the large hill, pale forms were crawling slowly into the night air.

Gilgoreth spoke to Faerie. 'He has to summon the human dead of ages past to make one old elf do his bidding. I refuse to submit to such a weak overseer.'

The lord waved his arm and the spirits disappeared. 'You will do as you are bid Gilgoreth.' He bound his mouth with a spell. 'Enough Dee. We have a bargain and you have kept your side of it. You have brought me a male in the prime of life. A pure spirit. Bring out the book and we will renew our contract.'

McKinley sought Teresa's eyes trying to convey his forgiveness and love. He was appalled to see how much pain she was in, his life seemed unimportant and he felt such great sorrow at his uncle's unnecessary death that he hardly noticed the mention of the book. He stood dazed and angry but heard Doctor Dee speaking humbly.

'I don't have the book this year, but we both know what is in it and it is only a book of account after all.'

There was a sudden silence and all attention focussed on the faerie lord.

'What! Only a book of account! This is a market, and it may be acceptable for the common folk to trade by a handshake and a wink but lords must have their contracts in writing.' Faerie's body was now crackling with power, his attention fully on Dee who backed away. Tell me why I should not take you instead?'

'Take me! I am more than willing.' Another man had appeared at the crest of the hill.

'Loveday?'

'I have followed you McKinley. I have anointed my eyes. I am ready to return to my people.'

'You don't know what you are doing!' McKinley shouted at him.

'This is ridiculous,' said Faerie showing many too many gleaming teeth. 'You have no book of account and yet I am presented with two offerings.'

At that moment Gil won back his freedom to say, 'Go all of you! The way is opening! It is time to return home!'

Everyone began moving at once and scattering in different directions. The fae started singing in their strange high-pitched voices as he had heard them at Pitdown Hall. Teresa staggered to him, holding her side and dragged him down to the grove that had hidden them earlier. She stumbled as they entered it and as he lifted her she cried out. He laid her as gently as he could on the bed of leaves and she lay motionless in his arms struggling to breath, her lungs filling with blood from the broken ribs that had pierced them.

'No, no, no.' He could not bear for her to die too. He wanted to take away the pain that he could see on her face. Tears slipped from her closed eyes, and he kissed her as his own fell to be mingled with them.

'You loved me so well,' she whispered. 'Your passion and mine together. I remember your smell and the warmness of your embrace, my love.' She gasped, and then the pain left her face.

He sobbed with grief at losing the woman he loved and his brave loyal uncle. Then a red rage overtook him and went in search of John Dee. He did not see Mariel as she went past him to tend Teresa's body. He saw Dee entering a cave on the side of the hill and there was no sign of any fae so he followed him at a run, intending to fling himself on the old man and beat him senseless for his despicable actions. He plunged into the pitch black hole.

McKinley's eyes, accustomed to moonlight, were blinded by the green dazzle of the forest that surrounded him. Through his left eye, green trees and grasses and sunlight slanting to the woodland floor. With his left eye he could see the old fae holding hands and being greeted by their people. Gil appeared at his side. He spoke quietly.

'I see you have joined us. You had better stay with me. I think the lord will not take you now that his pact with Dee has ended but it would be wise to stay out of his way. Have you been hurt, there is blood on you, and tears?' he said, fascinated.

'It is not my blood and not all my tears. My uncle and Teresa are dead. I want to kill John Dee.'

Gilgoreth took him by the hand and led him to a small clearing where they entered a quaint hut. He made him sit in a rocking chair and spoke to him kindly.

'You are in shock and, I think, not recovered from your injury. You must rest.'

'Where am I?' asked McKinley.

'This is where we live. It is a refuge from the world of men.'

'But the light and the trees?'

'You see them and smell them and feel the breeze so it must be real, yes? But it is not as it seems, and it is the power of the lord of the fae and his magic that maintains the glamour,' said Gilgoreth as he looked around the room. McKinley could see that he was uneasy and remembered the source of that power.

'What will happen to Loveday? And Dee? What will happen to him?'

'I will find out. The offering will be made and if the god is satisfied then the lord's power will be renewed and the glamour of this world can continue.' He paused, 'At least that is what we are told. But what I have seen over the past weeks in your world have changed my views. Perhaps this is not how it has to be, maybe the time has come for our own revolution against a feudal system. The real world is different and we hide in this memory of things past.' His grey green eyes glinted and he looked around. 'There are no fae at home today for they celebrate the return of the stolen ones. You must remain here and be quiet and I will see what is happening and come back and tell you.'

McKinley could not argue with him, he was overcome with grief and exhaustion. Before he left Gil turned and said, 'You must not eat or drink anything in this world, remember that. Everything here is an enchantment. If you leave with it inside your body it will kill you.' With that he was gone, and the quiet brought with it the sound of distant laughter like tinkling bells. He sat with his head in his hands and relived the past few hours so far as he could remember them, and allowed himself to weep some more.

He was thirsty and there was a jug of what seemed to be water on the sideboard, the range had a pie on it, cooling from the day's baking. He must not think about his hunger and thirst. He must master them or leave, assuming he could find the way out. Wooden stairs led up to a loft and a feather mattress. If he slept then time would pass, and he would not be tempted by the

279

enchanted food. It provided much needed oblivion, at least until the nightmares began.

He seemed to see pale grey walls around him; had they found him and cast him into a prison? There were marks of cutting and scraping and he could make out pictures among the gloom. He saw them with the eye of an artist, there were animals rendered in earth pigments, bison and horses, drawn with sparing elegance. He was stunned by the simplicity and power, admiring the skill but also the story that they told. Herds of animals running and fleeing, never grazing and sleeping, always pursued by something.

He remembered that he too was hunted and needed to flee, and soon he was running and leaping over tree roots along a pathway and downhill until he came to a gathering place, but it was empty. He looked around searching with his right eye for his own kind and with his left eye for the fae. He was not sure if he was safe so he hunkered down and tried to make himself small. He crawled into a tiny space with a low ceiling.

A cool hand touched his arm and he woke.

'Sleeping, very sensible,' said Gilgoreth. 'You have eaten nothing?' McKinley shook his head. 'Then I will tell you what has transpired. Your friend Loveday was very acceptable to the god and our Lord Faerie was pleased. He was not only willing, but also a virgin, it seems, so doubly precious.'

'But he was not in his right mind,' said McKinley. 'He believed himself to be a changeling, he thought he was returning to his own people. What has happened to him?'

Gil shrugged with that annoying insouciance that meant it was outside his control so he dismissed it. 'Maybe he was a changeling.'

'You don't believe that,' said McKinley and saw again the reluctance to take responsibility that would always mean that the fae would be marginalised and live in the glamour of unreality. 'I saw the walls of chalk and flint and the pictures painted on them of animals. It wasn't faerie art was it?'

Again Gilgoreth shrugged and declined to confirm his suspicions and McKinley accepted that he could never rely upon a straight answer from the creature. 'I am sorry Gil. Please tell me what else you have found out.'

The elf sat crossed legged on the bed and recounted his tale.

'First, I found the returned ones and their people rejoicing and singing and feasting and the lord of fae sitting on his high throne as though he had made it happen, taking all the credit for what was my hard work, escaping and flying alone all around this strange country and its appalling human inhabitants. Well, I doffed my cap and bowed to him and requested an audience. He grumbled but could hardly refuse as he was presiding over the show.

'I told him what I had seen in the land of men and how the world was in revolution. He squinted at me and asked how I had enjoyed it and I had to admit that I did not enjoy it at all. Then he asked me what did I want in order to keep quiet about it. He knew what had been going on, his personal bodyguards venture out in daylight and bring back food and other things he considers necessary. Fripperies usually. It is how he met Dee in the first place, a-robbing of his warehouse he was.' Gil paused. 'But that's another story and a long time ago.'

'What did you ask for, to buy your silence?' said McKinley dully.

'One thing I asked was that no faerie life should ever be enslaved to human forms again.'

'Then what will happen to Doctor Dee?'

'You must be careful of him Mr Robert. He has great power even without the magic of the fae. You saw those poor souls he called from their thousands of years' rest. He can do that and will use it to his advantage if he can find a way. I saw him watching the celebrations and no doubt plotting his next ventures.'

McKinley had seen enough of fairieland, the glamorous and the real. He wanted to get back to his own life. He must make funeral arrangements for Ewart and would need to explain to the family how his uncle had died, and they had promised to visit Nicolas Weber and recount the tale to him. That would be a sad day.

He had no doubt that Teresa's mortal remains would have changed form and become a beautiful animal. How he wished he could have watched over her and perhaps she might have been a creature he could keep and cherish; a cat or a dog or a little fox as red as her beautiful hair. He would have kept her with him always. His anger had torn him from her side and he regretted it.

There was also the matter of Avery in the care of Miss Salter and Katherine who was bound in one of the wagons and who had tried to help him by seducing young Mr Penny. He asked Gilgoreth what would have happened to them.

'Ah, they are likely to have aged and died if they are not with Doctor Dee in this world or the human one. They could not survive without him because he has the elixir of life.'

'The elixir really exists?' asked McKinley.

'Well it's a dirty clay stuff that he keeps in a hollow sword hilt and wears about his neck, but yes something very like it exists and prolongs his life and allows him to prolong that of his people. He has it and they do not. And now you must go.' Gilgoreth pulled McKinley from the bed and waited for him to climb down the ladder.

The desperate need for a drink of water pulled the man to the jug but Gil pushed him out of the door and towed him up a path and through stands of trees with the suggestion of a blue sky above but no glimpse of it. He did not see the door but was propelled outside with the following phrase ringing in his ears.

'By the way, I also asked his lordship that he keep Doctor Dee here for a bit longer so he doesn't bother you. Good luck to you Robert McKinley.'

McKinley turned to thank his saviour and to see where the door was concealed, but he could see nothing. There was nothing to distinguish this piece of Cissbury Hill from any other. He stood alone on the prehistoric henge in the mist of a November morning and resolved that he must find Michael Flaherty and Mariel and then they must account for the dead.

*   *   *

He climbed wearily to the top of the hill looking for signs of the bloody battle that had taken place the previous evening. There was nothing but sheep-cropped turf. It was light but there was a thick fog surrounding him and he could not see far, so he walked around the henge until he came to the place where Teresa had died in his arms. There was no sign of her. But a woman walked through the trees to meet him and for a moment he thought it was her dear ghost come to take him into the other world and he would have gone willingly.

'Mr McKinley, you are tired and thirsty. I have brought water and a little food.'

He recognised the voice but not the figure and as she drew nearer he saw that it was Mariel.

'Mariel, you look … beautiful', he was going to say older, but she was beautiful, her hair worn in a long plait down her back and her gown unconventional under a warm cloak. She was taller and her figure fuller. Her brown almond shaped eyes were thickly lashed and her skin clear and glowing. She gave him a flask of clean spring water and he gratefully drank it.

'Where is …' he looked at the place she had lain, knowing that she was long gone into another world of animals.

'She became a bird and flew into the sky.'

'Oh, I thought she might have waited for me.'

'It has been seven years Robert, since you went under the hill.'

He remembered then that one day for him had been seven years for the mortal world. It would explain how Mariel had grown up

283

and become a woman, whereas he was still the same, except for his aching heart.

'My uncle, where is he? How did you explain his violent death?' said McKinley.

'That could have been difficult for us, Michael being an Irishman and me a girl of mixed race, so we buried him in one of the ancient flint mines hereabouts. Then we returned the brougham and travelled to London to see your uncle's clever friends and asked them what we should do.' Mariel said. 'Mr Weber was very helpful and contrived to tell the story of a venture abroad made by you and Dr Ewart McKinley with a view to discovering the pygmy marsupials of Australasia. You would be gone a very long time and letters were received recounting your uncle's illness and death and burial in a far distant place. I don't know how he managed the letters, but they were very convincing.'

'I must go and see him and explain what happened.'

'I'm afraid that won't be possible Robert. Mr Nicolas died earlier this year. He asked me to give you his deepest affection, but he was ready to go on the last great adventure.' Mariel said gently.

'You grew to know him?' asked McKinley.

'I was his housekeeper these past five years. He remembered me in his will, and thanks to him I am a woman of independent means now.'

'I am pleased for you Mariel,' he said, 'What happened to the other rogues who died that night?'

'They were taken by the faerie lord's servants and we heard nothing about their transformations. We managed to avoid curious locals asking about the disappearances of so many people in one night. And because they were travellers, nobody was surprised to see they had gone. We could not do that for poor Katherine and we went straight to that camp site before returning the brougham. She had grown old and died, peacefully I think, on the bed where Teresa and I had tied her. We bought her a Christian burial in Chichester, she did not transform.'

McKinley took a few minutes to absorb this. So many people gone in one night and Doctor Dee retained in the realm of the fae for how long, he wondered?

She said, 'If you are refreshed then we should go now.'

Mariel held his hand and led him down to the path where a horse waited patiently for them.

'Marshall!' he cried out in delight and the old horse searched his hands and smelt the odour of the fae on him and snorted contentedly. They led him back down to the village and everything had changed and yet in some way it seemed the same. The servants at the Gun Inn recognised him and asked about his travels, they sounded the same but looked older. The autumn was not so advanced this year, it had been a mild October and the golden leaves were still on the trees.

Mariel could see that he was in a state of shock and grief and she accompanied him to a large comfortable bedroom where they dined and talked at length. He read a letter written by George Macey telling her how one morning in November 1848 Miss Salter had attended to her 'gentleman guest' as they called him and found an old man who had passed away in the night. He was afforded burial in a church in Stourbridge, and she placed flowers on his grave every Sunday. Macey had been told the truth about that night on Cissbury Hill and knew when he wrote his letter that it would be some time before his friend would read it. The progress of his consumption was becoming a danger and in 1851 he had gone abroad to the warmer Mediterranean climate and was now settled in Egypt where he had renewed his interest in archaeology.

Mariel helped McKinley bathe and undress, they seemed not at all embarrassed, and she sat with him until he fell asleep. He had lost seven years of the time when he was supposed to be alive. It was now 1855. His uncles were dead, his parents and siblings wondered what had become of him. The three young artists he had known at Pitdown Hall were famous as the Pre-Raphaelite Brotherhood and had shaken up the world of art with their mysterious spiritual paintings. They had done everything they had promised, revolutionaries of the art world, scandalous in their private lives. She had told him so much.

He woke in the night and saw moonlight through the curtains and felt the cool crisp autumn air. He moved and felt a warm body in the bed with him. He turned and faced her.

'How did you persuade the landlord to let you stay with me?'

She said, 'I told them I was your wife. You have been abroad and obviously 'went native' as they say, and brought me back with you.'

They lay quietly, each delighting in the sounds of the other's breathing and becoming comfortable together. Then he said:

'Tell me I did not sleep with you seven years ago.'

He felt rather than saw her smile in the secretness of the bed covers. Then she kissed him.

[i] Hávamál", *Norrøne Tekster og Kvad*, Norway, archived from the original on 2007-05-08.
Larrington 1999, p. 37

Printed in Great Britain
by Amazon

65217707R00169